TAMING A MAVERICK

THE STERLING SHORE SERIES
by
USA Today Bestselling Author
C.M. Owens

Taming A Maverick
Copyright © 2017 by C.M. Owens

No part of this book may be reproduced, or stored in a retrieval system or transmitted in any form or by any means, electronic, mechanical, photocopying, recording, or otherwise without express written permission of the author. This eBook is licensed for your enjoyment only. It may not be re-sold or given away to other people.

The story in this book is the property of the author, in all media both physical and digital. No one, except the owner of this property, may reproduce, copy or publish in any medium any individual story or part of this novel without the expressed permission of the author of this work.

This is dedicated to the Sterling Shore lovers, and just to you. Thank you for making this series what it has been.

Prologue

Salem - Age 13

"Take the banana and bring it with us."

"I really just want to go play," I tell my mother, trying my best not to make her mad.

She sighs before pinching the bridge of her nose.

"You didn't wear your training bra today. You didn't wear the clothes I laid out for you, and you didn't take your purse. I swear, Salem, you'd think you were a boy instead of a girl. You have to start playing by the rules, or so help me…"

She lets her voice trail off, and I swallow hard while hiding my grease-stained hands. So what if I'd rather tinker with cars like my brothers? So what if I don't like dresses? Is it really the end of the world?

I swear she's a drama queen.

I always hate these stupid talks. And now she's married to another jerk who loves leaving me at home with some random nanny, while he whisks her away for extravagant weekends.

Not that I mind. At least I'm not subjected to her never-ending lectures when she's absent. But the nannies act like I'm an idiot kid who can't do anything without supervision, and they watch me closer than she does.

It's annoying.

"I don't think I'm a boy. I know I'm a girl. I just don't like purses or bras."

She rolls her eyes, giving me a pointed look thereafter. "Sweetie, you need to learn this stuff. Sex is important to be educated on. And I'd appreciate you not making me a grandmother so soon."

My stomach roils at the thought. Sex? How did we get on this conversation? Did I miss something? We were talking about bras!

"I'm too young to talk about this," I whisper, feeling my whole body burning with embarrassment.

"Your head thinks you are, but your body has a different opinion. You're already getting curvy, and Mother Nature has now bestowed upon you every woman's curse. That's why the school sent you home. You and I discussed this, yet you still freaked out. Ladies don't freak out and tell the entire class they're bleeding to death."

I swallow harder, already humiliated. Does she have to always rub my nose in embarrassing moments?

"Take the condom," she says, pointing to a black package on the counter, "and the banana, then follow me. There are lessons you need to learn now. I'll make an appointment tomorrow for birth control."

Make an appointment for what? And what the hell is birth control?

***

MAVERICK - Age 13

"So your parents are splitting up for real this time?" Corbin asks me as I recline back on the bleachers of the almost empty stadium.

"Yeah," I say, not taking my eyes off the pretty distractions in short skirts.

"That sucks."

"Not really. Less arguing. No more drama."

He doesn't say anything else, because there's not really much left to say on the subject. It's not a shocker that Dad and Mom didn't work out.

"Did you see that new chick Dane started hanging out with today?" he asks instead.

"The cute blonde? Yeah. She's cool. I think she's Tria's sister."

He gives me a weird look. "Tria has a sister?"

"Edward screwed the maid," I point out, shrugging. "Rain's not the untouchable princess snob that Tria is, though, at least not from what I could tell. And Tria pissed Dane off by having everyone make fun of Rain for being the maid's daughter. You know Dane hates that kind of shit. Tria might lose her perfectly popular spot if she pisses him off too much."

He laughs his ass off. "Yeah right. Like Tria is ever going to be scared of anyone. She won't back down."

Bored with talking about girl drama, I remember something that is actually important.

"Dude, I got the new Madden game," I announce while we continue to watch the cheerleaders stretch.

"Sweet. What time should I be there?"

"Anytime. Mom said it was cool to invite everyone over."

***

Salem - Age 16

"I need you to stop causing scenes, Salem. Kevin is still furious about the tantrum you threw at his last party."

I swear it's not natural to hate anyone as much as I hate her.

"Kevin is a pervert!" I hiss, shuddering at the memories of what he said to me.

"He says you misunderstood him," my bitch mother announces as though I'm being melodramatic. She knows I'm being serious. She probably has the whole thing recorded on one of her many spy cams, but she'll withhold it until she can milk him for the most money.

"You've known him for five minutes, and you believe him over me?" I growl, daring her to choose his side—to choose his *money* over me.

"I believe there are times and places for everything, and you shouting out to the entire party that your stepfather is a dirty pervert isn't the way you handle these things."

"You did this on purpose, didn't you?" I ask her, tears teetering on the edges of my lids. "You knew he was a sick freak, and you married him thinking he'd make a move on me."

She glares at me like I've crossed some line, but I just keep the challenge in my eyes. "I swear, Salem, he won't touch you. I won't let him. But you have to trust me to handle this."

Talking to my mother always makes me sick at my stomach.

"I don't trust you. How could I?"

She cups my chin, forcing me to look at her. "With this, Salem, you can trust me. And you can be sure that he'll be destroyed when we're gone. Just like he deserves. Trust. Me."

✳✳✳

MAVERICK - Age 16

"Maverick!" Mom yelps, quickly shielding her eyes while Chloe squeals and rips the covers over her head.

"Shit, Mom!" I yell, scrambling to get the sheet wrapped around my hips.

"Damn it, Maverick!" Mom gripes, her hand still over her eyes. "Get her out of here and get some clothes on."

I groan as she shuts the door, and then I start laughing when I see how pale and scared Chloe looks while poking her head out from under the covers.

"You said she wouldn't be here!" Chloe hisses, and I just laugh harder while putting my hands behind my head.

"You said you wouldn't care if she was," I remind the fake badass, grinning over at her as she glares at me and jumps up.

"My mother is going to kill me, Maverick. This isn't funny."

I continue laughing, taking my time to get on my clothes. "We're practically adults," I say, pulling a shirt on over my head.

"I'll remind you of that when my dad tries to kill you like a man."

I burst out laughing while she finishes up, and then I pull her to me to give her a goodbye kiss.

"Call me?" she asks, her irritation with me already falling away.

"Nope," I tell her, giving her one last kiss. "We talked about this. I'm too busy for a girlfriend. I'm taking dual enrollment classes so I can get college credits in high school, but I have to keep my grades up. Then there's football, basketball, and baseball…you know."

She bats her lashes before rolling her eyes. "You'll call, Maverick. They always do," she says on her way out the door.

I smirk before tugging my shoes on. Chloe is hot, but not hot enough to keep me interested through the drama. No fucking drama. And girls are full of drama.

I jog down the stairs, and then I stumble to a halt when I see Dad. Mom never invites Dad over. Hell, she can't stay in the same room as him.

"Dad," I say, grinning as I finish the stairs to reach him.

He bites back a grin when Mom says something I can't hear, and then she storms off, leaving a blaze of fury in her wake.

"Your mother called and said she just caught you and your girlfriend together. I saw her leaving. Macintosh girl?" he asks.

I nod, still grinning, and then say, "She's not my girlfriend, though."

He laughs to himself, but smothers it when Mom growls—actually growls—loud enough for us to hear her all the way from the kitchen. Dad clears his throat, trying and failing not to smile.

"Think we need to talk," he says, motioning with his head for me to follow him to the den—away from my mother's ears.

As soon as we're tucked inside, he leans against the back of the couch, and starts talking.

"Your mother wants me to talk you out of having sex."

"Figures," I say with a shrug. "You gonna to try?"

He laughs while shaking his head. "No. I'm not stupid. I was sixteen once. I *am* going to give you the safe-sex speech again. But first, let's talk about women."

My grin grows. "Hell yes. Talk away."

"None of them are the same," he says, and I nod in agreement, silently ticking off the differences: blondes, brunettes, redheads… "Some of them are looking for fun, just like you are right now. Some of them are curious, just like you once were. But some of them…"

He blows out a harsh breath before seriousness sparks in his gaze.

"Don't be an idiot, and never be a dick," he says, surprising me. That's not where I thought this conversation was going.

The hell?

"What?" I ask, confused.

"Always be upfront with them about what you want," he continues. "Be honest. It won't win you the prize every time, but it'll keep someone from getting hurt. Find a woman who wants what you want and nothing more. If you ever break a woman's heart…"

His voice trails off, and he clears his throat before he can continue. "Well, it'll make you feel like shit. Unless you know for sure you're ready for something real, don't find a woman that expects something real. Understood?"

Something tells me we're not really talking about me anymore, but I nod anyway. Whatever I need to do to get away from this weird side of my dad. He's the cool one. Mom's the serious one.

We have a system, and he's totally throwing it off center.

"Sure."

"Good. Now, make sure the girl isn't just telling you what you want to hear. Sometimes they say one thing, but they mean another. Some will try to tame you, make you think you want what they want. Hell, I think most girls just want a project, so they find a man they want to change into something else."

There's my dad. Thank God. I was starting to worry he was turning into Mom.

I laugh, shaking my head. "Why the hell do they want someone if all they want to do is change them?"

"Because, Mav, women are the most complicated fucking things in the world."

∗∗∗

Salem - Age 18

"Men are the simplest things in the world," Mom says, smiling down at a check. "Always wear makeup—no bare faces allowed. Make sure you only wear the sexiest lingerie. Dress up at all times, even before going to bed. Never, ever talk to them about anything negative or wrong in your life. In fact, don't talk about yourself at all. They don't care. Always listen to all they say, and pretend to be fascinated. Pour on a little Southern charm for an added bonus, and they'll eat out of the palm of your hand. They think with their dicks—not their heads. As long as they like what they see, they give up everything they own."

Apparently she's not listening to me, because that has nothing to do with the question I asked.

Looks like the child support just came in for one of my brothers. Or maybe it's a new settlement she's conned her way into. Who knows? All I know is that nothing besides money makes her smile like that.

"So, do you think it's too soon?" I ask, reminding her that I actually came to her for a reason.

She puts the check down, and she turns to face me. "Too soon for sex? No. The boy is poor, though, and you wasted your one-time V card on a man who will never be anything more than a local high school coach at most. With a face like yours, Salem, you should be focusing on boys like Cameron; he's going places."

I shudder at the thought of that dick. "Cameron is a major jerk. James is sweet. I think…I think I might love him. Or at least, I think I could love him. One day."

My stupid smile comes up as I think back to how gentle he was with me. But my mother's cold eyes snap me out of my trance when I see the disapproval rolling off her in heavy waves.

"You can easily fall in love with him, but he's never going to love you, darlin'. You're just too pretty. Pretty girls don't get to fall in love. Pretty girls are the ones the guys want—sometimes for a really long time—just to show off or brag about. Pretty girls get screwed. Not loved."

Which makes perfect sense…said no one ever.

"Too pretty?" I ask dubiously. "To fall in love?"

"Salem, like I said, men are simple. They're not like us. They have no loyalty, no virtues, no honesty…eventually, they'll break you the first chance they get. They're only good for one thing. Well, two, but only one thing that sticks with you—money. If you want something nice, you have to give them something nice. On occasion, you're going to enjoy yourself. But that's it, baby. It's only ever physical. Let them into your body, but never into your head or your heart. Don't give them that power."

I shake my head, biting back a few choice words I'd like to deal her. Why did I even bother coming to her? I knew better.

I keep thinking that one day she'll start being a normal mother.

"Not all of them are like that. James is good. He's so, *so* good. He wouldn't hurt me. And he's coming over in an hour, so I need to get ready. Please be nice."

I'm just ready for this conversation to be over. But James…James can get me out of here—away from her. We'll figure out a way to take Sean with us.

We can leave this small town and all the constant rumors that my mother has tagged to our names. I can move past the judgmental eyes that all think I'm no better than her.

They don't know me. I'm *never* going to be like her.

I don't know why she insists on moving back here after each breakup. This town hates us. I've changed schools like most girls change underwear, and this is the one I hated the most. I'm just glad I've finally graduated.

Now onto college. With James.

James is real. He made my body feel things that I couldn't have felt without the concern and care he put into every gentle touch.

"Sure," Mom says, seeming lost in thought. "But if he's coming over, then I need you to run and grab some fresh fruit. You know I like to serve fresh fruit to all guests before dinner. Hurry up and get ready, then run and grab it."

Rarely ever does she relent, so I take this as a blessing and run upstairs to grab some clothes. James will prove her wrong.

Salem – same day

Finally, I'm finished. Mom had about ten errands to add to my list before I even managed to buy her stupid fruit.

I drive up in her Mercedes, stopping well away from the garage. I'm too scared to park her car in the garage, because she loves each new car more than her four children. And that garage is rather narrow.

Tyler slams the door on his way out of the house, and I give him a confused look while he stalks toward me.

"What's wrong with you?" I ask my brother, but he shoves me back toward the car, pushing me like he's trying to get me out of here.

Since he graduated and started college, he comes to visit a little less, so I'm both surprised and excited to see him, but now his anger is confusing.

"By any chance are you dating a James?" he asks, his nose wrinkling in disgust.

"Yeah…" I drawl, letting the word trail off.

"Let's go. We'll come back later."

"No," I say, jerking away from him. "What's wrong? Did something happen to James?"

He grabs for me again, but I break free, pushing him away while racing toward the door. He trips and curses when he falls, giving me more distance from him. I barge through the door, racing through the house, just as Mom walks out of her room, tying her silky black robe together.

James comes stumbling out behind her, his shirt clutched in his right hand while he frantically tries to do his pants back together. Mom just stares at me, an unreadable look on her face, as tears waver on my lids.

James's head snaps up, and his eyes go wide when he sees me. Tyler curses while trying to pull me back outside, but I shrug him off. Since he doesn't want to risk hurting me, he relents.

"Fine. If I can't get you outside, then can I kick his ass?" he growls.

I stare at Mom, barely offering James a second look.

"I told you they have no loyalty," Mom says in a soft whisper, acting as though this is hurting her. "They all leave."

Tyler berates her, once again reminding her that she's screwed up in the head, but all sound disappears as James slowly tries to sneak out.

He slept with my mother? It's not like he was here for long without me. That's all it took to make him throw me away for my damn mother?

Pretty girls don't get to fall in love. They get fucked.

Tyler ends his rant and argument with our mother long enough to shake my shoulders. "Can I kick his fucking ass or not, Salem?" he growls.

"Yeah," I mumble, numb and still in shock.

Tyler doesn't hesitate to run out, and I continue staring at my mother as she wipes a tear from her cheek. Tyler will and can break James easily.

"I had to show you, Salem," she says softly. "They're only good for one thing. If you're only using them, then they can't use you. All I had to do was touch his hand, offer him myself, and he barely even hesitated. One touch and a few words, Salem—that's how easy it was. Do you understand?"

Until this moment, I only thought I hated her. But, twisted as she is, she showed me that I really am naïve.

She just proved two things: One, my mother gets whatever she wants when she wants it, and she doesn't give a damn about the collateral damage. Two, my heart is too fragile to go through this again, because it hurts. It hurts real damn bad.

Pretty girls really do get fucked.

***

MAVERICK - Age 18

"You look exhausted," Dad points out, dropping down beside me and handing me a beer that I gratefully accept.

"Long day. Rain's out of surgery, though, and everything looks good. So that's the good news."

He nods, frowning. "Little young to have to worry about that sort of reality," he says on a sigh. "You need to go over there?"

"Dane's with her right now. She's in good hands."

He smirks for some reason, then props his feet up on the table.

"Hey, did I see you talking to Martha Jameson the other day?" he asks randomly.

This time I smirk. "Yep. She wanted to see me again."

He sputters his beer before coughing and pounding his chest, and I swear he turns pale.

"The hell, Dad?" I ask, cocking an eyebrow.

"See you *again*? You slept with Martha?" he asks in an unusually high octave before clearing his throat.

"Yeah. She's smoking hot."

His eyes widen. "She's thirty-four!"

Since when is he such a damn prude?

"And? I repeat: she's smoking hot. Besides, there's that whole fine wine thing. What's the big deal?"

He groans while scrubbing his face with his hands. "*I* slept with Martha just last week."

This time I choke on my beer, and bile rises to my throat.

"What?" I ask, my own voice hitting a higher octave.

"Yes. Last week. When did you…"

He lets his words trail off as we both turn a little puce.

"Last Thursday."

"Shit," he mutters. "I slept with her on Wednesday!"

Of all the fucking luck—no pun intended. My stomach roils and he scoots away from me at the same time I scoot away from him. This is seriously messed up.

"New rule," he says, grabbing a pen and a piece of paper from the coffee table. "From now on, don't screw someone older than you by five years. I don't screw women younger than thirty… Obviously, that age will go up as I grow older. This shit can't happen again."

I nod in agreement as he hands me a different pen and a piece of paper. "What's this?" I ask, still feeling nauseated from our accidental bonding experience.

"Write down your wish list. I'll do the same. It'll save us some problems in the future in case the age thing becomes an issue."

Thank God. He's brilliant. I'm so glad I have a normal dad.

Chapter 1

Present Day...

Salem

Silk is where everyone has told me to go for a fun time since I got into town, and now that I'm standing here in the middle of the madness that can only be described as amazing, I completely understand why.

Talking to people is always complicated, because they ask questions I don't want to answer, which makes meeting people difficult. But dancing...there isn't a lot of conversation when you're dancing.

And the beach view...just wow. It makes this ungodly move worth it.

I like how big Sterling Shore seems to be, even though it's still relatively small. But not small-town small.

Here...I have the freedom to breathe and just be me.

My thoughts are broken up when I see something I can't stop staring at. I've seen sexy men all over Sterling Shore. Silk seemed like the best place to come find the ones who are on the prowl, which is another reason I came.

I want a good time with no strings—something dirty and semi-scandalous.

And I just found exactly what I want.

Inky black hair is tousled and wet—due to the rainstorm outside. My hair is still damp from the rain I endured on the way in here. But he makes wet hair beyond sexy.

He's tall, at least 6'2, maybe even taller. And he walks like he knows exactly how sexy he is. Good. I love it when they're cocky.

As he moves through the entryway of the club, people greet him, and he flashes them a smile that could easily prompt a girl to melt or throw her panties at him like an offering. After the few customary fist bumps and typical dude nods, he moves toward a back booth that rests higher on a platform area.

The seats are too high for me to see the people he's standing in front of and talking to, but a waitress basically rushes over to him, bringing him a beer he couldn't have ordered. Apparently, he's a regular.

That's good to know.

His shirt has an odd logo on the front, something that looks like a band name. His jeans are dark and frayed in some places, hanging low on his hips in all the right ways. Muscles flex beneath the semi-tight shirt he's wearing, and he's not even trying to flex them. He'll definitely do for a night of fun.

It's only right I have a proper introduction to Sterling Shore.

It becomes obvious that I'm not the only one interested when several girls wave at him, and he gives them a wink. But his interest returns to that damn booth. I can't help but be curious who is back there. That platform section is roped off as *VIP*.

There's not a bouncer keeping people away from it, so I could always wander up there and act as though I didn't realize it wasn't open to the lowly public.

Never mind. There's a bouncer now. I could just flash him. That always works. Besides, he's letting all those other girls through just from a little cleavage.

The second another girl runs her hand up his arm, basically inviting him to fuck her with just her touch and her eyes, I start to realize he's not going to be too easy. He has options — too many of them.

Leaning back against the bar, I observe him, studying him, and sizing him up as my prey. I'll need to make him come to me. A guy who gets chased would prefer a little chasing of his own.

It'll be a bit hard, considering most of these women are absolutely stunning and dressed to slay a man. That's a lot of competition.

I'm dressed as a predator and not the prey, so this should be an interesting challenge.

No way can I pull off coy or innocent like this.

My short leather shorts are barely below my ass. My top is a little flashy, considering it's barely a top at all. The back is completely missing, tethered to me by only a small string across the shoulder blades, and the front hangs loosely, stopping just above my navel. No bra in this thing. I might as well be screaming *easy one-night-stand*.

See my dilemma? I'm trying to be a challenge now, and there's nothing challenging about this attire.

"Not that one," a woman says from behind the bar.

I turn just in time to see a pair of dazzling white teeth behind a red-lipped grin.

Shiny, dark, mahogany hair drapes around her shoulders, looking freshly dyed. And she slides a beer down the bar to a waiting hand that snatches it up.

"Were you talking to me?" I ask unsurely.

"Yep. You're eyeing that booth, aren't you?"

I nod, shrugging casually while glancing back once again. This time, the unknown guy's dark eyes turn to meet mine at the exact same moment, and he bites his lower lip while shamelessly raking his eyes over me from head to toe.

Hmmm. Maybe I was wrong about not being able to get his attention.

Heat floods my veins, and I start to wonder if I can handle him the way I thought I could. He's not even touching me, and I'm already on fire.

"Ah hell," the girl says, and I force myself to look away.

He knows I exist, and now it's obvious he's interested. A little game of cat and mouse should seal the deal, hopefully.

"What?" I muse, half listening.

"That one is the worst. If you're going to mess with someone from that group, I'd tell you to pick Dale. But Dale just got engaged, so that's a no-go."

"And is the guy I'm looking at a dangerous guy?" I ask, considering it's not exactly safe to take someone home from a bar.

She snorts out a laugh. "Not physically, but he'll damage you emotionally if you get attached."

"Personal experience?" I ask her, even though I probably shouldn't be so nosy.

She smirks and shakes her head. "I'm not a bitter ex warning you off. I've never slept with anyone who hangs with that crowd. My friend Raya has, but her experience was different from mine with the rich crew. Girls like me and you…we don't belong in the mix with money and egos. Those guys can have anyone they want. Don't expect them to want you for longer than a hot minute."

I've seen that happen more than once, so I don't doubt she's telling the truth. I like this girl more and more. She's not judging or criticizing, but she's offering life experience.

However, she has me pegged wrong.

"I take it these people are regulars?" I ask, even though I still haven't seen anyone inside that private, high-backed booth.

"Yep. That one's cousin owns the club. All of them own the city. Meet the elite of Sterling Shore. Back there is Corbin, Ruby, Tria, Kode, Jax, and the one you're staring at is Ma—"

"Ember, I need you to keep up!" a man behind the bar shouts, and the woman talking to me rolls her eyes.

"I should have never come back," she sighs. "I need to get back to work. Steer clear of him. He's a handful that doesn't stick around for too long."

As she walks away, I find myself smiling. She was sweet enough to think she was warning me. All she did was cement my plans for the night.

It's highly unlikely I'll be in Sterling Shore for long. I need to have as much fun as possible before I get shipped back to Georgia or end up in yet another random state.

When you are constantly stared at and judged, you grow used to feeling eyes on your back. I don't know if it's him who's watching, but I hope so, because I definitely feel the burn of someone's gaze.

Several guys ask me to dance on my way to the dance floor, but I just ignore them, making sure I look damn hard-to-get to the predator seeking prey. I chance a glance over my shoulder, and sure enough, he's watching me with intrigue, slowly sipping his beer while leaning against the wall with his back turned to the booth.

I smirk, deliberately staring into his dark eyes, and I turn back around, moving my body to the music while I wait. And then I move away from some random's groping hands to wait some more.

And I continue to wait. And wait…

Seriously? Is he honestly going to just keep watching and not make a move?

Chapter 2

MAVERICK

"Who the hell is she?" I ask Corbin as he gets up, coming to stand beside me as I watch the girl I've never seen in here before.

She's wearing shorts that fit her perfectly round ass like a glove, and the high-heel, leather ankle-boots are doing a number for my dirty mind right now.

With that shirt, she can't be wearing a bra, which has me itching to stick my hands up there and find out how real those perky breasts really are. And the way she was looking at me lets me know she wants me. But she sure as hell isn't from around here, or I would have seen her before now.

"I don't know," my cousin says with a shrug. "But she looks like she's ready for a good time. You chasing?"

My smile dies a little as I scan the club, noting that more and more women are wanting my attention since Corbin lost his balls and settled down with Ruby. Everyone wants to tame Maverick Sterling now.

I hate it.

I miss the good times and fun sex before all the women assumed I was going to follow the rest of the Sterlings and settle down. This girl, fortunately, looks like she just wants to play.

"I plan on it. She wants me, but I can tell she thinks she's running this little game. I'll wait until her confident little bubble bursts, and then I'll surprise her. Then I'll find out what it's like to fuck her with nothing but those shoes on."

Corbin laughs, but Ruby groans as she wedges in between us. "Could you be a bigger slime?" she asks.

She's never happy with my honesty.

"Would you rather I be a liar?"

She rolls her eyes as Corbin kisses her on the head.

"No," she says on a sigh. "At least you're upfront with the women who want to go home with you. Besides, if the girl wants a night of fun, who the hell am I to judge?"

Ruby is definitely my second favorite woman. Well, it's a tie between her and Tria for second place. Tria has Kode under her thumb, which makes our outings *so* much easier. Fewer fights, less drama. Ruby is badass, even though I partially hate her for stealing my favorite wingman.

"How can you possibly know if she likes you?" Ruby asks, acting as though that information just dawned on her.

"She was looking at me from the bar. I got the I-want-you-to-chase-me-look. I know it well. But she'll think she's in control if I just jump to it."

Corbin snickers, because he knows damn well what I'm talking about. He's just as educated on this game as I am. Of course, now all of his skills are worthless.

"Has your Dad called?" Ruby asks.

I shrug, not really wanting to talk about this. I can't believe my father—the one who taught Corbin and me all the tricks of the game—finally got married again. It's as though the world has flipped off its axis.

"Not since he called to say he was married. It was a spur of the moment thing. I haven't even met the woman—Kelly? I think that's her name. He said he didn't want a wedding, so they did it with a JOP."

"Think it'll last?" Corbin asks, knowing I don't want to talk about this.

"Doubtful. But the woman must be hella sexy to have gotten him to put a ring on her finger. Can't wait to meet my stepmom," I answer, waggling my eyebrows at him.

I'm joking, of course, but Ruby still mocks a gag. The only way to keep from sounding annoyed about the entire situation is to turn it into a joke.

Because that's what the hell it is anyway.

Kode and Tria are all over each other in the booth right now. I don't know why they bother coming out.

"It's just not like Ian to up and marry someone," Ruby says, pointing out the obvious, but it's more like she's talking to herself than me.

I answer anyway. "Dad is probably going through a midlife crisis or something. The new will wear off, and he'll go back to being the man he really is."

At least he had a pre-nup ready to sign. I'd have kicked his ass if he married a woman and threw his life's work into a grinder.

"How'd your mom take it?" Ruby asks.

I've changed my mind. Tria is definitely my second favorite woman, because she never flogs me with a hundred questions.

"My mom? Mom doesn't care what Dad does. Their relationship has always been great since they got divorced. No drama. How do you think I turned out so normal?"

It's not the truth, but Ruby doesn't know the situation well enough to see through my words. But this is the best thing for my mother.

She'll stop waiting now.

Just that thought has my annoyance with my father immediately ebbing. Maybe him getting married isn't such a bad thing after all.

Corbin and Ruby climb back into the booth when he ushers her in. She might not care that I don't want to talk about this crazy shit, but he does.

My eyes fall back to feast on the beauty with her back turned to me as I lean against the wall.

I need a good distraction tonight, and she's perfect for the job. Her drink is getting low. I'll wait until it's almost gone, and then I'll make my move.

Chapter 3

Salem

By the fourth song, my glass is empty, and a waitress walks by to grab it, not slowing down long enough for me to order another. I'm worried if I turn around that *he* will be with another girl, and that would just make me feel ridiculous.

It's obvious he's moved on even without seeing it for myself.

Just as I'm about to set my sights on easier prey, a hard body is pressed against my back, and a drink slowly comes in front of my eyes. The large hand holding it is very possibly his, but I hold my breath in anticipation.

"You were running low. Long Island?" he asks, his voice layered with sex, velvet, and deep tones that all mingle together in delicious harmony.

Apparently he found out what I was drinking, and I resist the urge to grin. "You did some research first," I say, feigning a heady dose of confidence while taking the glass.

No, it's not safe to take a drink from a stranger, but I have no plans to drink it.

"Damn," he says on a breath. "Where the hell is that accent from?"

Now that I have his attention, I turn around—mostly to make sure I'm right about who he is.

Oh shit.

I should have stayed facing the other way. He's so much sexier up close.

Those dark eyes are actually a deep brown, and his inky black hair is slowly drying, but it looks just as sexy. And that mouth…I could have fantasies for years about a mouth like that.

Those full lips are etched in a knowing smirk, and he radiates confidence and cockiness, riding a fine line between the two. If I wasn't already interested, I sure as hell would be right now.

"Small Town, Georgia," I say with a grin, watching as he moves a little closer and thumbs my lower lip.

He's not shy, and I really like that.

He doesn't mask the hunger in his eyes, the dirty thoughts in his mind, or the fact he obviously wants me. This is going to be a good night.

"Why are you in Sterling Shore?" he asks, his eyes coming down to my lips as he starts moving his body to the music, keeping his hand on my face until it slides back into my light brown hair that is streaked with subtle touches of red.

We could do this—both of us pretend as though we give a damn about getting to know each other—but I'm not willing to risk actually liking him. Then again, he could end up having a personality that won't allow me to even have a good time. It's safer to keep it physical and only physical.

"Does it matter?" I ask, pushing closer to him as he tilts my head back, and I purposely bite my lip, hoping it's as sexy as I think it is.

His free hand slides down my side, while his other remains fisted tightly in my hair, his grip just shy of painful. When he uses his hold to pull me closer, I hold my hand out that has the glass, and let my other dangle to my side, giving him full control.

Our fronts touch, and I fight really hard not to shiver against the instant heat that floods my body with tingles of anticipation.

"Not really. I'm just looking to know you for tonight. I'm not someone you want if you're looking for more than that."

And he knows exactly what I want to hear.

He controls our movements to the seductive music, his eyes still on me and not on the stage where burlesque dancers own the crowd.

His honesty is sexy, because it's exactly what I'm looking for. I'm not looking for a night of false romance and sugar-coated lies. I want something fun, freeing, sinfully dirty, and extremely temporary.

"Turns out, I'm looking for a one-hit wonder," I quip, keeping the banter up.

His grin is one of scandalous intent, and I push closer, enjoying the way his grip tightens on me.

"Just because it's one night, that doesn't mean I'm a 'one-hit wonder,' baby. I can promise it'll be the best night you've had in Sterling Shore."

I don't burst his bubble by telling him that's not hard to do since I've only been here for a day and a half. Or that his egomaniac line is sort of…not sexy. He seems very attached to his ego, after all.

"You seem to know exactly what I want to hear. I hope you can back up your words," I tell him, daring him to make a move.

And he does. His head dips, and he takes my mouth in a kiss that has my damn knees trying to buckle, my heart racing, and everything inside of me tries to combust.

Okay, so now that ego makes sense.

My mouth opens, giving him access, and he doesn't waste time.

His tongue is possessive, claiming me in a way that has me making sounds against my will. My free hand slides up his arm, feeling the muscles hidden beneath the thin fabric. His hand on my side slides down to my ass, and he tugs me harder against him.

When I feel the hard bulge in the front of his pants, I shudder. He tugs my hair harder, bending my head back so he can thoroughly explore my mouth with his expert tongue.

By the time he pulls back, my lips are swollen, my thoughts are scattered, I'm dizzy, and quite frankly, I'm a hot mess. I barely even notice him handing my still-full drink to a waitress, and then my hand is firmly pulled into his as he tugs me back against him.

"Are you all talk, or are you ready to get out of here?" he asks, his smug grin proving he's damn proud of himself.

I'm sure I look like a starry-eyed fool right now, all because of a kiss. *A. Kiss.* It promises to be a good night if he fucks as well as he kisses.

"Lead the way," I manage to say, even though the words are breathy and broken. Still a hot mess, people.

I felt so much more confident about this before that kiss.

Refusing to feel inferior or waver in my resolve, I get as close as I can while he holds my hand, moving us toward the exit.

"Hey, Mav," a guy calls from the platform on his way down. "You leaving?"

I take in the girl hugged against his side, her tattoos streaking down her arms like colorful warnings. His arm is draped around her shoulders protectively, drawing her closer.

"Yeah," the guy holding my hand—whose name is apparently Mav—says in response.

The other guy is not bad looking, but I wouldn't have messed with the girl on his arm to get to him. Not to mention, this *Mav—whatever kind of name that is*—has had my attention for over an hour. He's by far the most attractive guy in this club—in my opinion.

The other guy gives him a knowing smile and a wink, and the girl on his arm surprisingly doesn't cast judgment on me with her eyes. Instead, she winks at me, grinning while tugging her man toward the dance floor.

I really like Sterling Shore.

"Dance with me, Corbin. Before I get too drunk and you have to carry me out."

Corbin smiles down at her before waggling his eyebrows, and then he claps Mav on the shoulder while walking away. The girl gets close to my side before whispering, "Have fun."

Have fun? That's it? No snorts of disgust, disdainful eye-rolls, or even a snarky comment?

Sterling Shore is officially my happy place.

Mav starts pulling me with him again, and he puts his hand on the small of my back as we make it outside. People have started lining up, proving I was smart to come before the late crowd.

I'd have to flash a bouncer to get in without waiting all night in that line. And despite the fact I've mentioned it twice, I actually hate doing that.

Mav wraps his arm around my shoulders, nodding and speaking to a few people as we pass through.

A couple of whistles follow our departure, but he doesn't acknowledge them.

"My place is just down the road. You're not one of those girls who steals wallets, are you? Because I lock my shit in a safe."

He grins, letting me know he's possibly joking.

"I make my own money, *Mav*. But feel free to lock your stuff up. I only want you for your body."

His grin grows, and I smile back at him, airing on the safe, sexy talk instead of delving into personal facts to put him at ease.

No, no. I don't do this all the time. But occasionally, a girl needs a wild, reckless, possibly dangerous night.

Especially me.

And I really deserve it.

Suddenly we're stopping. "You got a car here? It'll be safe to leave it if you aren't up to following me. My cousin owns the place. He keeps heavy security, and he doesn't mind overnight parking, as long as he knows about it."

I frown at the sporty BMW in front of us. Not because it isn't frigging gorgeous. I've never been a BMW person, but right now, I'm actually a little in awe.

But I don't want to ride with someone who has been drinking.

"I didn't drive. You've been drinking. Can't we take a cab?"

He smiles over at me as he clicks the button and unlocks the door. "I've only had one beer. I was a little busy watching you. I swear I'm sober."

That's not good enough for me. I don't trust him enough to believe the one-beer tale. I've heard that before.

Yes, I realize it's dangerous to go home with a stranger, and it's hypocritical to focus so intently on the drinking and driving issue. But putting my life at risk is better than putting others at risk who don't have a say.

"I've changed my mind; I'd rather just go home, and I'll take a cab to get there."

I turn around, but the fast footsteps behind me almost startle me. "Hey, whoa! If driving is a deal-breaker, I'll grab a cab. There's always a line of them around the side. They know fare is easy here."

I breathe out in relief, and he reaches down and strokes my cheek with his thumb. "Come on," he says sweetly, that cocky grin back on his face.

I go without resistance, letting him lead me around the parking lot to where there really is a line of cabs. He slides his hand over the bare skin of my back, and like an unpracticed idiot, I shiver against him.

"You sure you want to do this?" he asks, already proving to me I'm acting like a novice to this situation.

I'm not expertly rehearsed, but I'm not blushing innocence either.

I'm sure that much is glaringly obvious by now.

Right now, I'm a girl without a halo of rumors over her head. The girl who can finally live up to her semi-deserved reputation without the fear of small town scandal.

"If you're not into it—"

"Oh, I'm into it," he says, spinning me suddenly and forcing me to walk backwards as his lips move to mine. My hands immediately go to the back of his head, my fingers threading through the unnaturally soft strands of his hair.

He breaks the kiss before I'm done, and opens the door to a cab for me. "After you."

I hop in, feeling excitement and nervousness unfurl in my body.

He rattles off an address, and he tugs me over to him until I'm straddling his lap. Just before my lips find his, he says, "There are definitely perks to taking a cab."

I grin lightly, but that smile disappears the second he captures my lips in a scorching kiss that has me forgetting how to breathe. I grind against him, happy to have him under me, and I kiss him without reservation or concern for the cabdriver.

Poor cabby. Unless he's getting into the show. Then *ewwww*.

When Mav's hands slip through the sides of my slinky shirt, I resist the urge to stop him. I'm used to taking things slower, but that's not what tonight is.

I suck in a sharp breath when he touches my breasts, kneading them in his hands as a low growl vibrates in his throat and chest. His hands feel firm and possessive, just like his lips, and I buck against him when he shows me just how good he is at finding all the right things to do.

"Your name would be nice," he says against my lips, tugging my hair back when I try to resume the kiss.

I can picture him pulling my hair for other reasons.

"Salem," I tell him, smiling when his eyebrows go up in confusion. Before he can ask, I add, "My mother named me without a real good reason."

It's not like he has room to talk; his name is weirder than mine.

He laughs while letting me resume the kiss, and the cab slows to a stop. The driver never makes a sound, but Mav removes his mouth from mine to pay the guy with cash, telling him to keep the change, before he opens the door and stands with me still wrapped around him.

I never see the house we enter, or pay attention to any of our surroundings. My eyes are closed tightly as I drink him in, kissing him with pure abandon. He holds me effortlessly, as though he could maintain this position for hours without strain. It's just as hot as his ability to kiss me senseless.

Suddenly I'm being lowered, and his body comes with me until my back finds a soft surface. I open my eyes as he pulls back, and I immediately regret it when he pulls his shirt off. The room is dark, illuminated only by a thin shred of moonlight that is escaping between the gap in the drapes that are off to the side, but that's all I need to see the body I wasn't prepared for.

Ripples of muscles line his chest, arms, and abdomen. A cut V forms and disappears behind the low waistband of his jeans, and all of that is complemented by the stunning face and daredevil smirk.

"I want you to leave the shoes on, but everything else needs to go," he says, watching me and waiting.

I'm supposed to just strip? Usually, a guy undresses me. Even one-nighters are ripping my clothes off. I suppose no-strings-sex with Mav means I undress myself.

Mentally slapping myself for my pointless inner thoughts that have me sitting here dumbly, I lift up enough to unclasp the top part of my shirt and toss it to the floor. His crooked smile kicks up, making him look even sexier, and I take in the few tattoos on his chest to keep from looking at his face while he stares at me.

There's another tattoo on his shoulder, but all I can see of it is *ling*.

My attention is quickly drawn away from the ink when he says, "I want your shorts gone, too, baby."

Shit.

His taunting grin only teases me when I look back up. With an exhaled breath, I stand up, and I start undoing my shorts while he watches me, his eyes regarding every movement with either amusement or fascination. Not sure which.

I'm glad it's dark when I feel my cheeks heating from the blush creeping into them, and I push my shorts down, carefully pulling them over the shoes and tossing them aside. Standing in front of him in a pair of slinky red panties and black, high-heeled ankle boots, I feel a little…foolish?

"Damn," he says softly, biting his bottom lip as his eyes hungrily rake over my body.

I fight really damn hard to keep standing here, letting him appraise me with a studious eye. I'm not usually self-conscious, but I'm also not one to be on display either.

Finally, he walks over to me, reducing the distance in just a few long strides. When he tips my head back, I happily surrender, letting his mouth claim mine in another kiss that goes into my archives of *things to never forget*.

"You in these shoes while being naked is going to be seared into my memory," he says, grinning as he picks me up and drops me onto the bed.

His body covers mine as he starts working my panties down. Once they're past my shoes, he leans back and looks me over one more time. It's really hard not to cover up, simply because of how long he stares.

"Definitely a good image to keep," he murmurs, more to himself than me—I think.

"Are you going to wear your jeans?" I ask, trying to sound flirty and not nervous.

Even though his grin is one of the most perfect features about him, I wish he'd stop showing it to me. His eyes dance with enticing hints of mischief as he stands up, and I watch as he undoes the top button.

The suspense is almost tangible, and I don't hide my mouth falling open when he drops his underwear and jeans in unison, stepping out of them with an erection that proves life isn't fair. One man shouldn't be this physically amazing from head to toe.

Maybe he's as dumb as a box of rocks to even things out?

It's a damn good thing I'm limiting myself to a tryst instead of allowing myself to entertain the idea of more. He's heartbreak wrapped in sex appeal.

Naked and so damn confident, he moves back over to me, sliding me up on his bed as he picks back up with that kiss. His lips will ruin me for all other kisses in the future. He has already set the bar too high.

His mouth moves to my neck, and some foreign sound escapes my lips as he works his way down to my breasts, drawing a nipple into his mouth. My body arches involuntarily, feeling the heat of his skin against mine, and those hard lines of muscle taunt me with every slide of his body.

When his finger finds a spot I wasn't prepared for him to touch yet, I squeal in surprise.

Way to be sexy, Salem. Bravo. Encore. No, do not do an actual encore!

His throaty chuckle only makes me feel like a bigger idiot, and his lips move back up to meet mine softly.

"Last chance to back out. You seem more nervous by the minute," he tells me.

Taking a deep breath, I shake my head. "No. No backing out. Do you have a condom?"

I hope so, because I forgot to buy any, and this can't happen without one. My occasional one-nighters are usually stocked on their own, never needing my condoms anyway.

His teasing grin doesn't amuse me. Is he silently making fun of me?

"I have all the condoms we could ever need, *y'all*."

I roll my eyes. "You used that wrong, and your fake accent is just insulting."

He laughs under his breath before reaching over to his nightstand, and I watch with rapt attention and a fierce heartbeat as he grabs the foil packet. My nerves gather in the pit of my stomach, making it tight as my whole body goes through a series of adrenaline-laced emotions.

It's thrilling and terrifying in one breath.

Why am I so freaking weird right now? It's the same as any other guy; he just happens to be a smidge hotter than the usual.

Definitely think that's what's throwing my game off.

He tears the pack open with his teeth, seeming too well rehearsed with that motion. And my eyes move down to that very…intimidating thing between his legs as he rolls the condom over it.

Licking my lips absently, I practically dissolve when those dark eyes find mine again, and he moves fast to take my lips, settling into the space between my legs and prodding my entrance ever so slightly.

Just as his tongue slicks into my mouth, he thrusts in, and I almost convulse right then. With hardly any foreplay, I'm more turned on than I've ever been, and it shows when I desperately start grabbing for him, raking my nails across his back, shoulders, and arms.

He growls as he thrusts in harder, angling my hips in a way that gives him depth, and I cry out, finding it impossible to catch a breath. Every thrust is harder and faster, and he leans up to his knees, looking down at me as he uses the bends of *my* knees as leverage, gripping them tight enough to leave behind bruises for tomorrow.

His jaw gets tense, and my back arches up as he hits a spot deep within. His vicious pace sends me spiraling, my mind goes foggy, and something between a scream and a praise falls through my lips unintelligibly as fever sweeps my body. The wild explosion starts at my core, and it spreads to every nerve on my body.

He grunts harshly as his rocking slows down, and his head drops back as he grits his teeth, silently following behind me. I pant for air, hoping the feeling in my legs comes back soon so I can leave.

He grins, keeping himself inside me, and leans down to kiss me again.

"Welcome to Sterling Shore, Salem," he mumbles against my lips, his voice husky and a little tired as he drops to the bed beside me.

I just laugh, and then I take a deep breath. Usually, either regret or surreal excitement spikes my blood, but instead, I'm just...calm. So calm. And tired. Very, very tired.

It's a first.

"Just let me go take care of this, and I'll welcome you from a different position," he crudely announces, kissing me again before lifting his muscular, toned body away from mine and heading for the bathroom off to the side.

It's just now that I take in how massive and lavish his room is. Judging by the car and this one room, I understand the bartender's warning about him being part of the *elite*. This is far more elite than anything back home.

As the light comes on and the door closes, I debate staying for another round. It'd be incredible—no doubt about it—but staying would mean eventually we'd talk. If we talked, I'd like him or hate him.

Neither of those seem like a good thing. Liking him would lead to me wanting more than the fun night I promised myself. Hating him would suck the air out of the wildest, most exciting night I've had in a really long time.

There's only one option.

Chapter 4

MAVERICK

"You look grumpy," Corbin points out, taking a seat across from me as I idly scan the faces at Silk. I can't believe I'm fucking looking for one particular girl.

"Not grumpy," I lie.

I'm pissed. All because of that girl I met two days ago. The girl was smoking hot, definitely into me, and she was fun as hell. I told her I wanted to have another round, and she disappeared while I was in the bathroom.

Salem. What kind of name is Salem? It doesn't matter what her name is; she shouldn't have just bolted without telling me what the hell I did wrong.

"Any reason why you're a thousand miles away?" Corbin prompts, waving his hand in front of my face.

Because I'm an idiot. Not even sure why this is irking me.

"Ever have a girl walk out after the warmup without saying a word? And I'm talking about after she got hers."

He snickers, apparently understanding. "No. Usually I was the one doing the leaving. What'd you do wrong? And what's a warmup?"

That'd be nice to know.

"Beats the hell out of me," I grumble. "And a warmup is the sex before the actual *sex*. You know, to get that first one out of the way."

Ruby mocks a gag, popping up out of nowhere and sliding into the booth.

"Didn't you plan on sending her on her merry way when you were finished anyhow?" Ruby taunts.

How long has she been listening?

"Yeah. But not until I was finished with her," I say, shrugging.

Jade or Mandy or… hell, I don't know her name, comes up to us, grinning as she leans over the table.

"You look like you could use some cheering up," she tells me.

This is the same girl who told me she'd never touch me again. I *do* remember that. She got pissed on Corbin's birthday after *she* propositioned *me*, and I did exactly what I promised. But apparently I'm an ass for being honest.

"No thanks," I state dismissively, looking back at the sea of faces, searching for the one in particular that is driving me crazy.

"Seriously?" Corbin asks me as whatever-her-name-is walks away, rolling her eyes and shaking her ass.

"Not in the mood," I tell him.

Chicks walking out apparently makes me cranky. Maybe that makes me a dick, but usually they leave happy—and after I've excused them. No one has ever just left.

This is just my ego. Has to be.

"Well, while you're searching for Cinderella's glass slipper, I need to talk to you about that—"

Corbin's words are cut off when my phone buzzes in my pocket. My dad's name flashes across the screen, and I quickly answer it, wondering if he's still on his honeymoon.

"Dad?"

The static on the other line makes all of his words almost indecipherable. Where the hell is he?

"Beach… for… help… house…"

The fuck?

"Dad, I can't understand a word you're saying."

It sounds like someone is playing white noise over his words, but he tries again. "Beach house… go… help…"

Shit. The call drops, and I groan.

"What's up?" Corbin asks me.

"Something about his beach house. I should go check it out and see if I can figure out what he's talking about. I'll see you guys later."

"Want us to let you know if we find the girl?" Ruby asks, seeming genuine.

"Yeah. Call me if she shows up. But *do not* tell her I'm pissed about her exit."

Corbin snickers while I walk away, and I head out to my car. I never even had a sip of my beer tonight because I was too intensely focused. Why is this driving me crazy?

Ruby's right; I would have just dismissed her shortly after, but I still prefer not to feel as used as I was. I know she told me that was the plan, but—

Great. Now I sound exactly like all the women I leave after we're done.

I have to stop obsessing.

It takes only a few minutes to make the short drive, but I'm confused when I see lights on inside the house. Dad keeps this place locked up tight. I bet that's why he called. Someone probably tripped the alarm while trying to squat here.

It happens all the time—squatters finding homes on the beach that are not in use. The cops should have already come after Dad was called to confirm he wasn't home. So why the hell aren't they here yet?

A jacked-up pickup truck with Georgia plates has me inwardly groaning. Great. A redneck. I better not see a fucking shotgun.

Heading down the side, I start looking through the windows, trying to see how many I might be dealing with. I'll handle it myself if it's just one or two.

Suddenly, I'm tripping, slapping the side of the house to catch myself from falling, because through the window, I see something that has my mouth watering, my eyes widening, and my blood pumping.

A girl with purple streaks in her otherwise light brown hair is standing in my father's bedroom with her back turned, and all she's wearing is a lacy thong and a matching bra. I lean in closer, watching as she opens the drawer, pulling out what appears to be shorts, but I'm too busy searching the tan lines near her ass to be certain.

This is one squatter I might not kick out. She'd definitely be good to use after the shot my ego took the other day.

And this is a bitch-slap from reality. I've gotten so damn bad lately, that I'm considering fucking a hot squatter who just broke into one of my family's homes. It's like my standards just keep sinking.

I need to take a break from damn women.

Never thought I'd say that.

Still, I watch, somewhat entranced, as she moves through the bedroom, her face hidden by her hair. But then she disappears into the hallway, robbing me of the view.

My eyes keep searching, waiting for her to come back, but as the seconds tick by, nothing happens. Just as I'm about to turn around, I'm yelping, stumbling, and landing hard on my ass, as a blast of cold waters pummels me in the face.

"Take that, pervert!" a feminine voice yells.

I gargle on the water, using my hands to shield my face from the stream that is shooting me relentlessly.

"Fucking stop! I'm not a pervert!"

Well, that's not entirely true.

The water assault ceases, and I try to see into the darkness as the girl holds the garden hose on me like a gun, her finger itching to pull the trigger again, but it's too dark to see her face. The moonlight is behind her, facing its beam on me as I continue to shield myself from the possible attack she could unleash at any moment.

She has on shorts now, but it doesn't look like she ever pulled on a shirt.

"Only perverts stare through windows while women change clothes," she hisses acidly.

"Perverts fog up the window with their hand down their pants, damn it," I growl, lowering my hands. "I was—"

"You," she says, sounding shocked the second she sees my face. Just as she moves farther away from the house, the security light finally comes on, shedding light on her face, and my jaw drops.

It's her. But no…

Her hair had red streaks, not purple. Right? Definitely right. I took my time taking her in the other night.

Before I can say anything, she continues, "Are you stalking me?"

Everything falls into place, and suddenly I get very fucking pissed. "Stalking *you*? At least now I know the reason you ran out of my house the second I left you alone. What'd you do? Sift through my shit and find my properties?"

Her incredulous expression is almost convincing. At least she has the grace to play dumb, but it's annoying.

"What the hell are you talking about? This is Ian Sterling's house."

My anger dissolves and morphs into utter confusion. "Yeah, doll. This is Ian's house, and I'm his son. This is my place, too, considering I'm the one who maintains it and paid for half of it."

Her face pales, and her eyes widen to the point where I realize she really isn't faking this. She honestly had no clue this was my place. But why—

"You're Maverick?" she asks in a rasp whisper. "Maverick Sterling?"

Well, shit. I never did give her my name.

This is the reason I need a damn break from women. I don't even bother giving them my name anymore, because I just assume they know who I am.

"Yeah. Now who the hell are you, and why are you in my house?"

And why the hell did you leave my house if you weren't trying to get something? That question can wait.

She groans long and loud, and then she pushes the heels of her palms into her eye sockets the second she drops the garden hose. That thing was meant for washing sand off boards and shit. Not for assaults on me.

"I'm Salem Wright. Oh, no. I'm going to be sick. No. No. No. This can't happen," she says, sounding truly horrified.

"Salem Wright? Is that name supposed to mean something?" I ask, completely and totally confused.

She pulls her hands away, and then she nibbles her bottom lip nervously. That's a distraction I don't need right now.

"Seriously? Your father hasn't mentioned my name to you?"

"Pretty sure I would have remembered it if he had," I mumble, now letting my eyes roam down her chest to where the black bra has my full attention. Her chest really is a work of art. Maybe we can—

"My mother is Kelly Lane—well, she's Kelly Sterling now. I'm Kelly's *daughter*, Maverick."

That has my eyes snapping up and my head tilting to the side. Then my jaw fucking drops when she adds, "Your new stepsister."

Chapter 5

Salem

How the hell did I manage to completely fuck up this bad? Maybe I'm being punished or something. The universe does love punishing me, after all. I'm its own little punching bag.

"No," Maverick says, shaking his head after several long minutes of stunned silence. "My father married a woman named Kelly, but he didn't mention a daughter, so this is a mistake."

Figures I wouldn't be mentioned. I bet Sean, Connor, and Tyler weren't mentioned either. Maverick has no idea what the hell his new family has become.

He's still on the ground, and he's still soaking wet. I knew I heard a noise, and then I saw him out of the corner of my eye while I was moving around in the bedroom. But I had no idea this was what I would find.

I really hate the universe sometimes.

"I'm definitely her daughter," I assure him with a tight smile.

Shit. Of all the men in this damn city, I chose my *stepbrother*? Yeah. I'm not chalking that up to coincidence. There's a conspiracy going on against me.

He groans while dropping his head back, and I cross my arms over my chest, suddenly feeling far too exposed in just my bra. When he saw me naked, he was a random guy from a club. Now he's my mother's new husband's son.

"I need a drink," he says, his sigh possibly layered in the same frustration I feel.

"I need something stronger than a drink," I mumble, sticking my hand out to help him up.

I ignore the unbidden shiver that runs through me the second he touches me. That's really not good.

As he climbs to his feet, he releases my hand, trying and failing not to let his eyes drop to my chest again.

Time to put on a shirt.

"I'm pretty sure we need to talk," he tells me, looking away from me completely and focusing his attention on the side of the house.

"Obviously," I scoff, turning to lead the way as he follows behind me. This is going to be a long night.

As soon as we're inside, he walks toward the kitchen, and I move toward the bedroom to quickly toss on the first shirt I come across. It's one of my random high school band shirts, but it'll have to do. And no, I wasn't actually in the band.

Deciding my shorts are far too short, I also grab a pair of yoga pants and toss them on.

When I head back into the living room, he's already on the sofa, and there is a large bottle of whiskey right in the center of the coffee table. He's already drinking a glass, and there's another one poured and ready for me.

Considering what happened two nights ago, I opt to sit on the other side of the large sofa—far away from him and his body that I'm overly acquainted with.

"What happens now?" he asks, acting as though I'm the resident expert on fucked-up situations.

I'm going to have to play this cool or look like an ass. Those are literally my only two options.

"We drink this whiskey, you call for a sober ride to come pick you up, and then we forget this ever happened," I state hopefully.

He snorts derisively. "You expect me to forget that we fucked. Just like that. And then see you at family gatherings?" he asks, eyebrow quirked.

Bristling, I nod. Then take a long sip of the whiskey, coughing and cringing afterwards because I can't drink whiskey straight.

A little smirk plays on his lips as I force down another sip and set the glass down.

"It shouldn't be a big deal. It was a hot quickie with—"

"It was a warmup," he interrupts, eyes narrowed on me.

"I'm sorry, a what now?" My tone is incredulous. But seriously, what?

"A warmup. It wasn't the main event. You left before we got to that."

A slow grin curls my lips as he continues to glare at me. His ego is a lot bigger than I initially realized.

"I said it was a *hot* quickie. I wasn't insinuating you were a minute man or anything."

His lips twitch. "I'm definitely not a minute man under normal circumstances. But I'd been hanging with my hand a little too long, and warmups are sometimes needed during those times. It wasn't a quickie."

He's really sexy when he's trying to redeem his manhood.

Nope. Not sexy. He's my *stepbrother*.

Yay! I love complicated shit...said no one ever.

"Anyway," I say, trying not to smile as he leans back, eyes on me as he casually sips his whiskey, "it's not like we're some star-crossed lovers who can't possibly move forward after our...*warmup*. We'll just pretend it didn't happen."

"After, of course, we have the main event," he goes on with a shrug.

I stare at him like he's an idiot for a full five seconds, waiting on him to tell me he's joking.

He doesn't.

He just continues to smirk at me.

"I want a redo," he finally says, only confusing me more.

"A what?"

Completely relaxed, as though we're talking about something as mundane as chicken or fish, he explains, "A redo. You caught me on a night when my game clearly wasn't on point. I want to start over, and this time, you'll be less inclined to run away before I'm finished."

I just blink at him. "Absolutely not."

He mutters something about that line apparently only working for Wren.

"Who the hell is Wren?" I ask.

"Not important. What is important is us trying this again."

"You're kidding, right? You heard the part about me being your stepsister?"

"We've already fucked once. Damage is done. The least we could do is have a—"

"I'm going to stop you right there, because I see what's going on here," I tell him, holding up a hand.

"What's that?" he asks, clearly amused and enjoying this for some reason.

I stare directly into his warm, chocolatey eyes. "You're still in hunter mode."

I'm not sure if he looks amused or confused right now "Hunter mode?" he asks.

I nod slowly. "Yes. Like back at the club. I saw it in your eyes that you wanted to do some hunting, since it was abundantly clear you had too many options coming to you. You wanted a little chase. I gave you that. Let you come to me."

His lips twitch again. "You *let* me come to you?"

"Part of the game, Maverick. You give a guy what he wants, and he'll rarely let you down. Now you see this as more chase, when really, it's a brick wall."

Silently regarding me, he taps a finger on his chin like he's thinking before he speaks again. I decide to go on while he's silent.

"This is no longer a game between us. Trust me when I say my mother would blow a tiny gasket if she found out I slept with you. You need to know something very crucial about my family, and that's the fact my mother will indeed become the center of your father's universe. Stepping in the way of that by drawing attention to us would prove stupid for me."

He continues to study me.

"I haven't met your mother yet," he finally says without concern. "But obviously she has skills if she got my father to put a ring on it and then he put you up here." He gestures around my temporary dwelling.

I narrow my eyes on him. "I put myself up here. I'm paying Ian rent each month. Two grand. I know it's not what it's worth, but he refused to let me find another place on my budget, which was hard to do in Sterling Shore."

His eyebrows go up. "You've met my father?"

That's what he asks? Really?

"No. I've only spoken to him over the phone, because I had to move out here when Mom married him."

Warm brown eyes travel down my face as his brow furrows. "Had to? How old are you?" The way he asks it means it's more of a condescending question than one of concern for the fact he thinks I'm too young.

Rolling my eyes, I decide this conversation needs to hurry along. I, unfortunately, know how to end any ideas he might have.

Never tell anyone everything about you, Salem. It makes you a bore. And men love a good mystery in a woman.

My mother's rules are always fun to break.

Besides, the sooner he's appalled by me, the sooner he will stop tempting me. Maverick Sterling is like a presence that can't be ignored. And when all his attention is focused on you because he wants you? Yeah. See how strong you can be.

"Okay, I'm going to cut to the chase. Your father has married a typical gold digger, and I give it five months—on the high end—before he realizes she's not as perfect as he thinks she is. Then *poof*—we're once again gone, and it'll be like none of this ever happened."

His grin spreads like I just said something he finds amusing.

"Figured as much about your mom. Wedding happened a little fast. But my father isn't an idiot. There'd be an iron-clad pre-nup, and no matter how good she is, he's just as good. Fair chance she's not faking it."

I'd normally laugh at a guy thinking my mother is actually catching a case of feelings, but this isn't a time for laughter. "She's not looking for money after the marriage. She has plenty of her own money, since she's been doing this for a while, but she likes to live off men who are stupid enough to let her. She'll live a life of luxury, sponging off him like a leech for as long as he lets her. She'll have him wrapped around her finger until he finally starts getting tired of all the perfection. You'll try talking sense into him, but he won't listen, because Kelly is damn good at what she does."

He still looks amused. What is wrong with this guy?

"Then she'll get the marriage annulled," I go on. "So that she doesn't risk maxing out her legal marriage count. She'll charm the hell out of him, you, and everyone you know. You'll hate her as much as you'll admire her."

A smile stays fixed on his lips, but it seems to be growing.

"Why are you telling me this?" he asks.

"Because you're still staring at me like this is all a game, and like you think I'm still on the menu. If you know just how shallow my mother is and what she's really after, then it's going to stop this chase."

"You're trying to turn me off because you don't want *me* to turn *you* on. Is that what you're saying?" He's really not acting like they normally do. I've done this with countless other step-siblings—the conversation. Not the sex. The sex was a first and, as you know, a total accident.

Plenty of steps have hit on me, but after this story, they always look at me like I'm something that's stuck to their shoe. Not something they still want a piece of.

On the rare occasion, we're friendly with the new family, but it's never like a real family. It's just making the best of an otherwise awkward situation.

"I'm telling you the reality of the situation," I bite out, frustrated.

The cocky guy just leans over, invading my space, getting so close I can feel his breath tease my lips. His eyes dart over mine, and he cocks his head.

"The thing is, Salem, honesty is one of my favorite qualities in someone. If you wanted me to walk away, you should have lied to me and said your mom is deeply in love with my dad because of the man he is, or some shit like that."

I shudder a little, feeling his closeness in all the wrong ways. Totally backfiring on me.

His gaze drops to my lips, lingering there, and I dart to my feet, quickly walking over to the chair that is across from him, putting the coffee table between us like a short barrier. He just grins, staring down at the sofa where I just was, before those humor-filled eyes find mine again.

"Why'd you follow your mother out here?"

"Because I love her and adore her," I say with a smirk.

His grin is so big that it transforms his face. I didn't think it possible for him to be even sexier.

"Lie," he states through his smile.

"I'm a pathological liar," I lie.

He shakes his head as a deep chuckle rumbles from his chest. He holds a hand up in surrender. "Fine. Fine. You don't want me to want you. I got it. But we will be seeing each other. It's inevitable. So we should at least be friends. Tell me why you really followed your mom out here."

He leans back, acting as though he genuinely wants to know.

"It's a requirement that I follow her no matter which place she goes. At the end of each *relationship,* we return home to Georgia for a few months or less."

"Requirement? Trust fund or something?" he asks, no judgment in his tone.

"Or something," I say with a tight smile, not willing to give him that information. "Why do we need to be friends?"

I don't think I can be friends with him, to be honest.

"Because I have rules. One of those rules is not to fuck friends. So if you're my friend, then you're safe," he says, that smile of his never waning. "Otherwise, I'm just going to keep trying to get into your pants. Habit of mine."

Trying not to act affected by the sentiment of those words, I take a deep breath.

"I don't do friends."

"Me neither. That's the point," he says, winking.

It takes me an embarrassingly long second to catch the joke. "Finally. A flaw," I say on a sigh.

His eyebrows go up. "A flaw?"

"You make the same jokes an eleven-year-old boy would."

To this, he laughs, getting more comfortable on the sofa as his eyes stay warmly fixed on me.

"You could have called me a player. A manwhore. Something along those lines. Girls usually like to point out that little flaw," he says, still laughing lightly. "Maybe tell me I have a Peter Pan complex for not ever settling down or growing up."

He stares at me expectantly, like he's waiting for me to take the bait.

"You like sex. Totally get that. Unless there's a wife, girlfriend, or fiancée I'm not aware of, I don't see what the problem is. I mean, obviously you use condoms, so you take safety precautions. It's your life."

He nods, the humor slowly slipping from his face.

"Why don't you do friends?" he asks, gesturing toward me.

"I meant that I don't have friends, because I'm usually not in one spot for too long. Goodbyes are never much fun."

I do have my brothers, and they're all the friends I need.

He glances around, noting all the boxes in the house. "So that means you have no help unpacking these, I assume."

Sean won't be here until tomorrow, and even then he won't be much help unpacking. I'll be lucky to keep him off his phone long enough to unpack his room.

"I always manage on my own. I just keep the basics."

He stands suddenly, moving toward the kitchen again. The open floorplan gives a view of the three main rooms — living, dining, and kitchen. I watch as he goes to a box, opening it up.

"What're you doing?" I ask as I stand, going to join him.

"Being your friend. Like I said; I don't fuck friends. And if we just keep sitting there, *not* being friends, I'm going to end up trying to seduce you again," he says with a shrug, as though it's no big deal.

I guess he likes being honest too.

Bluntly honest.

Swallowing the knot in my throat, I resign myself to the fact that free labor and muscle like he has wouldn't be such a bad thing. The house came fully furnished, which is fortunate. Even though things are a little upscale for my tastes.

"Got a special place you want this stuff?" he asks, not looking back at me as he starts unpacking some of my pots and pans.

"Just keep the cookware close to the stove or oven. Other than that, no particular plan."

Skeptically, I go to pick up my own box, as he begins stocking a cabinet like this is any other day.

"Pizza would be good. I'm fucking starving," he says, causing me to smile a little.

"I ordered one fifteen minutes ago—right before I caught you perving through my window—so you're in luck."

When he flashes a grin my way, I have to remind myself that he's decidedly off-limits. I also have to ignore the stupid pang of disappointment that he's no longer *trying* to seduce me.

Don't you love it when you contradict yourself?

Maverick Sterling is going to be a terrible friend for me.

"So if I'm your friend, you magically lose all interest in me?" I ask him, aiming for casual conversation.

"Yep." He continues unpacking a box, never glancing in my direction. "That little tactic has worked all my life."

"You implement it often?"

"Every time I have to be around a girl I'm attracted to for extended periods of time, I become her friend. Attraction dies down pretty damn quickly, and soon, I look at her as one of the guys."

Not sure why that makes me smile.

"Why?" I ask, only because I'm genuinely trying to understand him.

"Friends last longer than hook-ups. I guess it keeps me from fucking up with the wrong person that could get hurt. Especially if it's someone I know I'll have to be around a lot."

Propping a hip against the counter, I study his profile. His shirt is still soaked from where I blasted him. I've been trying to ignore the way it clings to his upper body, showing off every line of definition there.

He looks my way, smiling when he catches me staring, and I clear my throat.

"You probably need to dry your shirt," I say like I just noticed it's wet.

He steps back, reaching an arm over his head, and tugs the shirt off right in my kitchen. My mouth tries to water. Then it dries. Then waters again. It can't make up its mind if it's Seattle or Phoenix right now.

In the light, his body looks so much better than I remember. Every defined line of his abs is on display and completely—

"Care if I borrow your dryer?" I don't miss the cocky mockery in his tone.

My eyes come up and narrow on his, while the sexy prick smirks at me knowingly.

Walking over, I snatch the shirt out of his hand, even as his smirk turns into a grin.

"You said you wouldn't try to seduce me."

"I said I wouldn't seduce my friend. We're not friends yet," he says, crowding my space as he backs me against the fridge.

My body really likes his body. There's no denying that.

I almost forget why we can't do this when his lips brush against mine while he cages me in, sliding a hand down to my hip to tug me in closer. My eyes flutter shut, ignoring my command to stay open. It's like there's a magnet drawing our bodies together, and I'm a slave to the pull.

But fortunately, before those lips of his do more than tease mine, the doorbell rings.

"Pizza!" I blurt out, my eyes darting open as I shove at his chest.

He chuckles under his breath while stepping back. "I'll get the pizza if you'll toss my shirt in the dryer."

I don't argue, because I need some space between us. As I sprint to the laundry room and toss the shirt into the dryer, turning it on, I hear, "Hey, Salem, can my pants go in there too?"

Maverick Sterling is going to drive me insane.

Chapter 6

MAVERICK

I'm grinning at her when she walks back in, a pair of sweats and a T-shirt in her hand that she roughly shoves at my chest.

"I doubt I can wear your clothes," I say, laughing as she backs up and crosses her arms over her chest, glaring at me.

"They're my brother's. Not mine. I steal sweats and T-shirts from him every time he visits me. So you're in luck."

"You mean *you're* in luck," I volley, loving the way flirting with her seems to really piss her off. It's a novelty. Never had that effect on a girl before.

Especially not one I've had sex with.

I mean, obviously I piss off all my female friends on the regular, because I'm awesome and fun like that, but not from flirting.

"Just put clothes on, or I swear the next pan out of this box will be cracking the side of your head. You said we'd be friends."

"Gotta work your way up to friend status," I remind her, unable to resist taunting her.

She turns her back when I start undoing my jeans.

"Are you seriously undressing in my kitchen?" she asks, her back rigid.

Dropping my jeans to the floor, I answer, "You saw every inch of my body the other night when I was buried balls-deep inside you, so I don't know why this has you flustered."

I can tell she's pinching the bridge of her nose as she shakes her head.

"I don't think friendship is in the cards for us," she grumbles, prompting me to laugh as I tug on the sweats. They fit almost perfectly, which means her brother is about my height.

Idly, I wonder if he's coming to stay here too.

As I tug the dry shirt over my head, I say, "I'm decent. Your shy little eyes can look at me again."

She gives an exasperated groan as she turns back, takes my jeans, and goes to throw them in the dryer. When she returns, she grabs the pizza box and flips the lid open. I grab a bottle of what looks like really cheap wine and pour us two glasses, working on hiding my inner wine snob.

"I'm not shy, but obviously I'm attracted to you, or we wouldn't be in our current predicament," she finally says.

I grin to myself, trying not to cross too many lines, reminding myself that she really should be off-limits.

"Has to be the weirdest one-night stand ever," I say mildly, hearing her laugh a little.

"Can't be."

Facing her again, I find her amused gaze on me as she takes a glass of wine and hands me a piece of pizza. I lean against the counter, eating a bite.

"Why?" I ask around a mouthful.

Really hope this friends thing works on her. Otherwise, my dick is going to revolt from the constant rejection.

She just grins. "It wasn't the weirdest one-nighter for me, so it can't possibly be the weirdest one-nighter for you."

My eyebrows go up. "We really doing this? Are we about to compare our worst one-night stands?"

She rolls her eyes. "I had a guy who stole my panties one time, and not for the pervy reasons you might think. He was actually *wearing* my pink thong. Caught a peek of them under his jeans when he bent over to put on his shoes."

I choke on my bite of pizza, and her grin grows.

"Your turn."

I can't believe I'm doing this. She really is trying to move us into the friend-zone, because there's not a lot of coming back from swapping war stories.

"Girl stole my house key one time when I went to the bathroom. She must have had like ten copies made, because I kept having to call the cops. Found her in my house doing domestic things all the time, and she kept trying to convince me we were in a relationship."

She shudders, and I nod.

"I know, right? Fucking creeped me out forever. I still don't know how she kept figuring out my damn security system codes. I swapped to keyless entry, and she stopped breaking in."

Salem sips her wine, studying me.

"This one time, I brought a guy home from the bar, only to realize I was his vehicle to my brothers, because he had a major crush on Tyler *and* Connor—wanted a threesome. They were both in town to visit me, and somehow this guy knew that. Totally creepy once we figured out his game. I stopped bringing guys home after that."

Gah, that's fucking horrible, but I still laugh, shaking my head.

"I tried to stop. But girls act apprehensive about taking me home sometimes. I'm never sure if it's because they don't feel safe, or if it's because they just want inside a Sterling's house. I risk it for their comfort, just in case it's the safety factor."

She chews another bite of pizza, leaning back against the wall.

"Worst one-nighter ever," she says, gesturing at me.

I have to think about that. "Probably the time I had a repeat and didn't realize it was a repeat until I saw the room full of fucking unicorns."

Her eyebrows go up. "What?"

"Girl took me home from Silk, and I had zero idea I'd ever been with her before. Until that damn room of unicorns. I swear, it was nothing but unicorns—all types, all sizes, all textures. I'd never found unicorns creepy until that moment. Now I hate the fuckers."

I give a full body shudder.

"It was like the Twilight Zone, because I seriously had no memory of the girl, but I had too many memories of that damn room. I left before things progressed, and got the hell out of there."

She laughs like she finds it funny. I still have nightmares about that fucking room.

She dusts her hands off, finished with her slice of pizza, and sips the rest of her wine as a comfortable silence falls between us.

"What about serious girlfriends?" she asks, going back to unpacking a box as though she's disinterested.

"Closest thing was Chloe Macintosh. We had a casual arrangement for years, but it was never a relationship. It ended fairly recently because she's not exactly someone I want to be cool with anymore, at least not until she chokes up a sincere apology to Dale's fiancée. Star Morgan was another semi-casual thing, but that nearly cost me one of my best friends. In other words, nothing serious."

"Nothing at all? Aren't you like twenty-seven or something?" she asks, understandably confused.

"I was busy with sports and school until I graduated. Then in college I was loaded down with courses, double majoring in business and marketing. After college, I went into business for myself, sometimes with my cousins. Casual works best for me, and since I'm not looking to marry, there's no reason to date."

She pauses working in her box, looking over at me with curious eyes. "You can date without getting married. I have zero intentions of ever marrying. I still like the occasional boyfriend, even though I know it'll end. It's worth the goodbye to get those early relationship flutters from time to time."

Clearing my throat, I look away, unpacking another box. "People get hurt when one wants to be serious and the other doesn't. Different end games and all. I don't want to be the reason some girl is in tears if I can help it."

When the silence stretches on, I finally look over at her to find her grinning at me, all her attention focused my way.

"What?" I prompt.

"Nothing. I just find it cute how you think we're so fragile that a girl would never bounce back from liking you, Maverick Sterling. Also, way vain. Your ego must be cramped inside this house."

I snort, rolling my eyes as I finish up another box and start on the final one.

"I didn't mean it like that," I mutter, causing her to laugh.

"People date. People break up. Nothing is so tragic that someone can't move on to another relationship. And no one is so epic that they rip the hearts from someone's chest, leaving them unable to move forward. Like ever. Everyone likes that connection of being with someone who wants to make them feel good, even if it is short-lived."

We'll have to agree to disagree.

"What about you? Anything serious?"

Her eyes get a distant glaze, but she offers me a tight smile. "Few times. I have terrible taste in guys."

I flip her off, and she grins genuinely.

"Our quickie doesn't count," she says, winking at me.

"Warmup," I remind her. "What happened with the serious ones?"

She looks away. "One slept with my mother, and one slept with my one and only female friend," she says, not looking at me as she slides the pizza box out of the way.

"That's...fucked up."

"Yeah. My mother didn't approve of me falling in love when she saw the way my boyfriend was constantly checking her out. Guess it's good she fucked him before I did fall in love. Would have sucked twice as bad, huh?" she asks, aiming for joking.

Girls with a past like Salem are usually bitter or bitchy. I find it a little fascinating that she's neither.

"Tell me something really personal about you. This usually helps the friend process to move along," I say, shifting the subject since she's gone quiet on me.

"Something more personal than my mother sleeping with one of my boyfriends?" she asks, a small smile ghosting her lips.

"Something a little lighter maybe. We jumped into the big stuff a little soon," I say, moving a little closer when she laughs.

"Seriously. Tell me something," I go on, unsure why I'm fucking going on with the twenty questions.

"I have an allergy to pet hair," she states automatically, never glancing at me.

I want to laugh at the irony of it.

"Your turn," she says, digging out more bowls.

"I have a hairless cat with a demon inside her."

She frowns as she faces me. "I never saw a cat when I was there."

"She was at the vet. Had to get her spayed. Really hoping that makes her sane or something, because that pussy is crazy."

She laughs like I'm joking.

I'm not.

I watch her as she stretches up on her tiptoes, putting a large plastic bowl near the top. Groaning inwardly, I try to tell the wayward appendage that I'm wearing her brother's sweats and that it's gross to be all pressed up against the front of them while I watch the unknown guy's sister's ass.

Who also happens to be my stepsister.

Fuck. When did shit get so complicated?

My phone rings on the counter, and I answer it when I see Kode's name. "What's going on?"

"We're heading to Dane's. Where the hell are you?"

Right. I sort of ditched them and never called them back.

"I'm at the beach house near the strip. I'm busy right now, so go on without me."

I catch Salem's head turn in my direction, but I only notice it from my peripheral.

"Seriously? You're the one who wanted us to all go out tonight, and you're just bailing?" he groans. "I could have been in bed with Tria, you fuckwad."

I hear giggling that I know is Tria, and I roll my eyes. It is shitty to bail on a night that I planned out.

"Fine. I'll head that way in a few."

"Gee, don't sound overjoyed, dickhead."

Hanging up on him, I turn to face Salem, who gives me a small smile.

"Feel like riding with me to a friend's house?" I ask her. "Well, actually my cousin's house. But we're all close like friends. Or brothers. Hell, we're tight."

I'm seriously fucking rambling right now. I don't like it. Not one little bit.

"Thanks, but I think I'm just going to stay in and eat some more pizza. Maybe catch a movie if I can find something worth watching."

Trying not to find that option more appealing, since it shouldn't be, I nod as I pocket my phone. "Care if I return the clothes later? I doubt mine are dry yet."

They probably are, but I need an excuse to return. You know, to be friends with her and all. Not to pin her against the wall again and get her loosened up enough to let me kiss her like she almost did before the pizza fucker messed it up.

"Sure," she says quickly, then clears her throat and bats her hand. "No problem. You're my stepbrother now, so you can borrow clothes when you need to."

She awkwardly punches my shoulder, like she's trying a little too hard for the friend angle. I smile at her teasingly, arching an eyebrow as she palms her face.

"I made that weird, didn't I?"

My grin grows. "Little bit."

She mutters a curse, and I restrain the laughter trying to escape.

"So I'll see you later then," she drawls, like she can't stop herself from talking.

The easy banter from earlier is gone now, replaced with this rapidly devolving, rambling version of herself. It's fucking cute as hell.

"Yeah. Later," I agree.

I start to step toward her, and she punches my shoulder again like a *friendly* but incredibly awkward gesture.

"Alright then. Have fun, buddy," she says in a tone a little too high-pitched.

A snort of laughter escapes me, and she crosses her arms over her chest before groaning. "I'll stop talking. And punching your shoulder. Like right now. Leave before I keep doing stupid shit."

I back away, holding my hands up innocently, and wink at her before walking toward the door.

There's no way in hell I can be friends with Salem Wright. This might just be the one time my tactic doesn't work.

Chapter 7

Salem

"You look fat," Mom sighs, pinching the small bit of softness on my stomach.

I'm not fat. I'm also not a rail.

Batting her hand away earns me a snort of irritation. "You look vapid. Guess none of us are perfect," I say with a dark smile.

She sighs again. "Careful, Salem. You have good genes, but you can still get fat if you try hard enough. Are you moved in?"

"Mostly. Where's Sean? You said he'd be—"

"He's on his way from the airport. His father cut their time short. Predictably. Hence the reason my honeymoon was cut short."

I hold my tongue.

Sean got about as lucky with life as I did. We're the only two out of the four offspring my mother has pushed out who have the absent father issue. At least mine has a good excuse.

"You said he'd be here, which is why I'm here," I remind her.

"I just told you he's on his way now," she says dismissively.

"If I had known you weren't picking him up from the airport, I would have gone to get him myself," I bite out.

"His father had to ride with him and walk him to the car I sent. Really, Salem, it's not as though I'm letting my child wander around a busy airport. Play your part, Salem. Happy daughter. Beautiful girl. Sweet disposition. Or Sean can just stay full time until you remember your place."

One day, I will be able to punch her in the face. Just as soon as she stops having kids, that is. I've never prayed for menopause to hit someone as much as I pray for it to happen to her.

She's not always terrible. And I know she has her reasons for all the shitty things she does, given her past and her experience. But those reasons are not always good enough to make it easy to bear her.

"Where's the new husband?" I ask her in deflection, carrying her away from the threats.

"He's somewhere," she says, gesturing around the huge freaking house. Very well may be the largest one she's scored yet.

Just how rich is Ian Sterling?

She starts guiding me through the home, and I slowly slip on the mask I've worn so many times for the new family. Well, the mask I wear when my mother is around, rather. She needs that Stepford illusion thing to keep them thinking she's perfection incarnate.

Just as we round the corner, a very gorgeous, older man comes walking out, though he doesn't look quite old enough to be Ian.

"Ian, darlin', there you are," Mom says, her face bright as she steps into him. His arms go around her, and *ewwww*.

He totally grabs two handfuls of ass right in front of me. She moans into his mouth as he kisses her, and I look around, you know, trying not to vomit and stuff.

"Oh shit," Ian says, drawing my attention back as he releases my mother. "Sorry. I didn't see you there. You must be Salem."

Wearing my practiced smile, I nod, extending my hand. He takes it, but just as our hands grip…I see someone I wasn't expecting.

Brown eyes meet mine over Ian's shoulder as my overly-familiar stepbrother walks out of a room. Maverick looks as surprised as I do, but a slow grin curves his lips.

Damn sexy lips.

What's he doing here?

Surely he doesn't still live at home.

"Really good grip," Ian says through strain, reminding me I'm squeezing the ever-loving-hell out of his hand.

"Salem, really," Mom scolds under her breath.

This causes Maverick's cheeky grin to grow.

I finally release Ian's hand, and he discreetly shakes out the pain. Maverick steps closer, joining the little awkward circle. See? I knew this would be weird. I totally wasn't expecting him to be here, and I didn't think I'd have to deal with the weirdness so soon.

"Maverick, this is my daughter, Salem Wright. Salem, this is Ian's only son," Mom says with every ounce of elegance she possesses.

I start to speak, probably to say something stupid, but Maverick beats me to it. "Salem and I are already friendly," the asshole says, his eyes sparkling with humor.

Mom's eyes slant accusingly toward me. Shit.

"Oh?" she asks, her voice deceptively calm.

"When you told me Salem had been here for three days already, I sent Maverick over to help her settle in," Ian says, saving my ass.

He brushes his knuckles over my mother's cheek, and she stops glaring at me as she relaxes. "You didn't have to do that," she tells Ian.

"I had nothing else going on," Maverick answers, his gaze flicking to my mother. "Besides, Salem is family now, right?"

I choke on air, and Mother cuts her gaze to me again. I'm really terrible at this discretion thing.

Maverick's laughing eyes tell me he's thinking the same thing.

"Bug," I lie, coughing one last time.

"There aren't any bugs here," Mom states dismissively, looking at me like I've lost my mind and probably wondering if I'm high or something.

"So, Maverick, were you just leaving?" I ask hopefully, my gaze moving back to him.

Subtle, Salem. Real freaking subtle.

His grin, as always, remains perfectly fixed on his stupidly perfect face.

"Actually, I was. Just dropped off all the business contracts Dad had me handling in his absence. We should do lunch sometime. Be *friends*."

Funny guy, this one. Real funny.

"I'm sure she'd love that," Mom answers as I glare at the grinning prick, who is quickly on his way to becoming the bane of my existence.

Mom is growing increasingly annoyed with my current ridiculousness, though the other two would never be able to tell it. But I can tell she's no longer suspicious of Maverick and me. At least there's that.

"We'll have dinner next week. Let everyone meet everyone. Though I hate that Connor and Tyler won't be here," Ian goes on.

He seems like a genuinely nice person. I hate that he got sucked into my mother's using web.

"Connor and Tyler?" Maverick asks, pretending I haven't spoken of them to cover just how well we've gotten to know each other.

"My brothers," I say with a tight smile. "Connor lives up north, currently in college. Tyler lives just outside of Atlanta."

He nods slowly, a smile coming up again. "Whose clothes did I borrow?" he asks me.

I'm killing him. Just as soon as I find something sharp.

"Connor's," I bite out.

"Clothes you borrowed?" Mom asks, confused, a little suspicion sneaking back into her tone.

"Little mishap with the garden hose left me soaked last night, and Salem was kind enough to lend me some clothes," Maverick tells her.

It's just enough truth to keep the misleading undertones a secret from my very shrewd mother, who relaxes again.

"Oh, I meant to show you something," Ian says to my mother, tugging her hand in his and guiding her away. "Maverick, I'll call you about setting up a dinner."

"Wouldn't miss it," Maverick says, grinning at me as my mother walks away.

As soon as they turn the corner, I slap Maverick across his really hard stomach, causing him to laugh and me to wince. That was definitely not the intended effect.

"Violent little thing, aren't you?" he muses as I shake my stinging hand.

"What was that?" I hiss, glancing by him, paranoid my mother will hear.

"My very sexy, rock hard abs. You think you'd know not to hit them," he deadpans.

Gonna be the death of me.

"Not *that*," I growl. "All that. You just flirted with me in front of our parents."

"That wasn't flirting. That was just me being *friendly*."

He waggles his eyebrows, and I glare at him, unamused.

Rolling his eyes, he steps closer, and I step back. "Relax. That's how I always am—with everyone. If I'd acted any differently, my father would have been questioning what happened when I went over there last night. Little does he know that I've already—"

I lunge and cover his mouth with my hand before he can finish that, looking past him to see if our parents are coming back yet. His hands go to my hips, jerking me until I'm slammed against his really hard body, and then the bastard *licks* my hand.

Licks. My. Hand.

Who does that?

I try to pull back, but he just holds me. I do, however, move my wet-palm hand off his mouth.

"Anyone ever tell you that you get a little too worked up?"

"Anyone ever tell you that you can't take anything serious?" I volley, still glaring, even though my neck is craned way back to see the tall bastard's amused eyes.

"All the time," he quips. "I really do need to be going, but I'll swing by sometime soon to return the clothes, *friend*."

He releases me, and I take a step back as he grins.

"No shoulder punches before I go?" the dick asks.

"The next thing I punch won't be your shoulder or your *rock hard* abs," I inform him with a cruel smile, letting my eyes briefly drop to his crotch to drive home my meaning.

He laughs, turning and walking toward the exit. I think. This place is massive and I have no idea how to navigate it.

I glance out the window nearest to me, finding myself watching him as he walks toward a silver Audi. Guess that's why I didn't know he was here. Of course he has more than just one car.

Rich guys.

Grrr.

He turns, his eyes colliding with mine through the window, and he grins again before getting into his car.

My inconvenient attraction to my stepbrother continues to be a pain in my ass.

But as he pulls out, I see a black sedan pulling in, and my smile spreads as the driver opens the door for a very familiar face. It feels like months instead of two weeks since I saw my youngest brother.

I dart out of the room, racing around to find the entrance, and…get lost. Because this house is freaking huge. And it's designed to confuse the Maze Runners or something.

I hear a door shutting somewhere, and I blow out a frustrated breath, hoping it is Sean.

"Marco!" I call out.

"Polo," he calls back, sounding like he's trying not to laugh.

"Marco!" I yell again, cursing a lamp that crashes to the floor when I accidentally bump into a table.

I'll clean it up and pray it wasn't a priceless piece of art.

"Polo!"

After I find Sean, that is.

And this is how my entire life has pretty much gone. It's what I call a pie moment.

Chapter 8

MAVERICK

"So your father is really married?" Mom asks me as I finally get her too-heavy picture hung. One of me, unfortunately. Because my chubby five-year-old picture had to be blown up to ungodly proportions and hung in the living room.

For *everyone* to see.

Can't wait to be ridiculed endlessly for that, and I'll bitch slap anyone who doesn't ridicule me, because obviously I deserve it for this monstrosity.

"Yes," I tell her, noticing the way she immediately fakes a shaky smile.

"I guess I should mention I have a date this weekend," she blurts out.

This is what I've been afraid of. I knew she was on dating sites, but she hasn't actually been dating. Because despite her denial, she's been waiting around for years for Dad to grow up and settle down for good.

Now he's settled down with someone else.

So she's going to fucking rebound with someone fourteen years *after* her divorce. Don't tell me she's probably been with others. I know. I just try not to think about it.

The point is, now she's telling me, and it's a new game.

"Please spare me any details," I say, kissing her forehead as she laughs.

"I just think it's time to maybe find someone."

Since she feels Dad is no longer an option.

As much as I hate the idea of her dating and then me dealing with the tools, I'd rather her find someone than keep waiting on him.

"By the way, Ruby said you're thinking of seeing someone," Mom goes on.

"Ruby is doing her best to drive me insane," I say with a roll of my eyes, prompting her to laugh.

"Speaking of, I got rid of all the peanuts. Finally. You have no idea how long it takes to get rid of anything with nut ingredients. Corbin and Ruby can finally come to dinner over here."

I glance at the time, deciding I should get out before she starts telling me what she's going to cook them for dinner. Then tell me what conversation starters they might have. Or what—

I can't believe I'm about to say this, but I think my Mom *does* need to get a boyfriend so I can take a break.

"Gotta run, but be careful with online dating. Some of those guys—"

She holds up a finger, the universal sign for *hold on*, as she reads a text message or something. "All the acronyms these days are really confusing. Why can't people just spell the whole words?"

"What *pesky* acronym is confusing you?" I ask seriously, though I'm holding in the age jokes.

"D-I-C P-I-C. What does that mean? Some guy is asking if I want one."

She blinks innocently at me as I jerk the phone out of her hand, ready to kill some skeezy motherfucker.

There's nothing here from any guy. All that's here is a reminder about taking the tuna casserole out at seven.

The hell?

When Mom starts laughing and her eyes dance with endless humor, I roll my eyes, groaning and feeling too damn gullible.

"You're so fucking hilarious," I state dryly.

"Just letting you know I'm not the one who's easily duped, son."

She winks at me, and I shake my head before walking out, deciding my mother just won that round, and nothing I say at the moment will be taken seriously.

Juggling the mini *zen garden* Mom decided I needed in my life, trying not to spill sand everywhere, I open my door, deciding on my next stop. My phone rings just as I get pulled onto the street. I answer when I see it's Rain.

"To what do I owe the pleasure?" I ask in a mock English accent.

"We're grilling out tomorrow. You coming over?" Rain asks me over the phone as I drive toward the beach.

"Not sure. I may or may not have plans, but I'll call you back and let you know."

"Hey, Ruby said you've been chasing a girl. Have you found a unicorn?"

Why that word? Does she not know it makes my skin crawl? And why does Ruby insist on falling farther and farther down my list of favorites?

"No, I have not found a fabled magical creature. She's just a girl, and…it's a long story. No worries, I'll tell you all about it. But stop doing your excited dance, because I'm not settling down."

"How'd you know I was dancing?"

"I didn't. I was just really hoping that's why you're getting out of breath."

"Har. Perv. You're so funny," she grumbles dryly.

Laughing, I take the next right, pulling up at my destination.

"I'll call you back," I say to Rain before hanging up.

With the borrowed clothes in my hand, I make my way toward the front door of my beach house—well, currently I suppose it's *her* beach house.

I knock. Wait. And then knock again.

Her beast of a truck is in the driveway, so maybe that means she's home. And what kind of a girl drives a truck like that? She's not tall, so why is it jacked up like it's meant for a NBA player's long legs?

The door swings open, and I turn toward it with a smile on my face. But…there's no one there.

"Can I help you?" a young voice asks, causing my eyes to drop.

Well, I guess there is someone here.

A kid.

Why the hell is a kid answering the door?

I take a step back, looking around at the house, then look back behind me. Yep. Definitely the right house.

My eyes land back on the kid with blond hair and an unimpressed expression. He can't be more than nine.

"Is Salem here?" I ask, confused.

His expression changes, his eyes going big. "Are you my daddy?" he asks, excitement in his voice.

Cold chills wash over me, and I clear my throat. Then clear my throat again.

Pretty sure I've had this nightmare on more than one occasion.

Still no words. One more time, I clear my fucking throat, remembering I only just met Salem and no way is this kid mine. Obviously.

"What? No, kid. I'm just looking for Salem. Is she—"

"Salem is my mommy! Are you my new daddy?! She swore she'd get me a new daddy!"

Since I have zero clue what to say—because what the hell do you fucking say to something like that?—I casually take a step back. Then another. Then another.

And then I literally turn and sprint to my car, jerking the door open, and drive out like hell is on my heels.

I can't believe a kid just sent me running for my life. Well, actually I can.

A fucking kid?

When did she get one of those? Well, obviously she got one about nine years ago, but she never mentioned a kid to me.

Am I okay with that? Shit, I don't know. The damn kid was asking me to be his daddy. That much I'm *not* okay with.

Moms are on my don't-touch list for obvious reasons. I'm clearly not father material, and moms expect a serious commitment. They have to.

What the actual hell just happened?

And how does she even have a kid that old?

Picking up my phone, I dial Rain. When she doesn't answer, I dial Bella. Then hang up before she can answer, because Bella will likely torment the unholy hell out of me and give me zero good advice.

Finally, I call Allie. The only safe option.

No answer.

Do you have any idea how many times they've had me move their shit? Where are these damn women when I actually need them?

Chapter 9

Salem

Cutting off the hairdryer, I walk toward the living room.

"Was someone at the door?" I ask Sean, who is lounging on the couch, his face on the screen of his phone as he plays a game.

"Someone trying to sell stuff," he says with a shrug.

"How many times have I told you not to answer the door for strangers?" I groan.

"How many times do I have to remind you I'm eleven and not five?"

"How many times do I have to remind you that I can take your phone away for being a little dick?"

He grins, but wipes it away, needing to stay cool and all.

"Sorry. Won't answer the door again."

I'm not sure I like the little smirk he's sporting. It's the I've-just-done-something-devious-and-loved-it smirk.

"Sean..."

"Salem..."

Rolling my eyes, I go back to the bedroom.

"There'd better not be any cops showing up!" I decide to warn him.

"I didn't do anything that bad," he assures me, though it's not entirely reassuring.

Quickly, I tug on my shoes and return. "Come on. I have that job interview."

His eyes come up. "In shorts that short?" he asks, cocking a judgmental eyebrow.

"Yes. These shorts have gotten me my past two jobs."

He rolls his eyes as he stands and follows me out the door, and I lock up as he waits.

"Using your body to get a job means you're not feminist," he points out.

"Yeah, well, my track record for sticking with a job is terrible, since we have to move so much, so it looks horrible on my applications. I look unreliable. I have to be feminist in other ways — such as supporting myself. Get in the truck."

He does, but I can tell my lecture isn't over. Did I mention he thinks he's my *older* brother sometimes?

"Besides," I say as I hop in the truck and crank it, letting him get his seatbelt on before I put it in reverse, "in my line of work, guys don't take me seriously until they actually see my work. This just gets me in the door to where I can prove myself."

"It'd probably get you into a strip-club, too. I bet they'd love for you to prove yourself there."

I glare over at him when we stop at a red light.

"Just sayin'," the little ass adds, still smirking.

"Just worry about starting your new school on Monday and stop worrying about the way I dress."

He bats a dismissive hand as I drive on. "Not my first time starting a new school. No worries."

It sucks that he's doing what I had to do. Getting dragged from school to school, from town to town. It's fortunate that he's smart, which has kept him from falling behind, even though he's attending some of the best schools there are. I can only imagine the brilliance that would come from him if he had stability in his education. And life, for that matter.

We pull up in front of Clanton Auto, and I park before hopping out. Sean follows me, and I head inside and to the right, taking the stairs up to the office — just as I was instructed to do.

There's an observation window that hangs over the garage where everyone below is working on cars. I pause, taking in the sight. It's a damn nice garage.

Sean pauses, looking out as well.

I put in for this job before I even moved out here. It seemed perfect, since the pay was awesome and the location isn't far from my house.

"Salem Wright?" a woman asks, her eyes dipping to my shorts.

Shit. I hope my interview isn't with her. It was supposed to be a guy.

"Yes, that's me. I'm, um, supposed to meet with Rye Clanton."

A few other guys are loitering in the waiting room off to the side, all of them glancing in my direction. One man even eyes one of the decorative, industrial poles then looks back at me like he expects me to dance on it. Okay, now I feel uncomfortable.

Sean is smirking, as if to say *told you so.* I ignore him.

Finally, the girl's eyes meet mine again. "This way."

She gestures toward an office, and I follow, taking a deep breath as Sean stays behind, phone in his hand in case he needs me.

I stumble a little when I walk in, because the guy who is standing up from behind the desk is...sexy. Very sexy. Was totally *not* expecting that.

"I'm Rye Clanton. I assume you're Salem?" he asks, his deep voice matching his roughly hot exterior.

"Yep."

Totally not getting this job, because he doesn't even glance at my very unprofessionally short shorts.

He takes a seat, gesturing to one of the chairs in front of his desk, and the girl from earlier comes in with a Coke, hopping up on the desk and looking at me.

"You're like *really* pretty," she says to me.

Okay…

"Brin," Rye groans.

"What? She is. Imagine how many guys would be plastered against that observation deck window if she worked in those shorts."

I hate to tell Sean he was right.

"Business would boom," she adds with a shrug.

Rye rolls his eyes. "Please don't sue us for her being incredibly offensive. She has no filter."

Finally, I relax a little as a smile spreads over my lips.

"I don't offend easily." He's got zero interest in me, so he's either with someone on a hugely committed level, or he's gay, or I'm simply not his type.

No job for me.

"Wrench went over your application. He was my lead mechanic until he got a job he couldn't possibly refuse. I don't have anyone planned full-time to step in for him, but he said you'd be the perfect temporary patch."

I perk right up, because it sounds like I might be in the game after all.

"Temporary?"

"Yeah, according to your previous employers, you only stick around for half a year at most. I'm assuming, given the fact you look healthy, that it's a family thing and not a health-related thing. I need long-term, but you'll work until I find someone else good enough to fill the role."

I nod slowly, wondering if this is really going to be this easy. I won't even have to feel slimy for flirting.

"Yeah. My mother moves a lot, and I move to be with my little brother."

He nods like that makes perfect sense, or he just gives zero fucks as long as it's not health-related.

"Wrench wanted to interview you, but he had to leave yesterday, which was two weeks earlier than planned. I need someone who can start as soon as tomorrow, because I can't handle the workload without an extra set of hands."

"Tomorrow works for me," I say a little too eagerly.

"You don't really have to wear the shorts," the girl—Brin—says, smiling at me. "Obviously I was making a joke earlier. But there is a dress code. No midriff or nipples. I think that's all. Oh, and steel-toes."

"Brin," Rye says again, a warning to his tone.

Brin just smiles at me, and I don't know if she's being nice and just joking good-naturedly, or if she's being mean with a smile. I'm from the South. It's not always easy to read between the lines, because we know how to slap you with a compliment and an insult, all in one sentence.

"I'll grab some paperwork for you," Rye says, cutting his eyes toward Brin before walking out.

As soon as he closes the door behind him, she scrambles off the desk and moves behind it, opening his drawer. I swear she's—*is that glitter?*

She's pouring glitter into something, but I have no idea what.

"Do you have a problem with occasional pranking?" she asks absently, her attention mostly focused on what she's doing.

"I...uh..."

"Just asking, because I started running the office after Rye's last office manager quit, due to the excessive pranking. Sometimes innocent bystanders get caught in the crosshairs."

"Any bodily harm?" I ask mildly, trying to act like I don't find her a little wacky.

"No. Not that extreme," she says seriously as she closes the drawer and tosses the empty container into the trashcan.

She scurries around to the front, hopping back up where she was, and training her eyes on me expectantly.

"As long as there's no bodily harm, I'm cool with pranks. Even if they get aimed at me. But I tend to get someone back. Fair warning."

Her grin blooms like it's the perfect answer. "Then I really hope you like it here."

Okay, so I no longer think she's mean with a smile.

"Thanks," I tell her sincerely, completely relaxed. Easiest interview ever.

Rye returns, taking his seat behind the desk, and he slides some papers across to me. "There are a few extra liability clauses and wavers in there since…I have an unorthodox office manager." He gives a pointed look to Brin, who bats her lashes innocently.

When he returns his attention to me, I decide there're not too many forms of wavers or papers I haven't signed before. All are pretty much the same.

"Do you have a pen?" I ask him, not seeing one near me.

He pulls open the drawer in front of him, but a loud *pop* sounds out, startling me.

Rye roars out a curse, Brin bursts out laughing, and I just watch with fascinated horror as the very huge man gets covered in glitter.

Yep.

Glitter sprays everywhere—mostly right in his face—like it's just exploded from something, and I'm positive it's purple. Definitely purple.

Rye shakes his head, and it looks like it rains glitter from his hair. Brin is still dying as his eyes narrow to slits, glaring at her.

Her laughter dies instantly.

"Oh shit!" She launches off the desk, and he makes an attempt to grab her, unsuccessfully, and coats me in a layer of glitter in the process.

Narrowly dodging him, Brin scurries out sideways like a cartoon character, and dives into another office that is directly beside us, slamming and locking the door in quick succession.

"That's for the stupid, stinky, poop-flinging mail you sent me!"

"It wasn't real shit!" Rye argues through the door, banging on it.

I hesitate, studying the papers before me, one of the wavers clearly stating that I won't sue in the event I become collateral damage in the ongoing prank war. Seriously?

"It was just as disgusting!" Brin calls back.

Do I want to work here?

Hell, it's paying too much not to work here.

The two call-backs I got while still in Georgia sounded promising. I never heard this in the background.

Shaking my head, I manage to find a pen under some papers on his desk and start filling out the paperwork as Rye says, "I'll fire you."

"I'll tell your daddy on you. You know he likes me better than you."

That has me grinning. I don't quite understand the dynamics of their relationship, but it at least sounds like it's a lot of fun.

"Fine," Rye growls. "But you have to come out sometime."

There's nothing about his posture or tone that makes me believe he's saying that with malice.

"I love you," Brin says through the door, mock apology in her tone.

"Then get all the glitter out of my hair when we get home. The last time it took me months to get it all out. Tag still fucking calls me Tinker Bell. And I swear I still see a sparkle from time to time."

A smothered laugh is all I hear in return from her, and Rye, looking utterly ridiculous in the copious amounts of glitter that continues to flutter from his hair, giving the illusion of purple dandruff, sighs as he returns his attention to me and sits back down in his seat.

"I swear this has nothing to do with Wrench leaving us, by the way. Are you certain you want to work here?" Rye asks me with feigned exasperation.

"I'll bring this back with me in the morning," I tell him, holding up the papers. "Seven, right?"

"Seven," he agrees, glaring at the door when it cracks open a little. It slams back shut, and he rolls his eyes.

Laughing quietly, I stand and start toward the door.

The sound of a chair sliding and slamming into a wall sends me turning around, watching as Rye grabs Brin mid-jump as she tries to escape. His arms come around her waist, and she bursts out laughing as he starts rubbing all over her, spreading the glittery love around.

He even shakes his head over her head, making it rain. Which has *Purple Rain* start playing in the background of my mind during all this. In my head, all this happens in time with *Purple Rain* as well.

And pathetically, I envy that moment. Their moment.

I've *never* had that moment, and this is probably just one of their many.

Her laughing as he blows raspberries on her neck, and him smiling against her after she has completely covered him in glitter. I don't look away until their lips connect, and then I start feeling less like a covetous onlooker and more like a skeevy voyeur.

I see so much of the fake stuff all the time that I often forget what it's like to see the real stuff.

Smiling a little dreamily, I turn and find Sean pinning me with an are-you-serious look, paired with a perfectly-executed condescending eyebrow arch. Cue record-needle scratch and the abrupt ending of *Purple Rain*.

"What?" I ask a little too defensively. And loudly.

A snort of derision answers that.

Little smartass.

Another few knowing stares are on me from the waiting room.

Rolling my eyes, I start down the stairs, and Sean follows with his judgy little eyes all the way behind me to the truck.

As soon as we're inside, he opens his mouth to speak.

"Don't you dare say it," I quickly caution, holding my finger up like it wields the power of the universe.

I crank the truck as he laughs to himself. Just as we get pulled out, he can't deny himself any longer.

Exaggerating his Southern accent, he asks, "How'd those shorts work out for ya, sis?"

"Hilarious, Sean. Real freaking hilarious."

"Bless your heart," he retorts mockingly.

The men in my life are always such exhausting smartasses.

Chapter 10

MAVERICK

"A kid?" Kode and Dane ask in unison.

I run a frustrated hand through my hair. "How did this happen to me?" I groan.

"You do realize that you only had sex with her less than a week ago, right? I highly doubt the kid is yours," Kode deadpans.

Dane chokes on a laugh, masking it with a cough as the other dickheaded cousin of mine smirks. I give him an incredulous glare.

"Sorry," Kode says, not sounding sorry at all as he rocks back on his heels, his hands in his suit blazer's pockets. "Had to be said."

"None of the girls I need to talk to are apparently available to talk to me right now, despite the fact that I'm friends with them for times precisely like this. I called you two assholes—"

"And you expect us to tell you to enlist to play daddy?" Dane asks me with a hint of laughter in his tone. "Maverick, you took my daughter to the park two weeks ago, and said you'd never do it again because too many single moms kept asking you out. And you can't do—"

"Can you stop talking now? You're sort of making me sound like an asshole," I interrupt dryly.

Kode turns away this time, trying not to laugh. I'm glad they find me so motherfucking amusing. I'll kick their asses later for this.

Fighting a smile, Dane goes on. "I'm just asking if you want to actually date this chick? It's sort of out of the blue."

I'm not sure what exactly about Salem has me so ramped up to begin with. Maybe it's because she doesn't expect anything from me. Or maybe it's because of the way she looks at me.

It's not just a hungry look. It's a look of torture—one where she wants more but doesn't want to risk it.

Something I can relate to.

Or maybe I'm just getting too fucking old to keep pretending like what I have is enough, and Salem is the breaking point for me.

"She's my stepsister, and I have to see her on a regular basis. Which means—"

"Stepsister?" Kode interrupts, and two pairs of wide eyes stare at me. I guess I glossed over that juicy little morsel during that summed-up story.

"Let's skip the shock factor, and the what-the-hells and yada yada and pretend this was common knowledge. The point is, I have to see her on a regular basis. For who knows how long. And she's in my head a little. I didn't expect to actually like her after I talked to her. No, I'm not in the market to be a dad. Hence my dilemma. I have to see her, and it's going to be a little uncomfortable when I go from stalking her to avoiding her upon discovering she has a kid."

"Ahhh," Dane says, leaning back against the desk in his office.

"That *is* going to be really awkward," Kode says with mock sympathy.

With an exhausted sigh, I say, "Thank you, Captain Fucking Obvious."

Dane, taking a little pity on me, claps a hand on my shoulder. "Ian will understand that you screwed your stepsister. Don't worry. It'll be all right."

So much for pity.

"We owe you at least two thousand more smartass remarks in return for the ones you've given us over the years for women," Dane says, grinning like a cheeky bastard.

Touché. "Can we put my tab on hold for five minutes?"

Dane grins tauntingly, but he says, "Be her friend. You told her that's what you were going to be. You're not going to catch a case of 'DAD' if you spend some time around a single mom."

I roll my eyes and flip him off. "Fuck you very much for your uselessness."

"Maverick," he calls, half laughing as I turn to leave.

Was I really this unhelpful to them?

Yes. Yes, I was. Many times.

Walking out now.

Of course, I flip them off one more time when they call for me again, never looking back as I head outside.

I start to call Dale, then halt myself. Every time I call, Harley has found some new toy to throw into their kinky damn sex life, and he wants to ask me about it, since he can't seem to fucking use Google like every-damn-body else in the twenty-first century. He clearly thinks my knowledge is far more extensive than it is, and he has to describe whatever it is in detail.

I have nightmares, people.

Night. Mares.

His fiancée created an app for him to use, and he *still* asks me questions!

Despite the joking around, Dane really did just unintentionally make me feel like an asshole. And all he was doing was repeating my words. Talking to Salem about the worst one-nighters also left me feeling like an asshole.

I told the story to be funny, but it wasn't so funny when I said it aloud to someone other than the guys. Telling a girl I've been with that I forgot about another girl I'd been with, but remembered her creepily decorated unicorn room…

I admit, I might have showered an extra ten minutes that night to wash that story off me.

Instead of calling Dale, I pretty much hear his voice in my head. I've had to hear hundreds of his unsolicited pep-talks/lectures in the past.

Uneasy feeling suddenly in my stomach, I pull out my phone, deciding to do something non-dickish for a change. And I order a pizza, while also hoping I'm not about to be an asshole in my quest to not be an asshole.

Chapter 11

Salem

Pumped from my successful interview, and loaded down with groceries for the week, I head inside with Sean. Just as I finish putting everything away, someone knocks at the door.

"I got it," I say to Sean, who is simply smirking on the couch for reasons unbeknownst to me.

I swing open the door, and my breath sort of does a shaky squeak thing. Maverick is standing there, sexy in a T-shirt that looks too soft, and a loose fitted pair of jeans. And two pizzas in his hands.

On top of the pizza boxes are the clothes he borrowed. My eyes swing up to find him smirking down at me.

"Too soon for pizza again?" he asks.

"Never too soon for pizza," I answer on autopilot, still a little stunned to see him.

"I can leave if you want, but—"

"No. No. Sorry. Come in."

Normally, guys I've been with don't get to meet Sean, but since Sean and Maverick are going to be meeting anyway, and Maverick and I are going to be FRIENDS, it's not like it's the same. I'm not sure how much Maverick will be in his life. Considering Ian seems like the family type—*bet Mother is loving that*—it could be a lot.

"Sean, Maverick Sterling is here. The new stepbrother I told you about," I call out.

Sean cuts his gaze toward me, eyes widening just a little before a ghost of a smile appears. Maverick stares at Sean, clearing his throat.

"We actually met earlier," Maverick says.

My eyebrows go up. Sean has been here all—

I cut my gaze to my brother to see his wicked-as-hell grin as he winks at me. "Is he going to be my new daddy?" Sean asks, throwing me off.

What the—

"Why the hell would he be your new—"

My words cut off, and I glare at my brother as his smile just grows.

Maverick, to his credit, just stands there a *little* awkwardly instead of *a lot* awkwardly.

"Maverick, this is my *brother*, Sean."

Maverick's eyebrows go up, confused for only a second, as Sean flicks a thumb at him. "For the record, I didn't know he was our stepbrother until just now. You now know he's probably a little too gullible this late in life, which makes him sort of too basic, if you know what I mean. You also know he's either into MILFs or he's a pervert. You're welcome for the breakdown."

Maverick glares at Sean, and I try not to smile, because obviously I'm not supposed to encourage bad behavior and all.

"Oh, you little—" Maverick's words bite off on his own as his face turns a precarious shade of red.

He thought Sean was mine and brought me pizza?

Yeah, sort of sweet.

No, I'll never tell him that.

Maverick moves to the kitchen, shaking his head as he drops the pizzas to the counter.

"Paybacks are hell, kid. Remember that," Maverick says to Sean, who simply laughs without concern.

"Is he always such a gem?" Maverick asks me, and I finally burst out laughing, unable to help myself any longer, even though I try to smother it with my hands.

He works really hard not to smile, because he's trying to hold onto that anger just a little longer. Finally he gives in and scrubs his face with his hands.

How lovely it is to know that my eleven-year-old brother has somehow already deduced the fact I slept with our new stepbrother. I'm such a great influence. Sadly, I'm the best one he has, besides Tyler. But Tyler has his own family and his own career.

Good thing Maverick and I weren't hopeless, star-crossed lovers who had to sneak around in secrecy. We apparently suck at discretion.

Sean gives me a knowing look that says he sees my thought bubble.

Creepy perceptive.

Sean returns his attention to the TV, and I look over at Maverick again.

"You said you had a brother near Atlanta and one in Boston. You never mentioned you also had one here," Maverick hedges, like he's accusing me of setting this up with Sean.

"That's because where I am, Sean is. I wouldn't live in a different city from him," I say, expecting that to be obvious to a guy who is still a stranger.

Getting just a little too comfortable around him.

Understanding dawns in Maverick's eyes, and he gives me a nod, finally getting the answer to his question about why I would move where my mother does.

Sean pops his headphones on, bobbing his head to music like he doesn't want to hear us talking anymore.

"So, pizza," I say when the awkward silence settles in.

"He stay with you a lot?" Maverick asks as I pull out a couple bottles of water.

He takes one, thanking me, and I glance back to make sure Sean is still distracted.

"Usually about two or three days at a time. Then a day or two off. Because we're siblings. Eventually we fight like siblings if we spend too much time together. And that's only as long as my mother allows it. When she wants me somewhere, I go to keep her happy. Hence the reason I'm attending this uncomfortable upcoming family dinner."

He flashes a grin, but it's a little weighted.

"Get all your boxes unpacked?" he asks randomly.

"I have a ton of bedroom things still to go up. Sean and I finished his room up earlier."

"I offered to help with her room but she's worried I'm too young for the things I might find," Sean pipes in, the little weasel faking with those headphones on so he can eavesdrop.

Maverick chokes out a laugh then turns away as I glare at my brother, who never even glances my way, eyes on his phone screen.

"Come on. I'll help you with your bedroom," Maverick says, pushing away from the counter. "Pizza is probably already cold anyway."

As we start to pass, my brother mocks us. "I'll just bet he'll help you with your bedroom."

I shove his head forward as I walk by, and he laughs at my back.

"I think he's me fifteen years ago, only twice as quick and doubly conniving. Really fucking terrifying thought," Maverick says as he shudders.

"You just met him," I say with a wave of my hand.

"Sorry. Didn't mean to—"

"No, I mean, you just met him; wait until about a month from now. He'll make you feel twice as stupid as him with just a look."

Maverick's grin returns, and I sit down, opening up a box.

"You know you don't have to actually help me unpack, even though your father told you to. Or do you?" I ask, prying as I study him.

"My father doesn't ever leverage me with anything, if that's what you're asking. Not our style. If he asks me to do something, and I'm able to help out, I usually do. But I never heard him ask me to help you. In case you've forgotten, I was shocked to find you here. Had no clue who you were."

"Right. Good point," I say, now feeling stupid.

Maybe he and my brother do have things in common.

"Family dinner in two days," I say when the silence stretches on. And it's just an awkward sentence tossed out without any preamble. I do this when I'm nervous.

Jealous, huh?

"Don't worry about it. I'll play it cool. I'm sure your brother has no problem playing it cool. And we're just friends," he says, shooting me a smirk even as he pulls out a stack of CDs.

"Didn't know they still made these," he muses.

Rolling my eyes, I snatch them out of his hand.

"On a scale of one to ten, how bad did you freak out when you thought I had a kid?" I ask him, giving him a mocking grin.

"Honestly? Nuclear meltdowns have probably been milder," he says with a laugh, shaking his head as he moves to hang one of my pictures on the nail already in the wall.

I guess he knows I'm not allowed to punch new nails in the wall.

Considering this is sort of his place.

"But you came back with pizza," I tell him. "Because we're really going to be friends."

That grin of his is definitely going to be the death of me.

"You sound very skeptical, Salem Wright."

We study each other for a moment.

"I can't stay too long," he finally says, looking away. "I have to go to my mother's to watch a movie with her tonight."

"Your mom? Is she like your Dad?"

He laughs like I've asked something funny. "Polar opposites. Sometimes opposites attract; however, they don't always stick together. But Mom is great. She'd probably like to meet you. She and my dad have been friends for the past few years."

"Did you just ask her to meet your Mom already? Clinger alert, Salem! Major clinger alert," Sean says from the living room, breaking up the semi-peaceful moment. "And, dude, seriously? Too soon. Just too soon."

"That kid is vicious," Maverick says, glaring at the wall like he can see Sean through it.

Trying not to laugh, I move the subject to boring things, not giving Sean any ammo or the wrong idea. We fall into easy conversation, which is sometimes like fun verbal sparring with Maverick, and then we're laughing by the time he stands to go grab a piece of cold pizza.

Sean has already eaten his fill, and Maverick glances at the time as he sticks a slice in the microwave.

It's always the most awkward when he's about to leave. Maybe I'll get to be the departer one day, and he can be the awkward one floundering around with how to bid farewell.

As soon as his piece of pizza is heated up, he smirks at me. "Is this where you punch my shoulder? Because I really do need to go."

"I'll never understand some generations," Sean decides to say.

Maverick grins at me, and I blow out a long breath, deciding to smother Sean with a pillow a few times tonight. Or dump a pitcher of ice-cold water over his head.

I go to tell Maverick that I'll see him later, or that I'll see him at the dinner, and can't decide which to say. So I say neither. Nope. Instead, I open my mouth and let stupid stuff fall out.

"Later, alligator," I tell him lamely, hearing Sean snort, and Maverick nods while trying not to laugh at me as well.

"After while, crocodile," Maverick finally says, sending Sean back into a laughing fit.

Smartasses. Everywhere I look, I see smartasses.

Two boys laugh at me as I turn and walk away. I'm going to Google *cool farewells*. Because I'm lame like that.

And to think, usually I'm good at this sort of thing.

But, outside of my brothers, I've never had a male friend. I'm the girl guys want to have sex with. Never the girl they want to settle down for. Never the girl they want to be friends with.

Okay. I'll stop whining now. Promise.

Chapter 12

MAVERICK

"So, Salem, what is it you do?" Dad asks as we sit down to our very awkward family dinner. I only just got here, since I was running behind.

Why was I running behind? Because the cat from hell decided my shirt was the perfect thing to piss on.

I really hope someone needs a cat. I don't know how much more I can take of the devil.

When I glance over, I can tell Salem and Sean would both rather be anywhere else.

Personally, I love a little drama. Keeps things interesting. As long as that drama doesn't involve me or a cat pissing on my shirt.

"I'm a mechanic," Salem answers, shocking the hell out of me.

Kelly bristles, and I can tell she doesn't like that answer.

"Salem was an excellent dancer when she was younger, but she decided she preferred to play in dirt like a boy." Even though Kelly says it with a smile, it's definitely an underhanded dig.

Salem doesn't seem fazed as she drinks her water. I'm sure she's probably used to the digs by now.

One of the things I like about her is how she doesn't seem to care what anyone else thinks about her.

"What about you, Sean? Any hobbies?" Dad asks.

Sean looks at his mother, who stares expectantly, and he narrows his eyes at me before answering my Dad. "I'm in dance."

A big-ass grin spreads across my face, and the little dick across the table glares a little harder, like he's daring me to say something.

"Dance?" I ask, leaning up.

Salem tries not to smile.

"Mostly breakdancing. Not ballet," Sean quickly supplies, as though that was paramount above all else to be told.

"But do you wear tights?" I ask, goading him.

He uses his middle finger to "scratch" his eyebrow. Pleasant kid.

Dad quirks an eyebrow, but Kelly seems oblivious. Clearing his throat, Dad redirects his attention to Salem.

"If you need a job, Maverick has a friend who was hiring," Dad offers. "May still be looking for someone."

Guess I could have thought of that.

"Well, I got a job a couple of days ago. It's actually a really nice place, and the work atmosphere is probably one of the lightest I've ever been in."

"Oh, Maverick, Salem made that pie on the table," Dad says, gesturing to the pie with whipped cream on top.

I shoot a taunting look at her, and she rolls her eyes. "I always make a lemon pie. It's Sean's favorite."

"Why'd you make pie?" I ask her.

"Because it's rude not to bring something when someone invites you to dinner," she states as though it's obvious.

I blink at her.

"Salem's lemon pies are good, but they are very fatty," her mother supplies dryly.

"Damn good; not just good," Salem says, her eyes on her mother.

I swear her mother *almost* smiles. "Language," she says instead.

Cue awkward silence.

Dad apparently grows tired of being the one to force all the conversation, so he looks over at me for help.

Kelly doesn't look old enough to have three grown kids, but she also doesn't look like the warm motherly type. I wonder what it was like for Salem to grow up like this. Constantly dealing with new family dinners and such.

"The prime rib is great," I state flatly, coming up empty for conversation topics.

Yeah. This sucks.

***

"See you after dance on Monday," Sean says over his shoulder to Salem.

"I'll be here tomorrow to help you study, ass face. Got everything you need?" she asks as he starts up the stairs.

"Always do, fuzzy head."

Fuzzy head? Salem's hair is always glossy and sleek, never a single piece of fuzz to be found.

Salem turns to face me as I cock my head. "He's staying here for two days?"

"He's starting school, so Mom wants him here to study for his classes, that way he's prepared on day one. She thinks I let him watch too much TV. I think he's already scarily smart."

I laugh to myself as I follow her out, holding the door open for her.

"So you're free to go to Silk? A bunch of us are meeting up. Thought you might want to make some new friends."

She hesitates, probably because of her no-friends rule.

"Are you being nice because you think we're going to have sex again? Or are you really trying to be my friend?"

A smile slides across my lips. "Both? Depends on which one we reach first, I guess."

She eyes me warily as she steps toward my car. "You can drive me there. Mom sent a driver after me since she thinks my truck is too obnoxious to be here, so my truck is still at home. But I'm taking a cab home from the club."

I wave off the driver who is waiting for her, and he nods before walking away.

"Fair warning, my friends are a unique and complex brand of crazy. It's like Skittles; there's a rainbow of options."

"Duly noted."

I open my passenger door for her, holding it, and she eyes me like I've lost my mind.

"Really?"

"I'm not a complete asshole most days," I say, still smiling.

She climbs in, still regarding me, and I close her door before walking around to my side and driving us toward Silk.

"Your mom is intense," I tell her.

"Always serious. Always planning her next ten steps. That's how she operates."

"I guess she tried planning your steps too, but you didn't let her."

She taps her nose. "Drives her crazy, but she deals with it. She doesn't like arguing. If she can't clearly and brutally prove her point, she'll give up with the argument and move on, never acknowledging who was right or who was wrong. What about yours?"

"She has a lot of rules," I answer, smirking. "Tons of them. She loves order in her house, but she still smiles amongst chaos, meaning she got used to me and my cousins constantly bringing disorder."

She smiles like she likes that answer.

"What sort of rules?" she asks.

"Typical things. You know."

"Not really. My mother's rules revolve mostly around how to carry myself in front of men. And what men not to bother with. And, well, you get the point. She doesn't believe in dating someone simply because you like them, and she really doesn't believe in 'being yourself' in front of them."

Something she said on the first night pops into my head as I turn us toward Silk.

"You said I was in hunter mode that night I first found you at the beach house."

"Some of my training. Always know what's on a guy's mind. Always know what he's looking for and give it to him. My mother is really sexist and tends to think men are painfully predictable. Thus, God gifted her with three sons who prove to be wildly unpredictable on a good day—her form of punishment, I think."

Not sure why that makes me grin.

"Yet, you pretty much figured me out."

"I didn't say a lot of her tactics don't work. They do. Women are just as predictable, though. We're all creatures of habit. It's not always so simple, though. You, for instance, threw me a curveball by being different than I pegged you. Unpredictability is preferred."

I start to say more, but we pull up to Silk, and she gets out almost as soon as the car is parked.

"I'm still not fucking you though, so we better figure out a way to nail down this friend thing," Salem adds as she joins me at my side, prompting me to laugh.

Without asking for permission and making it weird, I drop my arm to her shoulders, guiding her in, bypassing the really long line. Base Masters is playing tonight, which means the crowd comes early.

However, as soon as we're inside, she ditches me to head straight for the bathroom.

A shock of blonde hair catches my attention as Rain spots me ordering two drinks at the bar.

"So...how's the stepsister seduction thing going?" she asks, unaware that Salem is in the bathroom.

"Dane has a big fucking mouth," I fire back dryly.

Her grin just spreads. "Come on, Mav. No judgment here. Stepbrother romances are huge right now," Rain is saying, and I open my mouth to speak when I see Salem stop walking, standing just behind Rain as she arches an eyebrow at me in question.

"Rain, it's not—"

"I mean, they *were* huge. I wanted to write my own, but as usual, the market dried up before I could figure out the perfect story. But seriously, it's just the right amount of taboo without the *ick* factor," Rain goes on, causing Salem's lips to twitch as she eyes me.

"Rain—"

My gaze stays on Salem, as Rain continues to talk over me. "Well, it *can* be icky if they grow up together, because that's a little too close for comfort. But in your case, there's zero ick involved. And there's also usually some innocent girl versus bad boy trope mixed in to make it twice as hot. You could totally pull off the bad boy thing. And the conflict is already there, given the forbidden nature of—"

"Rain, for fuck's sake," I say, my eyes imploring her to shut the hell up.

Her expression sobers. "She's standing right behind me, isn't she?" Rain asks flatly.

Pretty sure she dies a little when I nod. Salem looks like she's trying not to burst out laughing.

"For the record," Salem says, looking at me as Rain's back stays to her, "I'm not all that innocent."

Slowly, Rain turns, plasters on a smile that is as transparent as they come, then grimaces when she realizes she can't pull it off. "Salem! Awesome to finally meet you!" she says, her voice two octaves too high. "I'm just going to go sew my mouth shut now before I lose any more of my foot in it."

With that, Rain darts off, leaving me behind with Salem. Her arms are crossed over her chest as she rolls her eyes.

"You told them about our quickie?" she asks incredulously.

"It was a warmup," I automatically defend. "And they were here the night I took you home. Then of course I told them about the bomb a little after it was dropped."

She groans while dropping her head back, and I step behind her so I can stare straight down at her, giving her my most innocent expression. In its slanted position, the crown of her head hits my chest as she glares a little, but I keep smiling, knowing she seems to give in easier when I do.

Someone bumps into us, and I grab her hips to steady her. She doesn't push away at first, but she finally does. "Are one of those mine?" she asks, pointing to the two Jack and Cokes in front of me.

"No, I'm an asshole who thought he needed two drinks even though you didn't have one."

She bites back a grin as she lifts one of the drinks to her lips, sipping it as Base Masters gets cheered for. Her eyes are drawn to the stage, and like every other girl in the room, she sways when she sees the cocky little guitarist start playing and singing.

I hate that guy some days.

And I should have learned to play a guitar.

"Come on, and I'll introduce you around," I say, pulling her out of the damn spell he weaves.

"Can you introduce me to him?" she asks, pointing at Base.

"Fuck no."

She grins at me, following as I guide her. She doesn't seem excited or nervous or genuinely concerned with meeting anyone. When we reach the booth, I see too many teeth in all the greeting smiles.

I'm starting to think my people are enjoying this a little much.

"Salem, I presume," Ruby says, grinning salaciously as Corbin smirks at me.

Yeah. I knew they'd all make this weird. What was I thinking?

"Yeah," Salem says while shifting a little. "I just found out that Maverick gossips like a teenage girl, so this is a little awkward now that I know how much he's shared with everyone," Salem tells them, causing laughter to break out as I throw my hands up like what-the-fuck.

"You do," Salem accuses, a taunting grin on her lips.

"I like her," Dale says, his arm around Harley as he grins wickedly at me.

"How about we drink and dance for a while. I like my friends more when I'm drunk," I tell Salem, tugging at her hand.

Won't be the first time I've danced with a girl who's a friend. I can totally behave. Never mind the last time we danced here ended with me leaving with her so wrapped around me that neither of us wanted to come up for air.

"Come find us soon, Salem. We'll make fun of Maverick with you," Kode tells her.

I flip him off, even as I smirk. That really could have been hella awkward, but Salem played it all off. Yet one more thing I like about her.

Now to see if I can play nice when she starts grinding against me.

Chapter 13

Salem

It feels different when you're dancing with a guy just for fun and not for seduction. I can't remember laughing as much as I have tonight.

Maverick doesn't care what anyone thinks. If he feels like dancing goofy, he dances goofy, despite the fact he has badass moves. I prefer him goofy, because he's way hotter when he's dancing for real.

He moves by Rain, dancing a circle around her, before rejoining me and…I think that's the "mashed potato" he's doing right now. I, of course, laugh like he's made me do all night as he waggles his eyebrows at me.

I vaguely notice when Rain decides she's had enough dancing, leaving us on our own.

We abandoned drinking about forty minutes ago, and his friends have danced with us a few times. Maverick is all smiles as he wraps his arms around me, tugging me to him as he dips me theatrically. I go with it, because I really don't care who is watching either.

As he swings me back up, he thumbs my bottom lip, sending a jolt of awareness through my very female body. Obviously I ignore that jolt, since this chemistry between us can't be revisited.

"Let's sit down for a while," Maverick finally says, his gaze on my lips for a fraction of a second too long.

He gives me a lazy smile before tugging me with him, not giving me a chance to object. I go willingly because I could use a rest. And some water.

The group makes room for us in the massive booth that could still hold more people if it needed to. But what has my head cocking to the side are two familiar faces.

"Salem?" Brin asks, grinning when she sees me.

"Hey," I say, confused.

"You know each other?" Maverick asks as he sits down beside me, his arm going around my shoulders like it's natural.

"Salem took over Wrench's spot at the garage," Rye says, looking at Maverick like he might hurt him. "And she's really good at her job. Fastest mechanic I've ever seen who does twice the quality work in half the time. We need her."

Not really sure what that's about—

"Maverick's already fucked her," the one they call Kode says in a bored drawl to Rye, prompting Maverick to grunt and bury his face in my hair.

Brin shoots a glare at Maverick, causing me to bite back a grin.

"Our quickie was memorable, but I survived the no-call the next day," I tell everyone, causing them to start laughing again.

"Warmup," Maverick says on a defeated sigh, his head still pressed to the side of mine as he leans on me a little. "And I didn't have your number since you ran out before I was done with you."

The others are watching the exchange with a little too much curiosity, more than likely getting the wrong idea, understandably so. I mean, I did drag him out of here and use him like he wanted to be used not too long ago.

That was before I knew he was Maverick Sterling. That *ling* tattoo on his arm? It's just half of *Sterling*. Wish I'd gotten a better look at it; this could have all been avoided.

Maverick reaches over and grabs Rye's drink, ignoring his protests before he throws it back, drinking it all in a couple large gulps.

Kode pulls his drink a little closer to him when Maverick eyes it. "You dicks are going to force me to be drunk tonight."

"We'll stop teasing," Rain says, batting a hand. "But you have to admit it—it sucks to be on the receiving end, huh?"

I can imagine Maverick relentlessly terrorizing them.

Maverick doesn't answer the rhetorical question, his face back in my hair as a waitress drops off a fresh drink for him and Rye, and also leaves a bottle of water on the table that I quickly grab. It's like they don't have to order anything. Mind-reading waitresses are totally awesome.

Then I remember Dane owns this place, and his wife is sitting at the table with us. I suppose they take a minute to pay extra attention to this table.

I glance at the bar in search of Ember—the bartender who tried to warn me away from Maverick. But she must not be on duty tonight, since I don't see her.

As Base and the band step off stage for a break, regular music starts playing. Maverick toys with some of my hair, using the hand that's not wrapped around me. It's an intimate gesture, but I don't point that out.

A song starts playing, and Maverick's grin grows as Corbin darts a glare in his direction.

"You fucking asshole," Corbin says over the music, while everyone else bursts out laughing.

Well, everyone but me, since I don't know what's so funny about *Shake that Ass* playing.

Maverick just grins like the cat who ate the canary, as Corbin slides out of the booth and moves to the edge of the platform we're on. Weirdly, he tosses his shirt off before he squats, puts his hands on his thighs and—

"Is he really twerking?" I ask, confused.

The table loses it twice as hard, but I'm so lost. Weirdly, he's damn good at twerking. He must do this a lot.

"Triple dare," Ruby says, grinning over at me. "He has to do this every time that song is played, as long as I'm nearby."

Sure. Makes perfect sense.

I really don't understand, but I still find his twerking fascinating.

Once the song ends and Corbin's twerking is applauded, he returns to the booth—shirt back on—and they all continue to talk, occasionally ribbing someone good-naturedly. I've never witnessed so many people who just fit like family. I already envied Rye and Brin with the relationship they have. Now I envy them more for the friends they're surrounded with.

By the way, Rye totally still has sparkly hair, though it's not as dramatic as it was when it was fresh.

Apparently glitter really is a bitch to get gone. I still have it in my hair too, and I barely got any on me.

This makes me miss my other two brothers. They're my best friends, and we have that easy friendship that they all do. We just don't get to see each other as much.

Maverick drinks, cracking jokes and taking his own jabs at people. I listen to them, sort of taking it all in, feeling possibly a little too comfy among them while pressed against his side.

"No, that was Billy. I've never heard anyone scream over a beetle like that," Rye is saying, talking about some story from the past.

"Probably had something to do with the fact his balls didn't drop until he was halfway to college," Maverick quickly inserts, causing the others to break out into hysterics again.

His arm is still around me, easily resting there like it's the most natural thing in the world. His thumb is tracing lazy circles on my arm near my elbow, an absent gesture he doesn't even realize he's doing.

Cozy, we are. Too damn cozy.

This is starting to feel like a date. Especially since I haven't seen a single tab for my drinks yet.

"So how old did you say you were?" Rain asks me, drawing me out of my thoughts.

"Twenty-five."

"And how old is your son?" Kode asks me seriously.

Maverick sputters his drink, coughing. How much did he actually tell them? And why isn't he correcting the misinformation?

"Totally forgot to tell you, since you were pointless in helping me, but she's sort of not the kid's mother. She's his sister," Maverick tells them.

"But he asked you to be his daddy?" Kode asks, genuinely confused.

"The kid is diabolical," Maverick announces, which of course, sets the table into a fit of laughter again. Even I laugh a little.

Sean's mischievous personality is one of my favorite things about him.

Even if he is a little too much at times.

The worst of his smartassery comes as a defensive mechanism. Truth is, he's just a normal kid who doesn't get the chance to make too many friends. He's also small for his age, which of course paints him a target to bullies.

His quick tongue and evil genius mind keep him from being someone's doormat.

Finally, Maverick leans back over to me, his lips brushing my ear and sending a shiver up my spine. "You ready to get out of here? We can go to my place and watch a movie or something."

"Netflix and chill?" I ask, rolling my eyes, ignoring that grin he wears so well.

"Friends Netflix and chill too," he argues, still grinning.

"Yeah, but friends didn't already fuck on your bed. I think I should probably just go home for tonight. But thanks for inviting me out."

I don't want to be just another one of his conquests anymore. See? I knew it was a bad idea to be his friend. He's hard not to like.

He studies me for a moment. "What're you doing tomorrow?"

Sounds like another date he's offering…

"Tomorrow I'll be helping Sean study for his first day of school in your old house, while my mother continues to keep your father in her thrall."

He really doesn't seem concerned with my mother and his father at all. As though he's not getting involved or something.

"I need your number. Or I can just keep showing up at the house if you prefer," he finally tells me.

Definitely feels like a date when I take his phone to program my number into it.

"If you get free time tomorrow, call me, and I'll give you the tour of Sterling Shore. After all, I'm the one who christened your arrival. Only fair I show you the town," he goes on, that cocky grin back in place.

Ignoring the heat in my cheeks, I stand when he lets me, knowing plenty of cabs will be waiting outside.

"Later, alligator," I tell him, causing him to smile as I start walking away, leaving him behind without an answer.

"After while, crocodile," I hear him say from behind me, the weight of his gaze on my back.

Then I also hear him catching hell for saying it, which has me grinning as I head toward the door.

Chapter 14

MAVERICK

I'm almost home Monday around noon when my phone rings. Not knowing the number, I answer warily.

"Hello?"

"I apologize if this isn't a real contact number for Sean Young, but we can't reach the other two numbers we have, and he said this was his sister's boyfriend's phone, Mr. Sterling."

The fuck?

Whose boyfriend?

"Sean Young?" I ask, confused. Then it dawns on me that he wouldn't have Salem's last name. She'll kill him for calling me her boyfriend. "I mean, yeah. Who is calling about Sean?"

"This is Misty, from the school, and um…we have a situation. Sean is being sent home early for disciplinary action. You're listed on his emergency relatives' page for school, and you're the only one we can reach."

Salem's phone is no doubt hard to hear if she's at work, and there's no telling where my father and Kelly are or what they're doing. Dad is flighty normally. I can only imagine what he's doing with a newlywed mentality and a gold digger who likes to shop.

"I'm on my way, but how much trouble could he be in? It's his first day."

She clears her throat. "The principal will fill you in when you get here, Mr. Sterling."

With that, she hangs up, and I roll my eyes. That kid really is a little monster. He couldn't even make it through a whole day of school.

✳✳✳

Sean looks bored and annoyed as I wait for the principal to explain why he's being sent home for two days, when he's barely been at school for half a day.

"He told one of the teachers that *tuna sub* spelled backwards was what he'd like to do to her face, Mr. Sterling." The principal's face turns red like he's a little embarrassed to even have to repeat that. "I'm afraid the lewd behavior is harassing in nature, and we simply don't tolerate it."

Tuna sub spelled backwards? B-U-S-A... Ahhhh. I choke back a laugh, and Sean's lips twitch when he sees me struggling.

"He's eleven. He doesn't even know what it means. He's likely just repeating something he saw on a meme somewhere," I state dismissively.

Principal Walker looks like he hates me already. Not the same principal I had when I went here, so he has no reason to hate me.

"It simply can't be tolerated. He's fortunate we're not expelling him for—"

"For making a joke?" I interrupt. "Two days is too much. He'll go home the rest of the day, get a lecture on what he can and can't say in the new school, and come back tomorrow with a different approach to how he handles situations," I state all adult as fuck.

What can I say? When my game is on, it's on.

"Not happening," the principal says around a huff of condescending laughter.

But I know how this school really works. So does he.

"Sterling alumni contribute a lot to this school. There's a library or two with our name on it. Hence the reason the kid got in on short notice, despite the several-year waiting list others are still on. He'll be back in tomorrow, because, as you've already read in his file, his mother recently married my father. And Ian is the largest contributor to the school."

He hates me worse now. Shit happens.

His jaw ticking, because it really isn't fair, and he turns to face Sean. "If another incident like this occurs, I will be calling in your mother and stepfather for a little chat. A certain level of decorum is expected of anyone attending our school, Sterling or not." His eyes slide to me. "Understood?"

Sean nods, acting like he doesn't give a shit, but I can see there's actually a little worry creasing his features, though he'd never admit it.

He grabs his backpack, standing, and I walk him out.

"You told a teacher you wanted to *bus' a nut* on her face?" I ask dryly as we walk out.

"She asked what I wanted to do with my life, made me stand up in front of the entire class. Seemed like a funny answer at the time. Didn't realize people around here were so sensitive."

Trying to keep my adult in place, I refrain from laughing. I'd have loved to have seen her face.

"Bet she doesn't call me out like that and make me look like an idiot again, though," he mutters under his breath.

Feisty kid.

Defensive kid.

"Truth," I decide to say instead of pretending like I have any right at all to chastise him. "I'll swing by Dad's and see if anyone is at home and just not answering—"

"I intentionally wrote down Mom's number wrong. The number they were calling is mine, not hers. I can't go home. If Mom finds out I got in trouble, she'll ground me from Salem's house for two weeks at least. That's the reason I got your number out of Salem's phone yesterday and wrote it down on the emergency numbers. You don't work. Salem does. And I know your secret."

This kid…

"First of all, I do work, thank you very much. Secondly, blackmail? I would have kept the secret without you tossing *my* secret in my face. Don't threaten me again with it, because that secret also hurts your sister." He slinks down in his seat.

"Probably *only* hurts her," he grumbles.

I roll my eyes.

"The point is, it's not a big deal, so long as you tell Salem what you did."

He darts a gaze at me.

"I mean what you did at school, because she's not going to be mad at me over your secrets. Not the blackmail threatening part."

He just looks away.

"Feel free to thank me any time now," I point out.

He snorts.

"Anyone ever tell you that you're an unappreciative little ass?"

"Anyone ever tell you that you're too old to still look like such a douche?" he fires back.

"Seriously? Douche?" I ask on a long exhale.

"You seriously going to pretend that's something you haven't heard before?"

I hate this kid. I really hate him.

We roll up at my house, since I know Salem is working and he can't go home.

"Who are you texting?" the nosy, paranoid little asshole asks.

"Dad. I'm telling him I'm picking you up from your first day, making sure they know you're affiliated with the Sterlings and blah blah blah."

"You play off your name a lot, don't you?"

"You can still thank me for that. It'd be hard to explain a two day suspension if you can't even go home today," I quickly remind him, which shuts him up.

Asshole still doesn't thank me as he gets out of the car.

"Pie moment," he says, confusing the hell out of me.

"What?" I ask.

I lead the way in, stopping to unlock the door, and then disarm the security system once we're inside. Devil Spawn walks on in, dropping his backpack to my floor like it's too much hassle to place it somewhere neatly.

"Pie moment. It's something Salem and I say, since she won't let me cuss. When someone is getting on my nerves, and I can't cuss, it's a pie moment. She says it when she's ready to throttle someone."

"What does that even mean?" I ask the future poster child for anger management issues.

"It means, you picture shoving a pie in their face, and it makes you feel better. Right now, I see your face in pie. Pie moment."

"Whatever, weirdo," I say under my breath.

I start to offer him a drink, since we're right at the kitchen, when a damn rebel, feline battle cry sounds out, and I duck, narrowly missing the flying pussy that zooms by my face when Bananas leaps out of my cabinets.

I swear her mission in life is to cause me cardiac arrest.

"I hate that fucking cat!" I snap, watching as the cat hisses at me before turning and walking out of the room, leaving behind her stench.

And what's the stench? That pussy farts more than any pussy ever.

"You totally squealed like a girl just now," Sean tells me, smirking even as he waves the putrid aroma away from his face.

"Lie."

He grins as he watches Bananas dart back into the kitchen, and I might squeal. That cat is pure evil.

I don't relax until she runs out again, doing her usual crackhead routine of trying to tear my house apart.

"Why do you have a cat you hate?"

"Long story short, I bought it as a long-running joke for one of my friends, left it to tear her house to pieces, and she got pregnant shortly after, so she dropped it back off with me. Now I can't get anyone to take her."

Another feline cry coming from the back makes me worry what she's up to. Hopefully she's just hiding whatever body she forgot to dispose of.

"Care if I borrow your phone to find mine? I think it fell out of my bag in your car, but I didn't see it when I got out," the kid says.

After unlocking it, I hand it over, absently picking up the paper that my housekeeper must have left behind for me. Devil Spawn walks out to go to my car as I read over the business section.

When he finally returns, he mumbles a reluctant *thanks,* and I smirk as I pocket my phone.

"Got anything to drink?" he asks me.

I gesture to the fridge, silently telling him to help himself, caught up in an article, when I hear the phone start dinging in my pocket.

The fridge opens and shuts as I ignore my phone, trying to finish skimming the article about Sterling Shore expanding. Lots of opportunities to buy up some land surrounding the city if they're about to expand.

"Got any rules?" the kid asks.

"Don't pet the cat. She'll claw you to pieces. And don't go in my room. My bed is sacred."

He snorts and walks away, and I try to finish the reading, even though my phone is starting to get annoying. When the dinging persists, I finally check the damn thing, wondering why so many people I haven't talked to in ages are suddenly texting me en masse.

The cloud is only good for saving contacts you forgot you even had.

Confused, I pull up my messages that are going haywire, and immediately curse when I drop my phone like it's on fire.

Hairy fucking balls!

Why the actual fuck is there a dick pic being sent to me by a guy who used to mow my grass?

My phone keeps dinging, and warily I pick it up, closing out of that message box. I end up dropping my phone to the counter again when I realize the guy who painted my house has also sent me a dick pic.

For fuck's sake, is it National Dick Pic Awareness Day and no one bothered to mention it before now? Is that a real thing?

By the fifth random—and utterly traumatizing—dick pic, and thirty new unread messages, I push my phone away, glaring at it as it continues to light up, possibly giving my inbox a few STDs along the way.

When it lights up with an incoming call, I almost don't answer, but decide to anyway, since it's Corbin. Maybe he's getting blasted with dick pics too. Sounds like one of those flash mob things.

He's laughing when I answer. Like full-on belly laughing.

"Are you getting a shit-ton of dick pics? Because if so, I'd like to know why you're finding it so humorous."

His laughter doubles, and he struggles to speak. I can't understand a damn word he's trying to piece together.

Finally, he gets his shit together enough to say, "I think you've been hacked."

My eyebrows knit together.

"I haven't been hacked. I'm just getting a lot of nasty fucking dicks sent to my phone."

"Twitter. Go read your last tweet," the prick says through his guffaws.

Pulling my phone back, I quickly go through the motions of pulling up my app, and I get a little nauseated when I read it.

@MavSterling: I want 2 start a collection of dic pics so hit me with your best shot if you got my digits. #dicpiclover4life

Then I get twice as sick when I see my fucking mother has gotten in on the damn fun.

@MommaQueenVictoria: @MavSterling I have a collection. When you're ready to swap notes call me. #AllTheDicks

I make a mental note to kill my mother later. Then I make another mental note to kill Ethan's mother when I see she's one of the many to have also responded.

@ArleneMommaBear: @MavSterling we can scrapbook when you get done collecting all you need. :)

Who decided to give these mothers Twitter? Who thought it'd be cute? Not me.

Then there's a tweet from Ethan.

@EthanNolesIDGAF: @MavSterling if you scrapbook dick pics with my mom I'll be by to beat your ass & not with my dick. #NoJoke

I'll throat punch him later for that. For now, I delete that damn tweet before shit starts to escalate. I almost forget Corbin is on the phone until I start muttering about taking Twitter away from anyone over the age of thirty-five, and he bursts out laughing.

"Who the hell hacked you?" he asks as I put the phone back up to my ear.

A cool wash of obvious slaps me in the face.

"That little fucker," I growl.

"Who?" Corbin asks, still laughing, of course.

"Sean!" I yell, but there's no answer.

"The kid? The fucking kid did this?" Corbin asks, and then laughter roars from him.

I hang up on my dickheaded cousin, leaving him to laugh in private as I hunt down that damn little ingrate.

"Sean!"

He still doesn't answer me, and I don't find him in the living room, den, or anywhere else for that matter. I should have checked my bedroom first. That fucking little—

I stop short in the doorway of my bedroom when I find the Devil's spawn lying on my bed and watching TV, casually sipping from a bottle of water. His other hand is petting the Devil's cat, who is thunder-purring for him as she kneads the bedding, looking content as hell.

That cat can't be touched! She's carrying around the spirit of Jack the Ripper, usually plotting ways to get close enough to tear your face off, yet he's petting her like she's a sweet little purring kitten.

Evil tames evil, I suppose.

As one, they both look at me—two versions of psychotic.

Sure, that's not creepy *at all*.

The kid gets a wicked grin on his face as I glare at him, and the fucking cat hisses at me.

"Get. Out. Of. My. Room!"

He chuckles as he hops off my bed—my sacred, precious bed. That cat is not allowed in my damn room! She destroyed my last bed!

Bananas shoots out, leaping up and almost slapping me in the face while airborne. I've learned to dodge the half-kangaroo devil cat during these moments. It always makes me feel like less of man when I'm bitch-slapped by that pussy.

They disappear from sight, and I take a few minutes to compose myself so that I don't kill an eleven-year-old.

Spotting the zen thingy my mother sent, I decide to test it out, raking the sand over and over and over… When is this thing supposed to make me feel zen? Because I'm totally not feeling it.

Giving up on raking away my fury, I walk out.

As I slam the door, I stalk toward the den to find the kid and cat on the sofa. Well, the cat is purring away in the kid's lap, acting like a *pet* instead of a nuisance.

That cat has never, *not once,* been nice to me.

Yes, I'm a little pissed off about that. I feed the damn thing and clean the shit out of her litterbox. The least she could do is purr for me on occasion. Instead of trying to shred my skin.

"Why?" I ask the sociopath who is petting the cat. "Just why?"

"Because you were stupid enough to give me your phone—unlocked. You're too gullible. I'm toughening you up, *kiddo,*" the condescending little bitch boy says, winking at me for good measure.

"I'm curious as to how Salem hasn't killed you yet," I growl.

He flashes a grin. "Who do you think I learned all my tricks from?"

"I bailed you out today, then kept your secret, and you repay me by doing this shit. All it does is make me want to never bail you out again. You realize I'm a better friend than foe, right?"

I can't believe I'm threatening a kid. This is a new low.

He rolls his eyes. "You're only nice to me because you want to bang my sister. Again." He wrinkles his nose as I shift awkwardly. "You didn't do her on the bed I was just on, did you?"

A dark smile graces my lips. No, it wasn't my bed, but he doesn't know that. "Make you feel a little closer to your sister now that you've been at the scene of the crime?" I ask the twerp.

A sense of petty triumph sweeps through me when he turns a little green and shudders.

"Should have thought that one through," I add, smirking as I take the small win and walk away.

"You're still a douche!" the kid calls out. "And from now on, that's a boundary you don't cross or I'm telling Salem!"

"You're still the Devil's spawn!" I call back, finding myself wondering how pissed Salem would be for that comment about the bed.

The last thing I hear him bite out is, "Pie moment."

I still find that weird as hell.

After that, the kid pretty much leaves me alone, though I admit I check in on him periodically to make sure he's not in the middle of summoning a demon or something.

It isn't until a little after three that he comes and finds me in my study where I'm going over some real estate options that I'm forced to acknowledge him again.

He hovers in my doorway, seeming awkward for some reason, and I pretend not to notice him. Finally, I get tired of him staring and not speaking.

"Yes?" I drawl, swinging my gaze up to find his.

"I have dance in twenty minutes," he says reluctantly.

"And?" I ask.

His jaw tightens. "Mom said she's busy with a fitting, and asked if you could take me, since you know, you told them you were picking me up from school and all. She thinks we're bonding or whatever."

Little sad that his mother trusts me so implicitly with her son, when she doesn't even know me. Then again, I'm sure by now a woman like her has thoroughly investigated everyone in my family.

She's shrewd.

I can see it in her ever-assessing eyes. I also see that, despite what Salem says, her mother also actually gives a damn about Dad. You can't fake things. You can keep yourself guarded though, and she does that heavily.

Reminds me of Corbin's mom in a lot of ways.

"So you treat me like shit then ask for a favor?" I ask, crossing my arms over my chest and arching an eyebrow.

He hates this. I love it.

"If I miss dance, I'll miss out on the solo I barely got. As soon as I transferred, a girl hurt her leg, and I had to take over her solo. I still have to work out all my steps. It's an important shot."

My lips twitch.

"Say please."

His jaw tics, and for the briefest of moments, I think he's just going to be stubborn and refuse.

"Please," he bites out.

"You can thank me from now on when I save your ungrateful little ass. Otherwise, I'm not going to continue. Being nice to you won't gain me favors with Salem, because if she thinks I'm using you—which I'm not—she'll hate me. Go ahead and get that straight in your twisted little psychotic mind."

He doesn't look pleased, but he finally nods.

"Got your tights here?" I ask him, and then grin.

He flips me off before turning and walking out.

"I'm not sure it's appropriate for kids to flip adults off," I call after his back.

"I'm not sure it's appropriate to look, walk, and talk like a douche, but you do it anyway," he volleys.

Laughing under my breath, I stand up and grab my keys, following after him.

"You're small for eleven," I tell him as he grabs his bag.

He glares over at me. "My dad was small until puberty. I'll have a growth spurt, and then I'll be taller than you. No one will pick on me ever again."

I smile because that chip on his shoulder is a little funny. And I'm an ass like that.

"What's the deal with your dad?" I ask without thinking it might be a sore subject.

He walks out with me, hesitant to answer, but finally does answer me when we get in my car. He buckles up automatically as he speaks.

"He got a new wife, and she thinks her kids shouldn't be around me. What she says goes, so he'll only get me for a few weeks a year now." He shrugs like it's no big deal, but the asshole tendencies are making a little more sense now.

I'm not sure what the hell to say to that, so I say nothing as we drive toward the rehearsal studio.

"Salem doesn't mention her dad either," I say conversationally.

"He's dead," the kid states with no emotion. "Died when she was little. He was drinking and driving."

Shit. Makes sense why she refused to get in a car with me even though I'd only had one beer.

"Dad said he wanted to have another family dinner," I ramble, since I'm sort of dragging us down with the bad dad talk.

"Your dad seems nice enough," he admits, though it sounds like a begrudged confession.

My lips twist in a smile. "He is nice."

"Must have been nice having him and growing up in a place where your name means something," he goes on, staring out the window.

I really liked it better when I hated him instead of feeling sorry for the kid.

"As long as you're here, my name means something for you, too. As you saw today."

"For now," he mutters. "Then it'll go away, and we'll be somewhere else. Or you and your dad will get tired of me hanging around. Salem is the only person who likes me all the time."

I grin, even though I can tell he doesn't like it. "Ah, you'll find I'm a clingy, loyal asshole, Devil Spawn. Even the worst of my family can't get rid of me when they're being dicks. Ask Kode. Or Corbin, for that matter. I stick like glue."

He tries not to smile, so he cuts his gaze away.

"Salem can't date you," he finally says.

"Why's that?"

Figures I'd pursue the one girl who doesn't want a relationship. I'm not even sure if I'm cut out for a relationship, so I'm not sure what the hell I'm even doing.

"Dating you would cause family drama and all that. Stuff like that is usually frowned upon, especially with your kind of people."

"My kind of people?"

"Society types," he supplies, continuing before I can mock him for how wrong he is about *my kind of people*. "Anything that causes drama within the new family is a no-go. Mom would punish Salem by not letting me spend so much time with her."

I nod like I get it, but they still don't understand how the Sterlings work. My dad wouldn't give a damn if I dated Salem, considering he knows me and how I am. If I'm in, I'm all in. I don't play with a girl's head. I've never considered being all in as much as I've been considering it with Salem.

She's so fucking easy to be around.

But discussing it with Sean doesn't exactly seem appropriate.

As we pull up to the dance studio in town, I idle near the curb, waiting on him to get out.

"I have to have an adult present," he finally says on a sigh. "It's the studio's policy. Probably don't want people thinking they're perverts or something, touching their kids when the parents aren't around."

I clear my throat, grimacing as I wheel into a parking spot and park my car.

Guess I'm going to a dance rehearsal.

When did this become my life?

Chapter 15

Salem

I'm a little greasier than normal as I wash up in front of the mirror. But I kicked some ass today. We're now officially ahead of schedule, and I think Rye is a little in awe of my latest transmission rebuild.

He's stroking it. Talking to it like it's a sentient being.

"My fiancé is officially in love with a transmission," Brin says, shaking her head with a small smile on her lips as she watches Rye pet the thing.

"To be fair, it's a—"

"Don't start rattling off how special that transmission is. I'll fall asleep quickly," Brin tells me with a grin.

"I need to get out of here. My brother is coming over after his—"

"All that's left is locking up," she says, dismissing me with a wave. "And by the way, thanks for coming in early, though I didn't expect us to get ahead of schedule. Way to be a badass," she adds.

Not good at accepting compliments, I just nod and head out, stopping by my locker to grab my phone and purse. But when I see all the missed calls from the school's number, I get a little nauseated.

I haven't checked my phone since eleven, considering I've been crazy busy and I finished lunch early.

A message from my mother doesn't clarify anything.

MOM: Maverick picked your brother up today and is taking him to dance for me. You may need to call him if you're wanting Sean to stay with you tonight.

Why the hell would Maverick pick Sean up and take him to dance? And why did the school call?

I check my voicemails, but the only message is from some nasally woman asking to speak with the sister or guardian of Sean Young—no details.

Even though I still look and smell like I've been dunked in grease, I hurry out and drive to the dance studio. I don't want to embarrass Sean looking like this, but I'm a little freaked out.

And I'm sure Maverick doesn't exactly like my mother dumping her responsibilities onto him either.

As soon as I walk into the studio, I see the huge window that allows parents to view the dance floor without interfering with the training.

My eyes scan the room, and I spot Maverick looking as sexy as he possibly can. I'm not the only one looking at him either. Pretty sure a lot of women are paying more attention to him than the kids they're supposed to be watching.

He's in perfectly tailored slacks that make his ass look better than I thought possible. He's standing, leaning against a pole, his eyes on Sean as my brother nails a front flip, going into a spin move onto his head directly after.

My eyes move back to Maverick to see him grinning as he watches, and a few women expire around him with audible sighs. If I knew what was going on, I might be under the spell as well.

His button-down shirt is a crisp blue, tucked into the gray slacks with what is a likely very expensive belt setting off the entire ensemble. I've only ever seen him in jeans or sweats.

I've never seen him this dressed up, and I swear it's not doing nice things to my current state—my current state being the fact I'm a hot-blooded woman.

His sleeves are rolled up on his forearms as his hands stay tucked away in his pockets. He looks relaxed and at ease, despite the numerous pairs of eyes on him. It's like he doesn't even notice or care.

Shaking off the girly flutters, I move toward him, watching him as he watches Sean. He turns his head toward me when I'm almost at him, and his grin spreads as his eyes rake over me.

We couldn't be more opposite in this moment. My cheap jeans are covered in dirt and grit, and my steel-toed boots are a stark contrast to his matte-black, leather shoes.

He looks spit-polished. I look spit on.

Others obviously take in the difference between us as well.

"He's good," Maverick says when his eyes come back up to mine, his grin spreading.

"He's very good. Why do you think he got in?" I ask him, gesturing around at the very talented kids who are all working on their individual routines for the upcoming showcase — or the group dance if they don't have a solo.

Pretty sure Sean did a private happy dance when he heard he was getting a solo, though he's horrified at the music he's supposed to dance to.

It's still his first showcase, though. Usually he misses the deadline or we've already moved when a showcase airs. This studio has more showcases than the norm, so maybe he'll get multiple shots.

Maverick starts to reach for me, but I take a step back, ignoring the judgy stares.

"I'm filthy," I point out.

Maverick waggles his eyebrows. "Totally hot, too. I like things a little dirty."

A few audible gasps from nosy eavesdroppers ring out, but Maverick just grins and winks at me as I roll my eyes and stand just beside him, careful not to dirty up his shiny appearance.

"Why did my mom ask you to take him? And why did you pick him up from—"

"I'll let the kid explain all that," Maverick says, grinning over at me. "It's his punishment. I'm not giving him the easy way out by being the one to tell you."

I groan inwardly. What has he done now?

I glare at my brother, who is oblivious to my presence, as he does a side aerial.

"If you have stuff you're supposed to be doing, you don't have to—"

"I'm free right now," Maverick interrupts, saving me from rambling on.

As Sean finishes up and the kids have their usual end-of-class meeting, Maverick turns to face me, leveling me with that hard-to-handle presence of his.

"Rough day?"

"Busy day," I grumble. "Sorry you had to deal with Sean. I don't know why Mom—"

"He didn't give the school your mother's real number. He gave them *his* number instead of hers on the papers he apparently filled out, to be more accurate."

I roll my eyes. "Of course he did. He usually fills out all his own papers and has Mom simply sign them."

"And he got my number from your phone to add me to the emergency contacts, since, apparently, I'd do anything in my never-ending chase for you. According to his philosophy."

His lips twitch when my face starts to burn, and he arches an eyebrow at me.

"I'll get that fixed immediately," I promise him, counting the ways I'm going to make Sean's life hell for this really awkward moment.

"Leave my name on the list. My schedule is more flexible than yours," he says with a shrug.

I'm tempted to tell him that's not necessary, but too desperate to have the extra security net to dismiss the offer. Instead of saying anything, I just resume staring at my brother as he pushes through the door that separates the viewing room from the dance studio.

Sean adjusts his backpack on his shoulder and pulls his hat off at the same time.

"What'd you do?" I ask with narrowed eyes as he approaches.

He swings an accusatory glare toward Maverick, who merely grins in return.

"Why'd the school call me over and over today?" I ask again.

Sean looks around the room for a minute before walking toward the doors. "I don't want to tell you in here."

Maverick chuckles as he follows us out, and I get a few looks of disdain as people take in my greased-up self.

"You know what would be the worst form of punishment?" Maverick asks as he sidles up next to me, his hands remaining in his pockets.

"Life without electronics?" I interject with a tight smile.

He smiles as he stares down, looking too damn sexy for his own good.

"I was thinking more along the lines of sticking him at the kiddy table at my friends' house. They're having a kid-friendly gathering tonight over at Kode and Tria's place."

"Y'all hang out a lot together?" I say before I can stop myself.

"Family," he says simply.

Instant pang in my chest.

"I try not to let Sean go places on a school night," I finally say.

Maverick nods even as his lips tighten. We stop in front of my truck, just sort of staring at each other, neither of us doing the awkward farewell thing.

"He has a collection of erotic novels in his room, and he has boyband music in his phone's library," Sean announces, arching a challenging eyebrow at Maverick.

Maverick drops his head back, exhaling heavily, and I swear I don't smile. Okay, maybe a little.

Maverick brings his head back down, eyes flashing. "Sean told a teacher he wanted to 'bus a nut' on her face.'"

My eyes almost bulge out of my head as I gawk at my brother, who immediately ducks his head and kicks at a pebble.

"They wanted to suspend him for two additional days. I talked them down to just sending him home for the day," Maverick goes on.

"Phone," I say, holding out my hand.

I know it doesn't seem like much, but trust me when I tell you that Sean is definitely hurting when his phone isn't with him.

With a little whimper, Sean hands over his phone.

"Not so much fun when it happens to you, huh, kid?" Maverick asks, goading him.

I give him a stare that says, *"Really?"*

And Maverick has the grace to look away when his cheeks redden a little. Obviously Sean wasted no time getting under his skin.

"Four weeks. You can have the dinosaur to make phone calls and answer texts from Mom and me."

"Not like I have any friends to call or text," Sean mutters, doing that thing where he tries to gain my sympathy. Not happening.

I reach into my purse, and I pull out the old, banged-up flip-phone that I have to buy minutes for, and hand it to him. He almost looks horrified to take it, and only pinches it between his thumb and index finger before dropping it into his backpack.

"That's epic," Maverick says, grinning, and earns a scowl from my very furious brother.

"And you're going back to Mom's tonight, where you'll be writing a five-hundred word—*minimum*—apology letter to your teacher, and another one to your principal," I go on, watching as his eyes widen.

"But—"

"No buts, Sean. Get in the truck. We'll talk more about it on the way to the house."

He side-eyes Maverick one last time before getting in the truck, and Maverick turns his cheeky grin on me.

"I'll pick you up in an hour," Maverick says, causing my head to tilt.

"What?"

"Your excuse for not hanging out with me tonight was because you didn't want Sean out on a school night. So I'll pick you up in an hour."

He turns and starts walking away, hands still in his pockets.

"But—"

"No buts, Salem," he calls over his shoulder. "One hour."

Damn him.

As I climb into the truck, Sean is smirking at me. "Not so much fun when someone does it to you, is it?" he asks, sounding suspiciously like Maverick.

"Pie moment," I bite out.

He grins, but banishes it when I narrow my eyes at him.

"For the record, I asked her to spell tuna sub backwards and said that's what I wanted to do to her face," he clarifies.

"Not helping yourself," I snap as I crank the truck and start driving toward Mom's.

"Worth a shot," he says on a sigh.

As we drive toward the house, Sean says, "He really does read erotica. I'm not sure how I feel about that."

I try not to laugh.

"I'm not sure how I feel about you knowing what erotica even is."

"You can thank Dad's wife for that. She has a collection of bare-chested paperbacks with titles like *Four Firemen: One Hose*. She told me to read something from her bookcase and be quiet. I tried reading that one. Had nothing to do with an actual fire hose."

"Stop talking. I think I'm going to have to call your stepmother," I grumble, hating the fact that I'm not even the worst monitor in his life. At least I try to filter the things he sees or reads. He doesn't even know about my erotica collection because it's only on my phone. Where it's safe and pretty and very well hidden.

Mom is better than his dad, considering his dad left him in the car two years ago while he went into a strip club—the reason my brother knows about strip clubs—and got so drunk he had to call his wife to come get them.

That was when Mom decided I was right about him needing a phone, and she finally let me get him one. Until then, she'd thought of him as too young for something that would 'rot his brain out.'

I idle near the front of the massive home, letting Sean collect all his things.

"Can we get a cat?" Sean asks me randomly.

"I'm allergic to pet hair," I remind him.

"What about a hairless cat?" he asks, not looking me in the eye.

Maverick said his cat is hairless. I guess he got to play with it today. I thought Maverick said it was evil.

"We'll talk about it after you finish up your sincere apology letters," I say noncommittally.

He nods before shutting my door and heading inside. I lean back, staring straight ahead for a minute, trying to calm down.

I need to get myself together better and be the best positive influence I can. On the bright side, Ian seems great. At least there's that. And Maverick was there today, but I don't know if I can trust either of them to be consistently reliable. It's not really their place to be.

And now I'm going to rush my ass home and look like I haven't been slaving away in a garage all day, because I'm fairly positive I'm going on a date.

Or maybe it's a friend date.

"Maverick Sterling is a confusing, sexy, confounding man," I grumble to myself.

I'm in over my head.

"Pie moment."

Speaking of pie, if I'm going to this thing, I'm also going to have to hurry up and make a lemon pie. It's just rude not to bring something.

Chapter 16

MAVERICK

Salem laughs, sipping her glass of wine, talking with the girls who don't let me down by making her feel like part of the group.

"I'm starting to think you're being domesticated," Corbin says, lips twitching as he sits down beside me.

"Not sure what you're talking about," I say with a shrug.

It's not like I'm trying to put a ring on it or something.

Hell, Salem doesn't even want to risk seeing me as more than a friend.

But I like being around her. And I like seeing where she is, because that way I don't have to worry about her finding someone else in Sterling Shore.

I don't want to talk about how possessive that sounds.

I'm sure it's perfectly normal to think about smashing another guy's face in just for looking at her. Like several of the dads were doing inside that studio. I wanted to kiss her in front of all of them, and did all I could not lose my shit.

She walked in with grease smudges all over her damn white T-shirt and tight jeans, and tan boots half untied. Motherfucking wet dream for every man who's ever breathed.

And she thought she looked filthy. It's the first time I've ever seen her act self-conscious.

I never pegged her for oblivious.

Rye is lucky I know he loves Brin and doesn't seem to notice other women, otherwise I'd punch him in the face for getting to see her like that all day every day.

See? I'm sure this is perfectly normal.

I take a longer sip of my beer.

"Right," Corbin finally says, patting my shoulder patronizingly. "Denial is a bitch to get through. Let me know when you've moved on to acceptance."

I flip him off as he laughs at me, and I keep my eyes on Salem. Her light brown hair has those purple streaks in it, and it all looks as shiny as honey. It shakes with her head when she laughs again.

"I think we're about to get out of here. The girls are monopolizing my date," I say as I stand.

"Thought she was your stepsister," Corbin says.

"Thought you wanted me out of denial."

I wink at him, and he laughs, even though we both know this isn't really a date. I do know I want another chance to test out the physical chemistry between us. It can't be as strong as I remember it.

I don't think I've ever kissed a girl as much as I kissed her that night. Usually kissing is a hit or miss thing, and it's something I only do right before the deed. But with her, once I got a taste, I couldn't stop.

"The cat was a joke for me," Bella is telling Salem. "But Maverick—"

"You want to get out of here? We can hang out at my house until the little bit of alcohol wears off. It's just a walk down the block from here," I say to Salem as I deliberately put my ass right in front of Bella's face, cutting her off mid-sentence and stepping in her eye-line to Salem.

"Damn you, Maverick," Bella grumbles. "Get your tight little ass—"

"Maverick Sterling, there'd better be a damn good reason your ass is that close to my pregnant girl's face!" Ethan calls out from across the yard, causing me to smile.

"You can just call me your girl. I think it's obvious I'm pregnant," Bella says petulantly. "It's not part of my identity now."

"Bella loves my ass in these pants," I say, only to piss him off. "Thought I'd give her some fantasy material for when you just aren't getting the job done on your own."

He simply rolls his eyes, standing up to come over to us. It's fun pissing off the possessive cavemen around here. You should see Kode when I fuck with Tria. He looks like the cartoon characters when the tops of their heads blow off and steam rolls out their ears.

Before he can reach me, I jerk Salem up from her chair, which earns me a little squeal of surprise from her, and I put her between us like a buffer.

Ethan glares at me over her head.

"Real manly," Salem states dryly.

I just grin over her head at Ethan and wink at him.

"He's just mad because Bella always has to tell everyone about giving me her hairless pussy," I say on a sigh, then realize Salem might not enjoy these kinds of jokes.

Much to my delight, Salem snorts and chokes back a laugh. I knew there was a reason I can't seem to stay away from her. She has a sense of humor.

"The cat, Salem! Not *my* actual pussy. My pussy was only magical for Ethan," Bella says from behind us.

Ethan glares at me, and I actually get a little worried this has gone too far. You have to remember that Ethan *has* hit me over a girl before, and though I normally wouldn't mind risking a shot, I really do have Salem between us.

"I never tried the magic pussy," I state, just to keep his crazy ass in check. Not that I think he'd risk hurting Salem, but there's a smidge of protectiveness slinking out, making me unable to take the nonexistent risk.

"He knows that," Bella states blandly from behind me, leaning around to grin at Ethan. "But it's still cute when he gets jealous."

Ethan gives her a look of sheer frustration, and I usher Salem along, getting us out of here before I continue to open my mouth and mess this up before it can get started.

"Do I want to know what magic pussy is?" Salem asks, amused as I drop my arm around her shoulders and start steering her through the party.

"Honestly, I never want to talk about anything my friends say. I'm a little traumatized from their oversharing tendencies," I say to her, loving the way she laughs and doesn't act bothered by my unnecessary touching.

I've always been overly comfortable with touching people—mostly girls—but with Salem, I feel like I *have* to touch her when she's around. Even get annoyed when she's too far away for me to touch. Still processing what I think about that. Not sure if I want to overthink it.

"After while, crocodile," Kode calls out to me, causing me to flip him off over my shoulder.

Salem chokes back another laugh, turning her head so that she doesn't let me see her struggle.

She fits right in with this lot.

Bunch of jackasses.

Yeah, I know. I'm one too.

"The girls are really nice. All of your friends are, really. They invited me for breakfast in the morning, but I'll be at work. Brin offered to let me go in late, but I don't feel right about that."

I nod, liking the way she feels against me. "They're nice when they're not vicious."

To this, she laughs.

"What are we going to do at your house?" she asks me, a teasing smile on her lips.

"I was thinking we'd start with foreplay, have a few mutual orgasms, and work our way up to the main event, since you like to slip out after the warmup."

She arches an eyebrow. "Or you could read some of your erotica to get me worked up. Maybe play me some Backstreet Boys to set the mood."

I groan as her sideways grin mocks me.

"That kid is pure evil," I grumble, prompting her to laugh again.

After a beat, she says, "You know we're not actually going to have sex, right?"

"Netflix and chill it is," I tell her, sighing. "But I am excellent at cuddling."

She grins even as we turn toward my house, walking up the steps. I listen on the other side to make sure the devil cat isn't tearing anything apart too close to the door, and then open it.

It's eerily quiet when we walk in.

"Bananas," I call into the darkness as I flip on the light.

Nothing seems destroyed. Other than the leather furniture I still haven't replaced.

"Why did you name the cat Bananas?"

"Blowjob demonstration gone wrong on a banana, and Bella choked. It was funny before the cat was stuck with me."

"Makes perfect sense," she deadpans from behind me. "*What is your life?*"

I laugh under my breath, pulling her with me as we move through the house, never spotting the devil cat. Maybe it's one of those rare, precious times that she's out cold.

Those are my favorite times.

"Hurry. My bedroom before she wakes up," I whisper-yell, causing Salem to look at me like I'm the lunatic.

She starts to go into the guest room, but I pull her back out.

"I thought you said your room."

"That's not my room."

"But that's the room—"

She stops and I grimace. Not the first time I've felt like a total dick weasel in front of her.

"Gotcha. We didn't fuck in your room," she says with a tight smile.

"You were just another girl that night," I stupidly say, guiding her to my bedroom, though the air between us has changed dramatically.

"I'm still just another girl, Maverick," she says with her back to me as she kicks off her shoes and starts crawling across *my* bed.

My eyes move with her ass as I lean against my door, shutting it. As she turns and sits down near the head of the bed, I arch an eyebrow at her.

"Then tell me why I can't stop chasing you."

"I have gypsy blood in my lineage, and the spell I used to get you to fuck me the first time is still lingering. Drink some vinegar and it should flush out the residual traces of the spell." She says all this with a straight face and so earnestly, that I almost believe she's serious.

Until she suddenly grins and rolls her eyes at me.

"You really are gullible."

"No," I say, holding up a finger. "I'm just trusting. Big difference."

Shaking her head and smiling, she leans against my wall of pillows.

"If I'd been in this bed the first night, I might not have been able to leave after the quickie. This feels so good."

Warmup. Not a quickie.

I shut my mouth, because I'm tired of trying to explain the difference.

"You're the first girl to ever be on that bed. Just so you know."

She gives me a condescending, *I've-heard-that-line-before* look, and I cross my arms over my chest.

"I'm serious. The guest room is used for hookups. Not even my female friends have been on my bed."

"Until now," she says, eyeing me suspiciously. "Because we're friends."

We're not friends.

"Until now," I agree. "My bed is sacred. It's extra special." I make sure she gets the meaning of that by looking at her pointedly.

"Keep spreading cheese around me, and you'll have to bring the nachos so I can eat my way out," she says with a daring little grin.

"Sean's smartassery is starting to make more sense now," I retort, causing her to chuckle as I move toward the bed.

As soon as we're side by side, I wrap my arm around her shoulders, drawing her to me, as I find the sappiest fucking romantic movie I can.

"I'm not watching *Titanic* with you," Salem tells me.

I shift to a different movie.

"I'm also not watching *Pride and Prejudice* unless it's the zombie version."

Another movie.

"Nope. *Princess Bride* is so not happening."

I drop the remote, giving up, and she picks it up, giggling a little as she starts looking up different movies.

"I don't do zombie movies," I say when she tries to pick one.

She moves on.

"Or alien invasion movies."

A little growl of frustration leaves her lips.

"Or super nerd movies."

She drops the remote and we both stare at the TV, trying not to smile.

"When does the chill part happen?" she asks, looking up at me.

"What if we just skip to the part where I'm subtly letting my hand drop lower and lower until I'm copping a feel?"

She shifts, her body pressing up against mine a little firmer as she gets comfortable, her head resting on my shoulder.

"Or we could just talk and get to know each other. You want to be friends. I'd like that. I've had tons of sex with guys I cared nothing about and guys who cared nothing about me. I've had very few friends."

The sincerity in what she's saying snaps me out of everything I had on my brain.

"You grew up in Georgia, right?" is the first question I blurt out.

A smile spreads across her face. "Mostly. It's the closest thing to a home I have. We go back there after each divorce or annulment. Usually we end up in the South somewhere even when Mom does find a new man. You've always been in Sterling Shore?"

"A Sterling is nothing without Sterling Shore," I tell her, twirling a piece of her soft hair around my finger as her eyes flick to my *Sterling* tattoo. "All the Sterlings stay here."

And for exactly three hours, I don't make a joke—new world record for me. I actually listen, and for once in my entire life, I'm serious with a girl.

Chapter 17

Salem

"One year on and one year off?" Maverick asks, working damn hard to understand my complicated family.

We've been talking for hours about anything and everything.

I don't think I've ever done this with anyone. And to be honest, I don't think he has either. At least not without a thousand jokes to lighten up the serious conversation and keep things from becoming *real*.

I have that habit too.

Call us kindred.

"Yeah. Both of them. They'd live with their fathers for a year, and live with Mom and me—and Sean, after he came along—for a year. Connor got a hockey scholarship up north. Tyler has a wife and four kids."

We're lying on our sides, a small gap between our bodies, as we stare into each other's eyes. Fully dressed, I might add.

"I still can't believe you said you hate sports, yet you grew up in the South," he says, shaking his head in mock disappointment.

His arm is under my head, but that's the only place we're touching. And though it has to have fallen asleep by now, he keeps it there.

I grin. "Stereotype much?" I ask, and he rolls his eyes. "I hate all sports, but I've always made time to go watch my two athletic brothers do things with balls and pucks. I take Sean to some of Connor's hockey games when I can. And we also go watch Tyler play basketball."

"Tyler have an office team he plays with or something?" he asks sincerely, since he knows Tyler is two years older than me.

"Something like that," I say with a secretive grin. "You went to the school where Sean goes now, right?" I ask him, shifting the subject.

He nods, smirking. "It was just a step above regular public school back then. The Sterlings made it a school that people all over the country try sending their kids to."

He's proud of his name. His lineage. His home.

I get it. I wish I had that.

His smile wavers. "Don't get mad, but the kid sort of told me about your dad. I didn't mean to pry behind your back."

Sean usually doesn't tell anyone personal things about either of us. Despite the fact he tortured Maverick, Maverick still must have done something to make my brother trust him.

"There's not much to the story, and no, my mother's cold influence didn't drive him to drink. He got drunk a lot. Even when he was married to Mom. He was her biggest score, because he was drunk in Vegas when he married her—no prenup—and she fought him for every dime she could when they had me and got divorced. He died about two years after that, leaving a casino too drunk to see, and figured he could still drive in that condition. Fortunately, it was just himself who was killed."

Maverick reaches up, brushing my hair out of my face. I hope he doesn't think I'm a cold-hearted woman like Mom just because this no longer causes me to have any emotion. I'm just desensitized to it from telling the story so many times, and I don't remember him at all.

Just a thousand pictures of his heavy eyes and drunken drool hanging out of his mouth are all I have of him. He never looked sober in any of the pictures.

"I didn't drink for a long time, worried I'd be like him. Then I learned there's such a thing as moderation. Not that it was all his fault. Alcoholism is a disease. He just chose not to treat the disease," I go on.

"We used to steal Dad's beer when we were sixteen and we'd drink in my basement—only at his house. He usually didn't notice—or if he did, he pretended not to. But Mom? Gah, she marked a line on her wine bottles so that she'd know if I'd stolen even a sip," he tells me, groaning, and my smile only doubles.

That's actually smart, and I should be doing that.

His phone rings, and he leans over, grabbing it and answering it without taking his eyes off me.

"What's up?" he asks, putting it on speaker.

"Hey, Harley just bought a—"

"No," Maverick says firmly, glaring at the phone suddenly.

"Damn it, Maverick, just tell me how to—"

"*Hell. No.* Use Google. Or that kinky app Harley designed. Do *not* ask me whatever it is you want to ask me."

"But you—"

"I'm currently watching two chicks on TV get to the good part, and my lotion is waiting, Dale," Maverick deadpans, almost convincing *me* that's exactly what he's doing, even though I'm perfectly aware of what he's actually doing. "My spank bank is still being replenished to override some of the images you've put into my head."

I grin as he shakes his head, rolling his eyes.

"Too much information," Dale says.

"Says the motherfucker calling me to ask for my knowledge on some new kink Harley wants to try out. Google, Dale. Save my dreams."

He hangs up, putting the phone far away from him, and turns his attention back to me.

"What were we talking about?" he asks, pretending as though all that didn't just go down.

"What just happened?" I ask, pointing at his phone.

"I don't want to talk about it. Really. I don't," he states flatly.

Obviously that only rouses my curiosity more, and I sit up, scooting closer. Not sure why I feel the need to be closer, but I do.

He moves over to his back, eyebrow arching at me when I casually toss my leg over his waist.

"You have to tell me now. That's like telling someone a joke, but withholding the punchline at the last second," I argue.

He points his finger at me. "No. Not happening. My dick will stay limp for a week if I start talking about it, and I happen to be in the minority of men who love morning wood."

I burst out laughing, and he winks at me, his hand going to my leg and running up it. I sort of regret opting to wear these shorts now, since the feel of his hand on my leg is a thousand times more intimate than it should feel.

He tucks an arm behind his head, angling it a little more, watching me. My laughter cut off abruptly when he touched me, and I've sort of just been staring a little obviously at him ever since.

"I'd be a terrible boyfriend," he says finally, confusing me.

"Who's asking you to be a boyfriend?" I muse, trying to sound sassy and not panicked.

Please, for fuck's sake, tell me I didn't just ask him to be my boyfriend!

I have this thing where I sometimes say things without realizing I said them, but I'm almost positive I didn't say that.

"That's the real reason I never had a serious relationship," he goes on, like he's explaining the question I asked so long ago. "My dad cheated on my mom when I was a kid. Ended their marriage. Before that, they argued all the time. Dad's a natural flirt, even though most of the time he's not actually flirting, if you know what I mean. It always drove Mom insane. After constantly being accused of cheating, he finally did cheat just to end things. Broke her fucking heart to pieces."

He clears his throat as I reach down, running my hand over his chest like I'm trying to soothe him, even though he doubtfully needs soothing. I feel like I'm supposed to do something, even if it is making this awkward.

"Anyway, fourteen years later, he marries your mom, and my mom finally decides to start dating again. She's been waiting all these years. He knows it. I know it. She knows it. The thing is, she wants him to be someone completely different. And she couldn't ever be secure enough in their relationship to trust him. Imagine how little trust there'd be now that he's broken it," Maverick goes on.

"That's why you don't care about our parents being married. Your dad marrying my mom means your mom will finally move forward with her life."

He nods, absently lacing our fingers together like it's a natural thing. "There's a good chance my dad is using your mom as much as she's using him. Because he knew my mother would never move on until she felt like he had. That's not to say my dad doesn't like your mom, but you get what I mean."

Desperate measures for a woman he cared about and broke. Sort of tragically sweet.

"I'm a lot like my dad. Flirting harmlessly, never meaning anything by it usually. Hell, it's how I talk to ninety percent of my friends. I even do shit like that with the guys. The downtown kink store thinks Corbin, Dale, and I have normal threesomes."

My eyebrows go up as a very hot image flashes in my head, and I barely pause my hand in the air to stop from fanning myself. His lips curve in a knowing grin.

"Obviously it's disgusting that your mind just went there," he points out. "We're blood-related cousins. I mean, I've heard rumors about kissing cousins in the South but—"

His words end on a laughing grunt when I slap him across the chest.

"In my head, you're just three strangers who met for the first time. In a honky-tonk. Chaps might be in this image."

He loses it, laughing so hard that he shakes the bed, and I watch like I can't look away. As his laughter tapers off, he tugs on my hand, studying it.

"The point is," he says, his eyes still on my hand, "I can't be someone else. And relationships are complicated. I'd never want someone to be as pitiful as my mother was during their marriage.

She's fierce now. Fully confident. She was a shell of that woman then, because she was so worried he was serious when he said something. Sort of like the things I said to Bella tonight."

My lips purse. "What you said with Bella was just joking around. Not flirting."

He gives me an eye roll. "You pointed out that I was flirting at Dad's house that day I accidentally ran into you, and I was doing the same thing then."

"No," I say, pointing at him. "Totally different. You were dropping all kinds of hints to me about our little encounter, and by encounter, I mean the quickie—"

"Warmup," he interrupts as though he's programmed to do it.

I fight my smile as he silently dares me to call it a quickie again.

"Anyway, that was flirting. When you make inside jokes about the sex you've had to the person you had the sex with, *it's flirting*. Joking around with someone you've never slept with and don't intend to sleep with, using double entendre and ass jokes is not flirting. Major difference. At least to me."

He studies me like he doesn't believe me.

"And you still change, even if you don't want to," I go on, shrugging. "Relationships do that. It's how you change that should tell you what sort of relationship you're in. If you go from a happy optimist to a miserable shut-in, there's a good chance the relationship is toxic. But everyone changes, evolving together."

He goes back to studying my hand like it's fascinating.

"Who's your dream couple?" I ask him, knowing this is dangerous territory.

He jerks my hand suddenly, and I let out a yelp as I awkwardly fall to his chest.

"Are you asking me a Brangelina sort of question?" he asks with a grin as I shove my hair out of my face and try not to focus on the fact that I'm lying on his chest. Or that my leg is still over his waist, making this almost like I'm straddling him very intimately.

"I mean out of your friends. Rye and Brin have this like crazy magical connection. If you tell them this, I'll hate you, but sometimes I just like to watch them."

He looks at me like I've sprouted a second head.

"What?" I ask defensively.

"Rye and Brin? The prankster couple from hell? The couple we all dread seeing, because there's a good chance we're going to end up with food dye in our mouths, or something else just as bad?"

I roll my eyes. "Not the pranks, though I do enjoy watching them get creative. It's the *after* that I like so much. The way he always catches her, and it always turns to something sweet, which makes zero sense. But it's…magical."

An embarrassing, dreamy sigh escapes me.

Maverick continues to stare at me like I've lost my damn mind.

"Forget it," I mumble, looking down at his chest and avoiding eye contact.

"Kode and Tria," he finally says.

I peer up to find him glaring at me.

"I swear, if you ever tell Kode I said this, I will hunt you down and shave you bald. I don't give a damn about the fact I love your hair. It will be gone in an instant."

Working to keep a straight face, I nod, accepting the very odd terms.

He narrows his eyes, hesitating as though he's not sure he trusts me with this top secret information.

"Kode and Tria because they are constantly together. Out of all the couples, they spend the least amount of time apart. Yet they act like they don't have enough time together," he goes on.

I run my finger along his chest, studying him.

"You don't like being alone very much, do you?" I ask, thinking back to how often I've heard about him out with his friends or out doing things. Tonight alone, he's told me about dozens of gatherings like tonight that he's gone to over the past month. Maverick is the only constant. They're not *all* always there. Just bits and pieces of them on different nights.

But Maverick is *always* there unless there's somewhere else he's at—somewhere else with people.

"You wouldn't be as pretty bald, so I suggest keeping that to yourself," he says, then eyes me when I grin.

"I'd be hot as hell bald. Britney Spears style."

A rumble of laughter escapes him, and he shakes his head. Maverick Sterling, the guy who makes a joke out of life and is always around for all his friends, and has a string of one-night stands, hates being alone. And he's the only single one left.

Besides this Britt chick I've heard of but still haven't seen. Starting to think she's a myth. But she's a lot younger.

He's the last of his cousins, which means they all have relationships, and he spends more and more time alone.

"If we're being honest, I'm not a fan of being alone either. I hate it on the nights Sean is at Mom's. Sometimes, I actually go over there just so I'm not at the house alone."

I sigh dramatically, because that really is an embarrassing confession. I expect him to laugh, but when I look back into his eyes, he's regarding me with something I can't decipher.

I'm not sure who initiates it. One second our mouths are inches apart, the next they're fused together in a desperate, bruising kiss.

In one fluid motion, he flips me so that I'm on my back, and he comes down on top of me, his weight settling on me in just the right amount. My fingers tangle in his soft hair as he takes his time, exploring my mouth with his tongue in a way that has me moaning.

I'm not sure how long we kiss, but I know my lips are swollen and my body is begging for more by the time he finally breaks the kiss and starts dragging those incredible lips down my neck.

"Tell me to stop, and I will," he murmurs against my neck.

"Don't stop," is the immediate response that flies out of my mouth.

I feel him grin against my chest as he works his way down, kissing me through the material of my shirt as he works it up with his hands.

He takes his time taking my shirt off, kissing all of my upper body, teasing me, dragging it out.

I lose patience.

"Maverick, if you don't fuck me, there's a good chance I'm going to your bathroom and taking matters into my own hands."

He laughs and kisses me again, as I reach between us, shoving my shorts down.

That's the thing that snaps his control.

Finally.

He rises up, tugging his shirt off without undoing the buttons—*hot!*—as I slip out of my bra, my eyes not moving from the hard planes of perfectly placed muscle. There's not an ounce of bulk on him. Every muscle is lean and sculpted, not too exaggerated but certainly not lacking.

He starts undoing his slacks, and shoves them down just enough to show me the part of his body…that is a lot bigger than I remember.

He's definitely ready.

My eyes come up just as he leans back from the dresser, a condom wrapper in hand, and he tears it open with his teeth, his eyes never leaving mine.

My gaze drops when he starts rolling the condom on, and I bite my lip in anticipation.

His lips find mine again as he thrusts in, filling me instantly and taking away the ache. I garble out some sort of unintelligible praise that flows from my mouth to his.

Each thrust seems to hit a deep spot inside me, finding everything in just the right measure. Each drag of him as he pulls out is almost agonizing, but he soothes away the ache on each return.

His thumb moves between us, applying just the right amount of pressure where I need it, and I cry out when the very quick orgasm tears through me. But Maverick's not done.

He drinks in my sounds, his hips not losing rhythm, as he drives in and out of me on a mission. When he breaks the kiss, his mouth lowers next to my ear.

"There's one. I want two more from you," he says in a tone that sounds like a threat and a promise.

Just his tone has me shivering against him, and my body tightening all over again, because Maverick Sterling is the master of sexy.

He coaxes another orgasm out of me in no time, and by the third orgasm, our bodies are starting to stick together because of all the heat we're generating.

As if he was just waiting on that last one to blow me apart, he finally thrusts in one last time, pushing his mouth against the curve of my neck as he releases a guttural sound.

When his body goes still against mine, a lazy, very satisfied grin spreads over my lips.

He gives a full-body shudder as he kisses the side of my throat, and I loop my arms around his neck, holding him to me.

"Tell me that was the main event, because I don't know if it can get any better," I say all breathily.

A rumble of laughter shakes his body, and he grins as he kisses my neck again.

"Bet you're wishing you'd stuck around for it now."

"The thought is weighing heavily on my mind," I concede.

Proud of himself, he raises his head, grinning lazily at me. As he pulls out and goes to the bathroom on shaky legs, I take in the very incredible view of his back—and his phenomenal ass.

His bathroom is a straight view, and I look away when he decides to piss with the door wide open. Maverick Sterling has zero shame, so I shouldn't be surprised.

I drop back to the bed, a stupid, goofy grin on my face that I can't wipe away, but seriously need to before he returns. I manage a respectable half smile by the time he wobbles back to the bed and collapses.

"See? We can be friends and still have sex," he says, causing my smile to suddenly turn fake. "I'm a damn good friend."

"Friend?" I ask.

Not sure why there's suddenly a sour taste in my mouth. Did I think we'd lie around and talk for a few hours, and then magically be in the bubble like Rye and Brin have? I didn't even want that until today, so I have zero clue as to why it's suddenly an issue.

"Yeah," he says, smiling up at me as he turns over, his arm around my waist. "I have to admit, having sex on my bed is definitely better than the guest bed."

Everything suddenly feels less real. Our bubble is bursting with each new dose of reality.

"I imagine. It's a great bed, after all," I say, forcing the words out conversationally.

"You were fucking killing me in those shorts. I've been thinking about being inside you since I picked you up," he goes on. "And that grease on you today was…making me consider getting some auto work done."

As he wiggles his eyebrows, I continue to force a smile, feeling more and more like I normally do after sex, and less like the girl I was just moments ago.

"Hey, do you care if I borrow your phone to call mine? I think it fell out of my purse or something."

He reaches over, grabbing his phone, and unlocks it before handing it to me.

"Who do you need to call? You can just use my phone."

I shake my head. "I need to get home. I have a pile of dishes that won't smell too fresh in the morning if I don't do something with them tonight. So I'm just going to call for a cab or something."

"I can drive you," he says, his hand sliding down my leg. I shouldn't flinch at his touch, but I do. I shouldn't feel dirty, but I do.

It's silly, and I realize this, but it's just how things are. Can't help how I feel.

"We had alcohol earlier. I'd rather Uber."

He blows out a breath. "Fine, but I swear I'm sober."

"Do you have some water? My throat is dry."

He presses a kiss to the inside of my palm, a sweet gesture I'm tempted to misread, as he gets up and goes to grab me some water.

I take a few slow breaths.

My mother's voice makes an untimely appearance in my mind. *Pretty girls just get screwed.*

Double pie moment.

Chapter 18

MAVERICK

"So tell me again what exactly happened," Kode says, a secretive smile playing on his lips.

"I'm not giving you details if that's what you're angling for," I tell him, rolling my eyes.

Weird as it sounds, breakfast tastes better than usual. I blame it on the fact I was left very fucking exhausted last night, yet oddly energized as well.

I can't believe I asked her to spend the night. I'm still not sure if I'm disappointed or relieved that she had to go home. It's hard to figure out what exactly I'm feeling around her, since it's all so fucking new and confusing as hell.

The waitress drops off refills for our orange juices, and I look around the table at all my cousins who are staring at me with odd little smirks.

"Then you did what exactly to make her leave?" Dale asks me.

It's just the five of us this morning, no women, since they're having their own breakfast, making up for the lunch they missed last Saturday. I should mention they're just a few tables away from us while having this breakfast, so it's a little weird.

"I didn't say anything to make her leave. I did the thing where I make her feel sexy afterwards, and I hinted that I wanted to see her again. If I'd had anything in particular to invite her to, I would have invited her."

"Tria just texted me, asking you to get the lemon pie recipe from Salem when she's talking to you again," Kode says, staring at his phone, then looking up.

I glance over to the table of girls who are all giving me judgy little stares. Tria is staring at me, as if waiting to see what I'm about to say to Kode.

"I'm sorry, but what? Salem and I are on phenomenal terms," I say as I look back at my dickheaded cousin, who looks like he doesn't believe me.

"You did nothing to piss her off?" Dane asks me, leaning up on the table, a smirk on his lips.

"I'm telling you, she was very happy when she left. I fucked her in my actual bed. That's a special thing."

"Yeah, that's not exactly a compliment to a girl," Corbin says, clapping my shoulder.

"Any chance you made it sound like it was more casual than it was?" Dale hedges.

"It *was* casual. And I'm sure we'll *casually* do it again. It's not like we can do the relationship thing. Her mom would be pissed at her and cause problems for her and her brother. And I'd suck at being a boyfriend."

"There it is," Kode says, holding his hand out to Corbin who groans and hands him a twenty.

"What the actual hell is going on right now?" I ask as Dane mutters something under his breath and hands Kode a twenty as well.

Kode and Dale divide the money up between them.

"We said you told her it was casual and downplayed the whole thing," Dale says, pointing between him and Kode.

"I guessed that you fucked her in the guest room and told her you didn't have sex in your bedroom because your bed is sacred," Corbin confesses, looking anywhere but at me when I glare at him.

"I had money on you saying something stupid—which technically you did—but I meant more along the lines of telling her she was hot and it was fun. Or something like that."

I did say those things. Not in those exact words, well…mostly those words.

What the hell is wrong with that?

"Someone want to tell me why you think I've fucked up?"

"Have you checked your phone this morning?" Dale asks me, causing me to dig my phone out of my pocket.

"Are you kidding? I barely woke up in enough time to throw on clothes and rush over here. Fortunately I took a shower before crashing last night," I grumble.

Seventy-two texts?!

I pull up the first message, and I'll admit I'm embarrassed by the shrill sound that escapes me when I drop my phone like it's on fire. It bounces on the table, and I point at it.

"What the unholy hell is that shit?" I demand.

Dane picks it up and smirks. "Looks like a zombie unicorn fucking another zombie unicorn."

"Who the hell would send that ungodly thing?" I growl.

"Some guy named Jack."

I don't remember a Jack.

Damn cloud.

"Want to see the half-unicorn half-spider creature on this next one getting it on with a centaur?" Kode asks as he takes my phone away from Dane and holds it up.

Another embarrassing sound comes out of me, and they all laugh as I clear my throat.

Corbin plucks the phone away from him, taking his turn. "Or how about two dudes with unicorn horns stuck to their heads and a lot of leather?" Corbin asks, shaking his head and shuddering.

"You should probably check your Twitter account," Kode tells me with a smirk.

I stab the button to clear away the weird fucking image when I pick my phone up, and pull up my Twitter. Then curse.

@MavSterling: Send me the dirtiest/sexiest/creepiest unicorn pics you have if you know my number. It's what FRIENDS do. #ILikeDirtyPonyPlay

Damn woman. I thought she liked the idea of being friends. Though in hindsight, it does sound like I basically asked her to be friends with benefits. Pretty sure that was really stupid to say *directly* after having sex.

I hate my life sometimes.

The guys all burst out laughing, probably seeing the resignation in my features.

I also want to kill my mother. Again.

@MommaQueenVictoria: @MavSterling you still like playing with ponies? #MyBabyWantsAUnicorn

And Ethan's mother. Again, who gave the mothers Twitter access?

@ArleneMommaBear: @MavSterling I already have a scrapbook for that. I can bring it to you. I have pics with you and ponies.

@EthanNolesIDGAF: @ArleneMommaBear that's not what pony play is. And @MavSterling needs 2 find a new fetish. #Neigh

@BellaHasABigBun: @MavSterling I had no idea you'd reached this level of debauchery. But here's a pic of two naughty ppl in unicorn cosplay for ya. ;)

"Do I want to know what pony play is?" Dale asks.

"No," the rest of us all say in unison.

I really regret talking so many people into finally getting on Twitter. Really, *really* regret it.

Though, it wasn't me who got the damn moms on there.

Fucking Salem. No wonder that little shrimp brother of hers is such an asshole. And I can't believe I fell for the same damn con *twice*. My phone is never getting borrowed again, damn it.

"Oh, I think I'm a little sick now," Dale says, his phone gripped tightly in his hands as I put my own phone away, vibrating with a little more fury than I care to admit. "This is why I don't Google shit. You get pony play images stuck in your head. I'll never be right again."

"In that case, don't look up pineapple porn," I say through a tight smile, trying to pretend like I didn't just have to delete that messed up tweet from my account.

"Why would you even be looking up something like that?" Kode asks me, brow furrowed.

"The same reason someone looks up *blue waffle*—someone else told them not to. I need to go," I tell them as I stand and toss down some cash for the bill.

"Roses are always… Never mind. They never work," Dane says, batting his hand.

"Fuck you very much, but this is just a simple miscommunication. Clearly I insulted her. I'll get it fixed, and you jackasses can kiss my ass."

They all try not to laugh at my back as I walk toward the door. Just as I reach the exit, some guy sitting at a nearby table neighs—*fucking neighs*—at me. When I turn to glare at him, he makes some other horse noise and winks at me before licking his lips and biting down on the spoon handle like it's a bit.

With every ounce of dignity I can muster, I pretend to not notice my cousins nearly bursting at the seams with their barely-contained laughter, straighten my sleeves, and walk out.

I'm not buying Salem roses. I'm fucking strangling her.

Yep.

Right now, as a matter of fact.

Chapter 19

Salem

My eyes fall on a leggy, sexy girl as she talks animatedly to Rye, though she doesn't look too happy. He seems dismissive of her, even nodding toward one of the other guys to come help him out.

One thing I respect about him is that he literally doesn't pay any other girl attention—*in that way*—because he's truly devoted to Brin. I've never witnessed that before on such a level.

When he turns and walks away, the other guy blocks the girl, stopping her from following Rye into the office. I turn away from the massive window overhead. It's meant to be viewed from there not from here.

But when I see Brin, I can't help but ask, "Who's that chick?"

Brin apparently didn't go to the breakfast, since she got here as early as I did. She rolls her eyes after flicking them up to where the girl is flinging her arms, pushing the guy away from him.

"Leah. Long story short, she's mad that Rye gave you this job, when she recently became a certified mechanic. She sort of hates me and is blaming it on me that she missed this opportunity. Honestly, she was probably going to try and sue for discrimination when he didn't hire her, so I'm very glad you happen to have a vagina. Helps thwart that."

Glad my vagina is doing something right these days.

"Why does she hate you?" I can't help but ask, because Brin is freaking nice as hell to everyone.

"Because I got Rye," she says with a shrug, and I exhale in understanding.

"Got it."

"She's on my nerves because this is the fourth time she's stopped by since Wrench turned in his notice. Girls like her can't understand why he's with someone like me. This is just her way of trying to get closer to him."

"You're beaut—"

"Don't lie or sugarcoat it," she interrupts, giving me a pointed stare. "You didn't think I was with him immediately either when you came in for the interview. I'm cute—not sexy like you and her. And Rye is…hot as hell. I'm not even going to pretend he's not. But he's also mine, and for some reason, he thinks I'm hot. That's all that matters."

I give her a brittle smile. "You have all the most important qualities that no one overlooks. And what someone views as sexy changes as they get to know someone. You're smart. You're fun. You're fucking amazing—"

"Are you secretly a lesbian? Because I don't swing that way, but my friend Maggie does. She's in a serious relationship, but she has tons of gay friends," she says, interrupting me with a serious expression, but then grins.

I roll my eyes. "What I'm saying, is that the overtly sexy girls just get fucked. If you're simply too pretty, that's all you're seen as—just pretty. Nothing else."

She studies me for a moment, probably thinking I'm a *pretty girl* asking for some sympathy. I'm not usually so whiny. It's irking me. I'm way better than this, damn it.

"You okay? You seem a little off today," she finally says, probably reading between the lines.

"Just tired. Had a lot of pie moments lately."

Her confusion is evident when her face scrunches up. "Pie moments?"

"Just something I say when I'm to the point of wanting to hurt someone."

She grins. "When I'm to that point, I usually do something terrible to Rye. Then we have incredibly hot sex to fight it out. Try it. It works wonders."

I snort derisively. "My vagina is officially on lockdown."

"See? I knew something happened. What'd Maverick do? He's never brought a girl around and been all over her the way he is with you, but since he's a novice, he's—"

"It's not what you think," I say tightly, not wanting to discuss this at work. "He and I just had a major miscommunication. I zigged and he zagged, and we missed the mark completely. No big deal. But for the first time since I was eighteen, I was really naïve and wanted more than I'm allowed to have. I'm usually not that girl. I just need to get my head on right and remember my role."

She nods like she understands, though I can tell she doesn't understand at all.

"I blame you, just so you know," I go on, and then walk off to start tinkering on the old Mustang 5.0 they brought in this morning that seems to be running hot.

"Me?" she asks, chasing after me. "What'd I do?"

"You have so many moments. I just wanted one of my own moments."

"Moments?" she asks, confused.

I face her and roll my eyes. "You know. That moment when you feel like you're in the center of the universe, and everything is aligned just right. You're in this enchanted bubble where nothing can touch you. There's nothing you can do but smile and laugh and just be happy, because *everything* is perfect. Everything is just like it's supposed to be. I almost had one of those moments. *Almost.* Mine missed the mark by one harsh burst of reality. Just a slip on my part. I won't let it happen again."

I turn back to the beast that is definitely rusted. I'm going to bust some knuckles on this if I don't find some gloves.

When I pull back to grab some gloves, I see Brin with watery eyes.

"What?" I ask a little too defensively.

She wipes under an eye. "That was just freaking beautiful." When she grins, I think about hitting her upside the head with the wrench in my hand.

"Go do something in the office far away from me and tools, please," I tell her as she grins broader at me.

"You'll have your moments, Salem. Mine didn't start coming overnight," she says, her teasing gone. "It was a lot of tears, pain, heartache, and then perseverance that got me here with Rye. You don't just fall into blissful happiness. You make your own version of it."

"Now who's getting mushy?" I retort, trying to drain this seriousness away before it gets too intense.

For no reason at all, I turn and look over my shoulder, seeing…Maverick. Talking to the hot chick—Leah. Who also happens to be a mechanic.

Now I feel even more redundant and unoriginal. I'm a pair of overalls and sports bra away from being a cliché.

Whatever he's saying to her has her smiling, when moments ago it looked like she was fighting mad and about to be dragged out. I turn away, pretending I don't give a damn that he's the panty whisperer.

"What's he doing here?" Brin asks as I go to town, busting out some rusted bolts.

"Probably getting something lined up for tonight if I had to guess." Yeah, there's a lot of bite to those words.

"Maverick isn't here to hit on Leah when he clearly had no idea she'd be here. Whatever he's doing right now is simply to calm her down and get her out of Rye's hair."

Pie. Moment.

"I'm sure he'll take one for the team. No worries." *Wow.* "Sorry. Total bitch comment. I didn't mean to take that out on you," I immediately blurt out.

She just grins. "You're totally jealous right now."

I glare at her. "Repeat that, and I will let a car fall on you."

"Why would I be under a car?" she asks.

"I have my ways, Brin Waters. I have my ways."

I cast one more look over my shoulder to see Maverick's back pressed against the observation window, and Leah propped beside him and angled toward him, still grinning and speaking about who knows what.

It's just closing in on ten, but I decide to take an early lunch.

"I'll be back. Taking lunch right now. Call me when he's gone, and I'll come back," I tell her, tossing down my wrench much harder than necessary.

She rolls her eyes. "Salem, I swear to you, he's not—"

"He doesn't owe me anything, Brin. We're just *friends*. But if you happen to have a bridle handy, do me a favor and give it to him for me, would ya?"

The confusion on her face is priceless, and I wink at her before striding out, hopping in my truck, and deciding to wash my hands when I get home. Where I'll be eating lunch and waiting for Maverick to get his ass far away from me.

It's not until I pull up at the house and see the car in my driveway that my stomach does flips. Only one person would rent a cherry red Camaro and be here right now.

I push my door open and practically sprint inside to see a face I haven't seen in too long.

"There's my favorite girl," the deep voice says. And I fling myself into his arms, squeezing like I can't let go.

Chapter 20

MAVERICK

Leah finally walks away, leaving her number behind in my phone, and she winks at me as she disappears down the stairs. I blow out a relieved breath, and then quickly delete her phone number.

That crazy chick is not going to be kept in my phone by the damn cloud.

Because I'm finding a way to delete it from the cloud too before I get a new phone and find that bastard there again.

That cloud is diabolical.

"She finally gone?" Rye asks as he walks out.

"Fucking finally. What the hell did you do to get her so worked up?"

"Hired Salem," he says with a grin. "Leah thinks I'm going after my new mechanic, because she still refuses to believe that I love Brin. Crazy bitch."

His expression sobers, and he leans against the glass.

"Now I have to go find Brin and make sure this isn't bugging her. If it is, I'm going to get a restraining order or something and have Leah's ass arrested if she comes back. Hate to resort to those measures, but Brin comes first."

This is the reason I'm in trouble with Salem right now. Rye says fucking sweet shit like that and then makes me look like twice the asshole when I open my mouth.

"Fuck you," I grumble.

"What'd I do?" he asks innocently.

"You hired Salem." I blow out a breath as he arches an eyebrow, and I turn back toward the window to see…Salem is not down there. Where'd she go?

"If you're looking for Salem, she took an early lunch," Brin says, piping up as she makes her way up the stairs, her eyes already scanning me.

"When will she be back?" I ask, glancing at the time. Definitely an *early* lunch.

"As soon as you're not here," she says, her look a touch scathing.

"Damn it. What'd you do? I knew this was going to happen," Rye says, eyeing me.

"I'm fixing it," I say assuredly, holding my hands up in surrender as I back toward the stairs. "I promise. I just apparently won't fix it here."

With that, I turn and jog down the stairs, hating Leah for a whole new reason. I had Salem within reach until I heard Leah threatening Rye within an inch of his life. I showed her attention for twenty minutes or less, poured on some charm, made her feel pretty again, and all was right with her world once more.

She's not quite as complex as Salem. Usually, I prefer simple.

There are tons of different types of women. Just like there are tons of different types of men.

I stop for a minute, staring blankly before blinking.

Damn it. I better not fit into the 'simple' category.

Cursing, I get in my car, refusing to call anyone for advice. I made the mess. I'll fix the mess.

And I'll stop making new messes along the way.

Hurrying home, I walk through my door, planning to Google any and all recipes for fixing a mistake with a girl that I'm not really dating. Because my life has gotten complicated.

Just as I reach my room, I realize my door is cracked.

I *always* shut it since the last time that hellion wrecked my bed.

Damn it. That cat better not have—

I sigh in relief when I push inside and see my bed is still in pristine shape. But...there's a distinct smell of disgusting in here.

I turn around, searching for the source, and find the sandbox—known as the zen garden—has a pile of cat shit in it, where Bananas decided it worked just fine as a litter box.

"That's not zen, Bananas!" I shout. "Not zen at all!"

I swear, sometimes I hear that cat laughing at me.

***

I can't believe I bought roses.

This is what I've been reduced to.

But she won't answer her phone, and I found her Twitter handle, but she didn't respond to that either.

Obviously.

But she should be home by now. Rye's shop closed a couple of hours ago, and her truck is in the driveway. So is a car I don't recognize...

I knock on the door, looking the red Camaro over with a shrewd eye. When the door swings open, I reach out with the roses, turning my head back with a grin that I hope does more good than harm.

But I end up staring at a half-naked guy in a towel instead of Salem.

A guy about my height. Light hair. A guy who works out.

A guy in a towel.

Did I mention the motherfucker is in a towel? Just checking. Because it's a really important fact.

He takes the roses, a grin on his face.

"You shouldn't have," he drawls, exaggerating a Southern accent.

I step back, look around, finding myself suffering a case of déjà vu as I make sure I'm at the right house.

"Is Salem home?" I ask through clenched teeth.

His eyebrow arches as he leans against the doorframe, roses still in hand as he crosses his arms over his chest. I hope he didn't just make his pecs dance on purpose. Because that's just weird.

"Maybe. Depends on who you are," he tells me.

While wearing that towel around his hips.

"Who I am," I say, laughing under my breath. "This is fucking ridiculous."

"You talking to me or yourself? Because I can give you a minute if you need to do your thing or whatever," the smartass says.

I turn my attention back to him.

"I'd like to talk to Salem now." With a modicum of calm that I barely possess, I add, "Please."

He shrugs, that cocky smirk still fixed on his face. "And I'd like to eat an entire chocolate cake all by myself. But training season is a bitch."

He's definitely making his pecs dance on purpose. Who does that?

"Losing my patience, Titty Dancer. Where's Salem?"

"I left her in the tub. Want me to get her for you?" he asks as though it's no big deal that he's about to die.

This is when I take two quick steps toward him, my fist already coming up, as I barge into the house.

"Fucking kidding!" he bursts out, laughter following as he stumbles back, and shields his face with the roses.

When I pause and glare at him, he continues laughing. Since I'm inside by this point, it's easy to spot Scan sitting at the table, a grilled cheese on his plate, and a shit-eating grin on his face.

"Told you he was gullible," the little ass says.

Loud music is thudding from somewhere in the house, but I barely pay it any attention when Titty Dancer—who has no water on his body, by the way—rips his towel off to reveal a pair of athletic shorts.

He's still laughing when he tosses the towel over his shoulder.

"I'm Connor. Your other new stepbrother," he says, sticking his hand out as he grins at me. "Sean put me up to it."

I cut my eyes over to the other pain in my ass, and he winks at me, as I shake Connor's hand.

"That's for the tuna sub," the little shit says.

Despite my murderous moment—which makes zero sense—I completely relax as Connor shuts the door behind me, still laughing lightly.

"I'd say it's nice to meet you, but this family has a way of pissing me off in ways that can't be healthy," I say with a dark grin.

"Touché," Connor says with a shrug. "Salem's in her room. Just follow the loud music."

"He knows where her room is," Sean says with a small laugh, as Connor drops my roses into a vase near the door

"Right. And gross," Connor says, going to join Sean at the table and stealing half of his grilled cheese.

His Southern drawl is nowhere nearly as thick as Sean's and Salem's; no clue why I even notice that.

"He called you Titty Dancer," Sean says, laughing with his brother, as I turn to go into Salem's room.

Before I can reach it, she walks out, her head down as she carries what looks like a game of Monopoly.

"Found it. Finally," she says, swinging her gaze up.

Our eyes collide, and she stumbles a step, nearly losing the game from her hands. A small smile cracks my lips, since I love it when she blushes.

"What're you doing here?" she asks, darting a glance past me to her two brothers, who are no doubt watching us openly, not even bothering to hide their prying.

My eyes drop to the game in her hands, and I rock back on my heels.

"Apparently I'm playing a game of Monopoly and getting to know yet another wonderful new stepbrother," I say with a challenging grin.

A few snorts follow that comment from the Peanut Gallery back there. Salem narrows her eyes on me as she walks over and thrusts the game at Connor. He takes it, grinning as he watches us with undisguised interest—knew it.

I just swivel my head to track Salem as she stalks around for a second before returning to me, taking me by the elbow and dragging me toward her room. Dragging is a bit of an exaggeration, since I go all too willingly.

"*Somebody's in trouble*," Sean says in a singsong voice.

As soon as she has me in her room with the really loud music, she shuts the door and cuts the volume down just a little.

I start talking before she can start berating me. "I get it. I somehow fucked up and insulted you yesterday, and I am really fucking sorry. I'm also never letting you or anyone else from your family borrow my phone again."

Her lips twitch, but quickly her scowl returns.

"You didn't fuck up, Maverick. It just wasn't a time for those words. They weren't as real as I thought that particular moment was."

This is so far above my experience level that I feel like a total rookie.

"I still don't know what I said wrong, because you're the one who has been saying you couldn't have a relationship with me because of your mother leveraging Sean over you," I decide to point out, and then realize that was not smart when her look turns a little condescending.

"You didn't say anything wrong. You just said it at the wrong time. I wasn't asking for a declaration of love or a relationship," she states dryly.

"Then what the hell did I do wrong? I thought things were good between us when you left," I groan.

"I just wanted that moment, Maverick. Just that moment," she says as though she's exasperated.

I'm so confused. Women really are complicated. I never understood how much so until I decided to let all the feelings and shit get involved. I'm terrible at this.

"That moment?" I ask, though I'll probably regret it.

"It was a really important moment," she goes on, the anger leaving her as her shoulders slump. "And you cheapened it by saying our friendship was going to be fun now, and I was hot and you'd been thinking of banging me since you saw me all sexed up in my grease-stained clothes—"

"Pretty sure those weren't my exact words," I decide to point out, since I sort of don't like the way that sounds either, and I know that's sure as hell not what I meant.

It does sound like it cheapened the moment, and that I spent all that time with her just to fuck her again.

She exhales harshly. "It had the desired effect. And it ruined the moment. It was a moment I've waited on for a really long time."

And I was thinking it was a damn good moment.

The difference between men and women: Exhibit A.

"And I was wrong," she mumbles, the words almost drowned out by the music, but I catch them.

"I'm sorry, what was that?" I ask, amused because her cheeks are flushed.

"I said I was wrong. I told you I don't get jealous, and apparently I do. I really hate Leah, and I've never even spoken to her. That's not me. That's not who I am. It's also not what you want."

Her eyes meet mine and her gaze levels me with accusation, like it's my fault she got jealous over misinterpreting a situation.

"I was just calming Leah down; not planning a date with her. But it's good to know you got jealous," I say with a grin, unsure why I find that fascinating, since that's usually something that would send me walking away real damn quick. "Because I almost punched your brother in the face when he answered the door in a towel and maybe insinuated you were waiting for him in the tub."

"Is this another jab at Southerners and blood-relatives doing gross things? Because that's all bullsh—"

"No," I interrupt, chuckling under my breath. "I didn't know he was your brother until I almost punched him and he started laughing. Apparently you're not the only one having an unexpected case of the green-eyed monster."

She fights a grin, losing the battle and settling for an eye-roll and a groan as a consolation prize.

She shakes her head, still keeping a safe distance between us. Considering I'm in trouble, I try to keep my eyes up and not notice the fact she's wearing some skimpy little pajama shorts and no bra under that camisole top.

It seems as though torture is on the agenda for now.

"I felt really stupid last night," she goes on, her eyes meeting mine, barely giving me a glimpse of the vulnerability there. It's so minute that I almost miss it.

I doubt she allows herself to be vulnerable too often.

I get that. Probably more so than she realizes.

One more thing I like about her.

"I didn't mean for that to happen. Obviously. In case you haven't noticed, I have no fucking clue what I'm doing beyond casual. So I thought I'd stick to what I knew best, and go from there."

Her smile forms again, even though she banishes it quickly.

"I felt duped. It's been a long time since I felt gullible, and —"

"Really? Because I seem to be having a reoccurring episode of it lately. Happened about the time your family crashed into my life," I say, this time causing her to laugh.

Finally getting somewhere.

"Can we start from here? Because obviously there's something that keeps drawing us together, despite the fact we're both putting up a damn good fight," I tell her, only fueling her softening state as she takes a step toward me.

"One condition," she says, peering up at me when I finally get her in my arms. I didn't even realize how tightly strung I was until she touched me and my entire body relaxed. I really am losing my mind.

Wish someone had told me what really happens when you actually like a damn girl.

"What condition?" I ask her.

"No sex. Not until we know what we want from each other," she says.

Saw that coming. I really wish I had just kept my mouth shut last night.

"No sex I'll agree to if you'll do one thing for me."

She cocks her head, waiting.

"Sleep with me. As often as possible," I finally tell her.

Her eyes roll, and she starts to push away. I'm not even sure why I said it, but now that the words are out, I mean it. I've decided it was definitely disappointment I felt when she left instead of staying.

It was also disappointment when I woke up alone.

I've never fucking slept with a girl, and…now I'm back to feeling like an asshole.

"*Just* sleep. I don't want to sleep alone tonight. If it doesn't suck, we can sleep together again tomorrow."

She softens again, her eyes studying mine. "No sex," she says again, firmly.

"No sex," I agree.

"Okay. Hope you don't sleep naked. That will get you slapped."

When I smile, she rolls her eyes, and I follow her out to the living room.

"You staying or going? We're making pasta," she tells me, gesturing to where Connor is at the stove, still shirtless.

His pec dancing doesn't bother me anymore now that I know he's her brother. In fact, I have zero issue with the guy, when only moments ago, I wanted to smash his face in.

Definitely going crazy.

"You kidding?" I ask, rolling my sleeves up. "I'm playing fucking Monopoly."

Chapter 21

Salem

Monopoly sucks.

Maverick is grinning as he collects yet another assload of cash from Connor, who is muttering something about never inviting the 'boyfriend' to Monopoly night again.

Maverick adds the money to his many piles that are already set out in front of him. I swear he has three hotels on so many damn spots that it's ridiculous. I've never been so thoroughly destroyed.

"Your phone keeps lighting up," Sean says, probably trying to distract Maverick so Connor can cheat. But Maverick is a man of intent and focus.

"Probably another unicorn or pony picture. I'd rather not look at it for a few days, to be honest."

I choke on my laugh, and Maverick flips me off without even looking up from the game.

"Did I miss something?" Sean asks, confused.

"Probably something to do with that random tweet I saw this morning that almost made me regret following my new stepbrother. Guessing she hacked your Twitter?" Connor asks, smirking.

Maverick nods, glaring a little at me, before lowering his head. I just grin. At least I won at that.

"This is why I hate being grounded from the internet," Sean groans.

I've been out of the game for the past hour, picking at my cold pasta as they finish up. Sean was put out of the game after me, but he's still at the table, trying to figure out how Maverick has thoroughly wrecked us in record time.

Usually a good game lasts us for days. Three hours with Maverick Sterling, and Connor is already giving him the very last of his money.

The final one bites the dust.

"How? Just how?" Sean asks seriously.

I'm the banker, and I cheated. I still lost first. Guess that gives clout to the 'cheaters never prosper' thing.

"The Sterlings built Sterling Shore," Maverick says absently as he grins, clearing off the board. "Real estate and investments are our thing. We were a true monopoly in the beginning. Now we share a little. It's been forever since I got to play the game, though."

Sean rolls his eyes, settling back in his seat, but I can tell he's impressed. Obviously, he'd never admit it aloud.

"Why's it been forever since you played?" I ask, sipping my only glass of wine for the night as Connor drinks his beer.

Maverick grins as he looks up at me. "Because my family outlawed it. We get serious about some Monopoly, and after the fourth fight that broke out between me and my cousins, my Aunt Elizabeth decided to ban it from all households. We tried it again when we became adults. It was a lot of brokering trades, arguing over hotel acquirements, and trying to develop alliances so we could team up against each other. After the first punch was thrown, we banned it from ourselves."

"Glad us less-than-business-savvy people gave you back your childhood joy," Connor says flatly.

Maverick just winks at me, knowing he makes even Monopoly look sexy.

"You need to get to bed, kiddo. It's already past your bedtime," I tell Sean.

He glances at the clock, groans, then stands and wraps his arms around me, giving me a hug for the night. He turns and does the same to Connor, hugging him a little tighter, since Connor has to leave in the morning. He literally flew out just to make sure Sean had settled into school and was doing okay with the new town.

He has college to get back to.

"I'll fly out again as soon as I get a day or two off," Connor tells him, kissing Sean's forehead.

Maverick busies himself with putting away the game, and I watch as Connor ruffles Sean's hair.

When Sean turns and opens his arms for Maverick, I grin. Maverick just glares at him. "I'm not *that* gullible," Maverick tells him.

A smile breaks across Sean's face, and he laughs before turning and walking away.

"Still up for debate, Maverick," Sean says before he shuts his door.

Connor just grins, sipping his beer.

"Monopoly is Sean's favorite game," Connor says idly.

"Was I supposed to let him win?" Maverick asks sincerely, looking up. "Because I'm terribly competitive at board games."

I'm not sure why that makes me smile harder.

"No," Connor says around a laugh. "Just figured you might be wondering why we would play Monopoly on my only night in town."

Maverick leans back. "Sorry. I didn't realize you were here for the one night, or I wouldn't have intruded."

Connor bats a hand. "I'd rather you be here. I wanted to get to know you anyway, since you're going to be around my younger brother. He doesn't have a whole lot of people he talks about, but he talks about you. Don't tell him I told you."

Maverick flashes a grin, and I ignore the butterflies in my stomach.

"He just likes playing with my pussy," Maverick finally says on a long sigh.

To this, Connor chokes on his beer, and I burst out laughing.

"I heard that," Sean calls out from his room, sounding overly annoyed.

Maverick chuckles.

"Speaking of which, care if we borrow your cat for a while? I know you want a break from her, and Sean—"

"She's all yours," Maverick says immediately. "Take her. I'll even pay you to take her."

Connor laughs under his breath, and we spend the next couple of hours just talking about hockey and such. Connor hated the time in Georgia, because, well, hockey isn't exactly a Georgia thing. It was hard for him to find places to play, but Mom usually found them no matter what state we were in when it was his year to live with us.

Despite her faults, she did some of the important things that did count.

Doesn't excuse the fact she slept with my boyfriend to teach me not to be gullible.

She used just as many harsh tactics on Connor and Sean, too. It's why they find it fascinating to dupe people.

Connor finally yawns, and Maverick stands to head toward my bedroom, not saying anything.

"I'm going to bed before I decide this dining room table looks comfortable. I promise I'll be back out as soon as I can get away," Connor tells me as we both stand.

I go to hug him, holding on a little longer than necessary, since I don't know when I'll see him again.

"Just worry about keeping your grades up and your scoring average awesome. I got this."

"Yeah. I know you got it. I just hate that it's all on you, while I'm off living my dream."

"I get to work on cars no matter where I move to. My dreams are just fine," I assure him, patting his chest as I try to alleviate his guilt.

Maybe I bat a tear out of my eye before he can see it.

He musses my hair, and I roll my eyes as I fix it back into place. "Don't bang the headboard against the wall. I'd rather not vomit in my sleep. I like sleeping on my back, so that'd be a choking hazard," Connor calls out over his shoulder.

I roll my eyes.

There will be no banging of the headboard.

No sex.

Just sleep.

Shouldn't be difficult at all.

When I walk into my room, I reassess that last thought.

Maverick is standing by my bed, texting someone, in nothing but his boxer-briefs that hug his ass and show off his—

Eyes up, Salem.

His body is just too damn hard not to look at.

"Got my alarm set," he tells me, as though I was going to ask who he was texting.

I wasn't curious, actually. I was using the opportunity to rake my eyes over the sexiest man I've ever seen, shortly after I instated a no-sex rule.

Lovely.

"Okay."

I move around to my side of the bed, wondering how to do this *not* awkwardly. The sleeping usually comes after the sexing in my world. I've never done this without the sex.

What am I doing?

As I shuffle under the covers, Maverick turns out the light, and he crawls in bed beside me, his arms immediately wrapping me up and drawing me against him, spooning me from behind.

It's like he's surrounding me with just his touch. His lips trail over my neck, innocent little kisses, until he reaches my ear. "Night, Salem," he says, a grin in his tone.

"Night, Maverick."

In some weird way, it almost feels more intimate to do this without the sex. More personal.

His arms stay around me, and I find myself drifting off without any lingering awkwardness because it feels good.

Told you Maverick Sterling was going to be a problem for me.

Chapter 22

MAVERICK

Sleeping beside Salem is both a blessing and a curse.

A blessing, because I didn't realize what I was missing until I suddenly had it. I fucking love the way she wraps around me in her sleep. I also like not waking up alone.

I don't care if I deserve to be slapped for thinking something as cheesy as that.

It's the truth.

A curse because…that one's obvious. No. Sex.

I never thought about sex this much until I was told I couldn't have it. Now I'm fourteen again, and I'm one step away from stiff socks hanging out in my bedroom floor.

Not really.

My phone goes off with a text from her as though she felt me thinking about her.

SALEM: Can you get me some tampons? And some mint chocolate chip ice cream too?

I'm sorry, but when did I miss the part of the conversation that said we'd escalated to tampon-buying? Because I'm pretty sure guys who buy tampons are getting sex.

It has to be in a rule book somewhere.

Cursing, I jog across the street to the biggest superstore in town, and walk straight back to the aisle I've managed to avoid my entire adult life—other than that one awkward time my mother was desperate.

It wasn't awkward to buy the tampons. It was just awkward to buy them *for my mother*.

It's a massive fucking wall on the back of the store. How many varieties can they possibly need?

As soon as I step up, I spot Kode, Dale, and Rye, which is really weird.

"Didn't realize we had super-secret Wednesday meetings here," I say to the trio who gawk at me like I've somehow committed a sin.

Rye snags a box of tampons and stalks off, acting as though he doesn't know me. "Bye, Rye Clanton! Hope Brin likes those tampons!" I call out loudly, snickering as he ducks and weaves when people start looking after him. Meanwhile, I sing the *"Plug it in, plug it in,"* song from the old *Glade* commercials.

Dale grabs a box, rolling his eyes and grinning at me. "Bye, Dale Sterling," I call out loudly. "Tell Harley to go easy on the Midol this time. Last time she put the nipple clamp in the wrong place!"

Pretty sure those eyes of his are condemning me to hell right now.

That'll teach them to walk off without speaking to me.

I turn to Kode, since he's the last man standing, and I gesture at the massive wall.

"Which ones—"

He grabs my arm, jerking me behind him as he guides me away from the wall of shame.

"This is not a place where we talk, understand?" he asks, pointing to the wall like it's even more shameful than I imagined.

A grin curves my lips. "Sorry. Didn't know there were rules for this secret brotherhood."

"The only rule is that we don't speak. Don't ask what kind of tampons. If she didn't tell you what kind, then you're stuck guessing. Like the rest of us have had to do more times than I care to count, because they think tampons are a general, common-knowledge thing. They're not. There's like a fucking million choices, and you'll go crazy. Then she'll send you back if they're the wrong ones, and you'll have a full description of what you're going to buy the next time around," he explains calmly. Sort of.

I'm fascinated, simply because it's Kode. And he's not happy about buying tampons. I've never seen him so riled.

Why did no one tell me this sooner? I could have been giving him hell for months.

"So don't talk, and just guess at what she needs. Excellent rules," I say, grinning. "Do you boys plan shopping trips together? Pencil me in for next month. Same time?"

He gives me that signature glare he's spent years perfecting. "We don't plan the trips together. We try to avoid each other if we can. Hence the no-talking rule."

I can seriously do this all day.

"I find it highly coincidental all three of you were there at the same time."

He rolls his eyes. "The longer the girls are around each other, the more likely they are to need them at the same time. That's how it works. Trust me; you'll learn things you never wanted to know. And it's like they can't be bothered to buy them *before* it happens, even though they know it happens at the same damn time every month. Nope. It's not until shit hits the fan that they send you to the store. Get used to it. And welcome to the motherfucking club."

He claps my shoulder a little harder than necessary, stalks to the wall, grabs a box of tampons, and stalks back off.

"*Plug it in, plug it in!*" I sing louder this time, and he flips me off over his shoulder.

I should have come to the wall of shame sooner. It's fucking comical gold.

Since I don't really give a damn who sees me buying tampons, I take my time trying to figure out which ones to get. Strangely enough, I see more men come and go at the wall of shame than women, and it's like a run and snatch sort of thing.

Sometimes they even have something to wrap it in, or they just bury it in the bottom of their basket like it's contagious or something. Pretty sure you can't catch a period.

Finally, I give up and grab a basket, and end up grabbing seven different kinds. By the way, tampons are expensive. Totally don't get how a woman gets screwed into bleeding to death for most of a week, and then has to pay outrageous amounts just to keep from ruining her clothes.

Total extortion, if you ask me.

I'm slightly traumatized by seeing "odor control" on some of those boxes because…what the actual hell?

Back on topic: These men could cut out so many trips if they bought more than a box at a time, but I guess it'd be harder to hide those blasphemous things if they bought more than one at a time.

I go and grab the mint chocolate chip ice cream. Just for good measure, and because I know how cranky these beasts make women, I also grab some Midol. Maybe I won't get slapped for that.

I'll tell her it's for the cramps so it looks like I'm an absolute piece of fucking perfection.

When I get to the register and dump out my basket, the guy blushes five shades of red and has those things rung up and bagged in record time. Fastest. Checkout. Ever.

I wasn't planning on going to her house yet, since I need to grab some more things from town. But if she's texting that she needs them, then she probably *needs* them.

And I'm going to look fucking awesome for being so thorough.

As soon as I reach her house, I grab the two bags of tampons and ice cream — *and Midol* — and knock.

Salem swings open the door, acting surprised to see me. Her hair is wet, and she doesn't have on any makeup. And again with the no-bra. Why did I think no sex was cool? I'm dying a little.

"I thought you said you wouldn't be here until later?" she says as she steps back, letting me in.

"Figured I'd go ahead and drop these off," I tell her, handing her the two bags of tampons, and the bag of ice cream — *and Midol*.

Her eyebrows go up as she peers inside the bags. "Um...thanks? I think."

See? Nailed it. Maybe I would be good boyfriend material after all.

"And the ice cream," I remind her, pointing at it. Not bringing up the Midol. It'll be a surprise for later.

"Thanks, but I don't really like anything with mint in it," she says, smiling at me. "It was a sweet thought, though."

My brow furrows for only a brief second, until Sean sweeps in and grabs the ice cream from her hand. He looks up and winks at me. "Thanks. Been craving this all day," he tells me.

As he turns and walks off, I glare at his back, wondering how many times a kid is going to best me before I realize I'm an idiot.

Salem catches on, and she doubles over, laughing so hard she struggles to breathe. Yep. I'm a sucker.

That'll be my next tattoo.

"Glad this is so hilarious," I drawl, grabbing her at the waist, and tugging her to me.

She's still partially laughing when her hands open on my chest and she stares up at me, amusement dancing in her eyes.

"Didn't realize we'd graduated so soon to the tampon-buying stage," she says, grinning.

"Har. You really shouldn't let him borrow your phone," I say, glaring at her.

"I didn't. But he's got his ways around that." She flashes me a grin. "First time a guy has ever gotten me an assortment of tampons. Kudos for outside-the-box thinking."

Deciding not to continue holding her this closely, I release her and stroll toward the door. "I'll be back. Keep your phone away from that menace so I don't have any more unplanned detours."

I never turn around, but I feel her watching me. Yeah. She'll cave.

She likes sex too.

Chapter 23

Salem

Cheesy as it is, I can't help myself from buying the DVD when I see it. Then I buy a couple more, even though it doesn't really make sense. I'm not even sure if Maverick has a DVD player, considering he has about five video streaming services.

He takes Netflix and chill to the next level.

Just because I can't help myself in this old store, I also move to the CDs and buy a couple of those. With the extra money I made last week just from overtime, I can splurge a little.

It's not like Sean needs anything.

Not that Maverick needs anything either.

But tonight my job is to distract him from his mother's date, even though he's pretending it's no big deal. I know better.

I move on to some other things, putting them in the basket as well. It's like a treasure trove in here.

As I get finished and checked out, I think back to him walking in the other day with that ludicrous amount of tampons, certain I'd needed them right then. It was probably the sweetest—and weirdest—thing a guy has ever done for me.

Sean is with Mom tonight, so this will be the first time I've had a night alone with Maverick since almost a week ago when we had sex.

I said no sex the very next day, but he took that to mean no physical stuff at all.

I mean, I never said anything about not kissing.

So I'm a little irritated with my own rule, because Maverick is being so respectful of it that he's being *too* respectful of it.

I leave and drive to his house, parking beside his car. He swings open the door before I can knock, grinning at me as he leans against the doorframe.

"Dane invited us to his house next Friday after you get off work for a cookout."

"Hello to you, too," I say, holding the bags in my hands.

He grabs the bags, grinning as he leans down. I almost think he's going to kiss me, but he just inhales against my neck instead. I think he loves torturing me.

"Damn, you smell good," he says, his lips just barely brushing my cheek as he pulls back and winks at me. "And hi."

I grin. Because I do that a lot. I'm a goofy, stupid grinner. "Next Friday after work will be fine. But Sean is going to be with me."

"They want to meet the kid, so no worries. What's in here?" he muses as he leads the way in.

"Not tampons," I deadpan.

He stops and looks over his shoulder at me, giving me an incredulous look as I shrug.

"Couldn't resist."

He goes back to prowling through the bag. "You shouldn't have," he says dryly when he pulls out a One Direction CD and a Backstreet Boys CD, holding them up side by side.

I just grin. He smiles too, though he tries not to. He goes back into the bag and pulls out the first DVD. "Top Gun? I guess you know I was named after that movie, right?" he asks.

"You told me that night we talked forever, and I figured you already had a thousand, but—"

"I actually don't have a single copy," he tells me, smiling in earnest now. "I keep meaning to get one, but never think about it when I'm out. So thanks."

Well, now I just stand here awkwardly, since I suck at accepting gratitude worse than I do with compliments.

He goes back to rummaging in the bags, and he pulls out some Top Gun memorabilia, smiling fondly at the little trinkets that aren't anything special.

Then he laughs when he pulls out *Princess Bride* and *Titanic*.

Operation Distraction is working out well so far.

I just have to keep him distracted until his mother calls him at the end of the date like she promised to do to let him know she's safe and sound.

It's the least I can do.

"For you, I will watch those movies," I tell him, grinning as he stands, putting the bags down.

He comes over to me, and he bends. I start to turn into the kiss, when he merely kisses me on the cheek. "Thanks. That was way better than an assortment of tampons."

I start laughing as he grins and steps back, tugging my hand in his. "So Netflix and chill on the couch, and Princess Bride is back on the docket. Should be an epic night. But seriously, we can go out if you want to. A new restaurant just opened in town."

I shake my head. "I'd rather stay in."

He cups my chin, thumbing my lower lip. "I know what you're doing."

"I have no idea what you're talking about," I say with faux innocence and doe eyes as he grins.

"Thanks for doing it," he says, smiling that smile that warms me to my core.

"She'll be okay, Maverick. Your mother is sassy and confident now. She's not the same woman she was back then, and she's letting go of the past."

He studies my eyes like he's searching for the sincerity, and he nods when he finds it.

"Thanks for that too."

Releasing the side of my face, he drops to the couch, and I join him, but then he stands abruptly and grabs all the stuff I got him, carrying it toward his bedroom. When he takes a while, I get up and pad down the hall after him.

His devil cat is now at my house, hanging with Sean when he's there. And she's really not a devil at all. At least not to anyone but Maverick. He swears she was also terrible to Bella.

Just as I reach the bedroom, I see him gently placing the little Maverick figurine beside the DVD that he has on a stand he apparently freed up. All the things I just bought him get neatly tucked away in the open cubby, all on display.

"You don't have to do that just because I got it, Maverick. It was just some fun gifts I bought while perusing the store."

He finishes putting everything where he wants it and steps back. "I like it," he says simply, shrugging.

When he takes my hand, I tug him back, and he turns to face me, eyebrows arched in curiosity.

"I said no sex, but you've been careful to barely touch me at all. You haven't even kissed me since—"

In one step, he's crowding my space, hand thrusting into my hair, and he tugs my head back as his lips come down on mine, hard and demanding. I moan into his mouth as he kisses me, his free hand sliding down my back to pull me impossibly closer.

It seems like hours pass, though I'm sure that's not right, before I finally break the kiss and lean back, admittedly a little drunk on the way he can make me feel. He gives me a lazy grin before brushing his lips over mine again.

"We're doing this at your speed. I already fucked it up once. I don't want to fuck it up again. So if you're ready to be kissed, I'll kiss you. Whenever you're ready for something, just tell me, and I'll give you whatever you want," he says, his words whispering over my lips.

Drunk again.

"Okay," I finally manage to say, trying to blink out of my haze.

His smug grin stays fixed in place, and he tugs me to him. "Now let's go watch a movie we both know you're going to hate."

As we're walking back toward the living room, a private grin forms on my lips.

I just had a moment. It was a small one. But it was real.

And Maverick doesn't even know he just gave me something so fucking beautiful.

As we walk back to the living room, I veer off toward the kitchen, and he follows me.

"What are you doing?" he asks me as I start opening his cabinets.

"Making pie," I say, finding the ingredients I stashed here. He has so many damn food functions all the time that it's necessary for me to buy supplies in bulk in preparation, since we're apparently doing this thing. Whatever this thing is.

"Why?" he drawls.

"Because you're a terrible faker, and you're still worried about your mother. So I'm making pie."

He grins as he watches me slowly assemble my pile of items.

"Pie is brought to keep from being a rude guest. Pie is used to define your angriest of moments. And pie is now comfort food. I'm starting to see a pattern here, Salem Wright. You make life sound simple when pie is the solution to everything."

I grin as I grab the pie crust I already made using graham crackers as the main ingredient. Yes, I pre-make the crusts when I'm bored. We've already established I'm lame.

"Pie is the solution to everything, Maverick Sterling," I say, using both his names since he used mine.

I get out the Cool Whip, and I scoop out a dollop on my finger, putting it out to him. Grinning, he leans over, sucking it off the tip of my finger, making it far more scandalous and seductive than necessary before pulling back.

"See? We haven't even made it to the pie yet. Just the topping is making you smile," I point out, causing him to laugh softly as he watches me work.

"Hey, Salem?"

"Yeah?" I answer distractedly.

"If you want me to keep my abs, you might need to figure out a way to make broccoli the answer to all life's problems."

When I start laughing and look over at him, he's already smiling. He smears a line of Cool Whip over my lips, and my laughter dies off as his lips come down on mine to clean it off, while he tugs me to him to gain closer access.

My arms go around him, grinning when he nips at my lips.

Just like that, I have another moment.

I waited so long for just one. I never thought it possible to have two in one night.

Chapter 24

MAVERICK

"Your mom won't mind us using this place?" Sean asks me as we walk into the large ballroom.

I snort out a laugh. "No. She's not going to care. Where's your music?"

He stalls, looking at me like he'd rather slit my throat than tell me the music he's supposed to be rehearsing to.

"Your showcase is in three weeks, and you've griped nonstop about not having enough dance time to work on your routine. You haven't been dancing to the music at all."

"I just need to work on the steps. The music—"

"Is a really important part," I finish the sentence for him. Albeit, it's not the way he wants it to be finished. "Why are you being such a pain in the ass? Just tell me the music you have to use, and I'll download it. Then you can rehearse."

"I'm not telling you my music just so you can help me and get ungrounded with Salem."

My eyebrows go up.

"I'm not grounded, first of all. And secondly, why does your music have anything to do with it?" I ask incredulously.

"I'm not stupid. I know you're grounded. You've been sucking up for two weeks. You brought her roses when Connor was still here. You ran after those tampons like a Bloodhound—pun intended. So you do something nice for me—because my sister loves me—and you get ungrounded earlier. I know the routine. Why do you think my room has been so clean? I want my phone back. That's why."

He narrows his eyes at me.

My lips try to tug in a smile, but I stop them. "You really have to stop thinking I'm using you to score favor with your sister. Using you would only be terribly fucking bad for me."

"Then why are you trying to help?"

"For fu—fudge's sake. I'm just trying to be nice."

"People aren't just nice for no reason. What do you want?" he asks, eyes still narrowed in scrutiny.

"At the moment, I wouldn't mind seeing you trip and bust your paranoid face on the shiny floor. But I'm seriously just trying to help you out so you don't mess up in front of everyone at the showcase. It's a big showcase."

He bristles, looking down.

"They had the music picked out before I was in the lineup, and they won't change it because it works with the theme and it's already printed on the program guides. I only got the spot because a girl broke her leg, and they held an emergency audition to see who could fill the slot."

"Doesn't matter how you got the spot. It's still a big deal, and you still earned it," I say, sounding like a badass pep-talker.

He rolls his eyes. "Of course I earned the spot. I've earned more than this one, but it's the first showcase I get to be in. The problem is I'm replacing a girl."

It takes me a second to follow his logic.

"Ahhh. The song is girl song, right?"

He just gives me a bland look. "Your powers of deduction astound me."

Fisting my hands and reminding myself that murder—no matter how good the reason—is not okay, I ask again, "What's the damn song?"

He mutters something.

"Didn't catch that."

"I said *La La*. Ashlee Simpson."

Adulting is hard this day. I promise I don't laugh. Maybe I grin too big, but I don't laugh.

"Pie moment," he grumbles, prompting me to laugh despite my attempts not to.

I download the song, sync to the Bluetooth speaker system, and blast the song. I even head-bang a little, which gets me a murderous glare.

"Ah, come on. I get to tease you a little."

He rolls his eyes before moving to the center of the room, preparing himself.

After he makes one pass with the music — and looks sloppy as hell — I decide to critique him. "You're ending late every time, and I'm pretty sure you'd do better if you took out some of the footwork toward the middle, since the beat of the music doesn't let it flow. Or maybe change it out with some of the spins, giving you more time between beats to finish it. And bring your knees closer to your chest on your flip. You'll get around quicker and it'll look cleaner."

He looks at me like I'm an alien invader.

"I took dance too, kid. Hence the reason I'm helping," I tell him with a smirk.

By the third pass, he already has the adjustments made, smoothing the flow, and he ends on the last beat. Three more passes, and he still looks sloppy, but some improvement has been made today.

"We'll pick back up tomorrow," I tell him as I shut off the music.

He's drenched in sweat and panting heavily, nodding as he grabs his bottle of water. As we walk out, locking up, he mutters, "Thanks."

I decide not to mock him this time.

"She only uses that thing when she hosts big parties. The rest of the time, it stays empty. Feel free to use it whenever, even if I'm not around. I'll give Salem a spare key."

He doesn't say anything as we walk through my mother's house. Fortunately, she's not home, and I stop by the fridge to grab him another bottle of water, that he eagerly accepts.

As we walk toward the door, he stops suddenly, and I turn to look, grimacing when I realize I forgot one really import thing.

"Think that picture of you could be any bigger, momma's boy?" the little dick asks, turning a mocking grin my way.

The massive freaking picture that took me two ladders and half a day to hang is glaring at us. My chubby cheeks and all.

"I don't want to talk about it. Hurry up. You're dripping sweat everywhere, and Salem is waiting on us."

"Where'd you say we're going?" he asks as we jog out and get in my car.

I don't answer until we're pulling out of the driveway and headed toward the garage.

"My friends do a big cookout on occasion. They've been wanting to meet you since you hacked my Twitter," I tell him.

"Cool friends," he says, grinning at me.

I simply roll my eyes, continuing to drive toward Salem.

"Didn't think I'd have time for a shower?" he asks.

"You're a kid. They expect you to smell. All kids stink."

"Sometimes I think you're nice," he says on a breath. "Then I realize you're just a dressed-up dick."

I start laughing as I park in front of the garage, and we get out to go meet her. Salem walks out before we reach the entrance. She looks freshly showered, and her silky hair is bound in a ponytail.

Guess Rye let her use the office shower.

"I'm driving," she tells me as she takes my keys from my hand, grinning as she passes me, a pie in her other hand. You know, because it's apparently rude not to bring food to somewhere there's already food.

It's her quirks that keep me dangling like a damn fish on a hook.

"We're all going to die," Sean grumbles as he moves to the backseat. "Cars are the devil."

I just hope I'm not as pale as I feel.

"I'm an excellent driver, and you're still in one piece," Salem quips as she gets behind the wheel.

I'm uneasy as I sit down on the passenger side of my baby, trying really hard to be okay with this.

Sean leans up between the seat and the window and whispers, "Told you that you were sucking up."

I shove his head back, and he laughs as I buckle up. Salem really is a terrible driver, but she thinks she's the next Vin Diesel.

She spins out, probably chunking precious pieces of paint, and I remind myself that I have tons of money. I can fix anything she breaks.

Woosa, motherfucker. Woo. Sa.

Sean's right. I am sucking up, because no way in hell would I let her drive my baby otherwise.

She giggles when she cuts a curve too sharp and we fishtail. I'm pretty sure my ass is never going to unclench.

"This is why Tyler bought her a truck. Trucks can't turn like this," Sean grumbles from the backseat.

"He gave me his old truck," Salem says dismissively. "And I'm going the speed limit."

I turn to see Sean shaking his head, letting me know it was apparently a plot to keep her out from behind the wheel of a car. I don't care how badly I want ungrounded; I'm never letting her drive my car again.

The abrupt squeal of brakes doesn't register until I'm snapped around, and the seatbelt is catching me. "Fucking shit, woman!" I snap before I can stop myself.

"Sorry! The brakes are way better than I expected!"

I look around, searching for the kid chasing a ball into the street, or the dog crossing the street, or the Chupacabra sighting, or what-the-fuck-ever has made her come to a teeth-clattering halt on the middle of the busiest road in Sterling Shore, as cars blow their horns behind us. There's *nothing*.

"Why are we stopped?"

"Funeral procession," she and Sean both say at the same time.

A few limos pass us, following a hearse or something. "So?" I ask.

More horns blare behind us, and a few choice expletives are thrown our way from the same direction.

"You have to stop when there's a funeral procession," Sean explains—or thinks he does.

"No, the hell you don't. This is rush hour. Someone is going to break my windows in if you don't get out of the damn road!"

"There's nowhere to pull over. I have to stop here. It's disrespectful to keep driving!" Salem yells back.

"How is it disrespectful? The guy or girl is dead!"

They *both* glare at me like I'm the idiot. Of course. Sure. Why not?

Let's just sit here and die or something. Maybe someone will pull over for our funeral procession as a show of respect, and the cycle will continue.

My eyes flick to the side mirror, seeing a very large guy—at least twice my damn size—stalking down the line of cars on his way to us. I reach over and lock the doors, even though they're already locked.

"Any day now, Salem," I say impatiently. I really don't want to fight that big motherfucker just because some dead guy is being driven down the other side of the road.

"We can't drive until they're all through. Their lights are on," she argues.

"Most all cars have lights on even during the day. It's not the fucking nineties anymore," I say, growing increasingly worried as I track the rapid progress of Big Foot, who only seems angrier by the second. I think he's getting bigger too, so Hulk might be a more accurate nickname.

"I think that's all of them," Sean says, and Salem floors the gas just as Hulk reaches out like he's going to pound my window with his fist. The abrupt acceleration has my head snapping back.

"Pull over at the ice cream store," I tell her, fighting the nausea.

"Can I get mint chocolate chip?" Sean asks from the backseat.

"Hell no," I grumble.

Salem does pull over as soon as we reach it, spinning up more gravel. How? I don't know. We're on fucking concrete!

"Get out," I tell her, causing her brow to wrinkle in confusion.

Still, she does as I say, and I circle around, tugging her away from the driver's seat. "I might want ungrounded, but not this badly," I tell her, only making that wrinkle more pronounced as her confusion grows. "I'm driving."

I sit down, my knees at my chest, and wait forever for my seat to scoot all the way back again so my legs have room. Sean chuckles, smothering it as Salem drops to the passenger seat, pouting.

"Everyone is supposed to stop for a funeral procession," she grumbles. "It's drilled into you at an early age and you physically can't help but stop."

I roll my eyes as I gingerly drive us toward Dane's house, whispering words of apology to my poor, abused baby—I'm referring to my car.

Salem is shooting me with daggers from her eyes by the time we reach the party, and I reach over and grab her damn pie to carry in. Weirdly, her pies have become everyone's favorite thing, and they're eventually going to demand she bring more than one.

Sean is still a semi-sweaty mess—*my car had better not stink because of him*—when we reach the front door. I don't bother knocking as I head on in, and Salem chastises me for not knocking.

"I don't knock unless they're not expecting me," I tell her without turning around. "And sometimes not even then."

I grin when she rolls her eyes, and we head through Dane's house, heading toward the back.

"Are all the Sterlings rich?" Sean asks quietly, his eyes taking in the lavish surroundings.

"Monopoly," I remind him, and he nods like that's a perfectly understandable explanation.

Just as I push through the backdoor, leading the way to the outdoor garden party, Salem stumbles to a halt, grabbing my shirt at the back and clinging to me.

"I'm underdressed," she hisses, her eyes taking in the absurd amount of people and all the decorations. "And I didn't bring enough pie."

I smile to myself.

"You have a dress upstairs," I tell her, turning to grin down at her as she glares up at me.

"You could have just told me it was—"

"Half those kids are from my school!" Sean growls, turning his own scathing glare at me. "And I stink!"

To this, I fucking grin. "Payback's a bitch, kid. By the way, this is your party. Sterlings tend to rally around one of their own and make it known to the rest who belongs to them."

Kid can't stop getting picked on for five damn seconds. But that's about to change. Not that I want him knowing I give a damn. It's just a small damn that I give. No big deal.

His eyes widen in horror. "But I stink!"

"As I said, payback's a bitch. Go make friends. You'll find it a lot easier here."

If looks could kill…

"You planned this party so Sean could make friends?" Salem asks, peering up at me with eyes full of warmth and appreciation.

Rain walks up, smiling over at Salem, and I gesture to her. "Rain planned it," I say, causing Rain to look over at me in confusion.

Their backyard is bigger than my backyard. It could hold more people. Besides, Rain is good at planning parties for kids.

Me? Not so much.

Rain turns back to Salem, her smile returning, thankfully not selling me out. "Your dress is upstairs if you want to change. No worries if you don't," she tells Salem.

"I think I need to change," Salem grumbles, gesturing down to her shorts and T-shirt.

"We'll be back," Rain says, tugging Salem with her.

Salem looks over her shoulder at me, and I wink at her before turning and finding four other Sterlings just staring at me with smirks.

"I must look damn good for all of you to be checking me out so thoroughly," I quip, walking down the steps with Sean on my heels.

"Rain planned this party?" Dane asks, not acknowledging my comment.

"Technically she did," I say with a shrug.

I notice Sean studying me as I speak to them. Kid is supposed to be mingling, not sticking to my side.

"After you asked her to," Kode remarks, giving me a dry look. "And you're the one who sent out all the invites."

"Salem doesn't need to know that," I say with a shrug.

I really don't want to use the fucking kid to gain favor with her; I wasn't just saying that to him.

"Any change of clothes for me?" Sean finally asks.

I give him a pointed stare. "Hell no. You're officially the stinky kid. Now go mingle and make friends."

He narrows his eyes on me. "I can't stink. Jenna Clank is here, and she's the—"

He stops talking like he doesn't want to tell me he has a crush on a girl, and a taunting grin forms on my lips.

"Trouble talking to girls, shrimp? Need advice on how to improve your game?"

He rolls his eyes. "Says the guy who's grounded because his game is so weak he's scrambling to buy roses and tampons to recover."

Smartass.

"Joke's on you, because the wall of shame doesn't give me the willies."

"The willies?" Sean asks around a snort. "The fifties sent a telegram saying you were too much of a douche to be stealing their lingo."

"Hell called and wanted its spawn back," I gripe, gesturing toward him.

"Doubtful. They were too afraid I'd take over so they kicked me out," the evil kid says with a wicked grin.

"It's like listening to a miniature version of you," Kode says suddenly, causing Sean and I to both glare at him.

"Never say that again," Sean and I say in eerily timed unison.

Our heads dart toward each other, and our eyes narrow.

"Just a little bit creepy," Kode drawls, amused.

"I don't like your friends," Sean suddenly says.

"For once, I might agree with you," I grumble, flipping the guys off when they all chuckle. "You have clothes downstairs. Should be a shower in there too. Just find Rain and she'll point you in the right direction," I tell the kid.

He turns and darts inside, and I swivel my head back to find my cousins still staring.

"Am I your fucking entertainment for the evening?" I ask flatly as I put the pie down on the dessert table.

A small smile graces my lips when I see the tin pan next to all the crystal dishes. What's in that tin pan will taste better than all the others, but you wouldn't know it from the outer-coating.

"He's smiling at a pie," Corbin stage-whispers.

"It's way worse than we thought," Kode adds.

Rolling my eyes, I turn to face them. "What are you assholes on about?" I ask, reluctantly taking the bait.

"You got it, you got it bad," Corbin starts singing, and then laughs when I shake my head.

"That all you got? I can remember being so much better at this than any of you. I mean, my mocking was on point. This is just a poor man's parody by comparison."

"Not even going to deny it a little?" Dane muses.

"Why bother? You just caught me smiling at a fucking pie," I point out, causing them to start laughing again.

"I seriously never thought I'd see the day when Maverick Sterling admitted he had a girlfriend without protest," Kode says, sounding genuinely surprised, and I hold my hand up.

"I said nothing about having a girlfriend," I point out.

"Annnnd there's the denial," Dale says, and they all nod like the world makes sense again, while I just stare at them blandly.

"I really don't," I go on.

"You really do," Corbin argues, an asshole grin on his face.

"She and I are just feeling things out. Dating, so to speak. We're—"

"For the past two weeks, how many days have you gone without seeing her?" Dane asks, cutting me off.

Bristling, I answer, "Well, I see her every day, but—"

"Is it expected that you'll see each other every day, or do you make formal plans to do so?" Corbin interrupts.

I have to think for a second before I realize the answer. "It's just expected because—"

"Are you hitting on other girls or fucking anyone else?" Corbin asks.

"Hell no!" I snap, surprising even myself with the vehemence in my tone. "But—"

"Are you sleeping over every night?" Kode butts in, eyebrow arched in question.

Gritting my teeth in annoyance from the multiple interruptions, I answer, "Yes, but that doesn't mean—"

"You have a girlfriend," they all say as one.

I look behind me, worried I'm going to find Salem and hear her heckle me for this nonsense. Fortunately, that dress must be complicated, because she still isn't back.

I do spot Sean leaned against a wall and talking to a girl twice his height. His hair is still drenched—like he jumped in the shower and hopped out, only drying his body enough to wear the clothes.

The girl is giggling and blushing. Little shrimp does have game after all.

Returning my attention to the cousins I'm considering disowning, I shake my head in frustration.

"Boyfriends get sex, and in case you've forgotten, I'm still on probation." *Boom! Drops mic.*

They can't possibly argue with that logic.

The look they give me is incredulous. "Boyfriends get punished by girlfriends withholding sex," Kode finally says. "Trust me. Worst weeks of my life were after that party where Tria shoved me into the pool."

Fucking eh.

I think I have a girlfriend.

When exactly did this happen? And how did I not see it happening?

They look behind me, signaling someone is there, and I turn just as Salem steps outside looking…fucking incredible.

The purple dress brings out the streaks in her hair, making her look almost edible. Okay, completely edible.

It's a fitted bodice up top, with a pixie like skirt at the bottom to go along with the casual dressy theme here. My eyes go down her legs, raking over every inch of exposed flesh.

Down, boy. You already got me in trouble once.

Okay, so maybe it was more mouth than dick that got me in trouble.

Her eyes scan over the party, unaware of my appraisal just yet. When she grins, I know she's spotted Sean without even following her gaze. Just like I know she's probably going to give him hell later. Just like I know she's going to secretly worry he's growing up too fast.

I've spent over two weeks not having sex with a girl I can't stop thinking about, and a girl who sees Top Gun and immediately brings me the things that made her think about me. The girl who smiles just because I look her way.

The girl who made me pie and kept me from going insane while my mother went on a date with a guy I know nothing about, other than the online stalking I did to research him, of course.

Salem kept me sane. And the next night, she kept me sane again, since my mother liked dating so much that she planned two nights of it in a row.

And Salem is the only thing keeping me from losing my mind that my mother has four dates set up for next week with four different men.

My mother and father have switched places.

My life is upside down.

Fortunately, I have Salem. Otherwise, I'd be sitting at my mother's house and making men disappear before she could go be an adult with them.

I haven't felt alone at all. Not once. No empty feeling in the pit of my stomach. Even when I'm not with her, I still don't feel alone.

And until they brought it up, I hadn't really thought about the fact it's just expected I'll see her as soon as she's off work. It's expected that we're sleeping in the same bed.

There're no talks or communication about it. It just…is.

This might be a little worse than I realized.

"Think he just figured out how far gone he already is," I hear Kode saying as I blink out of my trance.

Before I can say something smartass in return, Salem's eyes finally find mine, and her smile spreads just like I knew it would. Like she's always happy to see me.

Returning her smile, I let my eyes rake over her slowly, this time just to let her know I'm taking in the sights. When my gaze meets hers again, she has an eyebrow cocked in feigned indignation.

I close the distance between us as she gives up the pretense of being annoyed, and she doesn't protest when my lips find hers.

By the way, thank fuck for that little green light, even though it leaves me wanting more all the time.

She's soft against me, her body pressed against mine without concern for the fact we're surrounded by people. Her hands slide up my sides, holding there as though she has to anchor herself.

That's what promises me she's feeling this as badly as I am.

Reluctantly, my lips move from hers, and I lean back, smirking down at her. "I think I want to see you in a dress more."

"Easy access?" she quips.

"You look fucking amazing," I say seriously.

Her eyes warm like I've just said something right—for once. This was the right moment for *amazing* and not *hot*. Duly noted.

Why does it feel like I'm being trained? Give the pup a treat when he doesn't piss on the floor or something.

"Well, that explains a lot," comes a voice that has Salem and I both stilling.

She turns to absolute stone, and I look up to see my dad standing a few feet away, his eyes on us as he smiles. Fucking hell. I'm going to kill him. He said they wouldn't be able to make it because of a party they were hosting.

It's the entire reason I planned this for tonight!

"Thought I'd seen your cars at the beach house a lot, but I didn't want to read into it," Dad goes on, as Salem stares across from us.

I turn to find her mother sipping a glass of champagne as her knowing eyes and enigmatic smirk take over her face.

I really better not have just fucked this up.

Chapter 25

Salem

Mom just looks at me, not acting too surprised to see me pressed against Maverick, his arms still around my waist as we both freeze like two teenagers caught in the liquor cabinet.

"Yeah," Maverick says finally, clearing his throat. "Not a problem with that, is there?"

His voice sounds as easygoing and unaffected as ever, as his hand gingerly slides down my back.

"Of course not. You're two adults who are capable of making your own decisions," his father says genuinely, giving me a breath of relief.

Mom won't rile him. It'd be worse for me to upset Maverick at this point than date him, since his father is perfectly fine with it. Guess Maverick was right to not be overly concerned with Ian's reaction.

"I thought you had a party to host tonight," Maverick tells Ian.

"We have one going on right now. We can be a little late. You said this was for Sean. I know why we do these sorts of parties, but I didn't realize he was having issues at school, since that kid stays with Salem more than he stays at home."

It's a little endearing how he immediately felt like Sean took priority over his own party.

"I'll be right back," I say to Maverick.

He smiles, though I can tell it's a little tight. He's worried for me.

I pat his chest, trying to tell him it'll be okay, but I don't think he gets the memo. Even as he speaks to his father, I can feel his eyes following me, protectively watching as I reach my mother.

"Given the genuine shock on your face, I suppose I should be insulted that you thought I wouldn't notice you've been slinking around with your stepbrother."

I admit I have been slinking, hence the reason I've avoided public dates with Maverick, though he hasn't seemed to mind.

"Didn't realize you were paying such close attention to me. I guess there's a first time for everything," I say, using the same backhandedness she taught me herself.

She sips her champagne, smiling at someone who passes by, playing her part.

"Honestly, Salem, I couldn't care less. Maverick is a big catch for you, considering you usually prefer to slum with men beneath your means. I'm just proud you finally found someone worth expending your time."

Backhanded compliments galore.

It's always like a game of chess—a conversation with my mother happens to be far more intricate and tricky.

"So this isn't going to be a problem?" I ask, just to make sure she's not playing me.

"Heavens no. Ian doesn't seem to be the least bit bothered, and from what I can tell, the Sterlings make the rules here. Be glad of that."

Well, then. That was easier than—

"As long as you're not gullible enough to actually fall for him, I won't cause issue."

So close. So. Damn. Close.

"No worries, Mother. I can assure you Maverick and I are just passing the time," I say with a cold smile, snagging my own glass of champagne off a passing tray.

"I'm not a fool, Salem," she says on an exasperated sigh. "You wouldn't have risked upsetting your arrangement for Sean over a man you were simply passing the time with."

Touché.

I roll my eyes, trying to play it off.

"The Sterling men are certainly a potent brand of charming," she prattles on. "I can understand how easy it would be to forget reality when the fantasy they supply seems so real. But it's not. You have to remind yourself of that at the end of the day. Otherwise, I'll—"

"Try to sleep with Maverick?" I chirp, almost finding it laughable. "Be my guest. I'd like to see that show. He's not an eighteen-year-old, horny boy with zero standards. And in case you've forgotten, you married his father. Believe it or not, family means something to them."

For the briefest of moments, she has the gall to look hurt. But it's gone before I can be certain.

"I can see you're clearly in no condition to be speaking, and this is certainly not the place."

"I'm fit for conversation. I haven't even had a sip of my champagne yet. But Sean's party is most definitely not the place for you to tell me how fake the Sterlings are, when they're throwing this party for him."

I gesture toward Sean as he runs and plays like an actual kid. He never does that. He's a miniature adult with the weight of the world on his shoulders, but today, he's just a kid.

Now I'm about to cry. Can't do that in front of Cruella. She'd beat me over the head with her Dalmatian coat for such weakness.

"Sean actually has friends now," I go on, then find it impossible to speak around the lump of emotion wadding up in my throat.

"Terribly inconvenient timing, this party," my mother says, blinking as she looks away from Sean, her eyes focusing on something else. "If I didn't know any better, I'd say Maverick purposely set this party up on the same day he knew we had a prior engagement."

I *knew* Maverick did this. He just refused to take credit.

Which makes me want him even more.

Maverick Sterling likes his stepbrother, and Sean is also getting attached. As terrified as that leaves me, because I know inevitably we'll have to give all this up, it still warms me. Sean needs this, even though it's going to hurt like hell to have it all taken away.

Fortunately, I don't have to respond, since Maverick and Ian join us. Ian draws her to him, kissing her on the head, and her smile is so convincing that I almost believe she's swooning.

Maverick stands by me timidly, hands in his pockets like he's trying not to touch me.

"Beautiful party," Mom says like the champion schmoozer she is.

"Rain did an incredible job," Maverick says before swiping my champagne and drinking it in a few swift gulps.

I stifle a grin as Mom stares at him like he's a heathen, and he deposits the empty glass on a passing tray, before grabbing two more full ones.

He hands me one of the full ones, and I take it and sip it.

"Maverick just told me that he met Connor," Ian says, looking over at me.

"Connor was here?" Mom asks, clearing her throat as her head darts my way.

"Yeah. He was just in for a day to see how Sean was settling in," I say with a shrug, trying not to make this awkward in front of Ian.

Mom's lips thin, and she looks down, blinking again for some reason.

"Well, if he gets a chance to come back, we'd love to have him over for dinner. We could get everyone together. I'd really like to meet him," Ian says so genuinely.

Mom doesn't say anything. She just stares off in the distance like this conversation isn't her favorite. Then again, Connor hasn't come to see her in a really long time.

"I'll tell him, Ian. But he stays pretty busy right now with college and hockey," I say diplomatically.

Maverick looks at my mother, frowning as she clears her throat again, never speaking on the subject. He looks at me, and I give a one-shoulder shrug, not wanting to get into their very strained relationship here.

Obviously.

Sometimes I think all the excessive blinking she does is her way of fighting off tears. Then I remember I've only ever seen her cry once, and that was over a lost necklace.

"There's Rygan. I need to speak with him. Excuse me," Ian says before stepping away and joining a man who looks very similar to Rye.

Has to be his dad, especially with that name.

"What time is it?" Mom asks, looking around as though she's going to find a clock.

"Just a little after six," Maverick answers without looking at her.

"I meant to call the caterers before we left. Ian has my phone." She eyes me, realizing I have no purse and no pockets. My stuff is still upstairs.

Her eyes move to Maverick, who's just sipping his champagne and staring around like he'd rather be anywhere else, but too sweet to leave me on my own.

I should probably make a note to thank him for that.

"Maverick, would you be kind enough to lend me your phone so I can call the caterers?"

Maverick's head swivels, and he looks at her like she just asked for his left kidney. "Hell no," he scoffs, narrowing his eyes, then turns and walks away to join Corbin, while my body shakes with silent laughter.

Apparently he thinks Mom is going to hack his Twitter too.

Mom just stares, as though she's stunned he was just so…Maverick. Obviously she has no clue why he was so adamant in his refusal.

"If he won't even let you borrow his phone, then at least we both know he'll never lend you his dick either," I chirp, then strut away when she releases an indignant gasp and hisses my name.

The look on her face, though…fucking priceless.

Chapter 26

MAVERICK

Salem is tucked against my side as we head into the Sterling Charity event, looking as though she meant to drive me out of my head tonight.

Her purple streaks have been replaced with a few red streaks instead, highlighting the red dress she's wearing like it was planned all along. And the dress? Stuck to her body, showing off every single curve, and a big fucking slit up the leg that stops on her upper thigh, just shy of being indecent.

I'd like to show her fucking indecent.

Tugging at the bowtie that's suddenly choking me, I look around at the party dwellers in search of my cousins.

"You hot or something?" Salem asks, concerned. I should probably not already be pocketing my bowtie and undoing the top two buttons on my shirt.

"Just a little," I say tightly, refusing to let my eyes drop to the top of the dress where there's a plunging neckline that hangs a little too loosely, teasing you with a lot of skin.

Her hair is in large curls and draped across one shoulder, and her lips have something glossy that will be making my lips glossy the second I kiss her. It's like she's trying to be as untouchable as possible, while looking like she's begging to be touched.

And it's now been a month. With no sex.

This fresh hell is not so pleasant.

Two weeks ago, we sort of went public, considering her mother busted us, but thankfully isn't causing any problems. I kept waiting for the other shoe to drop, and it took me a full week to realize it wasn't going to.

The no-sex rule has become a nonissue, for the most part. Surprisingly enough. But when she dresses like sex in heels, it's hard to not think about sex.

I clutch her hand, guiding her through the throngs of people until I finally spot Kode and Rye. "How did you get lassoed into coming?" I ask Rye.

"Dad is co-hosting this year with your dad, and Brin insisted we come to support him," he grumbles.

Salem flashes a smile, obviously pleased with seeing Rye miserable. It's no secret she's team Brin.

"Thought you were going to propose this weekend," I say to Kode, who chokes on his champagne.

"What?" he asks through a cough.

"You said you were finally putting your plan into action this weekend. Thought that meant you were proposing."

He rolls his eyes. "No. And no. I have a plan, but not for this weekend. This weekend's plan was just to feel her out on Dale recently getting engaged."

"And?"

He shrugs a shoulder, bristling. "She said she hoped it worked out for them. Nothing more. I don't get it; Ethan said he talked to her and explained her Dad's shit. But she's still not pro-marriage."

Salem looks around as though she's really uncomfortable. Right. She had no idea Kode's been trying to propose for months to a woman who doesn't approve of marriage. Sucks to be him.

But I do find it amusing to see him struggle. It's Kode; it's okay to be an ass to an ass.

The subject changes quickly when Tria returns from the restroom, and we all stand around talking for a while, and then peruse the silent auction items up for bid. Salem looks over a Samurai sword for a long time, which means she's thinking of Sean. He might have mentioned they needed one over the fireplace like they used to have in one of their old apartments before it broke.

As she walks off, I go to make a bid on the damn sword, not questioning my motives. Hell, Sean sexually harassed a teacher and got his privileges back before me.

Just as I look up from my silent auction box, I spot Kade Colton and his fiancée—Raya Capperton—moving toward me. Kade grins, and I know what he's going to say before he says it.

"There's this rumor about you having a girlfriend, but I figured someone was exaggerating and you just got a new pet or something instead."

Raya covers her smile, and I roll my eyes.

"You're late to the party. I'm already past the point of being mocked."

"Yes," Dane says, sighing as he joins me and claps my shoulder. "He's already risen above the heckling. Now we're just waiting for him to royally fuck up again. He's done so well for a month."

"Ah, then he's due," Kade agrees dutifully, giving me condescending eyes. "But major props for making it a solid month."

"When you wake up in the middle of the desert, covered in tar and mysterious bite wounds the night before your wedding, with no memory of how you got there, I want you to remember this exact moment," I say dryly.

He laughs under his breath, glancing around. "So where is she?" he asks.

My eyes lift, finding that red dress in two seconds, then…I start taking in the face of the man I'm going to kill.

"Oh, she's in the red dress," Dane says. "Looks like she's talking to Steve Golland."

Steve Golland is about to be etched into a gravestone if he keeps touching her arm like that and leaning in like he can't hear her unless he's pressed against her side. She can speak the hell up or he can go buy a fucking hearing aid.

His hand slides down to her elbow, and she takes a slight step back away from him like she's uncomfortable.

Done.

"This should be interesting," Kade says, laughing under his breath as I start walking rapidly toward Salem.

I quickly join them, finding Salem's back, and move behind her, wrapping my arm around her waist maybe a little too possessively, and pull her right up against me. The Gollum or whatever his name is, just leers at her, not even acting as though he's noticed I'm standing here.

Salem looks up at me, winking like she approves. Thank fuck. Because this could have been awkward if she reminded me she doesn't belong to me. I'm one step away from pissing a circle around her as it is.

"I don't believe we've met. I'm Maverick Sterling," I tell the Gollum.

"Steve Golland," he says, still leaving a sleazy slime trail with his eyes on her for a moment before turning his attention to me, smiling bitterly.

I feel like I should rush her home and put her in the shower.

"You know Salem?" I ask, even though I know he doesn't.

He gives a grin I don't particularly like, as his eyes shift back to her.

"Trying to get to know her would be more accurate."

My hand flattens on her stomach, pulling her tighter. "She's taken," I state like a jackass.

Salem still seems fine. She doesn't go stiff until his eyes drop to the split on her leg. And the reason she goes stiff is not because he's looking. It's because that's when stupid happens.

What's stupid? The answer is ME.

I'm not sure how it happens or even why it happens. I just know that for some reason, I lose a few thousand years of evolution and turn into a Neanderthal.

Chapter 27

Salem

Maverick's hand slides lower as he gets a little stiffer behind me. He's pretty freaking adorable when he's staking a claim.

Well, that is until he decides it's perfectly acceptable and civilized behavior to stake his claim by suddenly grabbing my vagina through the dress.

That's right.

My. Vagina.

In front of everyone.

I think I hear glass shattering and prayers for forgiveness being raised as Maverick Sterling cups my vagina through my barely decent dress, and *holds it*.

Holds. My. Vagina.

At a *charity* event.

It brings the entire party to a standstill.

Pie moment.

Chapter 28

MAVERICK

She slams the door in my face when I try to step into her house behind her. I narrowly dodge a broken nose by rearing my head back at the last second.

Probably deserved that.

I push through anyway, holding my hands up defensively in case she or the cat decide to sneak attack me.

"You grabbed my vagina?!" she yells from across the room as I slowly shut the door behind me, ready to finish this argument we've been having since we left the party. Abruptly. And drove straight here.

"He couldn't take his eyes off your damn chest! Then they dropped lower! And that dress barely covered—"

"Stop before you say something that makes this worse," she cautions, and I shut the hell right up. For a second, anyway.

"You want to be possessive?" she asks, taking a threatening step toward me. "Fine. Lucky for you, I like a little alpha in a guy. Drape your arm around me like a normal damn caveman and grunt a little. Do *not* grab my vagina! Who even does that?"

I'm not even sure why I'm arguing. I completely agree with her. But it's like my inner *male* survival instincts are in full swing, and I can't just bow out gracefully. Something is telling me that my very manhood hinges on winning this ridiculous argument.

"Maybe if that split hadn't been so close to your vagina, then I wouldn't have gotten such a handful!"

That was stupid. Yep. Real fucking stupid.

She goes to grab one of the nerf footballs, and I decide to run, since I have no idea how good at aiming she is. Or what kind of arm strength she has. Just as I get outside, she rushes to the door, launching it at me. If I'd been standing ten feet to the right, it might have hit me. She releases a little frustrated sound, and I sort of want to laugh.

"This is not funny!"

"Your aim is terrible. I thought you were a tomboy."

She's not as amused as I am.

"Either admit you shouldn't have grabbed my vagina, or you can go sleep in your bed by yourself tonight."

Obviously there's a clear choice right here.

"It let him know you were mine, didn't it? You're being totally irrational right now. I bought you Midol for a reason." *Dig, dig, digging up holes. Diggin' em' deeper.*

I promise I hear the indefensible stupidity running from my mouth. I just can't seem to turn it off. Blame the endorphins. Or the testosterone. Or whatever.

Bright side? She's really fucking beautiful when she's pissed. Can't help but enjoy myself a little.

"You are such an ass," she bites out, turning and stalking back in.

"Since you're clearly wrong and know it, does this mean makeup sex?" I call behind her. In response, she flips me off and slams the door.

"I'll settle for angry sex!" I yell louder.

She opens the door and another nerf ball is hurled out, missing me by another long mile. Cursing me like it's my fault she can't aim for shit, she slams the door again.

Get a girlfriend, they said.

It'll be great, they said.

You'll have lots of hot sex all the time, they said.

Motherfucking liars. All of them.

I go home, more annoyed with myself than anything else. Looks like I'll be buying more pointless roses and making another tampon run.

I'll skip the Midol this time. That probably didn't score me any bonus points.

Stupid fucking Gollum.

As soon as I'm out of my suit, I drop to my bed and put my arm over my head, wondering when exactly I got this fucking dumb? I blame *her*. I never got blinded by jealousy and made an irredeemable ass of myself before *her*.

Her and the stupid fucking way she draws me in. The way she has invaded my world. The way she takes me in stride and laughs with me. The way she gives me hell whenever she can.

And the way she looks like she could set me on fire when she's really pissed.

I blame her for the reason my bed sucks without her.

Pie moment. (I blame her for that too.)

Chapter 29

Salem

I'm jarred awake when two arms come around my waist, and I deny the smile that tries to form.

"I shouldn't have grabbed your vagina. It was the single stupidest thing I've done in my entire life, and I have zero clue why I even tried to defend it," comes the soft voice near my ear, his breath fanning my shoulder as I continue to fight the grin and burrow back into him.

"You're really lucky I can't sleep for shit without you anymore," I say on a putout sigh, even though my smile slips free.

I feel him smiling against my shoulder as he kisses it, our bodies lined up like two interlocked spoons.

"I am really damn lucky. And I'm sorry."

I pat his hand that's on my stomach. "That was hard to say, wasn't it?"

"You have no idea. I think it's the most fucked up, ridiculous apology I've ever given in my life. And that says *soooo* much."

Unable to stop myself, I start laughing, and he tugs me over to my back as I continue to shake from my laughter. Grinning, he leans down, shutting me up with a kiss that weirdly turns this second in time into another *moment*.

Didn't see that coming.

Chapter 30

Salem

I'm wringing my hands as nerves take me over. Maverick was stuck in traffic on his way back from the gym after a nasty wreck that jammed up most of the city. He was supposed to come to the house, change, and we were going to arrive together.

But he's still not here. Because he's still stuck in traffic, coming directly to here now.

Rain is beside me, along with a lot of the other girls who were able to get here without going through the middle of town. Not everyone from Maverick's group could make it, but I'm shocked at the turnout.

Sean is up next, and Maverick has been working with him almost daily this past week to make sure his routine is solid. Sean would never admit it, but he'd be devastated if Maverick missed it.

My eyes scan the crowd as a girl and her mother/dance-partner near the end of their duet performance, bringing Sean's debut even closer. My eyes scan the crowd, spotting my mother and Ian near the front. I'm two rows behind them.

Still no—

"Did I miss it?" Maverick asks, breathing heavily as Dane heaves for air behind him, along with Corbin right on their heels. They're all still dressed for the gym; a stark contrast to the fancily dressed patrons surrounding us.

His ball cap is facing forward, likely covering his messy hair, since it looks like he literally ran from somewhere.

Personally? I wouldn't care if Maverick was wearing a pair of chaps and a bra right now. As long as he's here.

Dane shuffles by me, taking the seat right next to me when Rain scoots over for him. Kode and Tria are already down there somewhere. Corbin sits with Ruby just behind me in the seat she's been saving for him.

"He's up next. Why are you so out of breath?" I whisper, trying not to disturb everyone watching the show.

He grins. "We left the car with Dale and ran the entire way. Traffic is so messed up that it could take hours to unjam everyone. Worst shit I've ever seen. I'm guessing someone probably stopped for a funeral procession."

"You ran all the way across town?" I ask in disbelief, ignoring that little barb on the end and focusing on the important part.

"Nonstop. Dane said next time he was volunteering to stay with the car."

I glance over to see Dane leaning forward in his chair, breathing heavily.

"He doesn't go to the gym as much," Corbin leans up to loudly whisper from behind me. "Depends too much on his naturally good genes."

I try not to laugh, relieved beyond words that Maverick is here, while Dane shoves at Corbin's face, pushing him back.

Maverick doesn't care when people glance over and eye his T-shirt and athletic pants. He simply puts his arm around the back of my chair as the act finishes up.

I bounce in my seat a little when Sean steps out, dressed in his track pants and new tennis shoes. His tight tank makes him look so tiny, which I'd never say to him, since he'd be mortified.

He twists his hat on backwards, and gets in position. I'm quite literally on the edge of my seat when they blast *La La*.

A few surprised chuckles escape the crowd, and Sean…freezes. His eyes go wide, and he just stares at me, eyes locked like he can't look away.

"Oh no," I say under my breath, freezing right along with him.

Another few laughs are smothered when he trips, trying to get started, and he just freezes again.

"Shit," Corbin says from behind us, probably feeling bad for my poor baby brother. "Do something, Mav."

Maverick stands abruptly, tossing his hat into my lap. I look down then back up as that song screeches to a halt. I start to ask what he's doing, when he pulls his loose T-shirt off, tossing it down to my lap.

Holy sexy man.

That's...um... why is he stripping?

"What are you doing?" I hiss.

"That shirt will drive me crazy," he says, retrieving his hat from me, and putting it on backwards as he jogs down and hops up on the stage with one jump.

Needless to say, several gasps and dreamy sighs sound out as a shirtless Maverick Sterling crosses the stage.

He walks over to Sean, saying something in his ear, and Sean nods with wide, grateful eyes. Then Maverick says something to another guy behind the music booth, who nods.

You want to know what can make a saint tempted to sin? Maverick Sterling in a pair of athletic pants that hang low on his hips, showing the top band of his underwear and that perfect V that draws the eye in. Along with lickable, defined abs that show up just enough. A chest sprinkled with tattoos that you can't help but touch if you get too close. And arm porn. Lots of hot arm porn highlighted with a STERLING tattoo.

His hat is on backwards, showing only snippets of his dark hair, and his smile is that of temptation itself.

Feel free to swoon. I won't get too jealous.

As Maverick comes up beside Sean, the music starts over, and...Maverick Sterling saves the day.

By dancing with Sean.

To a girl song that no guy should be able to own so well.

And making it look like it was planned all along.

Sean grins as Maverick and he keep perfect time, even with the trick moves. Maverick sometimes mirrors Sean instead of duplicating, giving the illusion of a new reflection.

When Sean flips forward, Maverick does a backflip.

"Showoff," Dane mutters with a smile, even as I grin so wide it almost hurts.

I think panties are combusting for miles away, because Maverick Sterling can move his body in ways that should be illegal, even though none of it is meant to be sexual. He just *is* sexual.

My brother feeds off the confidence that is radiating from Maverick. It makes Sean's dancing so much stronger, and there's zero hesitation in his steps.

They do a couple of slow motion moves that have people screaming like groupies. I admit, it's badass.

Maverick looks over as he and Sean work their way up to the big finish.

Two side-by-side side aerials and one head-spin later, they finish in some really hard-to-hold pose on their hands, with their legs straight out and horizontal from their bodies.

On the last beat before the fadeout, they jump to their feet and end on a very undignified hip thrust that has me laughing to myself.

Everyone is up on their feet, applauding, whistling, cheering.

Sean's smile couldn't be bigger right now.

"Now that was hot," Ruby says, then grunts a laugh when Corbin says or does something.

I don't know what they're doing to be honest. I'm too busy staring at Maverick as he trots back to me, leaving Sean to finish taking the bows on his own.

The second he reaches me, my hand goes to the back of his neck, and I pull him down, feeling his smile when I kiss him. His arms go around me, pulling me close, kissing me back.

I only break the kiss to look around the room. Sean is off stage, and there are five more acts to go before they bring them back for a final bow.

"Come on," I tell Maverick.

His grin grows as he follows me, then takes over leading the way when he realizes I don't know my way around this massive theatre-like building the dance school rented for the occasion.

Maverick pulls me into a massive stock room full of props from plays and such, and his lips come down on mine, kissing me just as hungrily as I'm kissing him.

He lets me climb up him, even helps me wrap my legs around his waist as he starts carrying me toward a short practice stage in the back. It's the perfect height when he sets me down on the stage, keeping all our best parts lined up as he continues to kiss me stupid.

"Now would be a time I want more. Like a lot more," I murmur against his lips, causing him to go still.

He pulls back, eyes searching mine.

"Here? Now?" he asks, a smile slowly turning up on his lips.

"I just had to watch you dance without a shirt on, so yes. Here. Now." I don't mention that I'm mostly in love with the fact he just saved my brother from utter humiliation. That would cheapen this moment for him, because he doesn't want me like that.

His grin grows as his eyebrows bounce teasingly, then his lips are back on mine with renewed hunger and excitement.

He shoves my skirt up on my hips as I kiss him harder, but he tugs me back, forcing my lips away from his. I'm not sure what's going on until he puts a hand to my chest, gently pushing me back.

"My skills on this aren't exactly that great. Not something I did too often in the past for obvious reasons, but something I've wanted to do to you for a while," he says, brushing his lips over mine as I try to figure out what he's saying.

He kisses his way down my neck as his hands work my underwear down my legs. I kick out of them, but my breath leaves in a rush when he suddenly pulls back and his head disappears between my thighs.

I moan when his mouth fastens around the spot I want him most, and I shove his hat off so I can grab handfuls of that soft hair I love so much. He makes a noise of approval, and the vibrations just drive the sensations that much higher.

Because I've been teased for over a month now, I'm not even embarrassed by how quickly I come. Or that I almost jerk his hair out. Or that I might call him a tongue wizard.

That last one is probably the reason he's laughing a little against my vagina. Odd sensation.

He kisses his way back up, his lips finding mine when I sit up again. Then he groans into my mouth like he's frustrated. He breaks off the kiss, his forehead pressing against mine.

"As much as I've wanted this moment, I'm in my gym clothes, had to run six miles to get here, so I'm completely unprepared."

I swallow down the knot in my throat as I slide my hands down the front of his pants, and he tightens a hand in my hair, his whole body shuddering once, when I stroke the warm, firm flesh in my hand.

"I'm on birth control, and we're both clean. We've had this conversation," I say on a shaky breath.

He goes a little still against me, eyes widening fractionally. We had that conversation as responsible adults. Not as a means of taking this to the next level.

Gingerly, like he might break me, he cups the side of my face, slowly kissing me again. I work his pants down around his hips, freeing him completely as I draw him closer.

Reaching his hand between us, he lines up with me, and with an agonizingly slow pace, he slides inside me, exhaling harshly like he's savoring every moment. His breath catches when he's completely inside of me, and he just holds himself there for long minutes as he kisses me again, tasting my mouth like it's the first time.

When he finally decides to start moving, I moan into his mouth, arching into him as he drives in and out of me, his speed gradually increasing.

His thumb slides over my clit, and with the perfect pressure, he sends me over the edge again, swallowing my sounds as I shudder against him. Apparently it sends him over the edge too, because he grunts, breaking the kiss, and buries his face against my neck as his body goes still.

Feeling a little too sated and limp, I grin over his shoulder at the dimly lit room.

"That was an incredible warmup," I say, grinning when his body starts shaking with soft laughter.

He leans back, his eyes finding mine. I love the way he's looking at me right now. It's completely different from the last time we were this intimately together. His touch is reverent, almost careful, as though he's terrified of losing this moment for himself this time.

Finally, after just simply staring into each other's eyes, I realize I sort of need to clean up, and apparently he thinks about it too, so he pulls back. When he scoops my underwear from the floor and hands them to me, I shake my head and put them in my purse.

"First time bareback was inside a store closet on a practice stage made for puppets or something," he says, grinning as he grabs his hat, dusts it off, and puts it back on backwards.

My eyes widen as I groan. "I'm sorry. I didn't know."

He laughs quietly as I make sure my skirt covers everything. "Please don't be fucking sorry. I'm considering buying this place and turning it into a shrine."

I'm the one to start laughing this time as I walk back toward the door. His fingers lace with mine, but he bumps into one of the racks.

Reflexively, he catches a costume whip when it falls, dropping my hand in the process. But just ahead of us, another prop falls, landing directly in front of us.

Stepping over it and across from Maverick, I barely contain the laughter when I see it's one of those pony heads on a stick that the kids play with to pretend they're riding a horse.

And Maverick is standing over it with a whip.

Still shirtless.

He looks at the whip in his hand then at the pony prop on the floor, and glares at me when I finally start laughing.

"Should I leave you two alone for the main event, Pony Boy?" I muse, and then squeal when he drops the whip and lunges for me.

Just as I scramble out the door, his front collides against my back, and his arms come around me as he playfully bites on my shoulder. My mother can't even sour this moment as she walks by us, water in hand, and sighs while shaking her head in disdain.

This is my moment, and she can't have it.

Maverick mutters something about fucking Twitter and damn phone cons and pony play, causing me to laugh again as I break away from him and go to the bathroom to clean up. He's still waiting outside the bathroom when I rejoin him.

He pushes off from the wall, sexy grin on his face, and he tosses his arm around my shoulders as he steers me back in. Dane glances up from his chair, rolling his eyes with a smile on his face when he sees us. He grabs the abandoned shirt from my seat and tosses it to Maverick.

Maverick winks at me before tugging it on, covering up that glorious body. I'm not the only one disappointed.

This is just a showcase and not a competition, so there aren't any scores or anything, but all the kids walk out, taking a bow at the end. Our section cheers the loudest when Sean steps up to take his solo bow.

Mom glances over, but I don't pay her any attention. I'm too busy whistling and *whooping*, doing all I can to embarrass the hell out of my little brother. Even though he secretly loves it as much as he hates it.

That little grin he's fighting says as much.

And this is that moment where pie becomes a celebratory dish.

Chapter 31

MAVERICK

The weeks seem to blur by, and seeing Salem becomes as necessary as eating or drinking. Fortunately for me, she seems to be just as addicted, so she doesn't care that I show up to take her out for lunch every day. Or that I've started driving her to and from work, because I'm terrified she's going to die if she keeps driving.

She also doesn't care that I've essentially started keeping clothes and hygiene essentials there instead of packing a bag. In fact, she even bought some stuff for me to use there.

She doesn't care that I bought her just as many supplies to have at my house, so that we can go to and from without needing something. She stays with me when Sean is with his mom. I stay with her the rest of the time.

Because this is real.

I can't even joke my way out of how serious this has gotten.

"Is there such a thing as a three month anniversary?" I ask Corbin and Jax as I finish grabbing my bag from the gym floor and toss it over my shoulder.

My hair's still wet from the shower when we walk outside.

"Yeah, back in eighth grade," Jax says with a taunting grin.

I glare over at him, and Corbin adds, "He has a point. No three month anniversary, dude."

"Where the hell have you been while the world has been evolving?" Jax asks around a laugh.

Why do I bother asking questions?

"It's because he's never actually had a three month anniversary," Corbin says with a fucking shithead grin.

"I'm glad I grew up an only child on days like this, because I might have killed you if we'd had to share a house," I say dryly as they both laugh.

"I'm glad you were an only child, too. You had a stepsister for two seconds before you were screwing her," Corbin says quickly.

I stop on the middle of the sidewalk just to glare at him, as he and Jax both laugh.

"You really want me to bring up your relationship hitches involving sisters?" I ask the two of them. That kills the laughter.

Maverick for the win.

"Didn't think so," I chirp.

Tossing my bag into my car, I walk around to the driver's side, waving dismissively when they both tell me *bye*. My phone lights up with Dad's name, and I answer as I start driving toward Salem's.

"If this is about the Jordan estate I just bought, don't bother. I saw it first," I say grinning; he wanted it too.

"That's okay. I bought the old grocery store outside of town with all that parking lot. Once Sterling Shore expands, that will be an excellent parking garage. Far better investment, if you ask me."

"Dick," I grumble as he laughs.

"I'm actually calling for a favor."

"I stopped hosting belated bachelor parties. Seemed a little desperate and just sad to call in strippers for an already married man. Guess you should have asked me before the wedding," I tell him, smirking when he laughs.

"It's actually about Kelly's birthday coming up in a few days. I bought her some jewelry, but it seemed impersonal. You have more female friends than any man I've ever known. Surely you can tell me what a woman wants."

A cheeky grin spreads over my lips. "Well, a woman wants—"

"Maverick," he interrupts, already knowing the direction I was taking with that.

Laughing, I tell him, "Something sentimental is the best way to go. It's easier when you know the person's past a little. Things that meant something then and now."

"Any chance you could ask Salem? I'm sure she'd know."

Here's my dilemma: Dad, for whatever reason, is really in love with Kelly. Kelly, for whatever reason, is determined not to love anyone. Hell, I'm not even convinced she loves her kids. And telling him that Salem likely doesn't know or care what her mother would find sentimental value in, would just hurt him.

I'm not ready to take away *his* moment.

"I'll ask her, but you would probably know if you thought about it."

"I can't think of anything or I wouldn't be asking you."

"I'm sure Kelly has mentioned something by now that would give you an idea of what would mean something. It wouldn't be something she told you directly to get. But it'd be something she mentioned while talking about the past."

He hesitates for a minute.

"I think I know what I'm getting her. Gotta make some phone calls. Bye."

He hangs up on me, and I shrug. I'm damn good at this boyfriend thing. Even my dad is calling me for advice these days.

I park at Salem's and walk in, past the point of having to knock anymore, but I end up stepping into the middle of a war zone, it seems.

"Because you're too young! And I already told you this, but you went behind my back and did it anyway!" Salem is yelling, pointing an accusatory finger at Sean and wagging it like he's in for it.

I cross my arms over my chest, and lean against the door, taking in the show.

"I'm not too young for bikinis!" Sean argues, confusing the hell out of me. "And I won them. I didn't buy them. It's not breaking the rules."

Is Sean wanting to wear bikinis? When did this happen?

"You won them because you mooned an entire bus of other kids. Which is why your principal called me at work. You're lucky they're not taking disciplinary action, since your friends are lying for you and saying you didn't moon anyone."

"It was a bet. I won the bet," Sean states firmly.

Fascinating stuff right here.

"The magazines, Sean. Bring the rest to me, or so help me, your phone will be mine for two months."

He narrows his eyes, but then sees me.

"Maverick, tell her I'm not too young for Sports Illustrated swimsuit edition."

Ahhhhh. Bikinis makes sense now. I was really dreading seeing him try to make his skinny little body hold up a bikini. Takes some ass to keep those bottoms up.

"Maverick will agree with me," Salem seethes.

Challenge accepted.

"Actually—" She levels me with a glare when I grin. "Actually," I start again, ignoring her adorable little attempt at intimidation, "I think swimsuits are fine. You see worse on the beach, which is right outside the door there." I point to the door on the other end of the house as if they need a visual reminder of its proximity.

Salem doesn't look away from me.

"The mooning was definitely over the top, though," I say, supporting her on that much.

Sean just grins. "I'm sorry for mooning the other bus. But does that mean I can keep the magazines?"

From what I can deduce, mooning someone won him a bet and scored him someone else's magazines. Yep. Sounds like a typical kid in Sterling Shore. He fits right in nowadays.

"No," Salem growls, facing him again. "You're too young."

"So you're never wearing a bikini again? Because I'm forced to get sick every time I have to see that and endure guys talking about my sister's butt and boobs. How's that fair? I'm too young for *that!*"

My eyebrows go up.

"Ignore what people say, but right now, this isn't about me, Sean," Salem says, still furious.

"I'm with the kid on the bikini. I think you should never wear one in front of other men again," I chime in, causing her lips to twitch even as she fights to keep her scowl in place and her attention on her brother.

Sean holds his ground. "Please? I won't even look at them. I just want to keep them because I won that bet, and it will shut them up."

"No," Salem says immediately.

"Surely the kid can keep them as long as he doesn't look at them," I say, butting in and getting another death glare from the saucy vixen across the room. "I mean, he's not hurting anyone by showing them his little ass either. It's highly unlikely they even knew for sure what they were looking at—might have thought it was the inside of a folded elbow or something."

"They knew it was my ass. Got a girl's number after that. She was two grades older, so it can't work out," he says, deadpan.

"Older girls are only fun if they know what they're doing, and you *are* too young for that conversation, so I'll shut up now."

Sean snorts, but Salem is totally not amused. Bananas just licks her paw, watching the action from a safe distance. Even she seems content to just be entertained.

"Do not team up on me," Salem states, gesturing between me and Sean. "That's not how this works. No magazines. And a written apology needs to be finished by dinner."

"Then you need to throw away your bikinis. If I can't have my bikini magazine, then I don't have to listen to what other guys say about my *sister* in her bikini."

"I'm still one hundred percent with the kid on that last bit," I pipe up.

"Pie. Moment," Salem bites out, glowering over at me.

I just grin, of course. It's fun as hell to rile her up. But in all seriousness, no one else needs to see her in a bikini. Ever. Just me.

"I've had five pie moments since we've been in here, because they're just bikinis! No different from what you wear. Some even cover more than what you wear," Sean continues.

"Why have *I* not seen these elusive bikinis?" I ask.

A sound of frustration leaves her as Salem whirls around, stalking into the kitchen. Laughing as Sean grins, I follow, turning the corner just as she rounds it again. Some sort of yelp leaves me just as something soft slams into my face and explodes, forcing my eyes to screw shut or get shit in them.

A choked laugh from Salem is smothered, and then Sean's riotous laughter carries around the entire room as I wipe the—I lick my lips, tasting my suspicion and am proven correct—*lemon pie* away from my eyes.

When I can open my eyes, managing to view the world through a funnel of creamy filling, I see Salem's eyes wide with horrified humor, her hands covering her mouth as her body shakes with suppressed laughter.

I lick my lips again, getting dessert before dinner.

"No fair," Sean says through his guffaws, clutching his side as tears of laughter slip out of his eyes. "You actually got to have a *literal* pie moment."

"I'm so sorry," Salem says with zero fucking sincerity. I lick more of the pie. "I didn't actually mean to do it. I didn't know you were right there. I was just going to threaten you with it, but...reflexes. However, I'll be honest; that was so much more satisfying than I ever imagined it would be."

I lick my lips again, then lunge without warning. Salem screams as she tries to dodge me, but I get her around the waist and cage her against the wall, kissing her all over her face as she tries to turn her head.

She laughs hysterically, as I rub the pie everywhere.

"Stop," she begs, still laughing. "I said I was sorry!"

"Lie."

She only laughs harder.

"Well, that escalated to *gross* quickly," Sean pipes in.

Salem and I both turn our attention on him, and matching evil grins light up our faces. Sean takes a cautious step back.

"Don't even think about it," he warns, narrowing his eyes as Salem and I both start slowly stalking toward him, pie all over our fucking faces.

"I mean it," Sean says, slinking backwards, scared to turn his back on us as he inches toward his door.

As if we timed it, Salem and I both dive for him, and he squeals while running toward the door. I leap completely over the couch, landing in front of him, and snatching him up.

The night goes on with wild giggles and threats.

Pretty perfect night, if you ask me.

Even the Devil Cat seems to have found her harmony.

Pie moment takes on a different meaning.

Chapter 32

MAVERICK

Family dinners are a little weird when your dad is kissing on your girlfriend's mom, because your girlfriend is also your stepsister.

Just sayin'.

When dad finally stops making us all uncomfortable, tearing his lips away from Kelly's, she actually blushes, eyelashes fluttering as she smiles at him.

It's moments when I see her look at him that way that I have a problem believing it's really all about the Benjamins.

Salem leans into my side, not particularly thrilled to be celebrating her mother's birthday. Sean acts like he doesn't care, but I can tell he wanted to be here. He even wrapped his mother's present that I took him to buy.

Salem brought her a pie.

I think she's secretly hoping to shove it in her face.

"Thank you. The ring is beautiful," Kelly says, smiling once again at Dad as she turns to open Sean's present.

Sean's such a wannabe badass, feigning aloofness, when he's secretly nervous about if she likes it or not. Of course she barely grins when she opens it and sees the two diamond, rose-shaped earrings—real fucking diamonds, by the way. I didn't tell him what it cost, since he only gave me forty bucks as a budget after picking them out. And then I snuck his forty bucks back into his room when he wasn't looking.

Sean said Kelly loves roses.

Which means Salem probably hates roses, and I need a new flower to buy her when I fuck up. Explains why those first ones never even got mentioned.

"Thank you, Sean," Kelly tells him, about as much warmth in her tone as a scoop of ice cream.

She also thanks me for my pen set—yeah, I'm impersonal when I don't particularly like you.

"I got you the pie," Salem says, a cold smile on her lips as she pushes the pie forward.

Kelly rolls her eyes.

"One more gift," Dad says, grinning as he stands and grabs a present and returns.

Kelly just smiles up at him, and then opens the necklace case. It's when her breath catches, her lips part, and her eyes glisten that Dad knows he hit the mark dead-on. It looks like just a simple diamond pendant necklace to me, so I don't understand the significance. That ring he just gave her easily has more carats than that necklace does.

"It's perfect," Kelly says on a shaky whisper, clearing her throat and blinking rapidly as though she's trying to compose herself.

Dad just grins like he's proud of himself.

"I had to go based on your description, so I'm glad I got it right."

She just nods, her smile turning a little tighter.

She pats his hand, leaning over to kiss him briefly this time. "I need to go to the restroom for a minute," she says as she stands. "Go ahead and start on the pie without me."

Salem and Sean need not be told twice. For once, I skip the fucking pie. My abs are trying to disappear. I blame *her*.

I'm not sure how she doesn't weigh five hundred pounds. Same for that little shit brother of hers. He eats more than I do on a daily basis and is so skinny that it's hard to find clothes to fit him.

Don't even ask how he conned me into taking him clothes shopping.

A lot has happened in three months.

My arm falls around Salem's shoulders, and she grins up at me before leaning over and kissing the side of my jaw. Dad winks at me when he sees it, grinning like he couldn't be happier.

I just wish Kelly was as genuine as Salem.

"So, Sean, I heard your other two brothers are pretty athletic. You thinking of playing any sports?" Dad asks him.

Sean shakes his head as Salem snorts.

I roll my eyes.

"I hate sports," Sean says. "Unless I'm watching my brothers play. Then I don't mind them."

Dad just grins.

"He's just mimicking Salem, because she hates sports," I say, gesturing at the girl still grinning beside me.

"Am not. I tried to like sports," Sean says dismissively. "Ball goes in hole. Ball misses hole. Puck hits net. Puck misses net. Seems redundant and I don't understand who wants to get punched in the face or taken out at the knees just to score points for no real reason. At least in dance no one is gunning for your face." He pauses and gestures to his face. "I'm going to need this to look good in a few years."

Unbelievable.

Dad chuckles. "Good point. Maverick played a lot of sports and did dance as well."

Salem's head whips toward me, and I wink at her.

"Overachiever," Sean mutters, smirking.

"My face is still fucking flawless despite the sports," I point out, causing Sean to roll his eyes dramatically. "I also had straight A's— *always*—and did some recreational rowing on occasion. And—"

"Just curious," Sean interrupts, looking toward Dad, "has he always talked so much about himself? Because I know more about him than I know about Salem, and I've known her all my life."

I glare at the kid, and Dad bursts out laughing, almost strangling on his drink.

"But did you wear tights?" Salem finally asks. "Back when you danced."

"Only when he took ballet," Dad says immediately, and I drop my head back, groaning, as Salem and Sean burst out laughing.

Dad fake winces, then gives me a taunting wink. Jackass did that on purpose.

My head comes back down as Sean unleashes a legion of 'men in tights' jokes that he's been apparently hoarding for a while. But I notice Kelly leaned against the hallway wall, standing in the shadows as she looks on at us.

Salem throws her head back, laughing at something Sean has just said, and Dad slaps the table, laughing so hard he can hardly breathe. All the while, Kelly just barely smiles, watching her children like she can't look away, and looking more human and less like an ice queen for the first time ever.

The second she realizes I've spotted her, she puts on her poker face, her forced smile, and comes back to the table, pretending to only be mildly interested in the conversations going on around her.

But I just saw something.

She's not as hardened as she wants the world to think.

I'm just not sure I understand why anyone would rather be hated than loved.

My phone chimes in my pocket, and I pull it out, looking at the screen.

DALE: Bella is having the baby!

I scramble up from my seat, juggling my phone like a cartoon comic strip of hot-potato before finally getting it under control.

"What's wrong?" Salem asks, looking up at me.

"Bella's having her baby!" I say on one rushed breath, pulling my keys out.

"I have a present at the house from us," Salem tells me as I lace our fingers together.

"Baby? You're on your own. I'll just stay here," Sean says.

Salem looks to her mother, confirming that's good with her.

"Just swing by tomorrow if you want to pick him up," Kelly says.

Salem and I leave, rushing out to my car. We quickly swing by her house, grabbing the little bag that says BABY in yellow letters.

I like that I never have to ask her to be a part of things. She knows I want her with me, and she's always prepared to be there. My fingers lace with hers, and she leans over, propping her head on my shoulder.

She talks about her moments from time to time. But this? For some reason, this is one of mine.

Chapter 33

Salem

@MavSterling: @SalemWithNoWitch did you really have to post that selfie of you in a bikini? #TooFarBaby

@SalemWithNoWitch: @MavSterling next time maybe you'll side with me. ^_^ #PieFace

@BellaHasABigBun: @SalemWithNoWitch @MavSterling Bikini selfie was hawt. #StepUpThatGameSterling

@MavSterling: @SalemWithNoWitch @BellaHasABigBun shouldn't you be breastfeeding or something?

@BellaHasABigBun: @SalemWithNoWitch @MavSterling I can multitask. Checking out the guys liking her pic now. #Competition

@MavSterling: @BellaHasABigBun @SalemWithNoWitch my cockblocking game is strong. #LookButDontTouch #MyGirl

@BellaHasABigBun: @SalemWithNoWitch @MavSterling is such a romantic… I think.

@EthanNolesIDGAF: @SalemWithNoWitch @BellaHasABigBun Mav doesn't have shit on me. #legend

@ArleneMommaBear: @EthanNolesIDGAF @SalemWithNoWitch @BellaHasABigBun none better than my boy.

@SalemWithNoWitch: @EthanNolesIDGAF if your mom says it on twitter then I guess it must be true. #ThatsSoSweet

@ArleneMommaBear: @SalemWithNoWitch you need to see his scrapbook!

@EthanNolesIDGAF: @SalemWithNoWitch you and @MavSterling deserve each other. #SmartassesUnited

@MavSterling: @EthanNolesIDGAF @SalemWithNoWitch #Soulmates #PowerCouple

@EthanNolesIDGAF: @MavSterling @SalemWithNoWitch #GagMe

@MavSterling: @SalemWithNoWitch @EthanNolesIDGAF is just mad because Isa Noles looks more like me...

@EthanNolesIDGAF: @MavSterling MY daughter is going to watch me kick your ass for that.

Laughing as I put my phone away, I glance at the door, wondering where Sean is. He usually doesn't make me go in.

Sighing, I get out and head up the front steps of Mom's, walking in since the door is unlocked.

"Sean?" I call out, wondering why he's not meeting me at the front door like he usually does.

When he doesn't answer, I jog up the steps, finding him sitting at the very top.

"Hey. Why are you up here? Do you not feel like coming with me and Maverick to see the baby again? We'll only be at the hospital for a second. I promise it won't be all day."

He just stares at the step beneath him, head hanging low. It isn't until I see a tear roll off his nose, drop the short distance to the stair and splatter that I get worried.

"Sean, what's wrong?" I ask, putting my hand on his shoulder.

"I hate her," he whispers brokenly.

Before I can ask what the hell she's done, I hear, "Salem? Come here. We need to speak."

A gnawing dread unfurls in my stomach. Apparently Sean has done something to piss her off, and now she's grounding him from my house for a while.

Mom is in Sean's room, sitting on his bed as she smiles timidly at me. "He just needs a moment. I think he liked this place a little more than some of the others," she says with no emotion.

But I'm not without emotion.

Confusion is the first emotion.

Denial is the second emotion.

Pain is the third.

"What?" I ask her hoarsely, then clear my throat.

"We're moving back to Georgia in two weeks. Our time in Sterling Shore has come to an end."

I shake my head. "No. No! That doesn't make any sense. Ian is still fawning all over you," I argue, not believing for one second this conversation is real. "It's like he can't look away from you. Why would you even want to leave?"

"It's not up for debate, and my reasons are none of your concern. Come or don't. Obviously, I can't force you."

She stands and starts walking away, moving down the hallway, and I take a few deep breaths as my heartbeat drums in my ears. Finally, I burst out of Sean's room, my shoes thudding against the tile floor.

"Like hell it's not up for debate. We've made a home here. This isn't some random drive-by, and you know it. It's different this time, for me *and* Sean," I snap.

She doesn't turn around, her heels still clicking and echoing through the halls as she turns into a room. I pursue.

"Is this because I'm with Maverick? Is it really pissing you off that much to see me happy and now you have to rip it away? Is that it?" My voice is raw, my chest is aching, and my tears are relentless.

"Don't be so melodramatic," she sighs.

She puts a necklace on the dresser, moving it away from her jewelry box like she doesn't want it around any of her other things. "Two weeks. That should be plenty of time to tidy up goodbyes," she says heartlessly.

My eyes scan over the necklace. I only saw it at a glimpse last night when Ian presented her with it. But upon closer inspection, I find it to be an almost exact replica of the one Mom used to have from her grandmother. It broke and fell off of her when I was about thirteen; she never could find it. I remember it, because it's the one and only time I've seen her cry in my entire life.

"This is about the necklace, isn't it?" I ask, piecing things together, even as my jaw grinds.

She feigns indifference, but I can see it in her eyes that she's struggling not to look at it.

"God forbid you feel anything for anyone," I mutter under my breath.

"What was that?" she asks, her voice even and not strained or emotional like mine.

"I said, God forbid you feel anything," I bite out, looking over at her. "Ian bought you something that meant something to you. Because he listens to you. Clearly you mentioned it, probably during one of your human moments when you unintentionally allowed someone to see who you really are. And you know he bought it because he cares. It fucking means something to you, and your icy heart just refuses to thaw. So you're running. Never mind that Sean and I love this place. Never mind it's the first time we've felt like we have a home. Just so long as you don't have to *feel* anything, nothing else matters."

Her bottom lip wavers only briefly before she recovers.

"I've emailed you the address to the house I'll be renting so that you can find appropriate housing nearby if you decide to follow us. Two weeks. Consider that a generous courtesy. Stay here if it's so important to you. Your brother will be going home with me."

I point to my chest. "My brother's home is with *me*. You know why? Because I'm the one who loves him. I'm the one who keeps him *warm*. I'm the one who works her fucking ass off to keep him from ever being a fraction as cold as you. And trust me, it's really hard when you constantly take everything away that he loves and work to make sure he can never form healthy attachments."

Her eyes go a little glossy, but as I said, my mother has only ever cried once.

"Say whatever you want, Salem. Get it all out. This isn't the first time you thought you loved a boy, and we both know that's why you're really showing out right now. Don't use your brother as a beard to hide your true, juvenile agenda."

I take a step back, more appalled by her now than I was when she screwed my boyfriend. "It's amazing to me that you managed not to turn us to ice. It must suck to never want anyone to care about you, since that leaves you always feeling alone. But don't you worry; Sean and I will be just like Tyler and Connor one day. Just *as soon* as Sean is old enough to break away. And we'll forget you even exist."

This time, I know her eyes water, even as her jaw tics with anger.

"And when you're all alone in that ice fortress you built so proudly…you can go fuck yourself," I say in disgust.

I turn, ignoring her as she shouts my name, and slam the door of her bedroom behind me. Mother doesn't chase. It goes against her rules.

So I don't worry about looking over my shoulder to find her coming after me.

Sean is right where I left him, and I drop down to sit beside him on the stairs. Neither of us say anything for a few minutes, both of us crying silently in the company of the other.

"We can't stay, can we?" he finally asks on a hushed whisper.

I clear my throat, wiping away my tears, but find I can't answer that.

"You could stay," he says even quieter.

The tears are making it impossible to see now, and I force myself to speak over the lump in my throat. With a monumental effort that comes straight from the most unselfish place in my body, I manage to force a smile for the sake of my brother.

Reaching over, I put my hand on his shoulder, shaking him a little. "You and me, kiddo. You can't get rid of me that easily. Besides, who the hell is going to love me like you do? I can't lose that."

I can tell my words have zero effect on his mood, though I can't blame him.

"Maverick loves you," he finally says on an exhale.

Freaking emotion starts choking me. "I'm going to go pack for Georgia and see about getting an apartment. I'll call you later, okay?"

He just nods dully, drawing his knees up to his chest and resting his cheek on them, his face away from me.

As I stand up, I hear him whisper again, "I hate her."

Usually I encourage him not to say that. Today, however, I just don't have it in me to be the better person.

Because I hate her, too.

Chapter 34

MAVERICK

"So these three are a little soft for my liking. They can't handle a good teasing without getting bent out of shape. But they are really nice looking. Almost too nice looking to simply scratch off," Mom says, currently in the process of traumatizing me for life.

She points to three other pictures she has hanging on her chalkboard in her old-school office. Under it — *I'm going to be sick* — the words "Well Endowed" are written.

"I think this category speaks for itself," she says with a nauseating giggle.

She points to another category that has KINK—

"Mom!" I say before she starts talking, shutting my eyes when I get worried what else I might see. "You need to call one of your friends for this. Not a mother/son thing."

"But you and your father always talked women. I'm late to the game, but—"

"Women," I groan, still keeping my eyes screwed shut. "Not men. And he was my dad. Not my mom."

"Maverick Sterling, I didn't raise you to be sexist," she says, sounding genuinely affronted.

I imagine she's glaring. I'm not opening my eyes. I'm still trying to unsee what I've already seen.

"Not even a little sexist, Mom. Not even Dad broke down this much detail for me," I tell her.

"Oh," she finally says, then sighs. "Will my friends think I'm a slut when I tell them about all this?"

I groan, hearing the word *slut* come out of her mouth. "Not the right friends," I assure her. "Call Aunt Elizabeth. Or maybe Eleanor. Or even better, call Wanda."

Seeing all these guys worries the hell out of me.

Carefully avoiding that nightmare-inducing blackboard, I ask Mom, "Are you being safe?"

Hell, these guys could be criminals for all she fucking knows.

"Of course, Maverick. In case you've forgotten, I'm the one who stocked your bathroom cabinet with condoms until you moved out, since it was apparent you weren't going to stop having sex. No glove, no love. Just like you used to tell the girls who came through here."

I turn a little puce.

"Not the kind of safe I was meaning, but thanks for completely ruining sex for me."

Her mouth forms an O and she refrains from laughing.

"No big deal. I'm twenty-seven, after all. I'm too old for sex."

"Now you're just being dramatic," she says, laughing lightly. "Of course I'm safe. I have a friend run a background check on all of them, and we meet at hotels for—"

"Stopping you there," I say, holding both hands up in front of me, pleading with my eyes for her to have mercy.

She swallows down the rest of her words before giving me a knowing grin.

"Fine. I'll call a friend for this. When is Salem coming back over for dinner? I feel like I've barely gotten a chance to know her."

"That's because I'm in the phase where I'm keeping her to myself as much as possible," I say before coming to drop a kiss on her cheek.

She follows me out, hand patting my back.

"I like seeing you in a meaningful relationship. It makes me not worry about you so much," she says softly. "I want you to know,

I'm searching for someone. This isn't just me trying to get my 'wild' out or anything. I'm just looking for the right connection."

Tossing my arm around her shoulders, I hug her to my side. "Yeah, I know. I'm trying to keep my nose out of it. For the record, it's damn hard to do."

She laughs lightly as I release her.

"I have to get home and grab some things before I go to meet Salem. We're going to see the new baby and then driving out to Raya and Kade's vineyard for the day."

"Oh! The baby! What'd they name her?" Mom asks as I put my hat back on backwards.

"Isa. Ethan thought it'd be a hilarious play on Bella's name—Isa and Bella. I think all the endorphins had gotten to her head, so she agreed to anything he said."

She rolls her eyes. "It's a lovely name. I'll swing by their house when they get home and drop off the baby blanket I made for them. Could have sworn they were having a boy, so it's a blue blanket. Oh well."

After a little more chitchat about Isa—why did I bring up a baby to my mother when I was trying to leave?—I finally get out and hurry to my house. But for some weird reason, Dad's car is in my driveway.

Confused, I get out and jog inside. "Dad?"

"In here," comes the slurred response.

I walk through to my den to find him on my couch, a dozen or more beer bottles on the table in front of him, and the scent of stale cigar smoke lingering the air. He's still in his wrinkled clothes from last night, and he quite frankly looks like shit.

"What the hell? Did you stay here last night?" I ask, confused. Usually if she doesn't have Sean, we stay here, but crashed at her place last night because she had to feed the damn Devil cat, then we were just too tired to go again.

"Figured it'd be safe, since you stay with Salem most nights," he says before burping.

Totally not my dad. He never gets sloppy drunk, and he never wears wrinkled clothes. He sure as hell doesn't smell like death on a normal day.

I've *never* seen him like this.

"What the hell is going on?" I ask him, and he blows out a heavy breath.

"I honestly have no fucking clue," he says, shaking his head. "I knew when I married her she wasn't in love with me. But I fell hard for her, Maverick. Not an easy woman to love, but that's what made her twice as special," he explains, only adding to my confusion as I go to lower myself onto the couch next to him.

He snags a beer from the table, drinking another long swallow.

As the bottle lowers from his lips, he goes on. "I thought it was my punishment. Finally finding a woman who made my world stand still, only to learn she was the one woman immune to falling in love with me."

He snorts, and I smirk at his joke about his arrogance. At least that sounds like him. Nothing else does so far.

"It was the times she let me in. Those moments her guard was down and she showed me the real woman no one else got to see…those moments were what made her so damn special and dragged me over the damn edge."

Unsure where this is going and why he's so out of sorts, I pat him on the shoulder.

"What happened?" I ask again.

"That's just it; I don't fucking know," he groans. "Everything was fine last night. We had a great time. Then after you and Salem left and Sean went up to his room, Kelly found me in the study and told me that it was over."

My skin prickles as my eyes widen.

"What?"

"I was so blindsided that I didn't even argue at first. And by the time I got my head wrapped around her words, she's was asking me to give her two weeks to get her affairs in order. She even packed me a fucking bag. Hell, all I could do was just let my jaw hang. I had no words. She was so fucking cold that it didn't even look like the same woman. I still have no clue what I did, Maverick. None."

I run a hand through my hair, and then scrub the same hand over my face. Salem warned me this would happen.

"I'll go find Salem and see if she can shed some light on all this," I tell him.

"That would be appreciated," he says on a long-suffering sigh. "And tell her she doesn't have to move out. I know she sent a text saying the movers would be there next week to collect her things, but it's not necessary. She's welcome to stay there as long as she likes."

My blood turns to ice in my veins as his words slowly sink in — as the entire situation slowly sinks in.

"She said she's moving?" I ask quietly, knowing damn well she hasn't sent that text to me.

"I assumed she was going to find somewhere not affiliated with my name on it, worried I'd take out my frustrations with her mother on her. But you know I won't do that," he says, not understanding the full gravity of this situation.

If Kelly goes, Sean goes. If Sean goes —

No!

Salem wouldn't just leave. She can't.

"I need to go," I say, standing abruptly. "You can stay here as long as you need."

"Thanks," he says on a sigh.

I pull my phone out as I stalk toward the door. I text three Sterlings to let them know their brother needs them right now, though he'd never call them himself. They're not as close as I am with my cousins who are more like brothers. But they're still there for each other when it counts.

Blowing out a shaky breath, I get in my car, try to get all my emotions in check, and drive to Salem.

We can fix this. There's always a way to fucking fix it.

Chapter 35

Salem

Sean walks in, the door shutting hard behind him, and I wipe away my tears, pretending as though I haven't been crying for the past thirty minutes since I left him with Mom.

"You want to grab some ice cream or something?" I ask him as he goes directly to his room, not bothering to answer me.

As I walk toward him, I notice the driver who drove him here is still idling in my driveway.

Just as I walk into his room, I see him putting Bananas in her pet carrier, her other belongings hanging out of a bag.

"What're you doing?" I ask him as he sniffs and wipes his nose.

"Taking Bananas back to Ian's house. I need to ask Maverick if he wants her back," he answers in a rasp.

My heart hurts just hearing his pain. I was wrong to let him get so attached to this place. I thought it'd warm him a little more, but I was kidding myself. Losing the things you love hurts so much that you can't help but grow a little colder.

"I'm going to leave early. Do some unplugging and rebooting while the movers get everything of ours out of here. Do you want to come with me? Or do you want to wait until I come back to get my truck?" I ask him gingerly.

He cuts his tear-filled eyes toward me, anger there instead of pain.

"No. I don't want to go with you and I don't want to see you when we get to Georgia."

I blow out a breath. "Sean, I know you're hurting, but—"

"Just shut up, Salem. I'm eleven, not five. You don't have to hover over me every second of every day. I don't want you there. If you come, I won't see you. And you know Mom won't make me."

Angrily, he jerks the strap of the bag over his shoulder.

He's lashing out. I'm familiar with this. But he's also doing all he can to keep me from feeling like I have to go. Because my brother, by some miracle, has his own warmth.

"Maybe I'm not going for you. Maybe I'm going for me. Because I don't want to let you go, kiddo. That's what happens when you love someone."

He narrows his eyes, even as his tears start to drip. "Love me from here. Because it's pointless for you to try and love me from there when I won't see you."

He lifts Bananas inside her carrier and shoulders by me, not looking back. I let him go, simply because I know he needs a little space.

It's crazy that a selfish woman managed to have four kids who all love each other so much they'd do anything to keep the other one from suffering. Give up everything.

He's willing to let me go just so that I don't have to let go of the home we've found.

That's how I know my influence isn't all bad.

Maverick...

How do I tell him this as I'm leaving town?

I pause by the fireplace, smiling weakly at the Samurai sword hanging above it, and fondly thinking back on the world's most ridiculous fight. Then I move to the kitchen island as the car pulls away, Sean tucked away safely inside, and I pour a large glass of wine before going back to the bedroom.

Staring blankly at the wall, I drop to the edge of the bed, sipping the wine as I try to numb myself. I need a little numbness to make through these next twenty-four hours.

Draining the glass, I put it down on the floor and lean forward, taking deep breaths.

The sound of the door slamming startles me, and Maverick's voice as he calls for me has me quickly wiping at my face, slowly putting on my mask. He's not the kind of guy to go down without a fight.

And I don't know how much I can be his opposition when I want to fight for the same thing he does.

"In here," I finally say, thankful the words come out stronger than I expected.

He immediately pops into my room, eyes raking over me as he keeps his distance, his stance defensive.

"One look at you, and I can already tell you're about to say goodbye," Maverick says quietly, an edge to his tone.

"We've known this was coming, Maverick. I told you in the very beginning this was coming. I gave you every opportunity to walk away without getting attached. It sucks, but you're too great not to be okay," I say without stumbling over the words or crying, mustering all my strength to bury my warmth for just a second.

"Just like that? You want me to believe this doesn't hurt you?"

My false bravado wavers, and I know he sees it, despite how desperately I try to cling to it.

His tone softens. "Salem, there's a way to fix this. I'll talk to my dad and find out what he's not telling me. Trust me, he'll fix this. He married her, and that does mean something to him."

The first tear slips. "I don't think this one had anything to do with what the man wanted this time. Mom wavered—and that's the thing she fears the most. Now she's not risking a slip. This has only ever happened one other time, but it just goes to prove that Sterling men know how to touch even the coldest of hearts."

He sags a little, but still looks so determined. "I can't accept this as it. Don't stand there and say 'goodbye' like you don't feel anything."

"I knew it was coming, Maverick." The tears finally win and start slipping free, but my voice stays even. "If I could have done something, I would have already done it by now."

"It's like you're saying this was all for nothing. I never wanted any of this until you, damn it. For the right person—"

"You're the right person, Maverick," I say, barely containing the sob on the tip of my tongue as the tears continue to fall. "You may even be the only person."

His look softens as I angrily bat the tears away.

"But just because you find the right person, it doesn't always mean you find the right time," I go on brokenly.

He takes a step toward me, reaching for me, and I stumble back. His hand closes into a fist before he drops it away, looking hurt. If I touch him, I'll lose my resolve. I'll be selfish. And I'll never forgive myself for it.

"Sean needs me more than you do," I go on, watching as Maverick tries to close himself off, and I'm unable to simply watch it happen. "He's just a kid. And if I'm not there to keep him warm, he'll go cold."

Emotion clouds his eyes as sympathy pools.

"I almost went cold," I tell him, choking on the words. "Tyler kept me warm. He kept me from turning into her. His father and stepmother were so warm, and he shared it with me. Connor had two cold families, but I kept him warm just as Tyler did for me. I passed it down. But when it was his turn to do it for Sean, I couldn't let him do it. He had such an amazing future ahead of him, and I couldn't let him give that up. He would have. Instead, I stayed with Sean, taking another turn. If he's alone, he'll go cold."

He shakes his head, clinging to the hope for the impossible. "No. There's something we can do. There's got to be a way, Salem. I'm not okay with just being done. I can't say, 'Oh, well, that sucks. It was fun knowing you.' I just can't."

Just over three months—that's how long it took for my world to shift. A fourth of a year. Three months can change absolutely everything you ever thought you knew. Three months should be such an insignificant amount of time in the grand scheme of things. A blink of an eye in life.

So tell me why it feels like I'll never get through another three months without looking back at this moment, this exact blink in my life, and know with devastating certainty this is when I blinked wrong.

The problem is, there's no *right* way to blink.

"I'm sorry, Maverick. There's no other way it can be."

"Stop acting like you're already finished without even thinking about it. We can just get a lawyer and you can get custody of Sean. She can't keep using him against you like this," he says so reasonably and with so much conviction that it physically hurts me to be the one to show him reality.

"Why would they take him away? He has the finest clothes. He's always supervised and well cared for. He's perfectly healthy and sees the doctor for regular checkups. He makes incredible grades at some of the best schools in the nation. She even pays for the finest dance teachers and goes to his showcases. She's always involved in the school and constantly keeping him focused on his studies, as well as making sure he's clean and well. Maverick, she's not a bad mother. She's not a monster. She's not even really a bad person. And on some very terribly sad level, she even genuinely cares for us. She's just…" I can't say another word, so the sentence just trails off.

"Cold," Maverick says quietly, finishing the sentence for me as his eyes drop to the ground and his shoulders slump in defeat. "Then I'll come with you. Go where you go," he says, tearing my heart right the hell out of my chest.

"And leave your friends? Your family? The home you love so much? I'd never let you do that, Maverick. Not for me. *A Sterling is nothing without Sterling Shore*—those are your words. You'd resent me one day, and I wouldn't blame you."

"Now it just sounds like you're actually ready for it to be over," he says accusingly.

It's better if he's angry. It'll be easier for him to be angry than to be in pain.

"Maverick, I'm sor—"

"We still have two weeks," he interrupts, glossy brown eyes meeting mine. "We have two weeks to figure something out. Right now…I just…I need to go right now. I'll see you in the morning, okay?" he asks through strain, backing toward the door.

"Okay," I manage to say.

He hesitates, starting and stopping, then looks at me again. "Salem, I l—"

"Please don't say it now," I interrupt on a near whisper, more tears leaking from my eyes. "That wouldn't be fair," I add as he tightens his lips, sparing me. "Because that would change *everything.*" Exhaling steadily to calm myself, I stare into his eyes. "And I wouldn't be able to walk away from that, no matter what."

Cursing and fisting his hands, he turns and walks out, punching the wall on his way. I blow out a pained breath, trying to steady my legs.

All of the sudden, he bursts back into the room, and my breath leaves as he stalks toward me, grabbing me before I can stop him. His hand painfully shoves into my hair, angling my head back before his lips crash down on mine.

My tears fall, sneaking into the kiss as I kiss him back, telling myself it's a proper goodbye so that my heart doesn't try to convince me it means something else. I kiss him hard, holding him to me as the kiss turns almost punishing. Angry.

Finally, he releases me just as abruptly, turning and walking out again without a backward glance. I jump a little and close my eyes when I hear the front door slam, punctuating the end.

Getting my breathing under control, I slowly open my eyes, steel my resolve, and shakily prepare for the wrong blink.

Reaching beside the bed, I grab the handle of the suitcase he never saw, and I start walking toward the door.

Obviously I don't look back. It just makes it worse to be looking behind you at everything you're giving up, when the pain hits you from the front, making sure you never see it coming; maximum impact.

You look forward for the simple act of self-preservation. Life doesn't go for the knockout. It goes for the kill.

Chapter 36

MAVERICK

Since this morning, I've been doing everything in my power to try and figure out a way to get custody of Sean transferred to Salem, but it's like a punch in the gut to realize just how right she is.

Hell, Kelly is a fucking saint compared to what it takes to be declared an unfit mother.

I'm still not ready to give up.

Fuck that. I can't just let her leave.

If I have to, I'll leave with her. Go to fucking Georgia. I don't give a shit what she tries to say. This is not the damn end. Can't be. We're just getting started.

And I don't just fall in love every-fucking-day. I'll never have this again, and I know it. Salem is it for me. All there is.

I know she doesn't want to leave, and neither does Sean. They've built a life here. So that's Plan A; find a damn way to keep them here.

I rub my chest, finding a hollow ache there, trying my damnedest to ignore it. It's trying to tell me it's over, but I know it's not.

Seeing her so defeated was too much to be around. I couldn't stand there and watch the fight be zapped out of her. But she's spent her life in this fucking cycle; her mother always dictating how life is lived, and Salem forced to go along for the ride because she loves her brothers.

Scrubbing a hand over my face, I walk out of my home office and grab my keys. I'm going to make Salem want to fight. Maybe I can't do anything on my own, but the two of us together have to be able to figure out something.

I hesitate by the den, seeing Dad lying on the couch and staring at the TV, though I don't think he sees anything. Blowing out a heavy breath, I reach the door, and stumble to a halt when I see three Sterling uncles about to knock.

"He's in the den," I tell them before weaving through their bodies and heading to my car.

I drive through town a little faster than necessary, returning to the beach house, and frown when I see Rain, Dane, Tria, and Ethan sitting outside like they're waiting on someone. Then I spot Rye and Brin as they come around the side, their feet coming to an abrupt halt when they see me sitting in my car.

They watch me as I get out, heading toward the door.

"What's going on?" I ask, confused.

"Just waiting on you," Ethan says with a tight smile.

I cock my head. "Why?"

Brin clears her throat as she does something on her phone then hands it to me. A text box is pulled up, but my eyes zero in on the last message.

SALEM: Be there for him. Please.

I read it five times, maybe more, before my vision starts to blur.

"She's gone, isn't she? Just like that?" I ask quietly, not looking up to see the pity I know will be on everyone's faces.

"Maverick," Rain starts, her voice oozing sympathy, but I wave her off before she reaches me as I shove Brin's phone back at her.

As soon as she takes it, I stalk back to my car.

"Mav!" Ethan shouts, but I crank my car and squeal out in reverse, punching my steering wheel even as I gas it down the street.

Her phone goes to voicemail five times in a row before I throw my phone to the floor, gripping the steering wheel tighter as I take another turn.

I drive to Dad's house, get out of my car, and burst through the doors.

Sean jumps when I barge into the living room and find him sitting on the couch with Bananas sleeping in his lap.

"Where is she?" I ask him, my jaw grinding.

His red-rimmed eyes water as he looks back down at the cat.

"She left. She needed to unplug. No phone. No internet. Nothing. She said she'd see me in two weeks when Mom and I get there. Connor or Tyler will be coming to get her truck."

I turn and stalk out of the room, jogging up the steps and start calling for the bitch from hell.

"Kelly!"

She comes out of a room, eyes wary when she sees me.

"You can't just fucking let them have something, can you?" I snap.

Her eyes go icy, her shield coming up.

"This has nothing to do with you, Maverick. I'm sorry for the personal inconvenience this might cause you, but—"

"Personal inconvenience?" I ask around a humorless laugh. "Really? I'm sure having my heart ripped out of my chest can be described a little more vividly than a *personal inconvenience.*"

She bristles, thinking about her words.

"Salem is choosing to leave. I'm not making her go."

"Then leave Sean with her and you go. Do something fucking right for your kids for once!"

Her jaw tics. "I realize you're in an emotional state right now, but that gives you no right to assume you know anything about the complicated relationship I have with my children after only knowing them less than four months."

I take a step back, shaking my head in disgust as I look at her, feeling sorry for the shell in front of me.

"I know that the only two who still even speak to you won't be around for longer than seven more years. I hope you treasure those seven fucking years. Because the second Sean's able to break away from you, they'll both be gone. And then what will you have?"

A flicker of humanity crosses her eyes, along with a hint of pain, but she backs away.

"Believe it or not, I am sorry for you and Salem."

"I'm sure you're real sorry," I bite out angrily. "Sorry that Salem is nothing like you. I'm sure it sucks like hell to see how hard she fights every day to make sure Sean turns out better than you, too."

With a trembling bottom lip, she turns and shuts the door, and I fight back the hot tears trying to prick my eyes as I turn and storm back down the stairs.

Sean is leaning against the wall when I reach the bottom of the stairs, his head down, likely having overheard all of that.

"I need a way to contact her," I say to him.

"I can call Tyler if there's an emergency. She's staying at a small cabin on his property. But he won't take her the phone unless it's an emergency."

"Tell him it's an emergency, because I really need to talk to her."

Sean looks up, that same defeat in his eyes that was in Salem's, all the fire gone from his usual mischievous self.

"She won't come back. I tried to make her stay. I'm sorry. It's my fault she won't stay," he says, tears leaking from his eyes. "And she'll never let you come be with her. Because she loves you," he adds on a whisper.

He wipes his tears roughly, looking away from me.

"None of this is your fault, kid," I say quietly, turning to leave. "None of it."

I feel like all the wind has been sucked out of me, and I almost function on autopilot. I don't even remember the drive home. Dad's gone, probably being glued back together by my uncles.

It seems Dad left behind two bottles of whiskey, so I grab one, taking it to the kitchen and pouring a glass. Restless and agitated, I take one sip, staring at the fucking pie crusts lined up on the counter.

She was going to make pie for Bella today to celebrate Isa.

Then we were going to go the vineyard and spend the day with Raya and Kade.

Tomorrow, after she got off from work, we were going to go with Britt to see this LARP thing she's gotten into.

We had plans that went on for months. Plans that we made with the certainty we had all the time in the world.

The glass flies from my hand and shatters against the wall. The fragmented pieces drop and clatter as I grip the edge of the island, not even acknowledging the sound of my door opening as I rake everything off the island at once, sending shit flying to the floor.

My chest vibrates, something hot and wet hits my cheeks, and I lose it, grabbing the fucking pie crusts and throwing them against the wall, watching all the crumbs scatter. Anything I can get my hands on is thrown, broken, or just strangled in my grip.

When there's nothing left to throw and I'm panting heavily, I slowly slide to the floor, leaning back against the wall and sitting down on broken shards, uncaring if I get cut or not. Might as fucking well bleed, too.

My eyes swing up, feeling someone's gaze on me, and I see all four of my cousins watching me silently.

Kode lifts a bottle of what looks like tequila, and asks, "Do you want to throw it or drink it?"

I reach for it, and he steps over the mess, crunching on things as he hands it to me. Still sitting in the floor, I throw the damn thing as hard as I can, hearing it shatter without seeing the mess.

Dane blows out a breath as he lowers himself to a half beaten chair, elbows on his knees.

"What can we do?" he asks seriously.

I laugh humorlessly, my head thudding the wall as I stare at nothing at all.

"Apparently, there's nothing to fucking do but get over it. At least that's what everyone keeps saying."

They say nothing else. They just stand there, giving me my space, being there.

As the weight settles on my chest, making every breath painful to take, I close my eyes, trying to shut it all out. I never realized anything could hurt like this.

Chapter 37

Salem

When I hear the door of the cabin open and close, I wipe my eyes quickly then pretend as though washing dishes is my favorite thing in the world to do, as Tyler lumbers toward me—all six-foot-eight of him.

"Okay, I've given you three days of moping," he says as he crowds me in the small kitchen, crossing his massive arms over his chest as he levels me with a glare. "Now it's time to talk."

"I don't want to talk about it, Tyler. And you can stand there and hover over me like a beast all you want to, but you stopped being intimidating when I caught you twirling in a pink tutu."

"I was eight," he points out dryly.

"Which means I've had many years of not feeling intimidated by you," I say with a flat smile, then turn my attention back to the dishes, scrubbing them much harder than necessary.

"I talked to Sean," he finally says, causing my hands to pause the excess scrubbing for only a brief second. "He told me what was going on. He also said that *Maverick*—we'll discuss that stupid name later—would follow you. So why are you here, hiding out, instead of with him?"

I drop the plate into the sink, giving up the pretense of giving a damn about the dishes, and turn to face him.

"Would you have let Monica follow you all over the continental U.S. back when you had to be there for me?" I ask him seriously.

His lips thin, but he doesn't answer.

"Didn't think so." I unplug the sink, letting the water drain, and start drying off my hands. "He has so many friends, and they're like this amazing, interlocked, support system-slash-family. They love him, and he loves them. Just like he loves his home."

"But if he's willing to be with you despite all that—"

"Do you have any idea how much I resent Mom every time I'm forced to start a new life? I still have seven more years left of this, Tyler," I say to him, clearing my throat. "Do you think he's still going to care about me in seven years after giving up control of his life to follow me from place to place?"

His look softens. "Salem, I can help with Sean."

"No, you can't. You have your own family—Monica and *four* kids of your own. They need you. Connor has an opportunity like you had—something so rare. You almost lost your shot by taking care of me. I can't let him lose his shot. So it's me. Just stop talking now."

I turn to walk away, and he follows me. "He can go see his friends any time he wants. It's not like you're going to lock him away," he argues.

I whirl around. "How often do we miss something important in each other's lives because of the physical distance always between us when I'm not in Georgia?" I ask him.

His lips thin again. That's what happens when he knows how right I am about something.

"Right now, he's a part of *everything* important. Little by little, he'd miss so much, and eventually, he'd hate me for taking those moments away from him. I can push through this. I can find a way to stitch myself together and aim for passable. Maverick has a huge group of friends and family. This way, he's only giving up two people he cares about—me and Sean. The other way, he's losing a small village. Which one do you think will hurt him worse in the long run?"

I can tell he's going to hug me. If he hugs me, I'll fall apart in his arms, turning myself over to be held up. I'll start crying again. And I'm pretty sick of crying.

"Look, the point is, Maverick Sterling will be just fine. He has plenty of people and love surrounding him. In a year or less, he'll look back on me as a fun fling."

I'm proud my voice stays even, despite the pain lancing my heart with the fear of the truth behind those words.

"What about you, Salem?" Tyler finally asks. "What happens in a year when you realize this was something you shouldn't have given up? Because I can tell by looking at you that you're barely holding it together, and I know how strong you normally are."

I force a smile, picking up a towel from the clean laundry, moving toward the bathroom to have an excuse to get away from him.

"You know me, Tyler. I have just enough cold in me to weather the storms. Eventually, I'll be just fine."

I turn and walk away when I see how sad his eyes look, and I lock myself in the bathroom, quickly turning on the shower and stepping under the spray. I can trick myself into thinking I'm not crying if there's water spraying on my face.

I can trick myself into thinking I'll be okay, so long as I know Maverick really will be.

A frustrated sound slips free before I can stop it, and I slam the side of my fist against the shower wall as my forehead falls forward, resting there as my body shakes with silent sobs.

One day, I can trick myself into believing I didn't blink wrong.

Chapter 38

MAVERICK

CORBIN: Silk tonight? Maybe getting out will do you some good.

ME: Maybe another time.

When my phone chimes again, I start to ignore it. But immediately there's another text, which probably means more than one Sterling is messaging me. They won't leave me the hell alone.

CORBIN: Fucking fine. I'll come over there. And you can kiss my ass if you even think about telling me not to. See you in two hours.

Running a hand through my hair, I groan, but don't bother texting back as I read the next one.

KODE: I'll be over later with beer unless you feel like going to Silk tonight.

Another text comes through. Even Britt feels sorry for me, and reaches out in her own bizarre, random way.

BRITT: Want to go elf ear shopping with me?

ME: Since I didn't even know that was a thing, I think I'll pass.

DANE: It's been a week, Mav. You need to get out. The world needs your pretty face.

I don't mind the texts. I don't care about going out. Currently, I'm evenly disinterested in anything going on around me.

This is what I like to think of as the calm before the storm. Because the storm is about to come. There's only one thing bugging the shit out of me.

I ignore the phone the next time as I toss it onto the counter and abandon it. Funny how I've spent most of my life avoiding being alone any way I could, only to find myself wishing my friends would give me one second alone.

Now I know why they wanted to punch me so much when I wouldn't just let them be while they were hurting.

You want to fix it when someone you care about is hurting.

You can't just let it be broken.

Sort of like I feel when I walk into my den and find my father lazily lounging on the couch, trying to grow a terrible beard.

"She won't even take my calls," he says, echoing my own issues. Salem, according to Sean, is *unplugged*.

"I think this is the universe punishing me for how I did your mom. Your mom was so amazing, but she was never *the* one the way I thought Kelly was. I'm not sure why I ever stopped living my simple life when I knew damn well how complicated women are," he goes on, repeating everything I've heard him saying all week.

He sighs heavily, his head tipping to the side as though he's thinking about something as I take a seat by him.

"I never even wanted this. Never wanted to settle down for just one woman," he prattles on. "I never thought I could be *that* guy. But for Kelly, I had no choice. I can't even look at another woman in that way. Hell, sometimes I think she put me under a spell."

I crack my knuckles, just listening.

"Those women are spiking us with some sort of love potion. That's the only explanation," he groans. "We were wolves, Maverick. Wild, untamable wolves. They used their sorcery to tame us and make us their pups so we'd stop howling at the moon. Then she kicked me away for no reason."

I say nothing. Per the usual. This week has been all about hearing him moan, and whine, and bitch.

Sighing heavily, he goes on. "I'll never love anyone like I love her. Makes me think of that song that says, 'You can tell me when it's over if the high was worth the pain.'"

At least he's sober. I want this to hurt.

My fist collides with the side of his cheek so hard that he flops off the couch, crashing onto the floor and groaning.

"What the hell was that for?" he asks as I calmly stand up, wringing out my throbbing hand.

He cups his jaw, blinking hard as he tries to snap out of his daze.

"For a solid fucking week, I've heard you moan and whine over Kelly, when she's right down the road at *your* fucking house. And you still haven't even *tried* to talk her into staying," I state conversationally.

He's lying on the ground, staring up at me like I've lost my mind. When I take a step toward him, he scrambles backwards like he's worried I'm about to pummel him.

My hand shoots out, and he winces, but I just leave it hovering, offering him a hand up. He stares at it dubiously before warily putting his hand in mine.

I help him up to his feet, and when I rear my fist back again, he throws his hands up in front of his face and brings his leg up to cover his middle while shouting, "Whoa! Whoa! *Whoa!*" He makes a karate-chop slicing motion with one hand, all while balancing on one foot. *"What* the *hell* is going on here?!" he demands. "Why are you hitting me?!"

I glare at him as I slowly lower my fist.

"She left me, remember?!" he snaps, cautiously lowering his hands while I'm not coiled for the strike.

"Yeah, and you're going on about how much you love her, yet you aren't doing shit about it. Instead, you're sitting around quoting Taylor Swift lyrics. Kelly could have already fucking left if she really wanted to. She's still here, riding out that stupid two week timetable. Salem left immediately because she was terrified she wouldn't leave if I had two weeks to try to talk her into staying with me. On some level, Kelly is obviously *hoping* you'll stop her. Stop being such a pussy and go be a fucking man."

I gesture toward him as I take a couple of steps back.

He scowls as he straightens his wrinkled shirt. Or tries to. There are just too many wrinkles.

"I mean it!" I yell, causing him to jump a little as he gawks at me. "Get a shower, put on clean clothes, and go over there. *Do* something." I turn and walk out, calling over my shoulder, "And shave off that shitty excuse for a beard!"

I slam my bedroom door behind me like an errant child before I drop to the bed, staring up at the ceiling. A stupid stress ball is by me, and I pick it up, pumping the fuck out of it several times.

For the record, stress balls haven't ever done shit to get rid of my stress. But it does keep my hand too busy to go punch more sense into my father. At least he has the option of trying.

After at least an hour of staring at my ceiling, I slowly sit up, staring across from me at the damn Top Gun stuff and various other random things Salem bought for me. Any time she sees anything corny or fun I might like, she buys it; it's like she can't help herself.

Well, that should obviously be past tense now.

Pushing off from the bed, I start to rip that shit out of there and stomp on it, but stop just short, blowing out a heavy breath.

Then I turn and stalk out the door, passing my father as he finishes buttoning up his shirt in the guest bedroom, looking freshly showered and shaved. "Where are you going?" he yells after me.

"To take my own fucking advice," I answer without looking back.

Right after I shove a hot coal into an ice heart.

✸✸✸

"Sean Wilson Young! You keep that cat out of my room," Kelly yells, looking completely frazzled in her robe, her hair sticking up everywhere, as she glares into the living room, unaware of the fact I've come into the house.

A familiar feline rebel cry sounds from somewhere in the house, and I note with some satisfaction that curtains are on the ground, shredded, along with a lot of furniture.

Apparently, Bananas is vibing off Sean and making the lives of everyone else hell to show her loyalty.

I've never seen Kelly less than pristine until now. It looks like she hasn't slept for a week.

Sean doesn't notice me either from this angle as he lazily changes the channel. His backpack is strewn across the floor, along with all its contents. It looks like he doesn't really give a shit about anything.

"I hope she pisses on all your stuff," Sean says flippantly, causing my lips to twitch.

"Sean!" she says on a gasp. "What has gotten into you?"

He shrugs. "I'm not letting you use Salem against me anymore. You want me with you, then I'm going to be with you. You want me to be like you? Fine. Here's what it looks like. And you lose the power you have over my sister in return."

Kelly just stares sadly at him, her arms hugging her middle.

"That's not what this is, son. I—"

"I don't have to listen to you. Like I said, I don't have to do anything, because you can't use Salem against me anymore." He flips her off, never even glancing away from the TV.

"You're too young for that. That's disrespectful!" Kelly hisses, then screams and ducks when Bananas flies in from out of nowhere. Pretty sure Bananas just bitch-slapped her across the face, but from this angle, it's hard to be certain.

"There's no reason to behave, Mom," Sean drawls, never acknowledging the hissing pussy as she struts away, feeling triumphant after eliciting Kelly's scream. "You get the me you've always tried to make me be. Bless your heart," he adds, exaggerating his accent at the end as Bananas scurries sideways down the hall to go line up a new attack—most likely.

I don't know if Kelly wants to cry or scream, but she ends up panicking for a different reason when she turns her head toward me. Her eyes widen and a bloodcurdling scream roars out of her as she clutches her heart.

Sean just smirks when he sees me, apparently having been more aware of my presence than I realized.

"Maverick," Kelly says a little breathlessly, trying to recover. "What are you doing here?"

She tries to smooth her hair. The bags under her eyes look to have tripled since I last saw her.

Either Sean's been giving her a lot of hell, or she's losing sleep over Dad.

Or both.

Or…Bananas.

"Let's talk. Now," I tell her firmly, not wanting to do this in front of Sean.

She clutches at her necklace for a second — the only jewelry aside from the wedding bands she's wearing — and I only glimpse it enough to know it's the necklace Dad bought her for her birthday.

Clearing her throat, she turns and guides me down the long, winding hallways until we reach Dad's office. I close the doors behind me and lean against them.

"I'm not sure what's left to say, Maverick. Salem isn't answering her phone because she's *unplugged*. I'm sure she'll—"

"Just leave him here. I'm only asking one more time for you to think about what's best for Sean, and leave him here." My words are calm, more exhausted than angry.

Her lips tense and her hand falls away from the necklace.

"My mother was an heiress," she says randomly.

"Good for her?" I'm not sure what she wants me to say to that.

"You think I'm a horrible mother, and I understand that. But I'm really not, Maverick. I want my kids to walk through life with their eyes open. I do care more for my children than you'll ever know. I've done things in my quest to keep them from being naïve that I really don't even want to think about."

"Like fucking your daughter's boyfriend? By the way, I wouldn't touch you even if you were begging."

She smiles cruelly. "I'm not trying to touch you, Maverick, and I'm aware that course of action wouldn't work on you. I'm good at reading men. That was not my finest moment, but Salem never got duped into falling in love with some user again."

I roll my eyes. "So the ends justify the means? Whatever. How do you justify this? You know they're rooted to this place."

"An unforeseen inconvenience," she states blandly. "But love, as I'm sure you know, given the fact your mother and father fell out of love as well, is fleeting. In time, you and Salem won't even—"

"I'd stop there. I tend to break shit when I'm upset, and I'd rather not start throwing shit in here," I tell her, holding my hand up.

She swallows then takes a step back, causing me to roll my eyes. I didn't threaten *her*.

"My methods have a purpose. My mother was an heiress, but she went against her family and married a man for love. Her family, in turn, cut her off, because the boy she married was a conman who'd already swindled my grandfather for so much money that it was embarrassing."

She clutches the necklace again, as though she's drawing strength from it.

"Obviously he divorced her after the first year of marriage when he realized she wasn't getting a penny of her family's money. So much for love. My mother went back to her parents, but was turned away. I was born five years later to a woman who had no clue who the father might even be. I grew up watching her take twenty dollars at a time from men who enjoyed her beautiful body, then dealt with the occasional man who didn't care if I was a child."

I grimace as she lowers herself to the chair behind Dad's desk, staring blankly at the surface of it.

"Beauty got her paid. And when I was sixteen, she decided I needed to help pay for things the same way." Her misty eyes meet mine. "My grandmother didn't know about me until shortly after that, when I went to her out of desperation. She took me in, gave me a necklace so much like this one."

She pauses, glancing down at the necklace, turning it over to reveal an inscription I can't read from here.

"Pretty Girl," she says with a tight smile. "Pretty Girl was all I was. Just like my mother. I just decided not to be poor while I faced a cold world. That necklace was the signal of a new era. I was never hurt again."

She clasps her hands together, and I snort derisively.

"Terrible story, really. I'm not trying to be insensitive, but you're no better than your mother," I state flatly, causing her eyes to narrow. "You fell in love with something that couldn't love you back—money. And you expected your daughter to do exactly the same. And because of you, she's hurting. Just like your son. All because you're too *scared* to fucking be human. You didn't just turn into your mother; you also turned into the man who broke your mother's heart."

She stares at me blankly for a second, so I impart one more bit of wisdom.

"Little advice: If you want your kids to love you, stop teaching them that love doesn't exist."

When a tear drops from her eye, I turn and open the door, sucking in a surprised breath when I see my father leaning against the doorframe, tears glistening in his own eyes after apparently having listened in.

He walks by me, eyes meeting mine briefly, before he looks over at her. Kelly is smoothing her hair down, tears leaking more fervently now as she tries to look anywhere but at him.

"Ian, you shouldn't—"

"Shut up," he tells her, a tight smile to his lips. "You got your turn to talk. Now it's mine. And you're going to fucking listen to everything I have to say."

I shut the door behind me, jogging out of the room, and whistle toward Sean. "Put your shoes on. We're going to do something that doesn't involve sitting inside."

Chapter 39

MAVERICK

It takes me a second to get out of bed the next morning.

I walk through the house, checking the guest room and the den, not finding any sign of Dad ever coming back last night. Hoping against all hope, I call Sean's phone, and he answers immediately.

"We're staying!" he shouts in my ear, forcing me to jerk my head back. But then a slow grin curves my lips before an immediate scowl follows.

"Sean, so help me, if you're just fucking with me to be an ass—"

"I'm not! Mom told me this morning to call Salem. We're staying! Your dad has been here all night, and they've been in their bedroom. I don't even care how gross that is right now, because we're *staying*!"

A full body sigh falls out of me. "So you called Salem?"

He grows quiet. Too quiet.

"Sean?"

"I called her," he says on a heavy exhale.

"And? Sean, stop leaving me in suspense."

"She's coming back next week. Said she'd call Rye and Brin."

My knees try to collapse as relief floods through me, but then an iciness slithers over me.

"Why next week? Why wouldn't she come back right now?"

Silence stretches for an uncomfortable, daunting minute.

"She said she needed some time to prepare herself to be back in Sterling Shore. Tyler said she's not going to risk getting too close to anyone this time. He said she's planning to keep her distance, and that I needed to call him if she looks like she needs a break."

"Fuck that," I say without thinking, constantly forgetting he's a child and not an actual adult. "Why? That makes—"

"She doesn't trust Mom. She thinks it's just a matter of time before we have to go through all this again. Tyler said she can't do it twice."

"I'll come over and you can call and get me on the phone with her."

He snorts. "Tyler will kick my butt. Besides, he said he wasn't telling her anything else unless it was an emergency because he was already breaking the rules by telling her that. But he thought that'd be good news. Until he thought it through."

I groan, running a hand through my hair.

"I need her address. If I can't get her on the phone, then I'll just go there myself," I tell him.

"Okay, but it's your funeral. Tyler won't let you near her if he thinks she's going to cry. He hates it when she cries. You know how Salem protects me? Tyler protects her."

"Tyler can kiss my ass; I'm going to see her."

I can feel him grinning.

"Why is that funny?" I ask him.

"No reason. I'll send you the address. Book a flight to Atlanta."

"Atlanta. Got it."

As soon as I hang up, I go straight to doing that.

"So, we're going south?" Corbin asks, scaring the unholy hell out of me.

He and Ruby are just lingering in the middle of the living room, staring at me. Not creepy at all.

"*We're* not. *I* am," I say dismissively.

"We're totally going," Ruby says, grinning.

"We're totally not," I argue.

Chapter 40

MAVERICK

"We need to stop and grab me something from somewhere that doesn't use nut ingredients, because I'm starving," Ruby says, leaning over my shoulder as I finish booking a rental car.

"Not sure why we would take someone with a nut allergy on a road trip," I say dully.

She playfully slaps my shoulder. "Because you and Corbin on the road together without any supervision is an accident just waiting to happen. And I sort of love him and want him back in one piece."

You know all those times when Salem said, *"Tyler lives just outside of Atlanta."*

Apparently, in the South, a two-hour drive is 'just outside of *insert major city here.*'

Corbin promises Ruby food, as we finally get in the rental car and try not to get lost in Atlanta. Which is not very fucking easy to do.

By the time we're out of Atlanta and cruising down the backroads, Ruby's stomach is talking ninety to nothing. But it's like there's *nothing* she can eat at the last three places we've stopped, since she can't eat there if they even serve peanut products because of possible cross-contamination. She's terrified of dying and all that.

Corbin is driving, I'm sitting shotgun, and Ruby and her talking stomach are in the back.

As we're driving, we start seeing little signs on the road, advertising — *wait for it* — nuts.

Nuts galore.

"Chocolate-covered peanuts, two miles ahead," Ruby says stoically.

Three miles later, another sign.

"Boiled Peanuts," Ruby says, her tone more nervous this time.

As you can imagine, she pretty much just starts reading every sign we pass with her tone growing increasingly horrified.

"Fried peanuts."

Another sign.

"Cajun peanuts."

Another sign.

"Roasted Peanuts. For fuck's sake, this is hell."

Corbin tries not to laugh, especially when her stomach growls again.

"Salem better have freaking food I can cook," Ruby finally says, and my humor dies at just the mention of her name.

"Or pie. Please let her have one of her pies," Ruby goes on wistfully, only adding to my thoughts.

Corbin cursing and slamming on the brakes is the only thing that jolts me out of my reverie when we're just ten miles out from our destination.

"What the hell is going on?" he demands, glaring at the three cars stopped in front of us for no seemingly good reason.

Corbin lays on the horn, and the guy in front of us gets out of his truck, rolling his sleeves up like he's about to kill someone.

"Sorry," Corbin says out the window uncomfortably to the beast who flips us off, calls us something that probably isn't too charitable, and gets back into his truck, slamming the door.

"What the hell is going on? And why was he pissed at me and not the ass out front?"

Slowly, my lips curve into a knowing grin when I look in the mirror to see a hearse leading a convoy, and on some level, I know it's really morbid to smile. "Funeral procession," I say as though it should be obvious.

"Why are we stopping for a funeral procession on the other side of the road?" Ruby asks as the cars continue to pass us, and we continue to sit still.

"Because it's a show of respect in the South," I say, my grin only growing as I see a small piece of Salem from the inside. "Can't go until the last car with lights on passes."

"Almost all cars have lights on during the day," Ruby says, sounding like a distant echo of my own conversation with Salem.

When we get to start moving again, it doesn't take us long to reach the private dirt drive with a cow pasture on either side and a gate right in the middle that is locked with chains.

I'm too determined to let that stop me, so I climb over it, ignoring Ruby when she hisses my name.

"Damn it, Mav. We can't just go in there," Corbin whisper-yells, as though the cows are going to overhear and charge him.

"This is the only way to get to that cabin," I argue, turning around to face him.

Cursing, he hauls himself up and over the gate. "I'm not going," Ruby says hesitantly. "I see the barrel of a shotgun in our immediate future."

"Don't be so dramatic," I groan, not willing to leave her here by herself.

Corbin either, by the looks of it, though he seems torn about me going off into the woods by myself.

"Dramatic? The fifty *No Trespassing* signs I can see from here are not an invitation, Mav. No thank you. I'll stay locked up in the car or some—"

She stops talking, because I swear—I'm not making this up— we suddenly hear the faint but distinct sound of banjos playing in the distance. Cursing, she immediately climbs over the gate and walks in her wedge heels quickly toward us, glaring at us both while we try not to grin.

"I still see a shotgun in our future," she grumbles as she walks right through us, driving forward.

"No worries," I tell her, lifting my phone. "I'll just play some twerking music if we run up on any shotgun wielding people. They'll either think we're insane when Corbin shakes his money maker, or they'll be distracted long enough for you and me to make a run for it."

Corbin flips me off as Ruby laughs quietly to herself. She stops abruptly and spins on her heel.

"One of you go first. There could be snakes," she says with a shudder as we reach the part of the dirt drive that cuts through the woods.

"You're thinking of Florida," Corbin says dismissively, taking over the lead spot.

"No. Georgia has snakes, too. Just not pythons. At least I hope there aren't pythons." She shrieks when a stick touches her toe through her shoe. "I sort of hate sounding like a city girl right now," Ruby groans. Then looks at me. "Are there snakes in Georgia?"

I shake my head. "I have no idea."

We seem to walk forever, all the while hearing the rustling of bushes. And *slap*. The chirping of birds. *Slap*. The mooing from the two pastures. *Slap*.

"Those cows aren't going to suddenly ram us or anything, are they?" Ruby asks, eyeing a group of them loitering at the edge of the barbed wire fence, heads precariously stuck through the fence as they eat the grass on the other side.

Slap.

"They can't get through the fence," Corbin says soothingly.

Slap.

"If they can't get through the fence—" *Slap.* "—then why have we passed three piles of cow shit?" she asks reasonably.

Slap.

"I'm more worried about the snakes than the cows," I say as I step over cow shit pile number four.

Slap.

"Snakes!" she hisses. "See! I told you they were in Georgia."

Slap.

"Really, Mav?" Corbin growls.

Slap.

Smiling to myself, needing to keep my mind off the knot of dread in my stomach that has me worrying about Salem's reaction, I keep walking.

"I promise this is the last time I whine, because I'm getting on my own nerves, but—" *Slap.* "—the next time we decide to go hiking in the woods—" *Slap.* "—someone grab four cans of bug spray." *Slap.*

"It's hardly hiking if you're walking a trail—"

My words cut off when we round the bend and there's a very, *very* tall guy with a shotgun over his shoulders, his arms wrapped around it like he's just hanging out. You know, with a dangerous, likely loaded weapon. In the middle of nowhere. On a trail in the woods.

Not ominous at all.

"Y'all must've missed the *No Trespassing* signs," he says, his Southern drawl a hair richer than Salem's.

Ruby swallows audibly from beside me. "I hate to say I told you so," she whisper-yells, "but I fucking told you so."

This guy is at least six-eight, has shoulders a little broader than mine, and his hands are fucking huge. He doesn't need the shotgun. He could strangle two of us at a time.

Dark eyes, a mixture of caramel and chocolate skin, and a devil-fuck-with-me smirk, he stands there like he has all the time in the world.

I think we trespassed on the wrong property.

"We're actually looking for someone," I finally say.

He's at least not aiming the gun at us.

Why does he look so familiar?

"I didn't figure you were out taking in the sights," he deadpans.

Slap.

Ruby curses a particularly pervy bug that gets inside her cleavage, and she slaps her chest for a minute. Not even that has him taking his eyes off me and Corbin.

"Salem Wright is supposed to be up here somewhere," I decide to say.

His eyebrows go up a little, and an easy grin transforms his features. "Ah, you're here for Salem. Why didn't you just take the driveway instead of coming up through here?" he asks me.

Ruby levels me with a glare as Corbin chokes back a laugh. I'm still trying to figure out where I've seen this guy before.

"I thought this was the driveway," I state flatly.

"About a mile down is the driveway. Takes you right up to Salem's cabin. This is just the road to the barn. And private property."

He gestures toward what looks like some sort of ATV with four seats.

"I just came out to check on my cows, and heard a lot of yappin' and slappin'," he adds, eyebrow arching at us.

Slap.

Ruby shrieks a little as she shakes her shirt, trying to evict the newest invader.

"And by the way," he drawls, "we have a lot of snakes in Georgia."

Ruby is probably going to kill me before I even make it to Salem. Or she'll kill Corbin. Maybe he'll die first and I'll have the chance to make a run for it.

"I'm assuming one of you is Maverick," he says, gesturing between Corbin and me, causing my brow to furrow. "Sean told me about you."

"You know Sean?" I ask, confused.

"Of course he does. We passed like twenty houses in an hour. It's one of those towns where everyone knows everybody and everything about them," Ruby says distractedly, stomping on another bug that is going after her. "I think they're after my lotion or something. Vicious little ingrates!"

The guy's eyes are still bouncing between us, completely unconcerned with Ruby.

"I know Sean," he says vaguely, his smile spreading wider.

Seriously, why is he familiar? Even that grin is familiar. And no, I don't mean that in a creepy way.

"I'm Maverick," I say, proffering my hand in greeting.

He glances down at it, still holding onto his shotgun, then grins as his massive hand swallows mine. I'm not a small guy. I'm over six feet. I'm usually considered tall and intimidating.

This guy makes me feel like a dainty little bitch.

"I'm Tyler Murphy," he finally says, still grinning.

Corbin chokes, Ruby makes a strangled sound, and my eyes try to bug out. Well, now I know why he's familiar.

"*The* Tyler Murphy?" Corbin groans. "We're trespassing on an NBA legend's land. How do you get us into these fucked up situations?" Corbin accuses, glaring at me.

My eyes narrow as I think back to Salem and her very vague ways. *Basketball.* She mentioned her brother played basketball and she always conveniently never referred to his last name.

"You're Salem's brother," I finally say, and he grins at me again. "Tyler. The one who lives *just outside of Atlanta*. And plays office basketball."

I scowl. He chuckles.

"Salem's mother hooked up with my NBA playing daddy right before his career took off. Salem hates sports, so she doesn't name drop for me or Connor if she knows someone's a fan of that sport.

Otherwise, they'll chat her ear off about things she finds utterly and miserably boring."

This is why that little pecker gnat—*yeah, I've picked up some lingo during our stops on the quest for nut-free food for Ruby*—laughed when I insinuated I'd kick Tyler's ass if he tried to stop me from seeing Salem.

Obviously that plan needs tweaking now that I realize he could very easily break me. I prefer to have a fair chance in a fight.

"Will you please take me to her? I need to see her." I go for sincerity.

His humor dies, and he frowns a little. "She's my only sister."

I nod in understanding.

"Mom is completely unreliable. Just because she's staying now, doesn't mean—"

"I just want to see her," I interrupt. Yeah, just interrupted a basketball legend. I'm in a mood.

He studies me for a moment. "Give me one good reason to," he finally says.

I start to tell him how I feel about his sister, and then decide I'm not ready to tell him before I even tell her.

So I go with my failsafe. My constant.

Picking up my phone, I turn on the song that Corbin wants destroyed. *"Shake that ass, bitch, let me see what you got."*

The words start blaring, and Ruby snorts before coughing. Tyler looks utterly confused as I hold the phone up, wiggling it at Corbin, as if to say, *"Well, then, get on with it."* Though I don't risk looking over there and being burned by the furious fire that's surely blazing from his eyes.

"You're fucking kidding me," Corbin snaps.

"Rules are rules," I remind him, once again wiggling my phone, prompting him to move this party along.

Even as he plots my murder aloud and maybe whimpers, he tosses his shirt to Ruby, squats, puts his hands on his thighs, and he fucking twerks like his life depends on it.

Right in front of a legend.

Tyler is torn between being fascinated and horrified, unable to look away from the train wreck that is my cousin shaking his ass to the beat.

"Reason number one," I say in answer to Tyler's question, "we're really fucking entertaining."

Chapter 41

Salem

I'm going to kill Tyler. I wish Maverick hadn't made *pie moment* a sweet thing, because before Maverick, *this* would be a pie moment.

I can hear that obnoxious Gator he drives around from here.

Wrapping up in a towel, I step out of the tub, abandoning my soothing bath.

I know damn well he's trying to piss me off if he's already driving back again today, after I already told him ten times that I just need some quiet time. The entire point of me unplugging is to get some quiet time.

And all he does is try to make me talk about Maverick.

I need distance from all those precious moments with Maverick. Not constant reminders.

Especially now that I have to return to Sterling Shore and somehow live around Maverick without being with Maverick.

If I didn't know better, I'd say my mother did all this just to break us up, knowing I'd be unable to go through it all again.

When I swing open the door, ready to ream my brother a new asshole, I almost trip. Almost lose the towel. And almost, *almost* go a little weak in the knees.

Because there're suddenly two arms around me, the spicy scent surrounding me with a familiar brand of heartache, and the lips on mine are devastatingly memorable.

I'm too surprised that Maverick is kissing me to remember I'm not supposed to be kissing him back. Or letting him walk me up against a wall. Or allowing him to slide his hands under the towel to grab me and pull me closer.

Not by my vagina either.

When I finally do remember, I shove at his chest, and he breaks the kiss, his forehead pressing against mine.

"Come home with me," he says softly. And my heart decides it's time to break all over again.

"You know I can't," I say with my eyes closed, my hand clinging to his shirt.

"You have to be where Sean is, and Sean is in Sterling Shore," Maverick says, his lips curving in a smirk that tells me he thinks he has it all figured out.

"I'll be coming back soon, but not with you. Mom could—"

He kisses me again, shutting me up, and for a very long second, I kiss him back. However, I find it in me to once again put space between us, though it's just a tiny amount he'll allow.

"As long as you're back, then I'll have a chance to fix all this. Find a way to make sure it's permanent. If I do that, there will be no reason to stay away, right?" he asks, his eyes intensely focused on mine.

"There's no way to make it permanent," I say on a sigh, wishing he wasn't pouring a little salt on fresh wounds.

Him being here, so close, is keeping the ache out of my chest, confusing my heart, tricking her into believing the world is right again. My heart doesn't have a brain; my brain doesn't have a heart; and the two of them refuse to be partners.

I haven't slept worth a damn in over a week since I left him behind to lick my wounds.

Now he's here. I'm exhausted. And all I can think about is wrapping up in his arms and sleeping peacefully for hours.

"I'll figure it out," he says with a confident grin that doesn't reach his eyes. "Until then, I don't want you avoiding me just to keep from getting close."

"Maverick, I barely walked away last time. If we keep going, then when Mom decides to—"

"I get it," he interrupts softly, his hand cupping the side of my cheek, his body still taking up too much of my personal space. But I don't have it in me to push him any farther away when my entire body is comforted by his mere presence. "But we can be friends until I figure it out—no avoiding me, Salem. That's all I'm saying."

I cock an eyebrow, and his grin grows.

"We suck at being *just* friends," I remind him.

"We can be friends when we know it's only temporary—until I figure out a way to make it okay for more."

I'm already struggling to be this close to him. How the hell am I going to be his friend? It'll be like having him all over again, minus the sex. Because Maverick became my friend. My best friend.

The friendship is what made me freaking fall in love with him, because it made us *real*.

Deciding not to unload all that, I keep my inner thoughts locked up. "You came all the way to Georgia to demand that we be friends?" I ask dubiously.

His smile falters. "No. I came all the way to Georgia because I needed to see you."

I'm kissing him before I can stop myself, and his hand goes into my hair, holding my head right where he wants it. I barely manage to shove at his chest this time, and he almost doesn't back away.

We're both a little breathy when we finally do put a few inches between our mouths.

"Already we suck at being just friends," I deadpan, causing a rumble of laughter to vibrate through his chest.

"I'll do better," he says on a long exhale, and then he takes a step back, woodenly, as though it's causing him physical harm to do so. I smile sympathetically, because it sucks.

I don't want to have to avoid him, but I sure as hell can't seek him out. Limited time together has to be a main priority.

It'll be like weaning myself off my version of crack. My crack being Maverick Sterling, in case that isn't glaringly obvious by now.

"Sorry to break this up," comes a voice I recognize, though it startles me just before Ruby pokes her head in, "but I'm starving, and I really have to pee."

Confused as hell to see her here, I gesture toward the open door, then remember I'm still in a towel when Corbin walks in.

I clutch the towel tighter as Corbin averts his eyes, looking at anything but me, as Ruby shuts herself in the bathroom. Tyler comes in last, smirking at me, and I glare at him, ready to kick his ass for not giving me any warning.

I'd probably need a stepladder to kick his ass.

"You might have mentioned your brother was an NBA legend," Corbin says with his back turned, sounding as though he's pouting.

"I never do to basketball fans—which you all are. Why are you so red?" I ask, noticing it looks like he's blushing.

Maverick grins, the sight doing strange and unexplainable things to my insides, as he cocks a hip against the counter I'm leaning against, once again invading my space as though we're two magnets pulling toward each other.

"He had to twerk in front of *Tyler Murphy*," Maverick says.

Pretty sure the tips of Corbin's ears are glowing red through his hair.

"Sean said your new people were weird," Tyler says through an amused smile. "He just never said how weird."

Corbin glares at Maverick just as Ruby comes out.

"Our flight doesn't leave until tomorrow. We got you a ticket, by the way," she tells me matter-of-factly, which has Tyler laughing at me with his eyes. "So what can we eat? And…where's the TV?"

"There's no TV out here, and there's only one other bedroom," I say quickly.

"I'll sleep on the couch," Maverick offers.

"Or you guys can come up to the main house," Tyler offers.

"Salem won't stay in this cabin with just me, and I don't want to stay in a different house with her just right here," Maverick says conversationally, as though he's not plucking at the heartstrings or anything.

Tyler turns away, a small smile on his lips.

"We have some board games here if you don't want to trek to the house. My wife and kids won't mind the company, though. She expects me to be out here bothering the hell out Salem, but she'd be thrilled to have everyone up."

I spent all day yesterday with Monica and the twins, and the other two. All are under the age of five.

"I'm good down here."

My brother refrains from grinning, understanding.

"Oh! Monopoly!" Corbin says, pulling out the board and causing me to smile. Again, before Maverick, Monopoly was just a game.

Maverick cuts a grin at me, letting me know he's thinking the same thing. Those moments I so eagerly and desperately collected now hang around like little haunting thought bubbles all the time.

"I haven't played this in forever," Corbin goes on, putting the game down on the dining room table.

Tyler pulls up an extra chair, and he sits down with the guys. Ruby works on making a large bowl of salad with the ingredients I fortunately have on hand. I go put on clothes so that I'm not standing in a roomful of people in nothing but a towel.

When I emerge, I tell Ruby, "Burgers are in there too. Tyler keeps all his grilling food in this fridge. Normally this is his man cave."

I feel Maverick's eyes on me, but I don't cave to the pressure of turning and looking at him.

Ruby gets excited, and she cooks and grills while the rest of us play the game. Of course, after a few hours, it's just down to Corbin and Maverick and the game is getting heated.

Tyler watches them with rapt attention, fascinated to the core as Maverick and Corbin talk shit to each other and start comparing the game to real life and the properties one got over the other and…I don't know. I tune most of it out.

I'm busy pretending that hearing his voice over and over isn't sending my heart into a constant frenzy.

The tears aren't even threatening to emerge. Why? Because I really am sinking into a blanket of false reconciliation. My heart can't understand that we're not back together.

Confusing.

Annoying.

Whiny, I sound. And done.

Standing, I snatch the board up before they get into a fight, and they both groan at me as I start packing it away.

"Can't play nice, can't play at all," Ruby says, drinking the wine straight from the bottle as she lounges on the couch, watching with a grin.

"I need to get back up to Monica. I guess, since you're leaving tomorrow, I'll come visit you soon," Tyler says, smiling as he reaches out and hugs me.

I cling to him a little, soaking in his warmth and comfort. Twenty-five, and I still run to my big brother when shit turns bad in my life.

Everyone is trying to send me back, after I was metaphorically dragged out kicking and screaming. It's like they don't understand how hard this is going to be. It's not just Maverick I'm irrevocably attached to.

As Tyler releases me, he bids everyone farewell, and the night creeps on.

I decide to go to bed a little early. Maverick gives me a knowing look, but he doesn't say anything as he makes a bed on the couch.

Ruby and Corbin go to the spare bedroom, leaving us alone in the living room.

"You sure you want to sleep on that?" I ask him, gesturing to the long leather couch.

It's actually really comfortable.

"It's not my bed or yours, but it'll do."

Yeah, not touching that.

I turn and go to bed, not saying anything else. Then I…toss and turn for several long hours. After four hours, to be exact, I decide to go confuse the hell out of us both and stick my heart in a blender.

The second I open my door, Maverick's head turns toward me, proving he's still awake too, suffering the same as me. He just watches me as I walk to him, and he helps me when I climb onto the couch and lie down on top of him. His arms squeeze around me as he blows out a relieved breath.

"We can be just friends tomorrow," I say softly, tucking my head under his chin. "I want to sleep for one night."

He kisses the top of my head, squeezing me a little tighter. "Thank fuck, because I could really use some sleep too."

And just like that, I drift off, cocooned in his arms, and tricking my heart for one more day, catching a reprieve from the pain that can wait until tomorrow.

Chapter 42

Salem

@**MavSterling**: @SalemWithNoWitch we're going to Silk tonight and so are you. #FriendGameStrong

@**SalemWithNoWitch**: @MavSterling I'm washing my hair tonight.

@**MavSterling**: @SalemWithNoWitch unless that's code for using your vibrator, then wash your hair tomorrow.

@**SalemWithNoWitch**: @MavSterling it was code. I guess that means I'm not coming out tonight.

@**MavSterling**: @SalemWithNoWitch that's just cold… And friends don't let friends vibrate alone.

@**SalemWithNoWitch**: @MavSterling have fun at Silk.

Yep. It's perfectly acceptable and not at all confusing to flirt with the man I love on Twitter, even though there's still no way we can be together. Distance. I'm supposed to be getting distance.

@**LegendarySWY**: @MavSterling @SalemWithNoWitch I think I need to stop following you both because UR gross.

@**MavSterling**: @SalemWithNoWitch @LegendarySWY is too young for Twitter.

Putting my phone away now. Far away.

In fact, I'm going to leave my phone here, and I'm going to take Sean out for ice cream. Far away from Maverick.

Who will be at Silk.

Three days back, and I've only seen him once for a few brief minutes when he and I ran into each other on my way out of a deli. I've been invited to three gatherings from his friends, because these people are obviously trying to put us in the same place at the same time.

I appreciate the sentiment. It means they find me worthy of the man they all love so dearly.

Brin's party is one I will be going to. And that's still a little while away, so that gives me time to prepare myself.

Sean and I are avoiding Mom, which means she's not picking him up from school. Once Brin realized I needed help getting Sean from school and taking him to dance—where an adult is required—she took over helping me, refusing to have it any other way. And my brother has given her ingenious prank ideas to use on Rye in return as payment.

This is my current life, people.

So when she asked me to come to a party, obviously I couldn't say no.

I haven't even bothered speaking to my mother, though she has called. Apparently Sean isn't in any hurry to go back to her, since he's reclaimed his room and ignores her calls too.

She hasn't sent a car for him or come to retrieve him herself, so we're just riding it out.

"Ice cream?" I ask Sean, who pushes off from the couch and closes his binder.

"Just finished all my homework, so yeah."

We drive all the way across town, and as soon as we get out, I realize the universe is conspiring against me. I see Victoria, and almost decide to dodge her so that she doesn't have to talk to me shortly after her son and I broke up. But then I realize she's not walking a straight line.

In fact, she's weaving and zigging and…is she drunk?

"Sean, go grab the ice cream to go," I tell him, tossing him my purse for him to dig out cash.

He doesn't argue as I jog over to catch Victoria seconds before she crashes into a bush.

"Salem?" she asks, her eyes glazed over and her smile too wide.

"What the hell is wrong with you?" I ask, worried as I steady her and put her arm around my shoulders.

"I have no idea. I was going to meet a date, but then suddenly…I just got worse and worse."

Sean is walking back out with two ice cream cones by the time I manage to help her weave to the truck. Getting her in the back is like an act of congress, and I curse myself for not getting this damn truck lowered when I have to grab two handfuls of her ass and shove with all my strength.

She giggles wildly, and I roll my eyes as I shut my back door.

"Sean, will you text Maverick and have him meet us at his house?" I ask.

"Sure," he says with a small grin.

"I'm just helping him with his mother," I tell the meddler.

"Sure you are," he agrees, but his tone implies he's being a smartass.

"You know we can't—"

"Ice cream!" Victoria shouts, startling the both of us as I drive us toward Maverick's.

She rips a cone out of Sean's hand, and she starts licking it like it's the last one on earth. Sean turns a little, making sure to guard his ice cream so she can't snatch it too, and he gets to eating it quickly.

"I've always loved it in the cone," Victoria says seriously, still going to town on that ice cream while I drive us toward Maverick.

She sways in her seat.

"Victoria, did you drink anything tonight?" I ask her.

"Of course not. I rarely ever drink. I have no idea why I feel so…airy."

Airy?

"Cones really are good. Waffle cones are better. I got a waffle cone once. Just once," she prattles on. "It had chocolate."

"Focus, Victoria," I say, feigning a modicum of calm when I'm secretly freaking out a little. "You didn't meet your date yet?"

"No," she says, then giggles. "He was a cutie too. But I didn't meet him yet."

"Did you take any medicine?" I ask, wondering if I need to go to the hospital instead of Maverick's house since she claims she's not drunk.

"Nope," she chirps, then eats more ice cream.

"Did you smoke anything?" Sean asks her, and I glare over at him. "What? I watch TV."

Rolling my eyes, I continue driving as Victoria giggles again. "Of course not," she tells Sean, leaning up to bat his shoulder lightly. "I'm so glad you're back, Salem," she says on a sigh. "And I'm glad your mother stayed with Ian."

"She's definitely stoned," Sean mutters under his breath.

"How do you even know what that is?" I hiss.

"I told you—TV."

"Maybe Mom was right about not letting you watch so much TV."

"*Mom* and *right* don't belong in the same sentence together," he deadpans.

"Ian loves her," Victoria goes on with a content little sigh. "It's so good to see him love someone. I also want to love someone like that. I always just wanted him to be the person I wanted to love instead of finding the man out there who was already what I wanted."

It's a little hard to follow that last bit, but I think I get the gist of it.

I really wish Maverick's house was closer than this.

"Maverick loves you, you know," she goes on, causing my stomach to tighten.

"She knows but she pretends she doesn't," Sean, the little traitor, says before biting into his cone to get to more ice cream. "She thinks we can't stay."

"You know the likelihood of this lasting more than a couple more months," I say under my breath.

"Mom is different since she made up with Ian. I still hate her for refusing to leave me behind when Maverick came to talk to her, but—"

"What?" I ask him.

He blinks over at me. "Maverick kept coming over. He finally won when he and Ian teamed up on her."

Victoria bursts out laughing. "Ian said Maverick punched him for being a whiny pussy," she says through her giggles, her body swaying as she almost tilts. "Oh, how I wish I could have seen it. Maverick made him man up and go after her. Then he asked when our son got so violent, because he has a mean right hook."

Her giggles only grow, almost infecting Sean *and* me when we chuckle a little for no other reason. Fortunately, we manage to pull up at Maverick's.

My breath stills in my throat when my lights shine on something too perfect. Maverick is leaned against the back of his car, his arms crossed over his chest as he smirks at us.

I turn off my truck, and Sean pushes his door open, hopping out.

"I was a little surprised you wanted to see me," Maverick says with a devastatingly cocky grin.

A loud cackle roars from my truck, and his brow furrows. Apparently Sean left out the most crucial detail of this little impromptu visit.

Maverick pushes off from his car and comes around as I open the back door to my truck, and he finds his mother with chocolate ice cream all over her face.

"Mom?"

"You called your father a whiny pussy," she says around a long cackle that ends up turning silent, though her mouth is still open and her body is shaking, tears leaking from her eyes as she laughs so hard she can't make a sound.

"Found her wandering the streets," I say, wiping my smile away as he stares at her with a horrified expression.

"I was trying to cross the street!" she informs him.

Maverick reaches in, and he manages to lift her bridal style, carrying her toward the house as I shut the door. Since I'm worried about her, I head inside. Sean's already inside and hanging out on Maverick's living room chair, turning the Xbox on like he's here all the time.

I decide to go wait in the den as Maverick carries his mother into the guestroom.

Just because I don't want to be in the way, I turn on TV, trying to pretend I'm not nervous about being in Maverick's house. With him in it.

It takes him a little while before he finally finds me, and he shuts the door, sealing us in alone, his face stuck in a stupefied expression. "So my mom is stoned," he says matter-of-factly, and I burst out laughing.

"She was hanging with Ruby's stepmom since she helps her with her blackboard—"

"Blackboard?" I interrupt, brow furrowed.

"Don't ask," he says with a full body shudder of disgust. "Anyway, she was at Wanda's and apparently took three big brownies for the road, since she was nervous about this date and chocolate always soothes her. However, those were not your average brownies. Wanda is notorious for just randomly baking 'fun' brownies and leaving them out like they're a treat for guests."

He sighs dramatically, and I wipe the tears from my eyes as I suppress the next burst of laughter.

"I have her tucked into the guest bed with half a gallon of water and a bag of Doritos," he goes on, and I lose the war, finally laughing as he comes to drop to the couch beside me.

"I've never even seen my mother drunk," he muses.

"She's going to be mortified tomorrow," I say as I wipe more tears from my eyes, still laughing lightly.

"Oh, I know. And I can't wait to give her hell about it," he says with a smirk.

Our gazes collide, and I realize how close we actually are when I feel his breath tease my lips.

His eyes flick to my lips, and…I dart to my feet like a spring is under my ass.

"I should get Sean back," I blurt out.

His lips twitch as he arches a knowing eyebrow at me.

As soon as I reach the door, he says, "Later, alligator," with a small little grin, not looking at me.

That stupid little farewell should not set butterflies loose in my stomach, but it does, and I walk out, muttering, "After while, crocodile."

Chapter 43

MAVERICK

"Thanks for getting all this for me," Dad says, a big, goofy grin on his face.

It's a little petty that I want to punch him this time for being so damn happy, when the cause for his happiness is the woman who surgically cut out my own happiness.

"Not a problem. Had nothing else going on," I say while pocketing my hands.

His smile wavers, and he clears his throat. "I thought about reaching out to Salem and Sean. It's been two weeks and they haven't come around. If I got them to dinner, would you be able to join us?"

Any chance I have to be close to her, I'll take it. Especially since I haven't seen her since she rescued my mother from her brownie-induced high a week ago.

"I'll be there *if* you can make it happen. But it's highly unlikely it'll happen unless Kelly leverages Sean, per the usual." Lot of bite there.

His smile vanishes as a crestfallen expression steals his features.

"I need to get going. I have to make a stop before I go to help Brin set up for tonight's party," I tell him.

He claps my shoulder like he's trying to give me some sort of show of support. As he goes to look over the contracts I brought by, I walk out, and make it almost to the door before I hear Kelly.

"Maverick!"

I turn around to see her moving quickly down the stairs, back to her usual pristine self, though she still doesn't look as rested as she should.

"Yeah?"

She clears her throat, probably embarrassed about pretty much running to catch up with me. That's not very *Kelly*. Normally she glides and expects the world to wait on her.

"I was wondering if you would—" She hesitates, swallowing like the words are hard to get out, but finally steels her resolve to ask. "I was wondering if you would be kind enough to perhaps ask Salem to speak with me? I haven't seen Sean in two weeks, and normally by now they've reached the point where they're arguing and he comes to stay with me for a few days."

She looks uncomfortable. She also looks a little humbled to even have to ask for help.

"Don't you usually just go over there and make demands? After all, he's your son, and you tend to do whatever whenever where he's concerned."

Shutters close over her eyes. "I'm trying to move away from those tactics. It's become apparent that my approach was a little—"

"Cold?" I supply.

She swallows down her pride and nods once. "Sean wasn't himself during his sister's absence."

"Sean was himself, just a more exaggerated version of himself. He wasn't playing a part since you had no leverage," I tell her, crossing my arms over my chest. "And anyway, you'd be hard-pressed to find anyone who can get close enough to have a serious conversation like that with Salem. She's keeping everyone at arm's length right now. Not just me."

Confusion crosses her features.

"I was under the impression you two would—"

"Immediately get back together when she learned you were staying in Sterling Shore?" I ask, then laugh bitterly. "Me too. But it turns out, when you rip the rug out from under someone and they fall and break something, they tend to not be so trusting of that rug again. So they might stay in the same room, but they never get comfortable enough to step on that rug again until they know it's glued down and not going anywhere."

She looks away, blinking for a moment, and takes a deep breath. "I see. I wasn't aware there was still issue."

"There wouldn't be if she trusted you wouldn't just tell them again in a few months that they're leaving. Sean is already on the rug again, but Salem is older. She's been around longer to see the worst of you. And she's not willing to have everything taken away twice. So she's living at a distance."

She nods, her lips tightening and her gaze not meeting mine.

"Thank you for letting me know," she finally says and turns to walk back up the stairs.

I should shut up and go, but it's like she brings out the lecturing motherfucker in me. I'm not sure if she's just oblivious or if she tries to pretend she doesn't know as much as she does.

"Sean doesn't come to see you because they start fighting," I tell her, causing her to look over her shoulder at me in clear confusion. "They fight all the time, because they *are* siblings. But they make up immediately."

"But they say—"

"They say he comes over when they're at each other's throats," I interrupt with a shrug. "That's the story they tell because Sean doesn't want to admit he wants to see his mother, and Salem lets him keep his secret."

Tears waver on her lids as she swallows.

"A kid shouldn't feel guilty about wanting to spend time with his mother, but since you act like he's just a chess piece on a board to control his sister, he does feel guilty. Very guilty. And to keep him from feeling like he's betraying her, Salem goes along with the ruse, because she's never wanted to keep him from you. She doesn't think you're a terrible person. She just thinks you're cold, and she's Sean's warmth—her guarantee that he turns out like the three who still want to find a home and love life."

When a tear escapes and rolls down her cheek she gives an imperceptible nod, possibly unable to speak, and turns to glide up the steps with her usual grace.

As I leave, I tell myself I'm seeing Salem at Rye's party tonight. That there's no reason to go get my creepy fix through that observation window. That there's zero reason for me to be parking at the auto shop.

That there's no excuse for me climbing up the steps, and going straight to the window.

Doesn't stop me from being seconds away from pressing up against the observation glass when I see her.

Her streaks have changed to pink now, and she's wearing a black T-shirt with "Clanton Auto" written across it. Her jeans are tight as hell on her ass, which has me inwardly groaning when she bends over to look under the hood of a GTO.

Then…I have to remind myself that violence is bad when I see a guy go over and prop up too close to her, smiling as he talks.

"Gonna go grab her vagina and stake your claim?"

I snap my eyes in the direction of Rye's voice to find him propped up on the wall, arms crossed over his chest, as he smirks knowingly at me.

"That was certainly entertaining the first time," he goes on.

"Who's that guy?" I ask, trying to sound casual and not murderous.

"Max. He's wheel and tires."

"I see no wheels or tires under the hood of that car," I point out. "Do your people not have supervision, or do you enjoy paying them to flirt?"

He snorts derisively, and then sticks his head out the door that leads down to the garage area.

"Max, stop flirting and get to work," he calls through the door.

Max jumps, startled, then pouts as he walks away. Salem laughs lightly, wiping her hands off on a rag as she turns to face us.

The second her eyes find mine, her smile disappears and a light flush colors her cheeks.

I wink at her, because it's clear I had something to do with that, so I might as well own it. Fighting a smile, she rolls her eyes and turns back around to resume her work under the hood.

Rye returns to my side. "Still keeping you at a distance?"

"It's hell," I confess.

"If it's any consolation, it's not just you. She's refused the girls' offer for lunch several times, and Brin said it feels like a wall is between them now. For the record, keep your stepmother away from Brin. She might very well tear the woman's head off if she gets a chance. She's gotten a little attached and protective of Salem."

I blow out a frustrated breath.

"She's easy to get attached to."

He grunts. "I just like her because she kicks ass in the pit. She finished up two jobs already today that should have taken at least a full day to complete. And she's likely to finish up that GTO in record time at the rate she's going. People fucking love her, and Wrench called to ask if she was really better than him. Think he's a little miffed and is now trying to redeem himself, even though he's happy where he is."

My eyes never move away from her as she climbs up, giving me a great view. If she has to pose like that to fix a motherfucking vehicle, I'm going to have to find a shop and buy it, make her the sole employee, and hide her from the world.

My knuckles turn a little white from tight fists as Wheel and Tire Boy trips over his own feet, eyes glued to her ass.

"Okay, she's purposely doing that, just so you know. There's zero reason for her to be in that position," Rye says, sounding amused. "Looks like she's fucking with you."

My lips twitch as I take a step back. "She always gets me back," I finally say, trying not to smile about that.

"Know that feeling," he mutters with feigned annoyance, even as he grins. "How about the kid? He shutting you out too?"

"No. He calls me daily to be a little smartass. Or accosts me on Twitter. Depending on his mood."

Rye laughs under his breath, and I shake my head.

"Well, at least you get to see her tonight. Thank Brin for that. She hounded her until she agreed."

"Doesn't matter how much I see her; it feels like torture not to touch her."

His expression sobers. "I get that."

"There's always alcohol," I say with a shrug. "I'll just get too drunk to care if I'm touching her, and maybe she'll take pity on me and give me a sympathetic back pat or something."

He laughs, and I force a smile, acting as though I'm joking.

When she spreads her legs, her knees bent under her, and bends way over into the car, I turn around and stalk out, ignoring the mocking laughter following behind me.

Definitely getting drunk tonight.

Chapter 44

Salem

The second I make it to the backyard, I feel a little queasy. I've managed to avoid the group as a whole for two solid weeks. Tonight? Everyone is here, along with some people I don't know.

Pie in hand, I shakily move to the dessert table to drop off my customary gift.

"Knew you'd be bringing pie." Maverick's voice is smooth, quiet, and really close to my ear as a body presses against me from behind, and a strong arm curves around my waist.

"That's a little overly friendly," I tell him, my voice managing to stay light and teasing instead of shaky and breathy as I put the pie down.

"So was your little performance earlier today," he says.

I can feel his grin, and I inwardly groan. I knew that was over the top.

Turning in his arms, I look up at him. His arm stays loosely fixed to my body, ending up on my back with the new position as he stares down at me with a smirk and glassy eyes.

"You're drunk," I say suddenly, a small smile curving my lips for no reason at all. I suppose it's because I've never seen him actually drunk. "Already?"

"I've been here a while helping Brin set up," he says, his other hand coming up to my face.

Okay, I have to get out of this position before I do something like drag him to the bedroom and take advantage, hoping he's too drunk to remember tomorrow.

Carefully disentangling myself, I put a few feet of distance between us. He rolls his eyes, but remains smirking.

"Does it bother you that I'm drunk?" he asks, his smile wavering. "We never talked about it, but I know your dad—"

I wave a dismissive hand. "Getting drunk and being a drunk are two different things. Even I drink too much on occasion."

He nods, his smile returning.

"I wouldn't object to seeing you drunk," he tells me with a daring little expression.

"I don't pole dance. It's actually dreadfully boring," I assure him, not taking the flirty bait.

"Where's Sean?" he asks me, looking around.

"He's having his first-ever sleepover with a friend from school," I say, unable to stop the huge smile that spreads across my face.

Maverick smiles, too.

"Girl or boy?"

I slap his stomach reflexively, and he grunts as he laughs. He rubs it, feigning pain, when we both know it didn't hurt him. I, on the other hand, resist the urge to rub the back of my hand that I used to hit him, because his abs have gotten a lot harder over the past few weeks in the absence of pie.

He grins as he brings the bottle to his lips, taking another sip of his beer.

I glance around, finding several people jerking their heads away when I catch them looking at us. They don't even bother hiding their smiles.

Meddlers.

"I was actually going to ask if you'd have a problem with me taking over Brin's task of shuttling him from school to dance and back home," he says, studying my eyes. "Don't you dare tell him, but I miss the little shit."

Warmth spreads through my chest, and even though it'll be hard as hell to see him daily, I wouldn't dare deny Sean this. I know he—though he'd also never admit it to Maverick—misses Maverick too.

"I'm sure he'd like that. What about Bananas? Do you miss her?"

"Fuck no." He shudders as I laugh quietly.

When the conversation stalls and we just stare at each other, on the verge of doing something more than just staring, I decide it's time to remove myself from his gravitational pull.

"I'm going to go find Brin and let her know I'm here," I say as a way of getting away from him.

He just continues to smirk at me, because I'm transparent to him. When you spend months in each other's pockets, never away from each other more than you absolutely have to be, you tend to get to know each other really well.

And fall really hard.

Shaking off the fact I can feel his eyes tracking me, I go to Brin, finding her also drunk already.

"Am I late or something?" I ask as she laughs at whatever Britt has said.

I take a seat by the redhead I barely know, as Brin smiles widely at me from across the table.

"Maverick and I played a drinking game. Then everyone started showing up, and they got in on the game. And now…blame Maverick."

My eyes inadvertently dart over, finding him saying something to Dane that has Dane scowling. No doubt he's being a gold-medaling smartass.

"If you don't want him knowing you're madly in love, you might want to stop staring and smiling, because he's drunk. He's likely to come over here and drag you out over his shoulder," Brin says, amused.

I snap my eyes away from Maverick and clear my throat as Britt and Brin stare at me with twin grins.

"So, where's this drinking game you speak so highly of? I have some catching up to do. I took an Uber for a reason."

She smirks and hands me what looks to be a Jell-O shooter.

"We just skipped to the fun part after a while. Bottoms up."

Music is playing over a speaker, and I take the shooter, then another, loosening up enough to sway with the beat of the song.

"You want one?" I ask Britt as I take another.

"Dane has a fit if she drinks, forgetting she's in college," Brin answers.

"He thinks I'll be influenced too much by the alcohol's effect and lose my virginity to someone without meaning to," Britt states with zero emotion, and I choke a little on the Jell-O as Brin giggles.

Britt remains stoic.

"Apparently inebriation is the key to losing my virginity, but I'd rather be fully alert when it finally happens," Britt goes on, not a hint of joking in her tone. "I just don't drink around potential sex partners. But I think I'm going to pick one of the guys from LARP—"

"LARP?" Brin asks.

"Live action role play," Britt explains. "Anyway, there are a lot of other virgins there, so I thought we could help each other out. Harley keeps saying two virgins shouldn't sleep together because it'll be awful, but the guys keep threatening everyone with any experience who seems interested in me. They think I don't know what they're doing, but Bella has briefed me on the truth."

Her tone never changes. Like it's monotone throughout. I just blink as Brin shakes with silent laughter.

Rain calls for Britt, who stands and leaves me alone with Brin, who is still laughing lightly.

"She almost made me believe she was being serious," I say as I take another shooter, and then decide to pace myself after it.

"She *was* serious. Britt is unintentionally funny and unabashedly blunt. It's part of her charm."

My eyes flick up to see Maverick laughing as Corbin twerks. It takes me a second to realize the twerking song—as I call it—is playing.

Corbin is glaring at Maverick, and Maverick is throwing a few ones.

"Funny how this is the first time I've seen him smile since you left. He wouldn't even go out with any of us. Yet you're here, and he's acting like himself. As though just your presence has brought him back."

I blow out a shaky breath, unable to look away from him. Obviously I don't respond to her. I'm too busy trying to remind myself how impossible it would be to walk away a second time.

I'm not strong enough to do it twice.

"Let's dance!" Ruby calls out to us, waving us over.

I struggle to stand the hell up. Apparently those shooters were a little stronger than I realized.

I join Ruby, Tria, and Brin, and I dance, closing my eyes, feeling the music.

When *La La* suddenly blasts over the speakers, everyone roars and whistles, mocking Maverick. But Maverick is hard to mock, because he owns things that would mortify most people.

Instead of cowering, he just grins, and catcalls and whistles emerge louder when he starts pulling his shirt over his head, his hips moving scandalously as he draws out the partial striptease.

Of course I watch.

He tosses his shirt at Kode, who catches it and rolls his eyes, as Maverick does some Magic Mike moves that spike my blood. This is cruel.

Kode's hands go over Tria's eyes, but she smiles like she can still see through his fingers. Corbin just laughs as Maverick dances toward me, his eyebrows bouncing as he gets damn close.

He mouths the words *La La* in time with the song, and I can't help but grin like an idiot. Kode tosses his shirt back at him, and

Maverick laughs when he catches it, ending the sexy dance as he tugs his shirt back on.

He goes to grab a drink, and I pretend I'm unaffected. Maybe we can be friends.

Two arms wrap around my waist as a familiar body moves in behind mine, and Maverick buries his face against my neck, making that last thought moot.

I barely suppress the shiver that tries to rattle my body. Brin grins and looks away as Maverick dances behind me, his body firmly pressed up against mine.

"I just need a crutch for a second. Legs are getting numb," he says against my neck.

When his lips brush the skin of my neck as he speaks, I can't suppress the shiver any longer. This. Is. Torture.

I really should be pushing him away. I should. No doubt about it.

Instead, I become his crutch as he continues to dance close to me, getting drunker and drunker as the night goes on.

Even after he finally lets me go and goes to lean against a wall while he's talking to Kode, I still feel his presence lingering.

Finally, Maverick is sitting in a chair, eyes almost closed. I've watched him all night, worried he was going to eventually pass out and get hurt.

Breaking off from the group of girls, I go over as Tag Masters bends, wrapping Maverick's arm around his shoulders, and helping him to stand.

Maverick's eyes lazily open, and he rolls them when he sees Tag helping him.

"I'm not ready to go," Maverick grumbles, even as Kode joins Tag and the two combine their efforts to help him toward the door.

I follow behind them, not saying anything.

"I can drive him. I haven't been drinking," Tag tells Kode, who grunts when Maverick's legs give out, forcing the two of them to divide his weight among each other and drag him.

It hurts my heart.

"I said, I'm not ready to go," Maverick slurs.

"I'll come with you, and I'll stay with him. He doesn't need to be alone right now. He could get sick," I say to Kode as I finally make my presence known.

Kode startles, having been unaware of my stalking, and Maverick smirks over at me. "Now I'm ready to go," Maverick says, causing Kode and Tag both to groan.

They put him in the backseat of a SUV, and I climb in beside him. The bench-like seat is perfect for Maverick to pull me up against him, his arms closing around me. Tag takes the wheel, and Kode climbs into the passenger seat, looking back at us as Maverick kisses against my neck.

I try to remind myself that he's really drunk, and that he's just in need of some comfort, not letting the lines blur as I pat one of his hands.

"You sure you want to stay with him? He's going to be all over you. You're literally all he wants right now."

Heart. Hurts.

Maverick grins against my neck. "She knows. No need to tell her."

Rolling my eyes, I say, "I'm not leaving him alone like this."

"I can stay with him," Kode offers.

"Hell no," Maverick scoffs, causing Kode to grin.

"I'll stay. I won't sleep at all unless I can see with my own eyes that he's okay," I explain, which only prompts Kode to smirk.

They know I'm in love with him. That's not a question, so it shouldn't be so surprising that I'm worried about him. The only thing stopping me from giving in and turning myself over all over again is the very brutal reality that it can all be gone again tomorrow.

Then I wouldn't leave this time.

And my brother…

It wouldn't be fair.

Tag starts driving us the short distance to Maverick's house, and Maverick continues to drive me insane by kissing on my neck.

"I've fucking missed you," he finally says on a sigh.

Reaching over, I thread our fingers together, finding it impossible to say anything.

As soon as we reach his house, the guys help him out, though his legs seem to be working a little better as the two of them get him to the bedroom. As soon as they drop him to the bed, I start taking his shoes off.

"You got it from here?" Kode asks, giving me one last out.

"Got it," I tell him, preparing for a night of pure torment.

I start working his pants down, and Maverick smirks at me as the other two leave.

He leans up, pushing them down himself. "I can undress myself," he says, grinning at me like he's amused as shit.

Now I feel a little stupid.

He wobbles as he swings his legs off the bed, and I go to steady him before he tips off completely.

"Now sitting and standing might be an issue though," he says, eyes widening a little.

When I start laughing, he tugs me to him, forcing me to stand between his legs while he wears a T-shirt and underwear.

"Sleep with me. Give me a night of sleep," he says so softly, raw emotion lingering in the words.

"Okay," is all I can say, because I don't have the appropriate strength to deny him.

The relief that coats his features is just one more thing that reminds me how much I love him, and how I keep hopping over the wall that's supposed to keep me distanced.

He pulls his shirt off, and he gets into the bed again, working the covers down until he can pull them over him.

I get down to my panties and T-shirt because I can't sleep in jeans. Yeah. That's my excuse.

Apparently, I'm a masochist.

As soon as I'm under the covers, Maverick pulls me to him, and I go willingly. His arms wrap around me, and then it happens before I can stop it.

His lips find mine, hungry and desperate, and I kiss him back as my leg goes over his waist, winding around him as we lie facing each other. His hands go to my ass, bringing my hips where he wants them, until he suddenly shifts, forcing me to my back, as he comes down on top of me.

My hands go to his hair, and I breathe him in, soaking in every bit of it, telling myself we didn't really have the best *goodbye* we could have had.

"We shouldn't be doing this," I tell him against his lips, finally realizing this is not a good goodbye. It's a terrible idea.

He groans into my mouth, ignoring my protests, since I'm sort of pushing his underwear down and contradicting my words as my hand wraps around the hardest part of his body and strokes. Strokes again.

He reaches down, practically ripping the flimsy panties off me, the second I feel him prodding my entrance, sanity and insanity war for dominance. His kisses move to my neck, rough and demanding as he touches all the erogenous zones he can.

"Just sleep," I blurt out, and he stills against me, his hands still gripping my hips, his lips freezing against my neck.

He exhales heavily before saying, "Really thought you were about to say *just the tip.*"

The thing I love the most about him is his ability to defuse any situation with humor, and I start laughing as he grins against my neck before dropping to my side.

Our eyes meet; his arm stays around me. I remain on my back, while he props up on his side. Then there's a little bit of awkwardness when his cock jumps a little, brushing my leg, since the underwear is still gone.

I arch an eyebrow, and he rolls his eyes.

"Ignore it. I am. It's going to take a minute for him to get the memo and go down."

Trying not to laugh, or get turned on, I just smile at him.

"If this is about you worrying you're taking advantage, you should know that my sober self would punch my drunk self for missing the opportunity to have you," he says, still joking around, doing all he can to suck the seriousness out of this for us.

Grateful for his incredible ability to do so, I play along, trying to do the same thing. "Make you wish you'd just asked for sex instead of friendship? No strings attached?"

A serious expression steals his features, and his eyes soften. "No. I'd give up sex as long as I get to keep you as a friend. I don't want just your body. It's not as much fun as having the rest of you."

A shaky breath leaves my lips as tears cloud my eyes. In that moment, I hate life.

Because it's a cruel, unfair bitch.

"You wouldn't let me say it before you left," he says quietly, and my stomach lurches.

"Maverick, do—"

"I'm doing all I can to deal with this fucked up situation, but I think it's owed to me to get to say the words. That's all I want. It's not like it changes anything. I know that. You already know it, so hearing it isn't going to be your downfall. I just deserve to say them aloud."

Tears start leaking down my cheeks, and he brushes one away. "Okay," I finally say.

"I love you," he says softly, his lips brushing mine in the gentlest of touches. "I love you," he says again. He kisses the side of my cheek, his lips moving over the tears. "I love you."

It takes every ounce of strength I have not to scream or sob or tell him how much I love him back. It's not fair that I'm even here. He'll never move on if I keep acting like a girlfriend but not being a girlfriend.

Fortunately, he goes to sleep—passes out, rather—in the next two seconds. I laugh humorlessly when he starts to lightly snore, and I stare up at the ceiling.

If I don't adopt some of my mother's coldness for at least a little while, he's never going to let me go. He's never going to move on.

And it's not fair to make him wait for a girl who isn't free to tell him how much she loves him back.

Chapter 45

MAVERICK

@MavSterling: @SalemWithNoWitch I think you're avoiding me. #JustTheTipWasTooMuch

@SalemWithNoWitch: @MavSterling Crazy busy week.

@MavSterling: @SalemWithNoWitch come out with us to Silk. #ProveWeRStillFriends

@SalemWithNoWitch: @MavSterling movie night with Sean. Sorry.

No teasing. No humor. No quick wit. Nothing but a straightforward answer. Per the recent usual.

She doesn't respond to my texts unless it's about Sean, so Twitter is my main source of communication with her. Especially since she's conveniently been in the shower every day this past week when I dropped Sean off.

Apparently, we're just going to pretend I didn't tell her I love her. We're also not going to broach the fact she couldn't say it back.

And we're going to pretend that she hasn't avoided me for the past four days.

Because I got too drunk and pushed way too damn fast.

I spin the coaster on the table in front of me, wishing I'd just stayed at home instead of coming to Silk.

"I hate to say this, but at some point you just have to accept the fact that it's over," Dane says on a long sigh.

"Would you?" I ask around a snort of disbelief. "You waited years on Rain, whether or not you admit it."

He glances around, eyes landing on Rain as she laughs and dances with Ruby.

"Fair enough," he says on a harsh breath. "But, until you can figure something out, at least act like you're still alive."

A familiar face is suddenly joining us in the booth, and I inwardly groan when I see Leah smiling at me. Our new VIP bouncer needs to start doing his damn job, because she's *not* VIP.

Obviously he didn't get the memo that I no longer want girls to have free access to me.

"Maverick Sterling, I think you forgot to call," she says, feigning an exasperated sigh.

"On purpose," I say immediately through a tight smile.

Her grin slips. I've already given up the pretense of even trying to be charming. Apparently my charm is not willing to be spent freely anymore.

"What?" she asks, annoyed.

"Sort of fell in love with the other girl mechanic. Makes you about as appealing as the disappointing sequel to an epic original," I say with a smirk, being a bit more dickish than I've ever been in my life, considering she's the fourth girl tonight I've deliberately been short with.

"There's something wrong with the guys in this group," she grumbles as she angrily slides out of the booth in a huff, stomping away.

I look over to see Dane grinning down at his drink.

"What?" I ask, exasperated.

"Never thought I'd see the day when you couldn't care less about flirting, even harmlessly. Hell, I don't think you've even looked at a girl since you met Salem."

I lean back in my seat, drinking a bottle of water.

"Get used to it," I say bitterly while clanking my bottle of water against his glass of Coke. "Blame it on the fucking pie."

Chapter 46

Salem

I'm returning the shopping cart at the front of the grocery store when I hear, "Salem!"

The voice turns my blood to ice as I turn to see my mother walking toward me, her determined strides bringing her dangerously close to power-walking instead of elegantly strutting.

I turn and walk briskly, hurrying my steps to my truck, unconcerned. She won't follow. It's beneath her to chase—

"Salem!" she shouts again, startling me when I turn to see her actually running across the parking lot in her heels.

I've never seen my mother run.

I'm so stunned by the sight that I forget I'm supposed to be escaping. She's out of breath, her cheeks are flushed, and she curses—my mother just said the F-bomb—when her ankle turns because her right heel breaks.

She doesn't even slow down—just kicks out of her shoes. Leaning against the side of my truck, I watch in unyielding fascination as my mother abandons her thousand dollar shoes in the parking lot and closes the rest of the distance between us—barefoot.

Obviously she walks on her tiptoes to prevent all of her feet from touching the ground, but still…my mother is barefoot in a parking lot.

She clears her throat when she reaches me, and stands there on her tiptoes, looking absolutely ridiculous.

A grin curves my lips unexpectedly.

"Is Sean with you?" she asks.

"He's with a friend," I lie.

The sincere disappointment in her eyes actually sends a pang to my heart.

"I know you really don't want to speak to me right now, but when you speak to Sean again, if you can put our problems aside, will you please ask him to answer my calls. I just want to hear…from him."

Her eyes water, and I cross my arms over my chest.

"He misses you," I decide to tell her. "But he's really pissed right now. This last little stunt hurt him as much as it hurt me."

She looks down, picking at her nails. My mother doesn't pick at her nails. It's inelegant and tacky.

"I'm painfully aware this situation was entirely more complicated than I realized." She looks back up at me and blows out a breath. "I want to go back to the night of my birthday dinner and do things differently, but I can't."

Her lower lip trembles, and I swear she looks human.

More human than I've ever seen her.

Hell, I've only ignored her just over a month, and I barely recognize her.

"What's going on, Mom? Why are you chasing me through parking lots and standing barefoot before me with tears in your eyes?"

My mother doesn't play on emotions like this, so I know it's not a manipulation tactic. She's too good for such mediocre tactics, and she's too proud for tears.

She straightens her shoulders, trying to gain some semblance of a respectable appearance. "It's been brought to my attention that I'm not an easy person to love."

I snort, and her eyes narrow in disapproval. At least that look is something I'm used to. This human side of her is creeping me out a little.

She stares expectantly, as though she expects me to comment.

"I'm sorry; was that not rhetorical? Because I found it to be the understatement of the century," I finally say.

She rolls her eyes, taking a deep breath, acting as though this is the most difficult conversation of her entire life. When her eyes meet mine again, she says, "I'm trying to remedy that the best I can. In my quest to keep you and your brothers from being duped by the cons in life, I may have suggested there is no such thing as love—"

"*May* have suggested?" I interrupt, laughing humorlessly at the hypocrite who loves to con. "You said those exact words, Mom. Numerous times."

She bristles. "Be that as it may, I never meant that all forms didn't exist. And I might have been wrong."

She says the last sentence quickly, as though if she says the words in a rush, I won't call her out on them.

"Did you just admit to being wrong?" I ask, clearly delusional by this point. I might even glance around for pink elephants on parade.

She heaves out a frustrated breath. "Ian is insufferable. He's relentless. And he's, as you put it…warm." Her eyes soften, and my heart kicks a little.

Is my mother seriously admitting that she's fucking in love? Are you kidding me right now?

Gah, it shouldn't piss me off so much, but I want to strangle her here in the parking lot for what she took from me, all while she plays house happily, as though she hasn't been on a mission to destroy all warmth.

"I see," I say around a cold smile. "Congratu-fucking-lations," I tell her bitterly, feeling the hot tears trying to breach my eyes.

Her eyes water as well. "I'm staying in Sterling Shore, Salem. Permanently."

Those words stave off my anger just because of the surprise.

"Even if Ian and I don't work out, it's clear Sean is doing better here than he's ever done anywhere else. He has friends. He has excellent grades—even better than usual. He's also in love with this place. I won't take that away from him."

Her eyes find mine, and I see the meaning in them.

"How can I trust that?"

"Because I'm many things, but I'm never intentionally a liar, Salem. You know this."

I do know that, but—

"Why the sudden change of heart? All because of Ian?" I ask, still wary.

She gives me a sad shake of her head. "Not just Ian. Sean is the only one of my children who doesn't cringe or run when he hears my voice. He's the only one who even seems to want to be around me. I realize this is all of my own making, and I don't expect sympathy. I might have realized that I'm not prepared to live alone in my ice fortress—" She pauses, sucking in a breath, as though she's struggling to finish the sentence. "—*fucking* myself."

My laugh is unexpected when I hear her throw my words back, and her lips twitch. Hell has frozen over. My mother just made a joke.

"You'll notice I haven't leveraged you against him in a long time. I really am trying to make appropriate changes, Salem," she goes on more seriously. "It's not going to happen overnight, but I am trying."

"We're really staying. No matter what?" I ask her, my heart fluttering inside my chest with bridled anticipation and cautious hope.

"We're staying no matter what," she agrees firmly. "Will you please tell Sean I would like to see him some time?" she asks, tears teetering on her eyelids.

Never thought I'd feel sorry for my mother. I really am too damn tender-hearted if this is happening.

I pound on the back window with the side of my fist, and Mom jerks her attention to the passenger door as Sean opens it. His eyes are red, as though he's been crying, but he acts unaffected.

Mom's tears fall as she takes him in, and she fights to stay rooted to her spot, her will to go to him almost palpable.

Sean looks over at me as he gets out and walks over to her. "I'm going home with Mom if that's okay. I'll come see you in a day or two."

I wink at him, trying not to also cry, because I know how much this means to him.

Mom messily wipes her eyes—no dainty dabbing—as she goes to him. For the first time in my life, I witness my mother hug my baby brother, and I see the same shock on his face as he warily hugs her back.

She's bent over, her arms wound around him tightly, as the tears leak from her eyes.

"I need to go," I tell them, shutting Sean's door and trying not to run to the driver's seat.

Mom smiles *warmly*—which just freaks me out a little, if I'm being honest.

Shaking out of the trance, I get into my truck, and I drive like hell, feeling my heart hit my chest so hard that I'm worried it's going to burst free and I'll die before I even get to tell Maverick how I feel.

Wouldn't that be one hell of a Before Maverick pie moment…

Chapter 47

Salem

Getting into Silk on a crowded night without the escorting assistance from a Sterling is not easy. I finally get desperate and go to the bouncer, wishing I had been coming a lot with the girls when they invited me. That way I was known.

"Please let me skip the line. It's really important," I tell him.

I can't call Maverick. This is not a phone conversation. And I maybe I already tried to call and it went straight to voicemail.

Yeah. I'm that pathetic.

"Sorry, but it's the line for everyone unless you're VIP," he says dismissively.

I really wish I had on something a lot sexier than jean shorts and a T-shirt. Groceries are wasting away in my truck, part of the sacrifice for tonight's rituals, as I glare at the man blocking my moment.

Who am I kidding? I know the way in.

I reach down for the bottom of my shirt, fully prepared to flash him. He grins in anticipation as I work up the courage, but suddenly there's a hand clamping down on my wrist.

"She's with us, Bert," Kode says, refraining from laughing as Tria covers her smile with her hand.

I blow out a breath of relief as Kode releases my hand, and Bert gives me a disappointed pout as he ushers us inside.

"Were you really about to flash the bouncer to get in?" Kode asks, damned amused.

"Maverick's phone was off, and I needed in," I tell him, cursing the blockade of people who are holding up my progress.

"Could have called someone else," he points out.

I pause and blink. Yeah, that would have been smart, but my mind is sort of only thinking of one person.

"Can't talk right now," I say as I start shoving through the people, tired of politely waiting on them to move the hell out of my way.

I leave Kode and Tria behind as I needle my way through very ungracefully.

My eyes dart to the booth, which is also blocked by a bouncer. The platform is raised, looking out over the dancefloor. It's only about chest high, so I run toward the back of it where I know he'll be. Or hope, anyway.

The second my eyes land on Maverick, I get a little queasy. In a good and bad way—nervous anticipation. He's talking to Dane, not looking particularly thrilled to even be here.

His dark hair looks like he just had it trimmed, and his face is smooth, showing off that one tiny dimple when he forces a smile for Dane. He's wearing a pale blue T-shirt and dark jeans, looking too sexy for his own damn good.

Dane sees me, and his mouth pauses mid-sentence. Maverick looks confused as he follows Dane's line of view, and his eyes collide with mine as his eyebrows go up in surprise.

Not even hesitating, he stands and moves to the edge, and I step back, allowing him the space he needs to hop down.

As soon as he's in front of me, he says, "Hey, I wasn't expecting to see—"

I launch myself at him, not even caring how ridiculous I look. He catches me, looking utterly bewildered until I grab him behind the neck and pull him down.

He doesn't hesitate to follow my lead, his lips crashing against mine as I start climbing him, needing to be as close as possible.

The sound he releases into my mouth is sexy, raw, and makes me want so much more. In a way, I'd rather say this somewhere more private, but I'm bursting at the seams. Also, this was where it all started, so it makes it somewhat poetic.

I break the kiss, even as he nips at my lips, holding me up by my ass as my legs stay wrapped around his waist.

"I love you, too," I say as tears stupidly leak from my eyes without warning.

He goes still for a minute, confusion clear on his face.

"What?" he asks, as though he's genuinely questioning his hearing capabilities.

"I love you," I tell him, kissing his stunned, motionless lips. "I love you," I say again, trailing my lips up his jaw. "I love you," I whisper right against his ear, and despite the music, I know he hears it.

He turns his head, his lips finding mine, and he kisses me harder than before, walking through all the people, bumping into who knows who all along the way. I never release him. Don't know if I could even if I wanted to.

I don't break the kiss even as I feel the night air on us, proving we've reached the outside.

"Well, that didn't take long," I hear Bert the bouncer scoffing, but I don't stop kissing Maverick long enough for him to ask questions about that snarky remark.

I'm not even sure how he's navigating us, since I'm on him like a spider monkey and holding his lips captive.

When he tears his lips away, I make a small sound of protest that has him grinning, even as he opens a door and, with great skill, maneuvers us into the backseat of the cab, me still firmly attached.

Since I don't want to leave him, I don't bother mentioning my truck is here.

The second he tells the cab driver the information, I start to kiss him, but he tugs my hair, halting me. When I maybe glare at him a little, he grins.

"Say it again," he whispers softly, just barely brushing his lips against mine enough to tease me as the cab starts driving us away.

Everything on me softens as my own smile grows. "I love you," I tell him.

He tugs at my bottom lip with his teeth, then soothes the slight sting with his tongue.

"And again," he murmurs, his lips brushing mine before turning into a kiss.

"I love you," I mumble against his lips, grinning like an idiot.

The kiss spirals out of control after that, and the cab driver is warning us that we can't have sex in his backseat. Understandable concern.

Maverick is quick to toss him cash, not even bothering to see how much, as we get out of the cab.

"Hey, this too much—"

"Keep it," Maverick says, his lips moving away from mine long enough to say the words as he carries me up his porch, fumbles with the door, then stumbles his way inside.

If he falls, I'm going down with him, because my legs are apparently never letting go.

I'm kissing my way around his neck, tasting every inch of him, as he kicks the door shut behind us and starts walking toward his bedroom.

"You had so much grace the first time we did this," I say, grinning when he stumbles again.

"The first time we did this, you were just another girl, and I wasn't a fucking mess," he murmurs, kissing me silent again.

My legs don't let go until he's lowering me onto his bed, and I move up, grabbing at him to drag him down with me until his body is on top of mine. His hands go to my head, gently holding both sides, as he breaks the kiss again.

"What changed?" he asks, his eyes studying mine.

I smile as tears cloud my eyes. "Mom let us have a home."

He runs his fingers through my hair for a second, before his lips come back to mine, softer this time, more searching, reverent even, as though he realizes I'm not going anywhere and he doesn't have worry about this moment disappearing.

He spins suddenly, pulling me on top of him, never breaking the kiss.

My hair falls like a veil around us, and he pushes me back until our mouths have a few inches of separation.

"So you're staying. For good?" he asks, his lips only growing wider in a smile. "I don't have to follow you all over the country?"

"I wouldn't have let you do that," I remind him.

"I wasn't going to give you an option. I figured you'd find my stalking too charming to ignore for long. I mean, stalking is trending these days, according to the books," he says with a grin.

"I love you," I tell him again, and he kisses me like he wants to taste the words.

Since we won't stop kissing, it's awkward to get my shorts and his pants off, but we manage. My underwear goes next, until only his buffer us.

He sits up, his arms around my waist, but breaks the kiss to pull his shirt over his head. I do the same, and he reaches around me, trying to undo my bra and…struggling with the warped clasp.

I didn't exactly plan for this, so my current underwear is not my finest.

I find myself giggling when he finally curses and has to look around me to see what he's doing.

"This thing is diabolical," he mumbles, only prompting me to laugh more until he finally gets it off.

The second his mouth starts showing attention to my freed ladies, I lose my sense of humor. My fingers dig into his hair as he moves his mouth between my breasts, trying to show them equal attention, all while I grind against him like an impatient teenager.

"I love you," he says.

"I was wondering if you were ever going to say it back," I murmur.

"I wasn't talking to you," he deadpans, staring *lovingly* at my breasts that he's cupping in each hand.

Laughter bubbles out of me again as he waggles his eyebrows and grins, mischievous eyes meeting mine.

"Does this mean I get more than just the tip?" he muses.

"It means you get as much as you want. As often as you want," I say with an impish grin as he smiles bigger.

"In that case, I fucking love being in love."

"As long as you buy me assorted tampons," I decide to add, trying to keep a serious face.

"I'll schedule an appointment to join the secret brotherhood as soon as possible," he says conversationally, confusing me.

Before I can ask what the hell that means, his lips are back on mine, and I forget how to do words and stuff.

His underwear gets pushed down, and he shuffles his legs, getting rid of them completely. No prep work is really necessary, since it's been forever, and my body is demanding his.

When I lift my hips, he thrusts up, apparently as impatient as I am. We both make our own sounds of relief, as though the world is finally in the right position again, as he buries himself inside me.

Every time I rock against him, his grip tightens on me, almost getting painful. It's as though he's still worried I'm about to disappear.

I moan into his mouth as I kiss him, and he moves my hips harder, letting me grind against him in just the right way.

When my core tightens, promising I'm already racing over the finish line, I try to break the kiss. But he won't let me, holding me in place, forcing me to give him every sound I make as I writhe with no rhythm. It feels so good that it almost hurts.

He spins, coming down on top of me, as my body tingles with the aftershocks of the orgasm, but his lips never leave mine. He thrusts in hard just a few more times before he follows me, his body shuddering against mine.

The kiss turns lazy, but he finally breaks it, dropping his head to the side and exaggerating a few pants for air, as I grin, kissing his shoulder.

"Didn't realize just how long it had been until now," he murmurs.

"It was worth the wait—"

My words end on a squeal when he suddenly flips me over, startling me, but I grin as I turn my head to the side. His lips trail over my shoulder, and he starts kissing his way across my shoulder blades.

"That was just the warmup," he tells me, kisses feather-soft as his lips move up to my ear. "I'm taking my time for the main event."

"And here I was thinking it was just a really hot quickie."

He bites my shoulder, and I giggle like a little girl, until his mouth makes me lose my sense of humor again.

This moment? This one right here? It's an After Maverick pie moment.

And there will never be anything to top it.

Epilogue

MAVERICK

I'm smirking as I near the wall of shame, catching a familiar sighting or two.

"So, should I grab super or super plus? Because she's really pissy this month. Maybe the pissier they are the more they bleed?" I grossly suggest, watching as Kode and Corbin look over at me in horror.

"No?" I ask, grinning bigger when Corbin flips me off, grabs a box of tampons, and takes off in the other direction like his ass is on fire.

Yes, this is still fascinating.

"You haven't seen my new super-secret handshake for our super-secret brotherhood yet," I call after him, watching as his face burns a little red.

"I think I liked you better all melancholy and shit last week," Kode mutters, snagging a box of tampons and tucking it under his arm like that magically hides it from view.

He shoulders by me, and I turn to follow him.

"You forgot your tampons," he grumbles.

"I was just fucking with you two; it's not Salem's time of the month. It seems she hasn't yet spent the appropriate amount of time with the other girls to sync up," I say with an extra dose of chipper while he pales.

"Can you just stop talking?" he growls.

I grin broader.

Britt walks out of an aisle, condoms and lube in her hands. That sure as fuck shuts me up.

"What the actual hell?" I ask, pointing at the very offensive articles.

"I read that even if you are aroused, that lubrication was still good for the vagina's—"

"Can you stop talking?" Kode and I both plead in unison.

She looks perplexed. "But you asked—"

"That's not why we were asking," I hiss.

"I wasn't asking at all," Kode points out, ready to kill someone by this point.

"Why are you buying that stuff? You're supposed to be a virgin!" I say this much too loudly, drawing the attention of every judgy eye in the store.

Britt, of course, doesn't care. She remains oblivious to social decorum.

"I'm still a virgin. I buy these things on occasion just to be prepared. Bella told me I'll want sex a lot in the beginning. It's just part of the process."

"Bella is going to die," I state emphatically.

"Painfully," Kode adds.

Bella is still championing for Britt's sex obsession, really hindering our attempts to keep her untouched.

"Why are we making Ethan a single dad?" Corbin asks as he walks up, his recent purchase now bagged and no longer causing him shame.

"I'm not sure what's going on here," Britt tells him with a sigh. "I just came to buy condoms and female-pleasure lubrication."

Corbin turns about as sickly as I feel.

Britt grins brightly. "I'll see you at the party," she chirps, then walks away like she didn't just ruin sex for all of us.

We stand there in awkward silence in her wake for a few uncomfortable moments.

Finally, Corbin says, "Let's never talk about this again," and turns to walk out.

I don't even buy anything; I just walk out as well, slowly walking down the street to where I had to park.

By some miracle, I put the whole incredibly wrong scene out of my mind by the time I reach my dad's house.

I can hear the party raging in the back, and I stroll quickly through the house, bursting through the doors and immediately scan the area for Salem.

It's Sean's twelfth birthday, and my present was a new phone that he already found yesterday because the asshole has no boundaries when it comes to looking for presents early. Wish Salem had bothered to warn me of that. It was awkward for him when he found the phone in the same bag as skimpy lingerie I purchased for Salem the same day.

Obviously neither of us are pretending that happened, since Salem would throttle me and he's just too disgusted to cross that line.

I spot about five pies that tell me Salem is definitely here somewhere amongst the madness.

I spot Kode and Tria—who apparently drove separately since I know his dirty secret and just left him.

By the way, how the hell did he beat me? He still had shameful products to pay for.

Then I spot her, and a grin curves my lips when I see her in a pink, pixie-style dress that matches the streaks in her hair. She's talking to Brin—per the usual—and smiling about whatever is being said.

"Could you look more whipped?" Sean drawls, popping up at my side.

"Could you be more annoying?" I volley.

"Only if I was you," he deadpans.

I still have days that I hate him. And the devil cat, too, who apparently only likes to scare *me*. Or shit in *my* shoes. Or attack *my* feet. Or bitch slap *me* on occasion if she catches *me* unaware.

Damn cat.

"I'm only looking at her like I'm whipped because she modeled the lingerie for me last night," I say with a cruel smile, crossing the unspoken boundary we had in place. "Ah, sweet memories."

He glares at me. "I hate you."

With that, he turns and walks away, and I grin at his back.

When I fist-pump the air, finally feeling victorious over the little ass, Dale walks up, rolling his eyes.

"I'm not sure it's dignified to celebrate outwitting a kid."

"You haven't verbally sparred with that kid yet. Trust me, I should be popping the cork on some champagne in celebration," I state matter-of-factly.

"Who's getting rid of the guy talking to Britt?" Kode asks as he joins us, gesturing to where a smarmy-grinning punk is hitting on our precious little cousin.

In my head, she's not out buying condoms and female-pleasure lube; I've replaced that image with her buying Barbie dolls and stuffed animals.

Dane walks over to them, and I grin.

"Looks like he has it under control," Rye pipes in, joining us.

"Motherfucker," Dale says under his breath, going to where Harley is as some guy talks to her a little too close for comfort.

"Caveman," I scoff.

"Says the guy who grabbed his girlfriend's vagina at a *charity* event," Kode states flatly.

I roll my eyes. "One time. I grabbed her vagina *one* time. At some point you really have to let that go."

"That's exactly what I was thinking when you grabbed my vagina." Salem's voice finds me before her arms wrap around my waist from behind.

I groan as the guys chuckle, walking off as I tug her around to be in front of me. She's smirking, of course. Because she's as evil as I am. Makes for an interesting pairing.

"There's a reason I love you. I'm just struggling to remember what exactly that reason is at the moment," I say as though I'm actually thinking on it.

She just grins as she steps into me. "Are you asking me to remind you in public? Certainly inappropriate for a child's birthday party."

I bend, kissing her, and she wraps her arms around my neck to pull me closer while getting up on her tiptoes.

She's the one to pull back, eyes sparkling with her smile. "So when are you moving in?"

I tap my chin with my free hand, pretending to think it over, while still keeping my other arm around her waist.

"Pretty sure my house is way bigger than the beach house. So it should be you moving in with me."

"But the beach house is on the beach."

"Where you wear your bikini in front of other guys," I remind her. "My house has no beach, therefore, no men see you in a bikini."

She rolls her eyes. "But the beach house also has the Samurai sword."

"That can just as easily be in my house. I have two fireplaces. I'll even buy another one and move the TV out from over the one in the living room."

She sighs as though she's putout.

"But the beach house—"

"Is also mine and I can evict you. Then I can be your knight in shining armor who keeps you from living on the streets when I offer to take you in."

"You're lucky you made pie moment a good thing," she tells me with a quirked eyebrow.

"My specialty is making bad things good. I mean, look at you."

I laugh when she slaps at my stomach, and I feign pain as I rub the spot, grinning as she gives me an unimpressed eyebrow quirk.

"I take it back. You can't have sex anytime you want," she says, starting to turn away, but she ends up grinning when I crash into her back and wrap my arms around her waist, kissing a trail down her neck.

"You really need to come up with a better form of punishment. No sex simply hurts you, too," I murmur against her neck, grinning when she shivers.

"You're right. Good thing I figured out your Twitter password."

I choke on air as she turns that daring little grin at me over her shoulder. "You didn't."

"Oh, I did, Pony Boy. Be more original than your name and birthday next time."

She did. She really fucking did.

She squeals when I lift her, tossing her over my shoulder, and she starts laughing as I tug her dress down, ensuring no one else gets a peek at her ass as I carry her toward the house.

Sean rolls his eyes, but he can't fight his grin when he hears his sister laughing uncontrollably in between insincere pleads for me to put her down.

The second I have her inside my childhood room — that is still untouched — I drop her to the bed and come down on top of her, silencing her laughter by kissing her.

"Did you really bring me to your old room to have sex?" she asks, grinning against my lips. "Are you going to give me your class ring next? Maybe give me a quickie and call it a warmup. Oh! Is that how all that started? Had to explain why you were so fast as a teenager and—"

"Salem?"

"Yeah?" she asks, still grinning.

"Shut the hell up and give me my moment."

For once, she listens, and it ends up being one hell of a moment.

THE END

Note from the author.

I've lived in northeast Alabama my entire life, yet I've never published a Southern main character with any Southern quirks. So in this book, I gave Sean and Salem a piece of me through that without trying to overkill it. (Hope that worked the way I intended!) Mostly it was infused subtly enough just to be relatable, but there were parts intended for maximum humor. Obviously.

Since I gave them a piece of me, I also had to share a piece of myself with Maverick. In case you haven't figured it out, we share a hatred of unicorns. ;)

There were other pieces of myself strewn throughout their book, including pieces of my own little ten-year-old boy who has a degree in smartassery. He's not quite as rude as Sean, but if he thinks he can get one over on you, he'll put in a ton of effort to do so. And he loves to mock. (Insert groan here.) That's just how our family rolls. I get a lot of banter ideas for my books just by sitting at a dinner table full of hecklers.

At the end of the day, I shed more tears writing this book than any other because I used so many pieces of myself—more so than usual—that I felt as though I was hurting right alongside them instead of just empathizing the way I usually do.

A lot of people wanted Maverick and Britt to be together, but that just didn't hold true to Maverick's character. For one, he'd never do that to Dane. For two, Maverick saw her as actual family, and it went against the nature of his character to see her as more than a young cousin. He wouldn't have even touched Salem if he had known she was his stepsister before he touched her which is why it had to happen before he knew. (Yeah, that sentence is a little confusing, but you get the idea.)

Keeping the magic of Maverick Sterling alive was my sole focus. I didn't want to lose anything that had made him so special. So he needed someone who he could be his smartass, cocky self with and not have to dial it back for fear of hurting someone's feelings or looking like a dick bully. Someone who was just as confident and ready to serve hell back on a plate and meet him step for step.

Salem was that girl. She comes off as cocky at first, but like Maverick, it's just a shield. They both keep their true vulnerabilities close to their chests, masking them with smartass humor to keep anyone from seeing through to the core.

That's what made it so special when they shared those pieces with each other. I wrote a lot of this book with a big goofy grin on my face. Hubs was discreetly taking pictures to mock me with later, because he's a creeper and a smartass like that.

Anyway, that's Maverick and Salem and how they came to be. This story was pouring out of me, and when it was finished, I was in love. I really hope it hit all the right feels for you, too.

Reviews are great and appreciated (also a major help in getting the book seen) if you wish to discuss the feels. Even if you didn't have the good feels, your opinion is just as important and respected.

Thank you so much for reading *Taming A Maverick*.

If you want to take a peek at Britt's book, please keep reading. Also, if you want to know more about Connor, stay tuned. His book will be releasing early 2018 to start the Cup Check Series (hockey rom-com), but I have a sample here for what's in store.

Eventually, I may write a prequel novella for Tyler and Monica to explain how they got together, which is one reason I left their relationship a little vague in detail. That possible novella will depend on if I can quit writing a thousand other books I have promised out. <3

Britt's book's title has changed. Again.

Anyway, here's the first two chapters for *Talk Nerdy To Me*, projected to release 2017.

TALK NERDY TO ME

Chapter 1

BRITT

"I can't believe Dane is letting you run the place," Raya says with a smile. "Is he freaking out?"

"It's just until he can get someone else in here to takeover. And only because it's *Under 21* weekend. No alcohol will be served. Thanks for coming and helping," I say diplomatically, since Dane isn't happy about letting me do this.

He said those exact words, so it's not just a case of me misreading tone or body language again. He's learned to be blunt with me instead of expecting me to read between the lines. I find it unnecessary to expect people to figure out what you're trying to say instead of just saying what you want to.

"Both his manager and assistant manager are down with some sort of virus. It's just temporary," I go on. "He's still in New York with Rain for the new book tour."

So I'm his final option, and I'm not even technically old enough to be in here on a regular night that isn't *Under 21* weekend, something he does once a quarter. Yet, I'm filling in, trying to finally prove to him once and for all that I'm not a child anymore.

"It's been a long time since I worked here, but I still remember the ropes, for the most part. Seems like all your help would rather congregate around the stage and watch the warmup," Raya says, smirking as I keep my features relaxed, trying not to show my irritation.

They don't do this when Dane's normal manager is here.

Or the assistant manager.

Dane said they'd run all over me if I let them. I just didn't realize what that meant until I got here and no one would work. Or do the stuff they're supposed to do. And I'm not even sure what they're supposed to do. There really should be a task assignment chart somewhere.

I take a deep, calming breath. Sure, the music is awesome, but we have jobs to do.

I'm not cut out to cover for him. The first day he's gone, one bartender quits, the other is on vacation, and the head bouncer calls in for the week. I haven't been in charge one day, and already everything is falling apart.

I picked the wrong adult assignment. I'm starting to think Harley was wrong about this idea.

"How long is Dane going to be gone?" Raya asks conversationally, distracting me from my thoughts.

"Two months. He couldn't stand not being on the book tour with Rain, so he finally left. I don't know why I told him I could do this. Between this and school and my internship—"

"It'll be fine," she says, smiling while rubbing my arm with her hand. "I'll call Bo. She used to bartend, so she can cover until I find you a replacement; she knows how to make virgin daiquiris, too. Jax can help with security. Until then, I'll help cover for the two waitresses that quit. Dane said he had a stack full of eager applicants. It won't be hard to replace anyone."

I forgot all about the two waitresses who quit moments before their shift.

And I refuse to call a Sterling for help. The point of this experiment and the reason Harley suggested I tackle it, is to prove to the overprotective Sterling men that I am an adult.

A nineteen-year-old adult, who can step in and be just as Sterling as them. Even though I can't serve beer. Or alcohol of any kind. Because I'm underage.

This is going well already.

It's Under 21 *weekend,* I remind myself. I don't need to serve alcohol. I just simply charge the same prices for the virgin alternatives.

Virgin. I'm essentially running Virgin weekend. Insert ironic snort here.

"I can wait tables, too." She smiles as though she feels she's successfully staved off my impending meltdown.

I look down, trying to figure out if we've done enough to recover from the abrupt issues. Harley is supposed to be here by now — without Dale Sterling.

Maybe filling in at my brother's club isn't the best way to prove how adult I am if I don't know what I'm doing.

In my head, this all worked out spectacularly. Harley and I even plotted out hypotheticals of every situation. Yet, we didn't plan for this. Couldn't have seen these hurdles coming due to the minute fraction of a chance something like this *could* happen.

As usual, the human element messed up the plans my head had.

"Hi," a smooth, male voice says from behind me, interrupting my conversation with Raya — who has already abandoned me, apparently.

How long was I looking over the schedule?

A throat clearing from behind me reminds me someone is beckoning for my attention. Remembering it's considered rude to simply ignore people here, I turn to face whoever it is. Before my eyes can even find my beckoner, I'm distracted by the burlesque dancers, who are stripping down to their lingerie to get ready for the stage.

They need their masks on. No one is supposed to get down to their lace without a mask. Dane specifically stated that rule to me five times, apparently forgetting I have an eidetic memory. Seems like it's them he should have been repeating himself to.

"Hi," I say, though my attention is still focused on the maskless ladies, who are joining all the other rebels by skipping simple rules. "What do you want?"

He snickers, as though something is funny, so I finally face him.

And I go a little…frozen.

I'm just gawking and standing perfectly still, eyes wide as I take him in.

Base Masters.

I've never had to see him this close before, and now I'm getting this weird feeling in the pit of my stomach. And lower. Oh, yes. Arousal. Recognize it now.

Being aroused has never left my body unable to function, though. My mouth is still parted like it expects to expel more words, but…no words. I'm just gaping in most every sense of the word.

What is wrong with me?

His dark hair is sticking up in short spikes that actually suit him really well. I think he has on eyeliner, but I could be wrong. He's a lot taller, so I'm still gaping with my head tilted back so that I can see him.

I'm sure it's not attractive at all, yet I can't stop the weirdness going on with my motionless body.

A black T-shirt that reads *"The Fallen"* is fitted against his body like he wants to hint to the lean contours of definition it barely conceals.

I'm still staring.

He's just smirking.

"Actually, I think I know the answer to my question now," he says, looking me over as though he's amused.

Don't trust my judgment on guessing moods, though. For all I know, he could be constipated. I've mistaken the two before—vice versa.

He shakes his head, though I don't know why. "That's a real shame," he says on a long sigh.

What?

"What question do you know the answer to? And what's a shame?" I ask as he turns away, the ability to speak returning with the loss of his attention, as though the two are linked.

A phenomenon I will definitely explore later.

He just laughs as he walks away, leaving me thoroughly confused, but I have more important things to worry about.

I have to prove I'm an adult and a capable Sterling.

Otherwise, my family, incredible as they are, is going to do all they can to prevent me from ever doing adult things.

Don't ask. It's a long story.

Chapter 2

BASE

"She's gay, and we can't compete with mostly naked women if she's gay. So we're good. Let's get ready. People are pouring in now," I tell the guys, still a little disappointed in the sexy girl with some of the most touchable hair I've ever seen.

"Who's gay?" Sticks asks while adjusting the height on one of his cymbals.

"The girl who wasn't hypnotized by us," Taylor snorts, rolling his eyes at me.

"You're so fucking vain," Sticks says pointedly at me.

"Label is coming tonight. Just needed my head on right," I say unapologetically. "Stage performance is fifty-fifty on talent and mentality. Everything needs to be on."

"This record label is the one. I can feel it," Randy says, tense and likely to fuck up five or six times each song.

He's not great when he's on. He's terrible when he's tense. Which means we need to sound twice as good tonight to cover for his less-than-stellar performance.

Sticks gives me a look like he's thinking the same thing. But we're a band. Been together since the eighth grade. It'd be wrong to lose Randy this late in the game, even though we can barely even stand him on a personal level anymore.

"You bitches just try not to mess anything up," Randy says as he winks at us. "I know how nervous you all get."

Groaning inwardly at how oblivious he truly is, and ignoring his typical arrogance, I roll my eyes and ready myself for Stick's kickass introduction.

One thing I love about Silk is that Sterling Shore only has this one club, and we always have a damn good turnout here. It's why we wanted the record label to see us in action in this element, when the crowd is fueling us.

The trance is always strongest here.

The doors have been opened, and the masses have flocked in, everyone is now packed in. Usually we don't play right at opening time, but since we're opening for Diamonds and Sex, a much larger band, I don't mind it.

I see the redhead from earlier as she walks around the stage, seeming to scold the other waitresses who have stopped waiting the now-full tables in anticipation of our set.

She needs to go back to waiting tables and ogling the burlesque dancers. The more people lost in us, the better. We need that damn trance to be on point tonight.

"And Base Masters!" Sticks yells, cuing me to get my ass out on stage, and I head straight for the mic, offering my best panty-dropping smile to the girls who have gathered the closest.

It's all part of the game. All part of the show.

Work the crowd.

Fire everyone up.

Feed the trance.

"Let's go," I say quickly into the microphone, and then I kick off the first song with the solo entry.

Stickhandling (Cup Check Series #1)
(Connor's Story)

PROLOGUE

People often ask me how I came to be friends with Connor King. I always remind them that we're not friends. Unfortunately, no one seems to believe me, because where I go, Connor seems to be close by. Where he goes, I seem to be close by.

How the hell did this happen?

Chapter 1

STASIA

"Psychology and economics go hand in hand," Professor Gander announces. He's wearing his *I can't believe you people are considered Ivy League material* face, which means he's about to hand out some shitty grades.

Not mine. Mine will be good, because I'm not a spoiled rich kid who can afford to flunk out of any course. Well, not anymore anyway.

And I didn't come here a sheltered child who can't resist the urge to break free and party like there's no tomorrow.

A loud snore sounds out from behind me, and I roll my eyes while refusing to turn around and see Connor King. His shoe is really pissing me off, because it's propped on my armrest, invading *my* space, while he does his usual sleep-through-Monday-class routine because he likely partied too hard this weekend.

"Saying that seems to be wasted," Professor Gander goes on. "Everyone here is focusing purely on the economics factor. We have numerous courses that offer just the straightforward economic facts. Please feel free to drop this class and choose one of the others, even though the cutoff means you'll have to accept a failing grade. If you want to be successful, I strongly recommend you actually intertwine psychology to better understand individual economics, as well as the consumer, and how it factors into each and every business worldwide."

He grows silent, and suddenly Connor King yelps before jumping up. "What? Who?" he says, disoriented. His booming voice echoes off the lecture hall's walls, and I maybe gloat a little.

Professor Gander glares at Connor, while I smugly smile. Why am I smiling? Because I'm the one who just stabbed Connor's ankle with my pen to wake him up. Yep. That'll teach him to put his stupid shoes on my armrest like he freaking owns the place.

"Are you in the wrong place?" Professor Gander growls, still glaring at Connor.

In a class of two-hundred-plus, it's unlikely he actually even knows Connor's name. Unless he's a hockey fan.

"No, sir," Connor says while clearing his throat. I hear the rustle of him sitting back down while several spurts of smothered laughter litter the air.

Professor Gander resumes his rant he thinks he's disguising as wisdom, and I chance a glance behind me. Blue eyes are glowering at me, and I go so far as to flash a triumphant smile at Connor and bat my lashes, as he possibly plots my death.

Turning back around, I resume taking notes, and I happily use *my* armrest for *my* elbow. Guys like Connor King think they own the world. Even though he's not too far from graduating, he still seems to think this is high school.

It's not.

Chapter 2

CONNOR

"I hate ECON," I grumble to Alek, while Jonas and Luke play the PS4.

"Well, I'd tell you to drop the class, but you've waited too long," Alek points out.

"Just because I hate it, doesn't mean I'm failing. My grades are solid. And I'm not stupid. I realize I missed the cutoff."

He covers his smile while shrugging. "Then deal with it."

"Thanks for the advice, dickwad," I mumble, leaning back. "Gander's class is too early on a Monday and too early on a Thursday for me to be able to focus."

Groaning, I scrub my face before blowing out a breath.

"Onto more important matters that don't include bitching," Luke says absently while his thumbs vigorously click the game controller. "We need a damn housekeeper and grocery shopper. I'm tired of the stench, and I'm tired of being hungry because we never buy the shit we need."

A housekeeper?

"Hell no. What if it's some psycho that smells our underwear or plants cameras in our bedrooms?" I point out.

He shrugs, still watching the screen. "Then you clean. No one even wants to come over here anymore. Four guys in one house who don't clean equals gross. I'm sick of it."

"House vote," Logan says, still watching the TV while clicking the controller. "I vote housekeeper."

"Seconded," Luke chimes in immediately.

"I'm in," Alek says, smirking when I curse.

"I know a girl," Luke says, still busy. "She makes a place shine, and I think she's also looking for a place to live. It'd be ideal to have her on hand, and it would give us someone to handle our shopping lists."

"What's her name?" I ask, sighing.

"Can't remember, but I'll call my friend and get her number. She's hard to get because she's actually good and keeps a tight schedule. But I'll see what I can do. Offering her a place to stay plus pay would ensure we get her, and she's trustworthy, which is something we'd really have to worry about."

He pauses the game and pulls out his phone. Ten minutes and fifteen laughs later, he's handing me a sheet of paper with a name and number scribbled on it—at least, I think it's a name. His handwriting is horrendous, but the number is legible.

"Why are you handing it to me?" I ask. "This isn't my idea."

"I know. But you were outvoted, which means the responsibility lands on you to get her. Besides, you're charming and all that shit."

The three assholes all turn to grin at me.

One day, I will smother them all in their sleep. After sliding my phone out of my pocket, I dial the number, and wait as some weird music plays. Finally, a girl answers.

"I don't know this number. You have five seconds, and I'm hanging up."

The fuck?

"Four seconds."

"Um…I'm calling about a housekeeper?" I say, even though it sounds like a question.

"There's a waiting list. I'm not going to be open until next semester."

Fuck.

"Can you recommend someone else?"

"There's a list for that. Several lists, in fact. Just look it up online."

This girl is a…word my sister would kill me for calling a girl.

"Um, so I—*we*—actually need someone trustworthy. That list has everyone who wants to make a buck on it."

"Some are cheap. Use them if you want to save a buck."

She hangs up on me, and I glare at my phone in disbelief.

"Couldn't get her to take us?" Luke asks in an amused tone.

I flip him off. "If you want someone to wash clothes and shit, I'll find someone who doesn't act like they eat kitten hearts for breakfast."

Other books by C.M. Owens:

*The Sterling Shore Series (Hooked on the Game, book 1, is free. Box set available for first 4.) Romantic comedy series. 12 (including #1.5) books available for this series as of now.

*The Death Dealers MC Series (Property of Drex #1 is free.)
3 books available for this series as of now. Semi-dark erotic romance series.

*Worth It (co-write with SM Shade) Stand-alone romantic comedy.

*Pieces of Summer – stand-alone unique romance with spurts of humor.

*Deadly Beauties Trilogy (Blood's Fury, book 1, is free.)
Trilogy is complete. Paranormal romance series.

*Deadly Beauties Live On Series (Dark Beauty is book 1.)
3 books are available for this series as of now. Please note: This is a spinoff from the Deadly Beauties Trilogy. Paranormal romance series.

*The Daughter Trilogy (Daughter of Aphrodite, book 1, is free. Box set available.)
Trilogy is complete. Paranormal romance series based loosely on Greek Mythology.

*The Curse Trilogy (Box set available.)
Trilogy is complete. Paranormal romance series. (Vampire dystopian.)

*The Gifts Trilogy (Secret Gifts is book 1.)
Trilogy is complete. Paranormal romance series. Spinoff from the Curse Trilogy.

*The Coveted Saga (Treasured Secrets, book 1, is free.)
4 books in this series, and it is complete. Paranormal romance. (Witches and shapeshifters.)

*Faders Trilogy (The Devil's Artwork, book 1, is free.)
Trilogy is complete. Science-fiction romance.

***

Upcoming Series for 2017 & 2018

The Wild Ones (lighthearted rom-com) and Wild Kids (middle school action/adventure/comedy). Two parallel and unique series that will allow your children to read about the same characters as kids that you're reading about as adults. The kid version will have the Wild Ones as children and searching for "treasure," but there's a Dennis the Menace vibe mixed with a touch of Problem Child just to take things back to old-school kid books. (Starting 2017)

Motorheads Series – A semi-rom com series similar to the SS series, but completely different as well. (Starting 2017)

Krux Trilogy (Set to release all at once in 2017 if all goes well). Semi-dark mafia romance.

Cup Check Series (hockey rom-com) coming 2018, starting with Connor's book.

And this is only a portion of what's to come. <3

About the Author

C.M. Owens is a *USA Today* Bestselling author of over 30 novels. She always loves a good laugh, and lives and breathes the emotions of the characters she becomes attached to. Though she came from a family of musicians, she has zero abilities with instruments, sounds like a strangled cat when she sings, and her dancing is downright embarrassing. Just ask anyone who knows her. Her creativity rests solely in the written word. Her family is grateful that she gave up her quest to become a famous singer.

You can find her on Facebook, Twitter, and Instagram.

Instagram: @cmowensauthor

Twitter: @cmowensauthor

Facebook: @CMOwensAuthor

There are two Facebook groups, the teaser group, and the book club where you can always find her hanging out with her fans and readers.

www.cmowensbooks.com

Sign up for my newsletter and get no more than one email a month with new release information and/or a list of my fave books from other authors and deals. (No spamming from me and no one else will get your email address from me.)

CPSIA information can be obtained
at www.ICGtesting.com
Printed in the USA
LVHW010247090720
660177LV00019B/1426